ALLEGIANCE

ASYLUM
BOOK THREE

SUSY SMITH

BABYLON
BOOKS

For Mom and Dad
Wikóⁿbla

Susy Smith

ALLEGIANCE

IN FREEDOM WE TRUST

BABYLON BOOKS

1

Monroe Farm, Osage County, Oklahoma

Secrets buried in darkness never remained hidden forever. Senator Thomas Monroe loathed to admit the truth in the old adage, but his wife's pitiful wails echoing down the farmhouse's small hallway begged to differ.

He loved her with a passion that bordered on obsession. From the moment he laid eyes on her walking down the capitol steps in Austin, he was enthralled. She wove a spell around his heart, binding them together. She was fresh out of college, and he was twenty years her senior. It didn't matter. He set out, a man on a mission to win her heart.

His enemies, and frankly his friends and allies, would be shocked to find his heart had the capability to love at all. They regarded him as a leader who ruled with a heavy hand and a big stick. He was feared by all who followed him, and he liked it that way. It kept everyone in a neat, tidy line.

He'd never considered Lacy his daughter, and the fact she knew the truth infuriated him. It would be political suicide if the world found out.

And yet that was the one thing that would alleviate his wife's pain.

What a disaster.

His wife, Geneviève, moaned as if her body suffered a physical ailment. The sound cut him to the core. He rubbed the heel of his hand against his throbbing forehead. He couldn't concentrate on anything except the memories he thought he'd buried for good.

He'd almost lost Geneviève when they'd given Lacy to his brother and wife to adopt. She'd fought him tooth and nail every step of the way. She couldn't understand his reasons for not wanting a child. His greatest fear was losing her, and if they'd kept the child, she inevitably would've loved it more than she loved him. He refused to share what he considered his and his alone.

The day they'd returned to Texas after dropping Lacy off with his brother and wife, she'd slit her wrists and almost bled out before he rescued her. The scars running along both his wife's wrists still rose thickly in stark relief against her otherwise smooth olive skin. He'd never forget the image of her, half-sunk in the bathtub, surrounded by crimson water.

It tormented his mind. What if she tried again? With a steely mental force he'd honed and perfected over the years, he shoved the image and troubling thought far from his mind.

He looked around the cramped kitchen in distaste. He'd been raised in this little piece of God's hell, and returning to the rundown, shotgun-shanty farmhouse had done nothing to lift his ever-present foul mood.

The brown porcelain sink under the kitchen window had more chips and stains than he could count. The four-pronged hot and cold knobs would only turn with great force. He shuddered as he glanced at the filth on the floor.

He couldn't stand the hovel and wished many times during his childhood that it would burn to the ground. He would've danced in the ashes.

Geoffrey Widdowson, neatly dressed in a '20's style, three-piece pinstriped suit sat across from him. The yellowish light of the room reflected off his hair, slicked down with some sort of oil. The man's unblinking stare unnerved him. He studied him like he was a God-damned circus sideshow.

He hated the man with his entire being, but he was a necessary evil. The militia men held a healthy fear for the man everyone called Widow which kept them in line. More or less. No one wanted to be on the receiving end of that man's cruel ministrations.

Monroe fisted his hands, wanting nothing more than to wipe the smirk off the weasel-faced man. But he had to tread with care. Although Widow worked for him, he didn't trust the man not to turn on him if the mood struck. Widdowson had garnered his nickname in medical school. He had no idea how the man got it other than the obvious abbreviation. Whatever he'd done must've been diabolical.

"The human spirit is surprisingly easy for me to break," Widow bragged in a cruel voice. "However, your *niece* happens to be one of the few people I've met with a strong sense of self. I have a few methods in mind I'd like to try on her. It will give me the opportunity I've lacked to perfect them."

Widow held his gaze with a slight smirk. He gritted his teeth over the snide way the word *niece* rolled off the man's forked tongue. By all outward appearances, Widow conveyed a picture of refined grace, but he knew from experience a monster lived inside the man.

"She will be a challenge," Widow continued, with a spark igniting his otherwise dull-brown eyes. "If you give me the green light, that is."

Another tormented wail reverberated through the thin walls. The sound scorched his veins. Her agony burned him alive from the inside out.

How had things gotten this far?

"I want her brought back here at once," he snapped. "She will pay for my wife's suffering."

"Don't you mean her *mother's* suffering?" Widow taunted.

His nostrils flared at the man's blatant disrespect. "Don't call her that. Geneviève hasn't been Lacy's mother in years."

"Of course." Widow acquiesced with a slight dip of his head.

He shot the man a withering glare. "Just bring Lacy back. And Jace. Take as many men as you need. Are you sure you can find her?"

Widow raised a brow. "Are you doubting my skills?"

The tone Widow used raised the little hairs along the back of his neck. "No, of course not," he demurred.

"When do you want me to leave?" Widow asked.

"Tomorrow," he said, searching both pockets of his slacks for the comforting pack of cigarettes.

He pulled one out, grabbed the lighter off the table, then lit the tip. Sucking the harsh nicotine into his lungs calmed his rattled nerves. He lifted his head and blew white smoke into the air, wishing he could turn off the thoughts that kept him up at night.

"Those will put you in an early grave," Widow commented with a dryness that rivaled a summer desert.

"I'd be in that grave a lot earlier without them," he snapped. "They calm my nerves."

He pulled a cheap, black plastic ashtray toward him and flicked grey ashes from the cigarette's tip. He took another long drag into his lungs, enjoying the temporary relief it offered.

A haunted moan filtered through his brief bliss.

"Dammit," he muttered, crushing the cigarette into the ashtray.

Determination to end his wife's suffering rushed through him. This had to stop. He pushed back the chair. One of the legs caught on the corner of a broken tile and he stumbled sideways, struggling to keep himself from falling. He scowled at the chair and almost gave in to the urge to throw it across the room. The satisfaction of seeing it break into pieces would only be a temporary relief, so he shoved his irritation aside.

"Come with me," he said to Widow. "It's time to sedate her until she can get herself under control."

"As you wish," Widow said with that ever-present smirk he wanted to smack off his face.

A knock at the back door drew him up short. His lips turned down and a V formed between his scrunched brows. Who the hell would bother knocking? All his men barreled through like the damn Charge of the Light Brigade. The guards posted there never stopped them. Worthless idiots.

"Go and deal with Gen. I'll be there shortly," he said to Widow.

Widdowson nodded, and walked down the hall with a casual, unhurried gait.

Monroe pivoted on his heel, strode to the door, and flung it open.

His eyes widened. Well, shit. If this wasn't the icing on the cake. Struck momentarily speechless, he stood in the doorway with his jaw dragging the floor. Texas Governor, William Fallon Sr., stared back at him briefcase in hand.

"Hello, Thomas."

This had catastrophic written all over it. Why the hell was he here?

With a resigned sigh, he motioned the governor inside then returned to his seat at the table. The governor pulled out the chair across from him. The legs screeched along the old linoleum tile, causing his temples to pound.

Governor Fallon began organizing a stack of papers. He shifted in his seat. The unexpected visit had him teetering on a cliff's edge. Geneviève's heart-wrenching sobs filtered through her closed bedroom door, pushing him that much closer into a free fall.

"We have a problem," Governor Fallon said, tone low and ominous. "A big one."

Concentrating was tough, but he forced his mind on the governor's words. The bombardment of conflict over the recent weeks weakened his iron-fisted ability to control his emotions.

The problem must be huge because Fallon looked ready to crack like plaster from a wall. The skittish man jolted as a gust of wind rattled the kitchen window. He raked a shaky hand through his thinning hair.

Placing his elbows on the table, he leaned forward. "Go on."

"The president just signed an agreement with the North Atlantic Treaty Organization. He's secured their support."

The ever-present frown on his face deepened. "What kind of agreement?"

"As you know, NATO has access to unlimited military resources, and they've agreed to wipe out any opposition to the president. That means *us*," Fallon stressed, unable to keep the tremor from his voice.

As if Monroe needed the reminder.

Clearly the governor's delicate constitution wasn't built for the harsh realities of politics. Sharks with sharp teeth and an insatiable appetite for the weak lurked in political waters. The evidence the president knew how to play hard ball was obvious with the NATO curve ball he'd thrown at them.

"What did the president give them in exchange?" Monroe asked.

Fallon's mouth puckered in distaste. "The president has agreed to make the Euro dollar the official currency once the new government has been set up."

Monroe blew a breath through pursed lips. "One step closer to World Order."

"The World Bank is backing the president. He plans to start releasing important people from the work camps to rebuild the economy."

The news lit his fuse, and he released a string of harsh curse words.

Damn Manuel Nieto. If the man had kept his word and sent

the army he already paid for, none of this would be an issue. As it was, he still needed a strong army backing his play to take over the country. Without Nieto's support, his plans would fizzle like dying embers in a fireplace grate.

He felt his blood pressure rise as tension flooded his head. He lacked one state in his endeavor to control the southwest part of the United States. Jace bungled the New Mexico mission, thus destroying any chance at using the southwest as a bargaining chip.

Manuel Nieto, a Mexican drug lord and human trafficker, wanted control of the United States southwest. He detested getting his hands dirty dealing with the man, but Nieto had control over the Mexican army. An army that could help him destroy all the president's militias combined.

With that army, he'd sweep in and take control of the country, rebuilding it according to the founding fathers. Contrary to the current leader's belief that the founding father's ideas were outdated and unrealistic, he knew without a doubt if they didn't return to those beliefs, the country would be lost.

New Mexico's governor, Mira Deschene, had disappeared like a phantom in the night, only to return with reinforcements from the Navajo Nation. Her line of defense at every border crossing into the state of New Mexico was impressive. It would take men he couldn't afford to lose to penetrate her stronghold.

It would take military aid only Mexico could provide, and Nieto was the key to gaining those reinforcements.

"Well?" the governor demanded, nostrils flaring. "What are we going to do?"

Monroe tapped a finger on the kitchen table. Another keening cry filtered down the hall. He was losing patience fast. Fallon shifted his gaze to the kitchen entryway, a question in his eyes.

"Will you excuse me, Governor? I'll just be a minute."

"Go ahead," Fallon said, waving a hand. "Our entire plan hangs in the balance, but family first."

The dig stuck. "I'll thank you to keep your opinions to yourself."

He strode to his wife's room without waiting for a retort. The governor could go to hell. He didn't need the man anymore. He could take the state of Texas away from him with a snap of his fingers.

He opened the bedroom door and knelt at his wife's bedside. Low light from the tiny hurricane lamp on the dresser barely lit her taut, withdrawn face. The enclosed room seemed heavy, depressing. Muggy air hung like starched sheets on a still day, stifling his breath. He grasped her hand, rubbing his thumb in slow circles against her wrist. She quieted. Tears from red-rimmed, swollen eyes trickled down her cheeks.

"I'll never see my baby again," she sniffled. "She hates me."

"She doesn't hate you, Gen," Monroe soothed, voice soft and hushed.

"Yes, she does," Geneviève lamented.

Widow walked in moments later. Frustrated, he rose and whirled on the man.

"I told you to sedate her," he seethed. "The Texas governor is here. He heard her for Christ's sake."

Widow gave a slight mocking bow. "I will increase her dosage."

"No," she whimpered. "Not another shot. Please, Tommy."

He ran a loving hand across Geneviève's forehead, ignoring her plea. "I'll be back soon," he promised, then walked out the door without a glance in Widdowson's direction.

The governor had refilled his coffee cup and sat back at the table, slurping the hot liquid slowly. The sound reminded him of a kid sucking up every drop of a milkshake through a large straw. He raised a brow.

The man's uncouth demeanor struck a familiar chord. Like father, like son. His assistant, William, was Governor Fallon's son, and the boy carried himself in the same boorish manner. Despite the time of day, the twenty-something young man always looked as if he'd just rolled out of bed. He did this with a consistency that stood in direct juxtaposition to his work ethic. Both father and son disgusted him, but he set his personal feelings aside.

Fallon straightened and gave him a pointed look.

"I think," Monroe started slowly, "I'll try to meet with Nieto again. Maybe we can salvage the situation. He has the gold."

"And if you can't salvage the situation?" Fallon queried, looking doubtful.

His chest tightened at the thought of failure, and he rubbed the heel of his hand against it. "I don't know."

"We could get a special ops team together," Fallon mused. "Take out the president. Cut the head off the snake."

He shook his head. "That's a suicide mission and you know it. Any team we send will come back in pine boxes. The president is too protected. We've been over this idea and rejected it."

"Perhaps. But it's worth a try. It may be the only move we have left," Fallon reasoned.

It seemed the man held no concern for the men they'd send. Expendable. That's what they were to him. Not that he particularly cared one way or another whether a special ops team made it home safely. But why waste time and resources on a fool's errand? He bet Fallon would change his tune if his son was chosen to be on the special ops team to take out the president. Not that it would ever be an option. The guy wasn't qualified to flip burgers at McDonalds.

Monroe pulled a chair from the kitchen table. The coffee he'd drank earlier that morning churned in his stomach. He stifled the belch rolling up his throat. He needed to wrap up this conversation and get back to his wife.

"Get a meeting set up with Nieto," Monroe said.

The Texas governor nodded his head. The tip of his pen scratched along the small notepad he'd retrieved from his shirt pocket as he took notes.

"Let's hope he's cooled down enough to meet."

Even as he said the words, he knew it was unlikely Nieto would be in a mood to negotiate. He'd held his son, Raul, thinking he'd be added leverage. It backfired, and in the end Raul had been shot when Lacy escaped from Nieto's clutches.

Lacy's brother, AJ, and his own personal pilot, Bryan, had gone to Mexico City and rescued her. He felt an odd pang of guilt but quickly shoved it away. He'd placed Lacy in a precarious situation when he'd sent her to Nieto with his payment for an army. So what if she was his daughter? She'd been a useful tool. Nothing more.

"I'll suggest meeting in Laredo. He has a lot of colleagues in the area," Fallon said.

He waved a hand in agreement, not bothering to voice the cutting retort burning his tongue. Nieto's colleagues, as the governor delicately put it, were nothing more than corrupt businessmen and priests who helped him traffic drugs and girls.

He might've been labeled heartless, ruthless even, but he always tried to stay on the right side of the law. Most of the time he succeeded.

Fallon pocketed the notepad and pen, glancing around the empty room. Fear bloomed in his eyes as he faced the senator.

"Look, Thomas, we're in real danger here."

Fallon cast a glance over his shoulder as if he expected an assassin to jump from the shadows and stab him.

He sighed through his nose, wondering if he could have another cigarette. He tried not to chain smoke, but in these circumstances, it was damn hard. Fallon needed to grow a spine.

"Take two of my men as bodyguards if it will make you feel better," he conceded with a slight eye roll.

Fallon set his empty coffee cup on the table with a thunk. "Thank you. It will. Watch your back, Thomas. The president considers you his biggest threat," he warned.

The president was too smart to come after him. Neither of them had resources to spare for that sort of endeavor—yet. If the president did have NATO backing him, those reinforce-ments would be astronomical compared to his small militia.

"If that's all?" Monroe asked with a raised brow.

He'd heard enough and tired of the man's company. He needed to check on Geneviève.

Fallon rose, gave Monroe a hard stare, then left without another word. He'd probably choose two of his best militia men, but if that was the price to get the man off his property, he'd pay it with a smile.

He sat for a moment longer, thinking again of Lacy. She was the cause of his wife's pain. He had no idea where she'd gone but finding her wouldn't be a problem. He could send Widdowson after her. The man had the tracking skills of a bloodhound. Her parting words filtered back to him.

"I want to get as far away from the both of you as possible. And if you ever try to find me again, I'll kill you."

He let out a dark chuckle. She could certainly try. Widdowson would find her and bring her back to him. She would make things right with his wife—or she'd never see Jace again.

$$2$$

———————

acy walked down the beach hand-in-hand with Jace. Soft, gritty sand squished between her toes only to be washed away by the breaking surf. The air, saturated with salt and seaweed, tickled her nose, and blew the hair off her damp shoulders. Simple pleasure slipped through her. Feeling the sand and sun against her body, mostly recovered from the recent trauma, gave her a modicum of peace. She cherished Jace's hand wrapped around hers. Miracles might not fall from the sky, but the gods had gifted them both a second chance.

A flirtatious smile lit her face as she looked up at him. "Are you sure we have to go?"

He'd announced that morning he was ready to move on as they shared a can of fruit cocktail scrounged from the kitchen pantry. They'd found a deserted beach house to stay in when they arrived at Coronado Beach a few weeks earlier and she'd grown attached to it. The skylight above the bathtub was her favorite thing. She'd miss time spent with Jace in that bathtub. The thought heated her skin.

She inched closer to him until her hip bumped his. His cobalt eyes twinkled as they met hers and he laughed softly.

"We could stay in bed all day," she continued, wagging her eyebrows at him.

He stopped and gathered her in his arms. "Having second thoughts about finding a preacher?"

His tentative question drew her up short. Why would he doubt her now after all they'd endured?

The week they'd spent apart had been the worst time of her life. Manuel Nieto had taken her prisoner when he found out her uncle, Thomas Monroe, had prevented his son from returning home to Mexico City. She'd been on one of her uncle's missions, delivering a payment to Nieto to secure an army. Her uncle wanted control of the United States and had proven he'd stop at nothing until he achieved his goal. Nieto and the vast trained-in-warfare soldiers to which he had access, were to join Monroe's small band of militia men.

She could still smell the stench of the small underground cell. She'd killed Nieto's man, Miguel, while trying to escape. It hadn't worked, of course.

The odds of escaping Nieto's human trafficking ring had been staggering. But Bryan and her brother, AJ, had swept in and stolen her and Willow right out from under his nose. Willow's cell had been next to hers in that underground hell. They became fast friends and when Bryan and her brother came to her rescue, Willow escaped with them.

It would take a lot of time to bury those memories.

She craned her neck to look up at him. "God, no. I'm ready. I'm all yours."

He grinned, showing off the dimple in his cheek.

She swiveled to face the ocean. "There is a reason I'm not ready to go just yet."

She said the words with quiet conviction. The wind blew around them, causing fine grains of sand to skate across the dunes. Beach grass rustled in response, and the raucous call of sea gulls pierced her ears. Jace was silent a beat too long, and she wondered if he'd heard her. Then, he placed his warm hands on her sunburned shoulders and turned her back to face him.

Concern formed lines between his eyes. She reached up and gently rubbed them with her thumb. She didn't want to be a cause of worry for him. Still, he said nothing, just waited for her to continue.

She dropped her hand and sighed. "It's just . . . I'm not ready to see my parents, Jace. I can't. Not right now."

Understanding lit his eyes and something akin to pity radiated from them. She stepped back, and his hands fell from her shoulders. She didn't want his pity. She'd rather not face the fact that Emmett and Lila were not her birth parents. God, that was a bitter pill to swallow. Added to that misery was the information her uncle, Thomas Monroe, and his wife Geneviève, were her true biological parents. The evil uncle who'd led her straight into Nieto's trap. How could he do that to his own daughter?

"Don't look at me like that."

She sounded defeated, pathetic, and hated it.

His lips tipped in a bemused half-smile. "Like what?"

She frowned. "I don't want your pity."

He sighed. "I don't pity you, sweetheart. You're the one wallowing in self-pity. Don't project your own feelings onto me."

Her chest rose and fell in rapid succession, eyes snapping. "They should've told me."

"Yeah, they should've. But they didn't. Can you really blame them?"

"Yes, I can!" she shouted. "Did they honestly think I'd never find out?"

"They probably hoped you wouldn't. What good has it done?" He raked a hand through his wind-blown hair. "These are the questions you need to ask them. You can speculate or have your questions answered. It's up to you."

Her shoulders fell, and as she blew out a breath, some of her anger leaked out. Her chest ached, and she absently rubbed it with the heel of her hand.

"You're still the same person, Lace. Don't lose sight of that. Your mom and dad love you."

They did, she allowed herself to admit. They'd given her everything they could, treated her no differently than AJ. She found no fault in how they raised her.

Her dad would go ballistic when he found out everything that'd happened to her, everything his brother had done. Maybe keeping the truth from her was their way of protecting her. Protecting her from her uncle.

"You can't avoid or run from the truth," he continued quietly. "You never run or hide from a problem. It's not your nature."

"There's always a first," she muttered, eyes downcast.

"You won't have peace until you sort this out," he said, wrapping his tanned, muscled arms around her.

She lifted her head and allowed herself to relax into his embrace.

Her eyes locked on his. "Yeah, okay, but will you stay with me? I need you."

His thumb swiped a tear running down her cheek. "As you wish."

She laughed at the famous line from *The Princess Bride*. She'd been obsessed with that movie as a kid and used the line to answer every question. It drove her mom and dad crazy. The thought shot a pain through her chest.

"You remember that?" she asked, a little floored he remembered.

"I've always wanted to be your Westley," he told her softly.

She studied him with solemn intent. "I wish I'd known."

"I was following what your mom wanted at the time. And she was right," he said, giving her a wink. "I don't know if I could've kept my hands off you."

Heat raced up her neck and desire pooled in her lower stomach. "Same."

Her mother's keen eye had observed Jace's interest, and because Lacy was three years younger, her mom had asked him to wait to pursue her. Jace honored her mother's wishes, giving her time to grow up.

He cocked a brow. "Do you like my hands on you?"

A shiver raced down her spine in response to his low, raspy tone. A fire lit under her skin as he trailed a feather-light finger from her shoulder to her elbow. She pressed her body closer to his, running both hands up his bare, muscled chest.

He tipped her chin and their eyes tangled. "Do you?"

"Yes," she whispered, concentrating on the rock-hard muscle under her fingertips.

His bright eyes searched hers. She didn't know what he was looking for, but whatever he saw caused his lips to turn down.

"I want to kill Nieto for putting his hands on you," he said harshly.

She tore her eyes away from his. "I never said—"

He cut her off, but his voice softened. "You didn't have to. I know you, sweetheart. You can't hide things from me. You have to tell me the truth, even if it hurts."

"He didn't rape me," she murmured.

"But he put his hands on you. He tried. Didn't he?" he pressed.

She stiffened but nodded in affirmation. "He tried. I was running out of time. If AJ and Bryan hadn't shown up when they did . . ." she trailed off.

"He would've succeeded," he surmised.

"No," she denied. "He wouldn't have."

His eyes narrowed. "What are you not telling me?"

"Nothing," she said, trying to step out of his embrace.

His arms tightened around her waist. "Don't run. Just tell me."

His words to her the day her uncle separated them at the border ran through her head. *Stay safe, stay alive.*

She sucked in a sharp breath. "I would've broken the promise I made to you the day we were separated. I wouldn't have survived another rape. I would've found a way to . . . to kill myself."

He pressed her head to his chest. And held her. His heart thundered furiously under her ear.

The wind continued to drive the surf to the shore, blasting tiny grains of sand against their bare legs. Sandpipers dove toward the water, searching for their supper.

"You don't get to leave me," he rasped, threading his fingers through her hair. His hand around her waist tightened. "Not under any circumstances. Got it?"

Comforted, she leaned into him and sighed. "As you wish."

3

A J leaned against the bedroom door, staring at his friend, Bryan.

"What's going on?" Bryan demanded.

"I don't think we can leave yet," AJ said, voice low and thoughtful.

Morning sunshine poured into the room from the dormer window that looked out over the Sinclair's front lawn. It highlighted deep lines around Bryan's droopy eyelids. He hadn't expected Bryan back from Oklahoma so soon, but it was damn good to see him.

"Why can't we leave yet?" Bryan asked, scrubbing a hand over his face.

"Did you drive all night?" he asked, ignoring his friend's question.

"Yeah." Bryan gave him a concerned look. "How do you feel?"

The gunshot wound he'd sustained while rescuing his sister, Lacy, from Nieto burned like wildfire. His chest felt as if it had been through a baling press. It crackled and popped with every breath. The swelling in his lower leg from the scorpion sting he'd gotten while lying in the sand, staking out Nieto's home, felt like it had a heartbeat of its own.

The harrowing escape from the human trafficker in Mexico City had nearly cost him his life. But it was worth it. His sister, back in the arms of his best friend, Jace Cooper, was safe. And hopefully happy.

They'd rescued Willow Sinclair, who'd been held captive with Lacy, as well. Recuperating in her home proved challenging because of his intense attraction to her. That was part of the reason he didn't want to leave.

But her boyfriend, Scott, had him worried. He couldn't put a pin on it, but there was something about the guy that just sketched him out, and he had a niggling feeling Scott had something to do with Willow's abduction.

"I'm fine," he answered, brushing off Bryan's concern with a slight hand wave.

"Why are we sticking around? I've got places to go, people to see," Bryan quipped with a smirk.

"Sure you do," he tossed back.

"Come on," Bryan urged. "Let's blow this stand."

He sighed. "I don't think I can. Willow's boyfriend is sketchy as hell. I think he might've had something to do with her abduction."

Bryan's nose scrunched. "Woah. That little skeevy guy downstairs with the weird hair?"

He huffed a laugh. "Yeah, that one."

Bryan turned thoughtful. "What are you wanting to do exactly? I mean, you can't accuse him of anything, can you? You don't have any evidence."

His brows rose. "Can I accuse him of being a colossal douche bag?"

"That goes without saying," Bryan said with a grin. "Seriously, though. What do you want to do? Hang around and make sure he checks out? The girls will want to know why we're not leaving."

"I know," he agreed. "I don't think Laurel will be too disappointed. She's trying to talk me into giving her information about Nieto."

"What the hell for?"

"Revenge," he answered grimly. Changing the subject, he asked, "How's my sister?"

Bryan's lips turned down, and a V formed between his brows. His pulse spiked. "What happened?"

Bryan schlepped his way to the twin bed and sat, folding his hands between his knees. He let out an audible sigh.

"Dude," Bryan said, shaking his head.

"What?" he pushed off the door. "Just spit it out, Bry."

"You better sit down," Bryan advised.

"I hate it when people say that," he groused, pacing to the window.

"Your uncle had Jace tortured."

He whirled around, causing the scorpion sting to shoot angry pains up his calf. "Is he okay?"

"He will be. But AJ, that's not the worst of it."

His heart sped up at Bryan's ominous tone. He swallowed convulsively with a sudden urge to throw up. Every muscle in his body tensed as he braced himself for what Bryan had to say.

"Your sister and I, well, we . . ." Bryan stammered to a stop, rubbing the back of his neck.

His eyes narrowed. "You didn't sleep with her, did you?"

Bryan's head snapped up. "What? God no! Why would you think that? That'd be like sleeping with my sister. Not to mention, Jace would kick my face in. I'd rather keep my front teeth if it's all the same to you."

He took a deep, calming breath, as he paced back to the bed. He lowered himself next to Bryan, careful of his ribs. Knowing his sister, she could've talked Bryan into just about anything. She was a wild card, always had been.

"What then?" he demanded.

"We sort of took your aunt," Bryan muttered, lowering his gaze to the floor.

His eyebrows shot to his hairline. "You did *what*? Why?"

"We had a plan, and it worked," Bryan said, defensively.

"Your plan was to kidnap Aunt Gen?" he asked, shaking his head in disbelief. "What did you expect to gain?"

"It worked," Bryan repeated. "We're all out from under the senator's thumb. Your sister found his weak spot, Geneviève, and used it. He promised to leave us alone."

"Okay," he said, drawing out the word. "Did Jace and Lacy go to California?"

"Sort of," Bryan hedged. "AJ, there's more."

"There always is," he said, sighing. He twirled a finger in the air. "Out with it."

"During the . . . standoff with your uncle, I guess you could call it . . ." Bryan's breath stuttered, and he let out a rough curse. "Your uncle told Lacy he was her father," he finally finished.

His ears burned with heat. It traveled in swift waves up his neck. What the hell? Why would his uncle say such a thing?

"Did she believe him?"

"Not at first, but eventually, yeah, I think she bought it." Bryan hesitated. "You think the senator is lying?"

He wanted to believe his uncle lied but remembered something odd he'd asked his dad about a few years ago. At the end of every school year, all seniors turned in a baby picture for the senior assembly slide show. He'd gone through several photo albums looking for one and noticed there were no baby pictures of Lacy. His dad dismissed him when he'd mentioned it, saying they were probably in another album. But now . . .

"I don't think so, but how the hell would I know? The guy's a snake and capable of almost anything."

"True," Bryan agreed.

He turned and leaned against the bed's headboard. "How is she?"

"Wrecked," Bryan said quietly.

He scrubbed his face. "Where are they if they didn't go to Tulare?"

Bryan shook his head. "I don't know. Somewhere along the Pacific, I think."

"Jace has got this. If anyone can get her through this, he can," he said, forcing himself to believe it.

Bryan stood and offered AJ a hand. He took it and rose to his feet, breathing through the pain.

"Let's go downstairs and see if those weirdos are still hanging around," Bryan said with a conspiratorial half-grin.

They closed the bedroom door with a soft click, then crept down the stairs. He gripped the banister rail so tightly his knuckles turned white. His body screamed for rest, but he ignored it, placing one foot in front of the other. He bumped into Bryan's back on the last step.

Bryan's arm rose, hand fisted into a military freeze position.

Voices carried from the living room. They snuck closer until they reached the wall dividing the foyer and living area. Pressing against the wall, they listened.

"C'mon," Scott cajoled with a whine. "It'll be a blast. You need to loosen up. Have some fun."

"We can check the cattle in the south pasture," Scott's friend offered. "That would help Olive out."

"I don't know," Willow hesitated.

AJ and Bryan looked at each other, puzzled. Why did they want to check cattle? It didn't make sense.

"Just ask Laurel," Scott pressed.

AJ motioned for Bryan to follow him, then walked around the corner. He gave Willow a confident smile.

"How's it going?" He addressed the two guys on the white brocade sofa.

Scott's brows lowered. "Aren't you guys leaving?"

"Not yet," he said, looking at Willow.

Willow's eyes widened, and he gave her a conspiratorial wink. Her face reddened. She lowered her gaze, shifting uncomfortably in the matching brocade wing chair.

"What were y'all planning?" he asked Willow.

She cleared her throat. "Uh, they wanted to take the four wheelers out."

"Sounds like a blast," Bryan said with enthusiasm. "Haven't been on one since I left home."

"Who's he?" AJ asked, pointing to Scott's friend.

Neither Scott nor his friend answered. Scott folded his arms across his chest, frowning.

"Diego," Willow answered for them.

"Well, Diego," AJ enunciated each syllable in his name. "Nice to meet you."

Scott rose to his feet. "I just remembered my dad asked me to run an errand for him." He looked at Diego. "Come on."

Willow's eyes tightened as she looked at Scott's thunderous face. She looked scared. He walked over and stood behind Willow's chair.

Scott's eyes narrowed on him as he said to Willow, "I'll be back."

"We'll be waiting," he answered, voice lowered with an underlying threat.

Scott's mouth pressed in a flat line. He turned, nodded at Diego, and they strode out, slamming the door behind them.

Willow rose from the chair, turned, and stared at him. "You were rude," she accused.

"Yeah, I was," he agreed.

She threw her hands up. "Why?"

Bryan sidled up beside him. "Want to follow them? See where they go?" he asked quietly.

He nodded. "Get the truck. I'll be right out."

Bryan left, and he turned back to Willow. "I don't have to be nice to that preening prick."

She snorted. "Ever heard of common courtesy?"

"He doesn't deserve it," he retorted. "What do you see in that guy anyway?"

"You wouldn't understand," Willow said, looking away.

"Try me."

A truck horn blasted in three short bursts.

Willow's brow rose. "Going somewhere?"

He gave her a terse nod. "Yeah, but I'd like to finish this conversation."

"Well, I don't," she muttered.

He touched her arm as she turned to leave, and she flinched. God, he hated that. Hated the men who caused it.

"Can we finish this later?" he asked, dropping his hand.

She pressed a palm to her forehead. "Whatever."

The horn blasted again.

"See you soon," he promised.

She nodded in reluctant agreement as he turned to leave. He loped down the steps, opened the passenger door and jumped inside the truck's cab.

"Took you long enough," Bryan said with a grin.

"Shut up," he ground out. "Did you see which way they went?"

"Yeah, but we need to hurry to catch them," Bryan said, throwing the truck into gear.

The tires ground into the gravel as he punched the gas.

He needed to focus on keeping Willow safe. And right now, that meant figuring out what the hell Scott and his friend were up to. He had a sinking feeling he wouldn't like it.

4

W illow slumped back down into the chair she'd just vacated, folded her hands, and stared at nothing in particular. She wanted to curl into a little ball and hide from the world, shut everything and everyone out until her heart calmed its constant staccato beating against her rib cage.

Scott's behavior unnerved her. Had he always been that controlling? Or was AJ skewing her perspective? But the way Scott treated her now made her question his interest in her. It was confusing to think about. What did he have to gain by dating her if he didn't like her?

His arrogance and the driving need to be the center of her attention regardless of the life-altering, shattering situation from which she'd been rescued, baffled her. He did control every conversation they had, steering it and twisting her words until she was nothing but a confused mess. When he asked her to go to Laredo and she refused, could he not understand it had nothing to do with him and everything to do with the fact she'd been abducted there?

She'd never been popular in high school like her older sisters. Never cheered for the football team, never went to games, nor participated in any extra-curricular activities. Her quiet, introverted manner seemed to turn off kids her age, as if she carried a horrible disease they didn't want to catch.

Most girls had lost their virginity by the time they graduated and were schooled in the ways of the world. Not her. Her naivety and innocence remained intact, so maybe that's why she'd agreed to go out with Scott the summer after they graduated.

She remembered the way his blond hair glistened in the sunlight the morning they bumped into one another on the sidewalk outside Cotulla's One Stop. Their eyes met as he hurried past.

He'd stopped abruptly, turned around and said, "Hey, don't I know you?"

With one foot inside the store and one out, she stopped and turned to face him. The smile he launched her way caused her heart to skip a beat.

She'd noticed him in school, but he'd been a popular soccer player. A jock. She was a nobody. Most of the time she liked it that way and avoided drawing attention to herself. She couldn't compete with either one of her sister's alluring gypsy looks or athletic ability.

Art had been her only escape. She lost herself when she painted—the way her mother disappeared into one of her novels. Nothing else mattered except the world she created on canvas. She was able to blissfully forget her problems at school—and the fact she felt like an ugly duckling swimming in a pond full of swans. Watercolor was her favorite medium, and she experimented in impressionism, realism, pop art, anything that caught her attention.

So, when he stopped her that morning to make small talk, which he'd never done before, she was more than a little surprised. When he asked for her number, she'd been dumbfounded. She gave it to him, but thought he wouldn't call. She was stunned when his number flashed on her cell phone screen that evening. They had their first date the next day.

She tried to think of a good quality Scott possessed, one of substance that had drawn her interest, but drew a blank. Had she only been attracted to his good looks? Was she that shallow? Or just that desperate for attention?

She needed to break things off with him. AJ's image popped into her head and a million butterflies took flight in her stomach. Breaking up with Scott had nothing to do with AJ, she insisted to herself. AJ's piercing green eyes seemed to laser through every wall she'd constructed in order to survive.

She twisted her hands in her lap, suddenly restless. After four traumatic months as Nieto's prisoner and being sold to a sexual deviant, she didn't think she had anything left to offer anyone. She'd been abused physically, sexually. But the mental torment her memories caused were the worst.

John, the man who'd bought her, was a sadist. He craved control. And he ripped everything away from her. Her virginity, her self-worth, but especially her control. If he told her to say, *'You're my master,'* she'd had to say it.

A shiver rolled down her spine as she remembered the few times she'd tried to defy him. She'd never forget the crazy, deranged look that manifested in his dead eyes when she refused to say it. It was like watching Bruce Banner transform into the Hulk. She swore he grew in stature, and his fists turned into steel hammers. He turned those rock-hard fists onto her and beat her as if she were a concrete wall he was trying to break through. He almost killed her. It was enough to never defy him again.

She'd never completely crumbled, though. She may have seemed like a pushover, easy to manipulate. But on the inside, she built herself a place to hide, to protect herself from every wretched thing he did to her. She was a survivor.

But being a survivor didn't stop the nightmares or the silent screams that often filled her head. She drew solace in the fact she'd shot and killed him. She'd given him exactly what he deserved. Although sometimes she wished she'd used the knife tucked into her boot on his disgusting white flesh and carved his back into ribbons.

Her troublesome relationship with Scott tugged her thoughts away from her time with Nieto. She'd break it off the next time he showed up. She had no business in a relationship with anyone at this point, and the odds of her ever having a normal romance that turned into marriage and kids were not in her favor.

"What ya thinking so hard about?" Olive asked, jerking her from her tumultuous thoughts.

Her sister sauntered to the couch across from her and plopped down with her usual effortless grace that defied her lazy actions. She stretched out her long, denim-clad legs, crossing them at the ankle.

"I'm going to break up with Scott," Willow blurted.

Olive raised a brow and gave her a knowing smirk. "Oh yeah? Hmm."

She bristled. "What's with the *hmm*?"

She lifted her shoulder in a careless manner. "Oh, I don't know. Would your decision have anything to do with your tall, dark-haired savior?"

The sudden urge to smack the smug look off her sister's face overtook her normal unflappability with startling swiftness. It wasn't her usual response to her older sister's teasing. Normally, she ignored her. She learned early on not to give Olive the satisfaction of a reaction.

Not this time.

"No, it wouldn't," she bit out with a fierceness that made Olive's eyes widen. "I want to vomit every time Scott touches me. I still see—"

She cut herself off before mentioning the bastard's name who'd bought her. He haunted her nightmares, stalking her there as if he'd been resurrected to torment her.

"Willow, I'm so sorry," Olive said softly.

Olive's words struck like steel on flint, igniting a raging wind of fire, devouring her heart as if it were made of nothing but paper.

"I'm not the same naive little girl. And AJ isn't mine," she finished, breathing heavily.

Olive's face turned thoughtful. She flipped the curled end of her rich brown hair over her shoulder and reclined back.

Willow's anger settled into a low simmer. Her dad said she'd been blessed with a level head. It took a lot to make her mad, and even then, it was like a flash in a pan. This time, her vexation didn't burn off. It lingered.

She was used to Olive smarting off. Speaking before she thought things through. Olive didn't mean to be insensitive. But the idea of AJ being hers . . . well, frankly it frightened her. The connection between them was undeniable, and if she hadn't suffered through such a horrific experience, she'd jump at the chance for true romance. Who didn't want a "happily ever after"?

But the ugly truth was undeniable, and she'd never forget the things that wretched man had done. It would taint any future relationship she tried to have. Pipe dreams would only lead to more heartache.

"I'm not so sure about that," Olive said, breaking the silence between them.

She glowered at her sister, wishing she'd shut the hell up.

"I don't want to talk about AJ," Willow blasted.

"You can't hide from the world, Will."

She clenched her hands into tight fists.

"And you gotta talk. You can't keep everything bottled up inside," her sister continued, not unkindly, but in a no-nonsense manner that had Willow grinding her back molars.

"Look, Liv, I know you mean well, but could you just leave me alone? I already told you the dirty details. I can't rehash them over and over."

Unwanted tears streamed down her heated cheeks. She jumped out of her chair, needing the conversation to end.

"You need a release for all that anger. You can't heal by hiding," Olive said.

"A release for my anger," she muttered under her breath.

Unbelievable. Her sister had no earthly clue what she'd been through. Sorrow tried to burn through her anger, but she wouldn't let it. She held onto her rage. It kept her from sliding into a pit of depression so deep, so dark, that when she looked into it, it seemed bottomless. It would be so easy to slip into the darkness. To let go and disappear. But the fear she'd never recover kept the battle for sanity raging. She had to hold onto the light inside her, however dim it might be.

"Yes, a release," her sister insisted.

She paced to the living room entrance, then turned and faced her sister.

"There's no hole deep enough to bury my anger." Her voice cracked. "You don't get it. There's nothing you can do to fix me, so just leave it alone."

She couldn't tell her sister how badly she struggled just to hold on to the tiny piece of herself that remained. Anger helped her with that. Her sisters worried about her enough. She didn't need to add to their burden.

Laurel's reaction to her ordeal seemed extreme. Insane, really. She wanted to kill Nieto and it wasn't an idle threat. She knew her sister well enough to know she was dead set on her plans for revenge. If Laurel knew how much she struggled, it would tip her sister that much further over the edge.

Olive rose, walked past her, then over her shoulder said, "Follow me."

Willow rolled her eyes at her sister's back. All she wanted to do was crawl in bed and hide under the covers. When she was little and scared in the middle of the night, she'd raise the comforter over her head, convinced the monsters couldn't see her there.

But she followed Olive anyway. They climbed the stairs to the second floor and walked down the hallway. Her sister opened the door to another set of stairs that led to the attic. Olive beckoned her to continue with a hand wave.

"What are you gonna do? Lock me in the attic again?" Willow sniped.

Her sister snorted. "Laurel and I only did that once. Dad made us cut our own switches from the willow tree down by the creek, you know."

Her dad had a dry sense of humor, and she laughed softly. "I remember."

"You spent a lot of time up here in high school, as I recall."

Willow's mind cast back to those lonely days. She had a handful of friends, but they lived in town, and she'd been stuck on the farm every day after school and most weekends. The attic had been her hideout. A place to think, write down her thoughts, and paint. Her journals were still hidden beneath a loose floorboard, along with a few other childhood treasures.

They reached the top of the stairs. Dust motes hung suspended in the still air. Bright sunshine spilled out of the room's dormer window, highlighting plastic tubs along the far wall. They held toys, old blankets, photo albums, and anything else her mother deemed worthy of keeping.

Olive walked across the unfinished planks and opened the window. Cool air blew inside, scattering the dust motes and old memories that clung to her like a second skin.

Willow's old easel sat by the window. Someone had found a blank canvas and set it on the stand.

"If you won't talk," her sister said gently, "maybe you could paint."

Olive gave her shoulder a squeeze, walked back down the stairs, leaving her to stare at the white canvas. Scattered images appeared, dark and ominous, begging to be released. Could she let out the dark mass of confusion and anger roiling inside her? Stare into the face of her own red-eyed demon? She shuddered, not at all certain she was ready for that.

Then AJ's image appeared.

She opened an old chest containing her oil paints, brushes, and a jar of turpentine.

She set to work, hours passing without her knowledge. She lost herself as swirls of mixed oil paints transformed the image in her head onto the canvas.

A short knock jolted her out of her creative haze, and she looked up to find AJ leaning against the door frame, watching her.

Her face flamed as she glanced down at her work. Panic filled her chest. What would he think if he saw what she'd done?

"Can I look?" AJ asked, pushing off the door jamb.

"No," she blurted. "How'd you find me?"

He lifted a shoulder. "Olive told me you were up here."

Her brows furrowed. "What do you want, AJ?"

She needed to get him out of here. Now. But how?

A challenging glint shone through his eyes. "Why can't I see?"

As their eyes connected, she wondered why in the world she ever thought them fascinating.

"Because," she answered on a shaky breath.

"That's not an answer," he returned, the corner of his mouth tipping into a crooked grin.

Frantically, she cast her eyes around the room, searching for the old sheet she'd used in the past to cover her work, but it was nowhere in sight.

She groaned as he prowled forward. "Why me?" she muttered.

5

Willow's brows furrowed in concentration, and a slight frown tipped the corners of her mouth. She dabbed the tiniest paintbrush AJ had ever seen into a swirl of bluish-black paint on a palette.

The palette sat on a high wooden stool beside the easel. Its wooden legs weren't quite flush with the seat, and he wondered how many times her palette full of mixed paints slid off. He glanced at the floor to find paint splatters in a bright array of colors, confirming his suspicion. The spattered paint created a rainbow-colored half-moon around her feet making it look as if it was done on purpose.

It occurred to him after he'd stood there a while, she might consider this an invasion of privacy. But his feet wouldn't budge. He just kept watching her.

She wiped her forehead with the back of her hand, leaving a streak of white paint behind. A sigh escaped her lips as she studied her work. The tiny paintbrush was dropped into a jar at her feet, containing some sort of liquid. He took a deep breath through his nose. A soft wind from the open window blew the strong scent of pine and citrus toward him. Turpentine maybe? She picked up a larger brush from a dark-stained wooden box.

He flipped his bangs out of his eyes and gave a short rap on the door's jamb with his knuckles.

Her head shot up. A flash of panic swept across her face, her cheeks flushing a deep red. Her lips parted, her breaths coming short and swift.

Curious, he stepped forward and asked, "Can I look?"

"No," she snapped. "How'd you find me?"

AJ shrugged a shoulder, trying his best to play it cool. "Olive told me you were up here."

His answer seemed to upset her. Her brows came down, and she unconsciously bit her lower lip in concentration.

Her gaze flitted around the room, then landed back on him. "What do you want, AJ?"

Holy hell. He loved his name on her lips and wished he could tell her exactly what he wanted. But he could never have her the way he wanted, so he deflected.

"Why can't I see?" he asked, his lips beginning to tip up.

"Because."

His small grin widened. More curious, he took a step forward. What had she painted?

"That's not an answer," he returned with an ease that matched his quick stride forward.

She glanced away, and he took advantage of her distraction. He took one more step. It brought him close enough for a quick peek of what she'd been working on with such intensity she hadn't noticed his presence.

Willow turned back and gasped when she realized he'd seen it. She wrenched the easel and canvas away from his gaze, almost toppling the whole thing onto the dusty wooden floor. She righted it, then turned a furious look in his direction.

He stared at her, knocked a little off center. He couldn't blame her violent reaction to him seeing it because . . . because she'd painted *him*.

Painted him walking down the main sidewalk in downtown Cotulla. He recognized Ben's retail store front due to its enormous, unique sign. The big brown boot sporting a cowboy hat, and the declaration, "A Texas Legend" was hard to miss. His head was partially bent, watching his shoes as he walked. That's the impression he got anyway.

But she hadn't left his head bent all the way. She'd lifted his head just enough for his eyes to stare straight out of the painting. And she'd painted his eyes a startling shade of green. How she mixed her paints to come up with the perfect shade of peridot was impressive.

In the background, a storm brewed in the sky, dark and ominous. Swirling clouds enveloped the sky above and wind kicked up dust at his feet. He wanted to look at the painting again, examine it. It was a window into her soul, he realized with startling clarity.

"What are you doing up here?" she seethed as she dragged the easel and canvas to the far wall, well out of sight.

"You're talented," he remarked.

Her eyes narrowed. "Yeah, well I'll probably just primer it and start over."

"Why would you do that?"

An unsettling tiny stab of hurt pricked his heart. He braced himself against the pain until it subsided, took a deep breath, and continued to study her. She walked back and stood by the doorway. They stared at one another until it became a battle of wills. Who would turn away first?

She crossed her arms, and harrumphed, but a smile tried to break across her face as she broke eye contact.

She stared back at the canvas. "I always strike my paintings and start over, in answer to your question."

"You never keep a painting?" he asked, incredulously. "Why not?"

She shrugged. "I'm my worst critic and besides, who would want them? My sister brought me up here because she thinks painting will help me heal," she said, using air quotes around the last word. "It's what I did in high school, because . . ." She drifted off.

AJ watched her mood turn from melancholy to morose and wondered what memory she'd dredged up from the past. He shifted on his feet, thinking.

His original intent for seeking her out was to talk about Laurel. She still wanted revenge against Nieto, and he wanted Willow's true opinion on the matter. Plus, he couldn't fight the constant urge to be near her, as if an invisible cord tethered them together. It was the most powerful thing he'd ever felt in his life, and the more he was around her, the stronger the feeling grew.

He cleared his throat. "Ummm, I actually came up here to talk to you," he said, drawing her attention away from the thoughts that made her frown.

She gave a dramatic sigh. "If you've come to talk about Scott, forget it. I'm tired of that subject."

"No," he drew out the word. "It's not that."

He couldn't blame her for thinking he wanted to harp on Scott again. He'd intended to sneak that into their conversation but now thought better of it. Judging her mood, he didn't want to stir the pot.

Besides, he needed to stay focused. He couldn't have her anyway. He wouldn't let himself. So, what did it matter if she painted over him? It shouldn't bother him the way it did, and if she wanted to stay with that preening, narcissistic jerk, he couldn't stop her.

The thoughts triggered other memories without warning. They exploded into his mind as if lightning struck the top of his head. He couldn't push them down fast enough, and a face flashed into his mind. The girl who used to own his heart. Quinn. And the reason he could never have Willow. He sucked in a sharp breath as her face swam inside his memories.

"What is it, then?" Willow asked, tapping her foot against the floor's wooden slats.

Her voice drove Quinn's image away, but the sharp, uninvited echo of her remained.

Averting his eyes, he said, "I just wanted to talk to you about Laurel."

She searched the tiny attic's corners until she found a dusty sheet. Shaking it out, she moved back to the easel.

"What about her?" she asked as she covered up the canvas with the paint-splattered sheet.

"She wants to go after Nieto," he stated.

He shook off the remnants of Quinn's memory. He'd go crazy if he allowed himself to dwell on her.

"I know," she said quietly.

"Do you want her to?" he asked.

"Does it matter?" she countered.

"It should matter."

She shook her head. "Laurel does what Laurel wants. No matter what. She's stubborn. And once she's made up her mind about something, you can't change it."

"She's asking us to go back to Mexico City. That's a huge risk."

"I know," she repeated. "You're not telling me anything I don't already know. Just because I'm quiet, doesn't mean I'm stupid or naive. I get it."

Taken aback by her sharp tone, he stopped and thought about his next words. He'd never taken her for a fool. A fierce protectiveness he couldn't explain rode him hard as if she was his to protect. She wasn't. But that wouldn't stop him from doing it.

He took a step toward her. "I know you're not stupid, darlin'," he said, gentleness infused into every syllable. "I just wonder why you let your sister have her way when it's obvious to anyone who cares to look that it causes you pain."

Her face flushed a deeper red, but she kept her eyes trained on his. "It wouldn't matter to Laurel if she knew it hurt me."

"Why?" he asked, scrubbing a hand down his face.

"It's a 'big sister knows best' thing. You should get that, right? You treat Lacy the same way. At least that's what she told me."

He rubbed the back of his neck. Dammit. Lacy and her big mouth.

"You're basing your opinion of me on one story? That football player had his hand on her ass. Did she tell you that? All I did was yell at him. I should've broken his hand."

She laughed despite herself. "She left out that part. But she could've taken care of the problem herself."

He squinted his eyes, the beginning of a headache coming on. "She could've. But what kind of brother would I be if I didn't say something? I understand Laurel's feelings. Man, I got them too. But it's reckless for her to go after Nieto. It could end up killing us all."

She threw up a hand in a helpless gesture. "What do you want me to do?"

"Try and talk her out of it."

"I already did. She *knows* this causes me pain, AJ. I've already told her. I was outvoted. Two to one. Even Olive wants to do this."

He cursed under his breath. "You're sure they won't change their minds?"

She sighed. "I'm sure. And they'll want to talk to you again."

The light burning through the window waned. Clouds shifted, the wind blowing them across the sun, diluting its rays. A gust of cool air blew dust off the floor, and the temperature dropped. Willow moved to the window and closed it, then picked up her paint and paintbrushes off the floor.

She walked to the door where he stood. "Where's Bryan?"

He rolled his eyes. "Last time I saw him he was bugging Olive about taking the four wheelers out."

She stepped out the door, and he followed. He shouldn't have followed her to her bedroom, but that didn't stop him. The invisible cord connecting them tugged him along, and his heart happily followed. It was his brain fighting, pulling back like a tug of war.

She walked into her bedroom then turned around. He leaned against the door jamb, his thumbs hooked into his front pockets.

"I'm sorry I snapped at you earlier," she said softly. His face must've mirrored confusion because she clarified, "About Scott."

He lifted a brow. "Okay."

Her eyes darted around the room before settling back on him. "I um—"

She looked nervous. Was it because he followed her to her bedroom? He instinctively backed into the hallway, thinking his presence must be the reason.

Her nervousness dissipated and curiosity washed over her features. "Where are you going?"

He let out a flustered laugh. "I don't know. You looked scared, so . . ."

"I'm not," she said in a serious voice. "I just wanted to say I . . ." She paused, taking a moment to look out the window. "I'm going to break up with Scott."

His eyes widened. Of all the things she could've said, he never expected her to say that. And then it hit him. As he searched her upturned face, mesmerized by her full, soft lips, he realized he was in trouble. The in-way-over-his-head kind of trouble.

Like it or not, Scott had been a barrier between them. One he needed to keep his distance. Now it was gone. Or it would be soon. After that, it would be harder than ever to keep his resolve not to claim her.

He couldn't have her, and he needed to remember that.

Shit.

This was a complication.

The drive along the Pacific Coast Highway stole Lacy's breath. The Santa Lucia Mountains rose in majestic splendor to the east, casting long shadows along the green earth below. As she gazed out at the rugged terrain, she half-expected to see Bilbo Baggins trekking across the peaks behind a grey-clad wizard. What would it be like to experience another life in a different era?

The sun played peek-a-boo, hiding behind white, fluffy clouds. When it burst forth again, the great expanse of the Pacific Ocean rippled with wave after wave of gold. She rolled down the window and breathed in the salty sea air.

The sharp odor of fish reminded her of racing along the Kaw Lake shoreline on her horse, Acer. She missed her horse, her friends, and the farm. What she didn't miss was her uncle and how he'd turned the farm into a military compound. She flicked the image of her uncle out of her head with a mental middle finger stuck in the air.

Gazing out at the ocean made her feel small, insignificant in the grand scheme of things. It was difficult to comprehend its enormity. She'd seen pictures deep sea divers published in magazines like National Geographic. It looked like an alien planet down below, beautiful with its rich rainbow colors, yet ominous and dangerous at the same time.

The wind whipped her hair, swirling it like a tornado. She grabbed it, then reached into her pocket for a rubber band. Twisting the black band around her thick hair without a brush to tame it was a test in patience. She finally managed a messy bun atop her head.

Closing her eyes, she breathed in the ocean air, teeming with a life of its own. Worries melted away. Hope for a happy, fulfilling life with Jace burgeoned in her chest. What would a life before the Big Crash look like with Jace? How would he have proposed to her? On a big screen at one of his college baseball games?

She sighed heavily, opened her eyes, and turned to find Jace grinning at her.

"You win the battle?" he asked with a chuckle.

"Har, har," she groused good-naturedly.

She turned to look out the window and her breath hitched as they approached Bixby Bridge along the Big Sur coastline. The open archway bridge was nestled between a large crevasse in the rugged terrain. It looked so natural. As if the land had naturally created the way across the Pacific Ocean below.

A little awestruck, he said, "I've never seen anything quite like this."

"It's amazing," she agreed. "So different from Oklahoma."

A contented sigh escaped his lips, and the sound made her ridiculously happy. The angry red slash around his neck from his time spent in the sadistic hands of Dr. Widdowson had faded into a pink, checkered line. He still woke in the middle of the night, covered in sweat. Nightmares of drowning haunted his sleep.

Nieto was the Freddie Krueger that preyed upon her dreams in the nighttime hours. Often, she'd already be awake when he started thrashing, fighting the covers like they were waves trying to pull him under. When he woke, she wrapped him tightly in her arms and just held him until the trembling in his limbs subsided.

After that, he'd kiss her, sometimes gently, drawing her into his arms. Other times, his kiss would turn desperate. Her stomach fluttered.

"What are you thinking about?" he asked, breaking her thoughts.

Caught in daydreams about him, she hadn't noticed he'd parked the truck in the middle of the bridge.

Heat rushed up her neck. "Nothing."

He chuckled as his hand cupped her burning cheek. "Why do you look so guilty?"

She let out a dramatic sigh, but her lips tipped into a smile. "I was thinking about you, okay? There. I've fed your egotistical dragon. Happy now?"

He leaned over and brushed his lips against hers. "You make me extremely happy," he whispered against her mouth.

He deepened the kiss, drawing her under his spell. His hand threaded through her hair, freeing it from the rubber band. She gasped when his grip tightened. His other hand wrapped around her waist, tugging her closer until her chest was flush against his. A laugh tickled her throat when he growled and pulled her onto his lap, facing him.

He leaned back. "Tell me," he began, his voice raspy. "What exactly were you thinking?"

She sobered, ran a hand through his shoulder-length, dark-brown hair. "I was wondering how I got so lucky."

He turned them sideways. In a quick, deft move, he laid her on the truck's bench seat, pinning her underneath him.

"I can't wait to change your name," he murmured in her ear.

She brushed her lips along his throat, kissing the mark Widow's rope had left there. "Put your hands on me, Jace."

He let out a satisfied growl and kissed her again.

After they'd spent time exploring each other, they got out of the truck and walked along Bixby Bridge. Lacy leaned over the bridge's pebbled concrete railing and her stomach flipped at the distance of the sheer drop. She tightened her grip on the cool, hard surface beneath her palms. Wind whipped through her tangled hair, blowing it behind her.

The shrill call of a condor echoed on the wind. She scanned the horizon until she found the majestic bird, flying along the coastline. The sun glinted off its wide wingspan as it swooped toward the ocean.

"Cut it out," Jace warned, walking toward her, his strides lengthening with every step.

She turned her head and grinned. "Does this scare you?" she asked, leaning farther out.

"Yes, dammit."

He grabbed the back of her T-shirt. Pulling her off the rail, he flipped her around to face him. The shit-eating grin on her face earned her a darkened scowl. She tried pushing him away, but he didn't budge.

"I was just having fun," she pouted, a smile pulling the corners of her mouth upward.

His eyes narrowed. "Find another way to have fun. I didn't get you back just to lose you again."

Normally, it irritated her to be bossed around, and the snippy remark on the tip of her tongue almost escaped. But the real terror she read in his eyes snuffed it out. He had a point, she conceded to herself. They'd been through too much for her to be reckless.

She wrapped her arms around his neck and changed the subject. "I'm hungry. And tired."

His expression softened. "Carmel is just up the road. We'll stop there."

"And find a preacher?"

He brushed a strand of hair off her forehead. "Hell yeah. I can't wait."

From the corner of his eye, AJ caught Willow's lithe frame dart into the kitchen. Her pretty, yellow-flowered sundress showed off her gorgeous neck and shoulders. He'd never thought about a woman's neck being sexy or seductive, until Willow.

The few days of nourishment and rest had placed the glow back into her face and skin. She still needed to gain a few pounds, but the bruises covering her body were fading. He didn't know about her internal scars, though.

Nightmares invaded her sleep. The thin wall that separated their bedrooms did little to muffle her screams. His heart tore a little more each night as she begged over and over for someone to stop.

She'd made an art form of avoiding him, her cheeks staining a bright pink each time they passed in the hallway. She was embarrassed about the painting and would probably rather tackle a porcupine than talk to him.

It seemed the more they talked, the tighter their mysterious invisible bond grew. He felt it. She felt it. Avoiding each other was for the best. It was a mantra he played over and over in his head. Still, his heart suffered over her silence.

Laurel cornered him at the kitchen's threshold, dashing his hopes of catching Willow before she disappeared again.

"I want to go undercover," Laurel said, voice low. "If you'd just tell me where he lives, I can—"

He scrubbed a hand over his face. Enough. If he heard that horrible man's name one more time, he'd end up driving his fist through the living room wall.

"No," he growled.

"We can beat Nieto at his own game," Laurel said, pointing a finger at him.

He knocked her hand from his face as he turned his gaze from the corner. Willow disappeared like a phantom as if his mind conjured her image just to torture him.

He sighed, gave his full attention to Laurel, and ground out, "No, we can't."

"We have to try!" she half-shouted, voice going shrill.

She took a step back, fists clenched at her sides as if the distance she put between them would keep her from beating him bloody.

He rubbed his ear, annoyed at her tone. "It's a suicide mission. Can't you be happy your sister's home? Take the win," he ended in a mutter, rolling his eyes.

Her face mottled an unflattering red. Blotches bloomed against her cheekbones, and on her nose. It looked like hives had broken out all over her face.

"If he gets away scot free after what he's done to Willow, that's not a win!" she shouted at the top of her lungs.

"If you feel the need to do something, go to the Mexican authorities," he said in what he hoped was a reasonable tone. "Maybe they can help. At least start there instead of premeditating a man's death."

She pointed a finger in his face. Again. He stepped back at the flash of fury in her golden-brown eyes. He could tell the thought of slapping the shit out of him was becoming a real possibility now. He'd never strike back but that didn't mean he wanted to take the hit.

"You *know* they won't help. Nieto probably has them in his back pocket."

He couldn't deny it.

"True," he said, drawing out the word, "but at least you'd try the right way first. You'd have a clear conscience."

"Damn you!" she yelled, spittle flying from her down-turned mouth. "You know nothing about my conscience!"

"True," he said again, eyeing her clenched fists. "You might be a sociopath for all I know. All you think about is yourself. You're blind to Willow's pain, or worse, you're choosing to ignore it."

"I'm not a sociopath!" she shouted, her arms flapping like chicken wings trying to take flight.

He smirked, knowing his next comment would get under her skin. "Sounds like something a sociopath would say."

The off-hand, taunting remark bordered on pushing Laurel too far. He knew it the second the decision to sucker-punch him flashed into her eyes. Her balled-up fist aimed right for his nose. It was easy to dodge. Anger made her movements slip shod. She stumbled a bit when her fist connected with nothing but air.

Catching herself, she smoothed her long, deep-brown hair, lifted her chin, and was about to spout something nasty when Willow marched around the corner.

Irritation set Willow's lips into a fine line. Fire flashed in her eyes, causing them to darken like a spring storm.

With hands on her hips, she turned to AJ. "Can you two knock it off? I can fight my own battles, so back off." Swinging on her heel, she faced her sister and said, "Laurel, I'm fine. Going after Nieto is crazy. Can't you just let it go?"

Her sister huffed a disbelieving laugh. "So, I'm just supposed to ignore what that piece of trash did to you?"

"Yes," Willow said, face softening.

Laurel took a long, drawn-out moment to look Willow over but in the end shook her head.

"I can't do that," she returned stiffly. "You deserve justice and there's no one out there who will fight for you. If I thought the proper authorities would take care of it, I'd turn it all over to them right now. But there's no one left, Will. No one but us will stand against what Nieto is doing."

"You can't even try?" Willow pleaded.

"Do you know what Dad would do?" Laurel asked, changing tactics. "He'd hunt him down and kill him. I have to do what I think is right. Mom and Dad—" Her voice cracked, and she struggled to clear it. "My *conscience* will not rest until justice is served."

Shaking her head again, Willow turned and left, striding toward the kitchen. A few seconds later the back door slammed.

AJ gave Laurel a withering look, then followed Willow outside.

She sat on the bottom porch step. He walked down and sat beside her, shoving his hands into his pockets in an effort not to reach out and touch her. His fingers itched to run down the length of her slender neck, feel her skin. Was it as soft and supple as it appeared?

She gave him a sidelong glance, running nervous fingers through her ponytail.

"I'm sorry I snapped at you," she finally said. "Again."

The words drew him out of his daydream, and he shrugged. "It's okay."

They stared at each other unflinchingly until she nodded and started to turn away.

He caught her wrist in a soft grip. "I said it's okay you snapped at me. I didn't agree to stop fighting for you. Just so you know."

Her shoulders sagged. "What is it with you?"

The defeated tone in those words made his stomach clench.

He wanted to wipe away the sadness on her face. He wanted . . . he wanted her. And it scared him.

"I . . ." He faltered as Quinn's face emerged from the recesses of his mind again, halting the confession from tumbling out of his mouth.

An admission he'd want to retract later, no doubt.

Quinn. The fragile, dark-haired girl that once held his heart with such completeness, it surprised him at first. She'd shattered it beyond repair. He'd tried to pick up the jagged pieces and put them back together, but it was never the same. He couldn't seem to close the gaping maw in the center of it.

Willow's impatient huff drew his attention back to her. He ran a hand through his hair, completely and utterly confused.

After Quinn, he'd bedded women without thinking of the consequences. Now, that "love 'em and leave 'em" attitude sullied him. He was unworthy of Willow.

He released her wrist, rose from the step, and walked away.

AJ TOSSED and turned on the lumpy, uncomfortable twin mattress. The house was quiet with a preternatural stillness that crept under his skin. Goosebumps rose to the surface on his arms. Too early for chittering pre-dawn birds, he strained to hear anything in the darkness. He needed something to latch onto to chase away the disturbing dream that had jolted him awake.

Too late. He was always too late. Born from past traumatic events he refused to face, his nightmares always ended the same. His subconscious was a brutal bastard. He wished he could at least dream of saving her. Saving Quinn. But maybe that would be worse.

His family remained unaware of his internal struggle. He kept his feelings close to the vest, wrapped in a safe cocoon in the furthest recesses of his mind. Sometimes, the cocoon split open and hatched a monster. Then the tedious, painstaking process of rebuilding the encasement would start over.

He flipped onto his back and stared at the inky black ceiling. What happened to Quinn was his fault. He should've been there. But he wasn't. He huffed out a breath, berating himself for dwelling on her.

A muffled scream interrupted his tumbling thoughts.

Willow.

He shot up, pain from his ribs barking in protest. He listened intently in the pressing silence.

Another scream, followed by whimpers and muffled cries.

Since their return, night terrors seemed to drag her kicking and screaming into a bottomless pit. Her screams slashed through his core like knives, and when she cried out for help, it was like salt being poured into those wounds. Every night he'd wanted to go to her, comfort her. But he hadn't.

He swung his feet over the side of the bed before he could change his mind. Pain shot up his side, drawing a low growl and a curse from his lips. He strode out his bedroom door not bothering to put on the crumpled T-shirt lying on the floor he'd worn for two days. His bare feet slapped against the hard wood as he walked the short distance to her bedroom door. He stopped and listened.

A pitiful wail drew him inside without a second thought. He didn't want to scare her awake, so he sat down beside her careful not to touch her.

"Willow," he murmured, soft and low.

He laid a gentle hand on her bare shoulder and tried not to ogle the thin pink camisole and night shorts that left little to the imagination. His thumb caressed her soft skin. She calmed at his touch, but her face remained pale and strained.

He began soothing her by speaking in a quiet, lilting voice. It was something he'd watched Jace do with horses. It didn't matter what you said. It was the tone of your voice that mattered.

"You're home, Willow. You're safe. I'll protect you from the monster chasing you. He's not real. You're safe," he repeated, swallowing hard. "You're safe with me. Stay with me, darlin'."

He stroked her forehead, brushing tendrils of blond hair from her eyes. Only when she'd quieted completely did he rise from the bed.

"Sweet sleep," he murmured, brushing a kiss on her forehead.

He padded on quiet feet to the door. Turning, he gazed at her one last time before shutting it with a soft click.

8

Willow climbed the attic stairs and opened the door, determined to strike the painting of AJ. The fact he saw it would haunt her for the rest of her life. She still couldn't shake her mortification.

Why did he have to seek her out? It was as if fate led him there right when she was swirling the last finishing touches on the painting of him.

The easel still stood in the corner where she'd hastily dragged it away from his prying eyes. Then she realized her paintbrushes were still soaking in turpentine. Dammit. She should've cleaned them. Her high school art teacher would've raked her over the coals if he saw the mess she'd left behind. Grabbing the jar, she hurried down the stairs to the bathroom sink.

Water flowed from the faucet in a soft hush. She cleaned each brush with punishing strokes and scrubs. An old plastic cup sat on the grey-flecked granite counter to her right. She dropped the clean brushes into it then noticed the water dripping from its sides. A wet greyish ring circled the base. Cursing, she grabbed a hand towel from the wire rack above the toilet and wiped it away. Laurel would complain if she left a stain, launching into a lecture about cleanliness and being considerate of other people who used the same bathroom.

She lifted the jar of turpentine to her nose. The fumes burned in a pleasant way. Memories of time spent in Mr. Rafferty's art room flooded her mind. She'd learned the importance of negative space and techniques of perspective. Mr. Rafferty made art seem effortless. She learned to appreciate all art forms, even though working with clay was not her forte. The lopsided jar she'd painted in monochromes of blue in her mother's kitchen was proof of that.

She screwed on the jar's lid and deposited it under the sink. She'd missed the familiar smells of her mixed media paints and paper. Even the musty odor of the attic held a special place in her heart.

Ugly memories of those long months spent in forced confinement tried to push their way forward. She shoved them back into the mental box marked Nieto. She had no idea how to navigate the healing process. If it was possible to take the Nieto box from her mind and burn it, she would. She knew it wouldn't be that easy. So for now, ignoring it was all she could do.

As for the painting, well, it had been foolish to place AJ in it. The concepts for her art came in the form of still-shots that flashed into her mind. She'd been thinking of downtown Cotulla. Antiquated and unkempt, it was nothing to write home about. But Ben's storefront sign, painted onto the upper levels of the red brick building, boasting of being "A Texas Legend," had snagged her thoughts like fish on a trout line.

Determined to get primer on the canvas as soon as possible, she shut off the water, grabbed the towel she'd thrown to the side and wiped down the counter and faucet knobs. It was sopping wet by the time she'd finished. Looking down, she realized the front of her favorite T-shirt was soaked with water and splattered with flecks of paint.

"Shit," she muttered.

She threw the towel into the clothes hamper, then strode to her bedroom and slammed the door.

Her twin sleigh bed sat against the far wall, dressed in a pink flowered comforter and matching shams. A pink Tiffany lamp sat on the black nightstand beside the bed. She turned it on and moved to the matching black dresser against the opposite wall.

She pulled an old T-shirt from the bottom drawer. It had faded to a light maroon, but her high school mascot, a man on a bucking bronco outlined in black, could still be seen. The shirt brought back unwanted memories.

Kids weren't exactly mean to her, they just ignored her. Sometimes she wondered if a slap to the face would've been better than being invisible. At least they'd know she existed.

She slung the T-shirt onto her bed and pulled off the soiled one. A knock sounded on her door, but before she could respond, AJ strode into the room. She squeaked, clutching the shirt to her bare chest.

"I'm sorry," AJ stammered. "I didn't think . . . uh, I mean I thought you—"

"Get out!" she shouted, face flaming.

AJ backed up, bumping into the wall. His eyes dipped to her chest, then back to her face. Desire swirled in his cat-green eyes.

Her thoughts scattered under his intense stare and her breath stalled. "What do you want, AJ?" she asked, barely able to punch out the words.

He arched a brow, and a slow smile spread across his face, but he said nothing.

Neither one spoke. She held her breath under his intense stare.

Finally, she pulled her gaze from his and said, "If you want to talk to me, I can meet you in the library nook. *After* I put on some clothes," she stressed.

"Okay," he said softly.

She didn't look back until she heard the door's soft click as he closed it.

"Oh my God," she breathed.

Heart pounding, her feet propelled her backward toward the bed in slow motion. She sat down, dropped the soiled T-shirt to the floor and stared out the dormer window.

A carrion bird circled in the distance below the low-hanging, dark grey clouds that filled the sky. Round and round it went, biding its time, waiting for some animal to take its last breath so it could feast. Its black wings fluttered, catching a cool breeze, and continued its orbit.

Cruel bird. Pity filled her heart for the poor, ill-fated creature lying on the cold, unforgiving prairie. It reminded her of Nieto, snatching helpless girls from their families and feasting on them for profit.

A burst of rage swept over her, and a metallic tang filled the back of her throat. Nieto needed to be stopped. On that she could agree with her sisters. But how could they possibly be the ones to do it? They weren't trained. Even though all three Sinclair girls had been schooled on guns by their father, it didn't qualify them to launch a mission to hunt someone down. This wasn't the movie *Taken,* and none of them were Liam Neeson for God's sake.

Her thoughts drifted to Scott. How did he play into all of this? He hadn't returned since Bryan and AJ essentially drove off him and his friend Diego. Scott wasn't stupid. He probably suspected the break up and was keeping his distance. He wasn't wrong. Again, she tried to convince herself that the decision to end things with Scott had nothing to do with AJ. She tried.

The nightmare from the morning flickered into her mind. She swallowed hard, throat still raw from screaming. Her sister's bedrooms located downstairs prevented them from hearing the screams that ripped from her gut every night, which Willow preferred. She didn't need them hovering over her like a terminally ill cancer patient.

And she certainly didn't need any more pep talks. Her sisters meant well but made things worse by trying to get her to bear her soul. Yesterday attested to this fact when they'd double-teamed her at breakfast.

"Hey Will," Olive had said in a cheerful voice that sounded too forced.

Wariness settled on her like a wet blanket as Laurel joined them at the table.

"We thought maybe you might want to talk," Laurel offered.

The pity in their eyes soured her stomach. They tried to pry more information from her, tried to get her to open up about the time she spent in Mexico City. They meant well. What they didn't seem to grasp was they were making the whole situation worse. She didn't want to talk about the horrible things she'd endured. She spent most of her days trying to forget them.

Some things she wasn't ready to think about, much less talk about. And some things she might never drag into the light.

She dressed, made her way out the door, and was about to descend the stairs when she drew up short. What did AJ want to talk to her about? He'd sure got an eyeful when he barged into her room. Her body had taken the reins from her brain as he perused her half-naked. His stare filled her with heat, butterflies, and a tingling expectation. Ugh. Add that to the list of reasons to avoid him.

At the snap of his fingers, every girl in his tri-state area probably jumped without even asking "How high?" The more she thought, the less she wanted to go downstairs where he waited. Had he ever been stood up? She huffed a laugh. Definitely not.

He had the looks movie stars would kill for with his perfectly squared jaw, straight teeth, and rock-hard body. As if the gods didn't bless him enough, they added intriguing peridot eyes, slightly upturned at the ends.

She desperately wanted to go down and see what he wanted, but she turned in the opposite direction and headed to the attic to primer over the painting of him. She wouldn't be the pathetic, moon-eyed girl she'd been with Scott. She couldn't be.

AFTER AN HOUR WAITING in the library nook, AJ couldn't deny it any longer. Willow had stood him up. He shifted in the red wing-backed chair and smiled. He'd never been stood up before. Never once been shot down by any woman he'd asked out or just wanted to— He shut down the thought before it could morph into something he'd brood about.

He could try and find her but decided against it. If she didn't want to talk, which she'd made glaringly obvious by not showing up, he'd respect that.

The back door slammed, and he heard Bryan and Olive move into the kitchen, arguing. Again. Bryan had agreed to help Olive with farm chores while they temporarily lived at the Sinclair Ranch. He couldn't understand why Bryan spent so much time with her. She was a bit of a loudmouth. And crass for a girl. Beautiful, yes, but salty.

She'd launch an insult at Bryan like a Russian missile. He'd bluster, then lob one right back at her. If AJ didn't know any better, he'd say Bryan enjoyed Olive's indelicate behavior.

He rose and strolled into the kitchen, curious about their latest sparing match.

Bryan's eyes darted to him as he entered. He gave him a head bob in acknowledgement.

Olive tossed a dusty black cowboy hat onto the counter and crossed her arms over her chest. "You're out of your mind," she declared hotly.

The grin plastered on Bryan's face widened, and he raised his hand in a Boy Scout salute. "I swear to God, me and my brothers tipped a cow once."

Olive blew out a breath through her nose. "It's physically impossible! And for your information, dumbass, cows don't sleep on their feet."

Bryan scratched his head in feigned thought. "Are you sure? They do where I come from."

He snickered. "He's playing you."

Bryan shot him a look that shouted, *Stay out of it.*

"Idiot," Olive muttered, bumping Bryan's shoulder as she strode out of the kitchen.

Bryan watched her leave, then turned to him. "Dammit, man. I could've kept her going for another thirty minutes. Why'd you have to rat me out?"

"Cow tipping? Really? You couldn't come up with a better argument?" he scoffed.

Bryan shrugged. "Nah. She'll argue about anything."

"You like her," he said, lifting a brow.

Bryan let out a noncommittal grunt. "I like to annoy her. She's funny when she gets mad."

"Whatever. Living in denial suits you," he goaded.

"What about Willow?" Bryan asked with a teasing glint in his bright brown eyes.

His eyes narrowed. "What about her?"

He'd walked right into that. Shit. He wasn't ready to admit he had feelings for Willow. Not to her and certainly not to Bryan.

"You like her, yeah?"

He rubbed the back of his neck. "Come on."

"So, you don't like her?" Bryan pressed, drawing out each syllable in dramatic fashion.

He stared silently at his friend, lips mashed into a thin line. The intrusive questions felt like being probed by an alien.

"Hmm. Maybe I'll ask Willow out," Bryan mused, giving him a sidelong glance.

The idea made him see red even though he knew Bryan didn't want Willow. He smothered the instinct to throw a right hook at the linebacker, but his fists clenched in response to the punch of adrenaline.

"Go to hell," he ground out and stalked from the room.

Bryan's laughter echoed from the kitchen. He knew his friend was just messing with him, but it still rubbed him the wrong way. He walked back to the library nook, picked out another book, and returned to his room. He spent the rest of the afternoon holed up, reading until he couldn't hold his eyelids open any longer.

Willow's crying woke him from a sound sleep sometime later. The book had fallen to the floor. He picked it up and placed it on the nightstand.

He pulled on a pair of sweatpants and padded out of the room. The hallway nightlight cast a streak of yellow light through the crack in her door.

The door creaked as he pushed it open. He tiptoed to the side of her bed and looked down. Her face was buried into her pillow, but her body seemed relaxed, her breathing steady. The mattress dipped and the springs popped as he sat beside her. In the stillness, he listened to the house breathe.

Willow turned. She stared at him, eyes glistening in the low light.

"Do you come in here every night?" she asked, voice thin and reedy from sleep.

He nodded. "I can't stand to hear you in so much pain."

He understated his feelings. Hearing her cry out in desperation every night shredded his soul. He wanted to help her, he just didn't know how.

So he did the only thing he could do. Offer her comfort. It wasn't a smart thing for him to do. She wasn't his to comfort. Not really. She was Scott's girlfriend. And he needed to remember that, keep his head on straight, and bury his true feelings for her. They'd both get hurt in the end if he didn't.

"Thanks," she said, eyes dipping shyly.

"You're welcome," he said, his voice gruffer than he'd intended.

She scooted over and patted the bed. An invitation to stay. And just like that, his resolve to keep his distance, bury his feelings, evaporated like water on a hot summer day. He knew better than to read more into it than she was offering, but he needed to make sure he understood what she wanted.

"What do you need, Willow?" he asked softly.

"You," she said on a sigh.

It was on the tip of his tongue to tell her she already had him. From the moment he saw her in the hotel garage in Mexico City. But he held back, and tried to remind himself he could never have her.

Instead, he laid down and gathered her into his arms.

9

Quaint buildings with gabled roofs and square pane windows lined Ocean Avenue in Carmel. Lacy rolled down her window, folded her arms on top of the truck's passenger door, and stared in awe at the shops as they drove slowly past. Most shops had red-and-white closed signs hanging from their windows. However, a few shop owners propped their doors open, allowing the flow of shoppers to pass through.

Fruits, nuts, and vegetables stacked in neat rows on wooden carts lined both sides of the street. Their vibrant arrays of red, yellow, green, orange, and brown attracted shoppers to the stands. A butcher stood, cleaver in hand, behind his table covered in butcher paper. A white apron with blood splotches enveloped his large, Santa Claus belly.

An old, white-haired lady with a tiny black poodle on a pink leash stood in front of the butcher, waving an expressive hand in the air. The middle-aged man barked a laugh, nodded, then left the stand and entered his shop.

Jace pulled into an empty parking spot at the end of the plaza square and cut the engine. Her eyes drifted to the small crowd gathered around an apple stand. She'd never been a big fan of apples unless they were in one of her mom's pies. Now, she'd eat a dozen of the juicy reds if she could get her hands on them.

They had no money. The only way they'd get food in their bellies tonight would be stealing or working. She chewed on her thumbnail. What were they going to do? She turned and found Jace studying her with a slight frown.

She tried to cover her worry with a bright smile. Jace had enough to think about. She wanted to share the burdens he carried, not add to them.

Escaping the work camps seemed like a blessing. She wondered, though, if they'd just exchanged one evil for another. At least they had a chance to survive on their own. Citizens placed in the work camps had no freedom at all.

He lifted her hand to his lips and placed a soft kiss on her upturned palm. "It'll be all right. We'll figure this out, okay?"

She nodded her head, biting her bottom lip. "What are we going to do?"

Her stomach cramped and rumbled out an angry growl. She laughed self-consciously and placed a hand against her middle. She trusted him. It was her stomach that held doubts.

"We'll stop and ask if anyone needs help," he responded in a reassuring tone. "We'll walk down this side, then up the other. Someone will have work or know someone who does."

They exited the truck and started down the tree-lined side-walk. Birds chirped merry songs back and forth to each other, performing their own musical. It wouldn't surprise her if a group of boys decked in lederhosen and girls donned in dirndls and clogs started singing in the street. She felt like someone from the future who'd stepped back in time when things seemed much simpler.

Jace laced his fingers through hers. An electric current ran through her middle at the simple touch and sent her heart racing. She chanced a glance at him and saw the boyish smirk playing around his lips. He knew how he affected her.

She blew out a breath and muttered, "Arrogant."

"You keep saying that," he replied, eyes twinkling with mirth.

She batted her eyelids at him and lifted her lips in a saccharine smile. "It's shameful how you take advantage of me like that," she drawled.

He chuckled. "You can't take advantage of the willing, sweetheart."

"Jerk," she said, laughing.

They stopped at a stand selling dates. She'd never tasted one, but they looked a lot like prunes. She grimaced.

A little girl, not wearing a dirndl, but a simple sky-blue dress with a frilly white apron, held out a date and asked, "Would you like to try one?"

Lacy bent down eye level with the girl. Fine blond hair did its best to escape the girl's pigtails. Her cheeks, stained with date juice and dirt, lifted as her rosy lips tipped into a smile.

"I've never tasted a date before," Lacy confided. "Are they good?"

The girl nodded, her light brown eyes round and solemn. She took the date, sniffed it, and popped it into her mouth. It had the chewy texture of a raisin but tasted a lot like caramel. Not awful, but not good either.

She rose to her feet and swallowed against her gag reflex, wishing for a glass of water to rinse the taste out of her mouth.

"Thank you," she told the girl, eyes watering.

The girl giggled and skipped back to her mother who'd watched the exchange with a friendly smile.

"We're looking for work. Do you know of anyone who needs help?" Jace asked the mother.

"No, I don't. I'm sorry," the woman replied.

"Thanks anyway," he said politely.

They moved down the walk and got the same answer at every stand. What were they going to do? The question ran in circles through her head. They needed a good meal, and the truck needed fuel.

When they reached the end of the market, they crossed to the other side and began their trek back up the street.

The rich aroma of yeast floated on the air, coming from a stand with freshly baked bread, croissants, rolls, and sweet breads. Her mouth watered and her stomach released another growl of protest. She skipped over that stand and wandered over to one selling honey. No sense in torturing herself over a cinnamon roll she had no way of buying.

Jars of liquid gold lined the red-checkered tablecloth. Jace walked up behind her and placed his hands on her shoulders. She leaned back into the solid warmth of his body.

An elderly man with patches of white hair limped over. "Can I help you?"

"We're looking for work. Do you happen to know of anyone needing help? We'll work for room and board," Jace replied.

"We'll barter for gasoline," she added, trying to plaster a smile on her face.

"Oh, and if you know of a preacher or minister in the area, we'd be grateful for directions to his—" Jace stumbled to a stop.

The man's rheumy blue eyes bulged at the couple as if they'd spoken to him in a foreign language. He cleared his throat and blinked a couple of times, then turned his head and spit tobacco juice on the ground.

"As a matter of fact," the old man began, then stopped and coughed.

He wiped his mouth on a blue paisley bandana. It was old and faded, and blood stained much of its surface.

"Are you all right?" Lacy asked, taking a step toward the old man, brow wrinkled in concern.

"Fine, fine," he said, waving her off. "I do know someone looking for help. But it's not here in Carmel."

"Is it close?" Jace asked.

The truck wouldn't make it much farther without fuel. Most stations were open for business which meant they couldn't steal it.

The man scratched a red, flaky patch of baldness on his head. "Pacific Grove's 'bout a fifteen-minute drive from here. My brother, Wyatt, owns Lighthouse Inn. It's a bit run down and he's wanting to spruce it up."

Relief flooded her system. "Sounds perfect."

The man smiled. "He also has a chapel on the property. They used to hold weddings there and such. He's got his license to marry and bury."

Jace grinned down at her. "You ready?"

"Hell, yeah," she said, giving his hand a light squeeze.

The man introduced himself as Wynn Gate and gave them directions to his brother's place.

"Thank you," Jace said, stretching out a hand. "Really. We appreciate it."

The man gave it a hearty shake.

As they turned to go, he hollered, "Hold up."

He walked around the stand, holding two Granny Smith apples and a small jar of his honey.

He held it out to them. "Looks like you guys need it," he offered by way of explanation.

Jace took the apples and honey and handed them to her.

Tears pricked the back of her eyelids. "Thank you."

Wynn nodded, then turned and ambled stiffly back to his stand.

They strode down the walk, eager to get back to the truck. Hope lightened her heart at the thought of marrying Jace. She couldn't wait.

10

AJ lay in Willow's bed, cradling her soft body against his. Her curves melted into him as if she belonged there. Her honeyed scent enveloped him, lighting the hottest fire in his blood he'd ever felt. With a feather-light touch, he brushed his fingers across her temple to her hairline. He stroked the length of her long hair down to the ends, curling a blond, silky lock between his fingers. Tenderness swept over him like a gentle breeze rolling across bluestem prairie grass.

Her steady breathing hitched as he played with her hair. His nearness caused her muscles to relax as she lay against his side. Yet she still hadn't fallen back asleep from her nightmare that dragged him from the dregs of slumber to her bed.

"Wanna talk about it?" he asked softly.

He released the blond strand as she turned in the circle of his arms. She placed warm hands against his chest. Her fingers splayed into his chest hair in tentative exploration. A euphoric thrill erupted as her hands moved down to trace the ridges of his stomach muscles. Closing his eyes, he drew in a sharp breath.

She lifted her gaze to his. The waning moon's light filtered through the window's pink gingham curtains, illuminating her eyes. The effect was ethereal. It wouldn't surprise him if she grew wings and sprinkled pixie dust on him so they could fly away together. The escape to another world would be a welcome one.

He took a second to calm his pounding heart. What would distract him from the hazy desire pooling in her eyes? She had no idea how alluring she was, nor how much she affected him.

"What's the point?" she asked, desperation edging her voice. "Why talk about something I'm trying to forget ever happened?"

Sadness swallowed her, shrouding the light in her eyes. Thinking about everything she'd suffered from her kidnapping came rushing back, hitting him in the chest like a cannon ball. He didn't know the dirty details, but it was enough to cool his heated blood. He placed a gentle hand on her cheek and sighed.

"Give yourself a voice. Not talking about it—" He stopped short, thinking what he was about to say.

He'd do good to take his own advice. He never once talked about his feelings to anyone when his girlfriend, Quinn, died. It wasn't his parents' fault he was so screwed in the head. They just didn't realize how invested he'd been in the girl. Lacy didn't either. If his family had known how close he'd come to losing it altogether, they would've committed him.

But they didn't know. His world changed the day Quinn died. He felt like a part of him just laid down and died with her. Demons arose from the ashes of guilt he carried, and they gnawed on his spirit, snarling and snapping any time he resisted them. He could never seem to escape their ironclad grip.

Then, he'd seen Willow for the first time in that dirty, gritty parking garage in Mexico City and light began to filter back into his world. The more time he spent with her, the brighter it became. He wanted to be the light at the end of her tunnel.

He forced himself to continue. "Not talking about it leaves the power in that bastard, Nieto's, hands. Take some of it back, darlin'."

"It's not Nieto I dream about," she confided, her voice barely audible over the fan by the closet, blowing gusty gales of stale air across the bed as it oscillated back and forth.

He tightened his grip around her waist, letting her know she was safe. She let out a slow breath, and her body relaxed against his once again.

"Who put all the bruises and marks on you?" he asked.

His sharp words sliced through the air. His skin pricked and tingled as anger swept over him. He didn't want the answer, but he needed it. The man didn't deserve to breathe. He might agree to Laurel's suicidal revenge plan after all. If Nieto hadn't done all the damage to her mind and body, then who the hell did? One of his men?

"About a month after I was kidnapped behind the restaurant in Laredo . . . Remember, I told you about that," she said with a tremor in her voice.

"I remember," he answered gravely.

He still couldn't shake the feeling her boyfriend, Scott, had something to do with her abduction. The guy didn't act like he cared for Willow. At all. Plus, what was the deal with him bringing his friend, Diego, around with him all the time? A real boyfriend would want alone time with his girl. Add his stellar narcissistic personality into the mix and one plus one definitely didn't equal two. His gut was telling him something was off about the guy. And his gut was never wrong.

He couldn't prove it. Yet. Bryan had suggested they surveil Scott's house in shifts, try to glean evidence that way. They'd started yesterday. He took the day shift and Bryan the night shift. Hopefully, Scott would lead them to some answers. The man's overconfidence would trip him up sooner or later.

"Well, about a month later, Nieto dragged me out of that nasty hell hole." A shiver rolled through her.

He'd heard a little about that too. His sister had been held captive in the cell next to Willow. Dark, dank, and dangerously dirty, it was a miracle neither girl had returned home with dysentery or some other bacterial infection.

"Where did he take you?" he prompted.

Her body stiffened. "To a hotel."

His heart beat like a war drum. "The one where I first saw you?"

He'd never forget the moment her blue-grey eyes landed on him in the parking garage. She looked like she'd strolled straight out of a fairy tale. The grey dress she wore hugged her curves down to the floor. Her blond locks, swept up, revealed a graceful neck he could spend every night of his life kissing. She carried herself with regal confidence. Then her eyes locked on his. One look from her had spun him off his axis.

"Yeah. Nieto owns the hotel. He keeps some of his girls on the top floor, either to sell or use for his personal friends and business acquaintances."

"Which were you?" he asked in a deceptively quiet voice.

Inside, his inner voice raged. Why Willow? What had she done to deserve this?

"He sold me to a man from the States, but the buyer had nowhere to keep me. So, Nieto held onto me for him. The man visited frequently. He was violent and sadistic. I was his slave, and he was—" Her voice broke, but she continued.

Once she started, the levee broke, and her story rolled off her tongue like water down a spillway. By the end, his stomach had churned itself into a foamy, acidic volcano. A pounding in his head banged against his skull, wanting to escape.

He couldn't think of a word shocking enough to describe what Willow had experienced. She trembled in his arms like a dry leaf shaking on a tree in the cold February wind.

"Shh," he comforted in a low, soothing tone.

If the fates ever gave him a one-way ticket back in time, he'd use it to prevent the horror, the trauma she'd suffered. If he could've offered himself as tribute in her place, he would've. It was a miracle she'd survived.

She scooted closer and laid her head against his chest. His pulse vibrated under his skin. Could she feel it?

"Can I ask you something?" he implored softly.

She nodded.

He swallowed against the lump in his throat, then asked, "Is this man alive?"

She shook her head. "I killed him," she stated in a flat, lifeless tone.

Her muffled words shocked him to his core. He wanted to raise that man from the grave just so he could kill him all over again. He thought of his sister. Had she faced the same gut-wrenching decision to take a life in order to survive her ordeal in Mexico City? The thought unsettled him deeply.

When she lifted her head, he realized he'd been quiet too long. He tangled a hand in her hair and guided her head back to his chest.

"How?" he asked, at a loss for anything else to say.

Did he want to know how she'd killed him? No. His anger and helpless frustration over the situation was already triggered. But he sensed she needed to talk about it, purge herself of the poison killing her from the inside out. If he truly wanted to help her get past the horrible memories haunting her, he needed to man up and listen. Even if it killed him.

"When Lacy killed Miguel, I swiped his gun and knife. When they came and took the body, no one noticed he was unarmed. Then, John, the man who bought me, came to visit. He bashed my head against a glass coffee table, then bit me." Her hand drifted to her neck where the purple mark lingered. "After that, he dragged me to the bedroom and threw me onto the bed. When he crawled on top of me, my mind sort of shut off. I pulled the gun I'd hidden beneath the sweatshirt I was wearing, shoved it into his navel, and pulled the trigger."

He closed his eyes. He couldn't comprehend the strength it took for her to kill the man. His mind reeled with information overload. His sister had killed someone. He'd process that later. He could only take so much before he exploded, and right now Willow needed him.

"I'm so sorry," he whispered. "So goddamned sorry you had to do that."

Her fingers combed through his hair. The sensation it evoked was innocent, yet sensual.

She let out a self-deprecating laugh. "Don't be. The world is a better place without him in it."

"Still," he said, rubbing a gentle hand down her back. "I wish it didn't have to be you."

She ducked her head as she whispered, "Me too."

They lay in the darkness with nothing but the whir of the fan and fell asleep.

AJ WAS BEGINNING to break from sleep's heavy bonds when he heard Willow's door open with a wild crash against the wall. Staying all night in her bed hadn't been his plan, but the feel of her warm, sleeping body in his arms was a hell of a bonus. He was drenched in her warm, honeyed scent and that alone sent a streak of heat up his back.

In the few seconds it took to process where he was and who he was with, Willow's sister, Olive, barged into the room. A shit-eating grin bloomed wide across her face, showing her straight, white teeth.

"Well, what do *we* have here?" she gloated with glee.

He sighed and cracked open an eyelid. Willow didn't need problems with her sisters stacked on top of the ones she already had. If Laurel found out he spent the night with Willow, they'd both end up on the receiving end of her sister's sharp tongue. How bad would this be for her?

Olive stood bouncing on the balls of her feet like a damn boxer ready to face the heavyweight champion of the world. Her face lit up like she'd just won the lottery. Dammit. How could he downplay this?

"It's not what it looks like," he muttered in a sullen tone.

Willow's body went stiff at his declaration, the only indication she'd awakened. She lifted her head and glared daggers at her sister who let out a loud raucous laugh.

"Isn't that what they all say?" Olive asked with an exaggerated sigh. "I think it's exactly what it looks like."

Olive gave them a suggestive wink.

Willow shoved him away with both hands, then sat up. The covers fell from her shoulders revealing the maroon oversize T-shirt she'd worn to bed. Was it hers? Or someone else's, like Scott?

He frowned as jealousy and feelings of unworthiness waged a vicious war inside him. He shouldn't care. But he did. He hated the idea of her wearing another guy's shirt. Would she wear one of his? He didn't have his clothes. They were in his truck Lacy had borrowed to go back to the farm to confront their uncle. But the idea of getting her into one of his T-shirts held an appeal almost too hard to resist.

A punch to his shoulder from Willow knocked him back to reality. "Did you hear what I just said?"

AJ cleared his throat and tried to rein in his wandering thoughts. "Uh, no."

Another punch. "Stop staring," she demanded.

Olive clapped her hands. "Oh, this is too good. Will," she sang, "I think he wuvs you!"

"Shut up, Liv," Willow growled.

"She had a—"

Before he could finish his objection, Willow pushed him off the bed. The unexpected shove landed him on his butt with an "umph." His ribs protested on impact, sending a jolt of pain through his chest. He ground his back molars, causing his jaw to ache. His head swam in a pool of confusion.

He pushed up onto his knees, casting his eyes up at Willow whose lips were mashed into an angry line.

"Why'd you do that?" he asked her, shaking his head.

She opened her mouth, snapped it shut and looked away.

What had he done? Nothing. Except, she might not like him the way Olive insinuated. But that didn't make sense either. She did like him. Years of chasing women had taught him the nuances of their body language and Willow's reaction to his touch gave her away.

Then it hit him. She pushed him when he started to tell Olive about her nightmares. She didn't want her sister to know about them. Her reasons were her own, and he'd respect them.

His irritation drained away as quickly as it came. The tightness around his eyes eased. She was dealing with a lot of crap. He didn't want to add to it, he wanted to help her.

Olive's grin drooped. "What's going on, Will?"

"Nothing," she said too quickly.

Olive folded her arms across her chest, clearly not buying it. Worry creased her brow three lines deep. She turned her attention to him.

"What were you going to say before she knocked you on your ass?" she asked him with a hint of a grin.

He studied Willow's expression and sighed. "Nothing. Not a damn thing."

He lifted himself off the floor as if he were a man three times his age. Pain ricocheted like a steel pinball banging against his ribs. Placing a hand on his side, he slowly stretched up to his normal six-foot, two-inch height.

He shuffled to the door. "I'm just gonna go now."

Olive gave him a contemplative look. "I'm going to figure this out. One way or another."

"You do that," he retorted with a smirk and walked out the door.

11

Beside the living room's fireplace was one of Willow's favorite places to be during the winter months. Logs in the grate crackled and popped, the flames dancing upward in merry motion. She dragged her blanket and pillow closer to the radiating warmth it offered. Nights spent reading by the fire or snuggled down in a pile of blankets watching TikTok videos from her phone had been the highlight of her days.

If her parents held any concerns over her lack of friends or a social life, they hadn't voiced them. In fact, she thought her dad preferred his youngest daughter at home instead of gallivanting across Texas as he'd accused her two older sisters. She missed her dad but was grateful to have spared him the knowledge of what happened to her.

She sighed. He'd eventually find out. That is, if she ever saw him again. Immediately, she shut down the thought. She wouldn't allow herself to believe she'd never see her parents again. Never getting to work cattle with her dad or bake cookies with her mom made her heart ache.

She laid her head down on a fluffy pillow. She'd been unsettled all day and couldn't figure out why. She'd painted only long enough to make a mess. She tried hanging out with Olive but that hadn't worked either. Olive's particular brand of coarse humor unraveled her last nerve. She'd walked away from her sister, leaving her alone with Bryan.

Then it dawned on her. She'd danced around the problem all day, but now, in the quiet, the stillness shined a beacon on it. When Olive caught AJ that morning in bed with her, he'd declared, "It's not what it looks like," and her heart sank to her feet. It stung. How could the attraction she felt for him be one-sided? Was it one-sided? Or had he blurted out the first thing that came to mind? How had she so grossly misread his actions toward her?

A sharp knock on the front door booted the gloomy questions out of her head. She hunkered down further into her blankets, hoping whoever was on the other side would take the hint and go away. Another impatient *rap, rap, rap,* came from the door. Sighing, she reluctantly threw off her covers and went to see who was interrupting her quiet time.

Peeking through the side window, she saw Scott standing on the porch, shifting from one foot to the other. *Well shit.*

She could feel his impatience through the thick outer wall separating them. It poured off him like water through a sieve. Diego didn't appear to be with him, thank the stars for that. She couldn't stand being in his presence. Not just because his ethnicity reminded her of the stolen months in Nieto's clutches, but because she inherently didn't trust him. He had an oily presence one associated with crooked car salesmen or bookies.

Her shoulders slumped forward. She let out a heavy sigh before opening the door. She'd been enjoying the long, quiet evening on her own. Olive and Bryan had taken off on the four-wheelers, Laurel was organizing her office, and AJ—her heart tripped over itself just thinking about him—well, she didn't know where AJ had gone. She hadn't seen him since he'd walked out her bedroom door that morning after she'd pushed him off the bed. She cringed. She'd apologize for that later.

She opened the door, plastered on a fake smile, and said, "Hi, Scott," as cheerfully as she could muster.

She wasn't ready for the brutal break-up conversation she knew needed to happen. So, she stood there and stared at him with a blank expression.

"Are you going to let me in?" he asked, irritation seeping into his words.

She shook her head, opening the door wider. "Yeah, of course. Come on in."

He followed her into the living room and took a seat.

She stood beside the couch, wringing her hands. Why was he here? All the courage she'd felt when she declared she was breaking up with him ran aground.

"Want some iced tea or something?" she asked, forcing herself to sound polite.

"No," he snapped, then added, "Who would want *iced* tea on a cold winter evening?"

Her head began to pound. He excelled at making her feel stupid. Inferior. She knew it was intentional. Why she couldn't see it before puzzled her. He was a master at the game they were playing. She had no idea what the game was, much less the rules. She wondered what would happen if she pushed back.

She crossed her arms and gave him a withering look. "If you're going to be an asshole, leave. I'm not in the mood for your shit, Scott."

The look on his face was priceless. Where was her Polaroid when she needed it? His eyes widened in shock and disbelief, then narrowed in heated outrage. For a split second she thought he was going to stand up and hit her. She'd never talked to him like she possessed a backbone. But, in a flash, his downcast expression smothered the anger as if the inferno she knew raged within him was nothing but a guttering candle.

He ran a hand through his hair. "Geez, Willow, what's wrong with you? I haven't seen you in a few days, so I thought I'd come check on you. And I get kicked like a dog for doing it."

Well, that wasn't the reaction she expected. Where was the angry blustering? She studied his face. His hurt seemed genuine, which confused the hell out of her. It was on the tip of her tongue to apologize, but something stopped her.

Think about it first, she counseled herself.

She sat on the chair facing the couch, leaned her head back, and stared at the ceiling. He'd been rude. She called him on it. Somehow he'd twisted the whole situation around where it was her fault, taking back the control he craved.

Shifting in her seat, she drew up her legs and tucked her feet underneath her.

"You were rude when I asked if you wanted something to drink," Willow pointed out.

"And I said iced tea wasn't something I wanted on a cold night," he responded in a slow patronizing voice.

She hated it when he talked to her like she was incapable of understanding, as if he spoke with an intelligence she couldn't possibly comprehend.

Picking at her thumbnail, she said quietly, "I can't do this anymore, Scott."

The silence in the room stretched, pulling taut anxious nerves from her body one strand at a time. She wouldn't be the one to break it. She'd said all she needed to say and didn't think he deserved a lengthier explanation.

He'd been a douche to her the entire time they dated. She'd been too naive to see it, too willing to accept his poor behavior because she thought it was all she deserved. But she was worth more than the lousy excuse for a boyfriend sitting on her couch.

Scott slapped both hands down on his knees and let out a sardonic laugh. "This is the thanks I get for giving you a chance."

She stiffened as sparks flew up her spine. "What did you just say?"

His voice rose. "I said this is what I get for giving you a chance."

"I heard that," she shot back. "What do you mean?"

"Do you really think you're pretty enough to date me?" he mocked. "Come on, Will. You're nice and I was between cheerleaders, so I asked you out. I was willing to overlook the fact you wear your hair in a ponytail and dress like a cowboy half the time. The other half, you're covered in paint."

His nose scrunched up in distaste as he spoke. She looked down at her faded T-shirt and track pants, then her hand rose to the ponytail in her hair. Some strands had escaped, framing her face. She tucked them behind her ears. His words were a hypodermic needle pumping poison straight to her heart.

"Maybe you're right," she said, lowering her gaze.

"He's not." AJ's voice boomed as he strode into the room.

Her leaden heart dropped to the floor like a stone in a pond. Bone-chilling mortification froze her tongue. AJ had a knack of showing up at the worst time. Why did he have to hear all that?

MURDEROUS RAGE SQUEEZED AJ's lungs, wringing out every drop of oxygen. His chest pumped up and down trying to replace it, but his head remained in a haze of anger as he scowled at Scott.

He'd surveilled the younger man all day, which amounted to sitting in the truck and staring out the window. A bend in the dirt road leading to Scott's house hid his truck but allowed him a perfect view of the blond-brick, two-story house. The way the asshole strutted around, AJ expected something more grandiose.

He hated the time alone with his thoughts and nothing to distract him. They bounced around like ping pong balls, dredging up memories he thought he'd scrubbed from his mind entirely.

He watched the sun sink into a bed of puffy orange clouds and decided to head back to Willow's. He'd just turned over the truck's engine when Scott walked out the front door. He cut the motor and hunched down. Scott got into a red sports car and drove straight to Willow's.

He watched Willow answer the door, let Scott inside, then waited a few minutes before entering the house through the back door.

What he overheard Scott say to Willow turned him inside out. How could he say she wasn't pretty enough? The thought was inconceivable to him. She possessed the most stunning features, from her striking blue-grey eyes to every dip and curve of her body. She was perfect.

A dark, ominous look crossed Scott's face as they squared off. He wanted to punch the guy's nose through his skull and imagined the immediate satisfaction of bones crunching and blood flowing.

Scott puffed out his chest, reminding him of a banty rooster. "What the fuck, dude? You wanna piece of me?"

"Don't tempt me," he growled, stepping into Scott's space. "Where do you get off talking to her that way? She's gorgeous and let me tell you, buddy, she's *way* out of *your* league. Just because you were captain of the lacrosse team in high school you think your dick is big enough to swing around wherever you go?"

Scott's face mottled an angry red. "I wasn't captain of the Lacrosse team, dumbass," he blustered. "For your information, I was captain of the soccer team. And," he continued, bumping his chest into AJ, "my dick *is* big enough to swing around so you'd better back off."

AJ barked out a laugh. "You're ridiculous. For the life of me, I can't figure out why Willow wasted her time on you."

Scott swung his fist out in a sloppy right hook. He moved to the side, and Scott stumbled forward, catching nothing but air.

The urge to beat the living shit out of the guy drove him hard. But it wouldn't be a fair fight. It wouldn't be a fight at all. The guy was a snowflake, and AJ had standards when it came to brawling.

"You don't want to start with me," AJ warned.

Scott turned his back on him to face Willow and jabbed his index finger at her. "We're done."

Willow glared at Scott. "That's what I just said."

"Yeah, but you didn't mean it," he said with an arrogant swag. "I do."

Willow jumped out of her chair and marched over to Scott. She raised her right arm and struck him square in the nose. "Get out of my house!" she shouted.

Scott grabbed his bloody nose and blinked several times. "You broke my nose," he shrieked.

AJ dipped his head, trying to hide his wide grin. He wished Bryan was here to see this. The guy shrieked, actually *shrieked,* like a little girl. A laugh burst from his chest. God, this was funny.

Willow gave him a wicked scowl. "You shut up."

She turned back to Scott. "You're a narcissistic asshole, and I never want to see you again."

Back ramrod straight, she walked to the front door and opened it. Scott stared at her in comical disbelief, shook his head and walked out. She slammed the door at his back and marched back into the living room.

"Darlin' that was the best thing I've seen in ages," he laughed.

Her eyes narrowed and his smile slipped. She was pissed.

"You have a bad habit of eavesdropping," she accused. "You had no right to interfere in our conversation."

"I didn't mean to," he said, sheepishly. "Honest."

"I can take care of myself, ya know," she declared hotly.

"Yeah, you can," he conceded, voice soft and soothing. "But you shouldn't have to."

"I don't *need* you to stick around for me. If you feel some sort of screwed up obligation to watch over me because you helped rescue me, then I release you from it."

She rubbed the heel of her hand against her forehead and released a breath with a loud whoosh.

His brows scrunched in confusion. "Woah, back up a second."

He had two choices. One, he could walk out the door, go

home, and try to forget about her. She'd given him an easy out. But something deep down warned him leaving would be a big mistake. He didn't think he could forget about her with a snap of his fingers. He doubted he could forget about her at all.

Which led him to the second option. As uncomfortable as it made him, he could finally fess up and tell her how he really felt.

He'd had all day to ponder why her attitude toward him had turned on a dime that morning. Her body turned stiff as a board in his arms when he tried to explain their sleeping arrangements to Olive.

"Is that what you really think?" he asked, brows raised. "That I'm sticking around out of *obligation*?"

She huffed. "Does it matter?"

"Yeah, it matters," he muttered. "Look—"

She held up a hand. "You don't need to explain."

He walked toward her but stopped an arm's length away. "I'm not sticking around because I feel responsible for you."

She dropped her arm. "Then why are you here?" she demanded.

He raked a hand through his hair. This was tougher than he thought it'd be.

"Because I—" He lifted his eyes to the ceiling, searching for courage, wisdom, anything to help him fumble his way through this. Then he dragged them back down, settling them on hers.

His lips quirked up. "Because I'm fascinated by you."

He took a step, then another, until he invaded her personal space, and cupped her cheek.

"Because the moment I saw you in that parking garage, I was hooked."

Her eyes lightened, and the stark lines around her mouth softened a little as she listened.

"Because I can't seem to stay away from you," he murmured.

He watched her intently, loving the way her lips parted and her eyelids fluttered.

"Because we have a soul connection," he continued. "I felt it the first time I laid eyes on you. It stole my breath. Scared the shit out of me. Still does. But there's something between us, and I can't walk away from it. From you."

Tears glistened on her eyelashes. "So these feelings . . . they're not one-sided?"

"Hell no," he said quickly.

"Why the mixed signals?" she asked, stepping closer to him.

A teasing smile lifted his lips. "You had a boyfriend until two seconds ago, and I'm nowhere near good enough for you."

"I don't have a boyfriend, and you are good enough for me. It's me that's not—"

He wrapped his arms around her waist and drew her into his chest. "Don't you dare finish that sentence."

She shuddered. "But—"

"No." He lifted her chin. "I understand you have things to work through. I can't imagine the pain you carry. But I'll help if you'll let me."

Their gazes locked and held. A million love songs had been penned about seeing forever in a lover's eyes, and he'd never understood. Until now.

12

As Willow stared into AJ's eyes, the truth of his words struck her heart, threatening to shatter her. Where was he when she'd dreamed of a man looking at her like she was the very air he breathed? Before she'd become a broken shell incapable, no, unworthy of what he offered her?

He admitted she had things to work through, which was just a nice way of saying, "Hey, I know you're broken." What if she could never put herself back together? She felt the connection he talked about, but was it enough?

He lowered his head. The light green in his eyes darkened with desire and she knew without a doubt he was going to kiss her. Looking into his eyes was like a shot of whiskey, going straight to her head. Her heart thundered in her ears like a thousand wild mustang hooves pounding the dry, dusty ground. Her whole attention zeroed in on him as he wetted his lips.

Could she kiss him, knowing she might not be able to follow through with anything more? He'd definitely want more from her than just kissing. She was afraid. Afraid the four months in Mexico City had ruined her. Afraid she'd never be able to love someone to the fullest extent.

Dragging in a deep breath, she placed a hand on his chest and took a tiny step back. She needed a minute to clear her head so she could think. The thought pained her but she needed to walk away.

He hadn't let go of her waist when she backed off. Instead, he moved his hands to the small of her back and drew her to him until their bodies were flush. Heat raced up her neck to her cheeks. His jet-black bangs fell over his forehead, and she had an irresistible urge to run her hands through it. She tracked his eyes roving from her eyes to her mouth. He ran feather-light fingers along her jawline, studying her lips as if they were the only thing capable of quenching the fire blazing in his eyes.

"AJ," she started, doubt creeping into her voice.

"Willow," he responded slowly, lips kicking up into a seductive smile.

"I can't do this," she whispered.

He lowered his head a fraction. "Do what?"

"This," she whispered, motioning her index finger between them.

She gasped as his lips feathered against hers.

"Willow," he breathed.

Her heart stuttered. "Yeah?"

"Shut up," he said.

His lips met hers, slow and seductive, silencing all her excuses. Impulsively, her arms wrapped around his neck as her body willingly melted into his. Her fingers splayed into his hair, drawing a low growl from him. The rumble caused a burning fire to erupt. It spread like lava to her lower stomach. It felt . . . euphoric, as if every nerve ending wound themselves into a tight spring ready to pop.

She'd never responded to anyone like this, never had a chance in high school because she'd never had a boyfriend. And Scott, she realized, didn't qualify as a boyfriend, and certainly never evoked these feelings in her.

A sudden flashback of the hotel room in Mexico City burned against the back of her eyelids. John's face, red with rage, loomed over her. His meaty hand grabbed her throat and squeezed. Fear bloomed like a mushroom cloud, smothering the flame racing toward a powder keg inside her. She whimpered, trying to break herself free of the vision.

Sensing her distress, he broke the kiss. His eyes blazed as he stared down at her. She sucked in a ragged breath, lowering her hands from his neck to push at his chest. Tears sprang into her eyes, causing his face to blur. She looked away before one fell and slid down her reddened cheek.

She'd lost herself within his kiss and, for a second, let go of the horror from the last four months. But only a few scant seconds. She stumbled over her feet as she tried to step out of his embrace. His arms tightened around her, steadying her.

If the soul connection between them hadn't existed, and if she wasn't so damn fascinated by him, that kiss would've been too much for her to handle. And as much as she wanted him, she didn't know if she could ever—

"Willow."

His voice, softened by an emotion she refused to acknowledge, washed over her. She lifted her gaze to his. The tenderness in his eyes caused panic to flare inside her. He cared for her. Too much. She would end up hurting him if they continued down this path because she honestly didn't think she'd ever get over what John had done to her.

"I'm sorry," she choked out, and when she tried again to step away from him, he dropped his hands to his sides and let her go.

Tension sizzled in the air between them like an electrical storm. She wrapped her hands around her middle.

"Talk to me," he implored.

She shook her head, tears burning tracks down her cheeks. No matter how hard she tried to talk about her feelings, the words dried on her tongue and tasted like ash in her mouth.

"I'm sorry," she said again and ran from the room.

She flew up the stairs, crashed into her bedroom and flung herself onto her unmade bed. A violent river of silent sobs flowed out of her as brutal memories flooded her mind. In cinematic fashion, they played on repeat.

John, the man who bought her, got off on bondage and torture. She massaged her wrists as phantom pain, biting and cruel from the medieval iron cuffs he'd used to restrain her, seemed all too real.

A scream crawled up her throat from the deepest part of her like a monster rising from the depths of the sea. She turned her face into her pillow, biting her lower lip until the metallic taste of blood flooded her mouth. By sheer force of will alone, she forced the monstrous scream back down her throat. It resisted the effort as if it were a live entity, digging its claws along the walls of her chest, seeking freedom.

Nervous energy skittered up and down her spine, playing it like a bow on violin strings. She could almost hear its dissonant screech inside her ears. The scream would not be silenced. It needed an outlet, or it would drive her mad.

She wished the trampoline her dad bought when she was twelve still sat in her backyard. When art no longer served to distract or entertain her, she'd traipse out the back door, climb up onto the suspended canvas, and just jump. She'd spent hours perfecting her back flips, concentrating on counting how many she could do in a row. The aimless monotony of counting one, two, three, and so on cleared her head, until she no longer remembered the problem that had driven her outdoors.

Needing to do something, she dragged herself out of bed. She checked her face in the ocher vanity mirror and wiped the remaining tears from her face. Grabbing a tissue, she blew her reddened nose then threw it into the small trashcan beside her nightstand.

The doors to her closet stood open. She glanced through.

Her running shoes, boots, sandals, and a pair of formal pumps filled a shoe rack to overflowing. A few dresses hung in the back, hiding like scolded children amongst more practical clothing. She hardly ever wore them.

The light teal-blue summer dress she wore once to her cousin's wedding, the slinky little black dress Olive insisted on buying for her that she'd never worn at all, and a couple of formal dresses hung at the very back. The formal wear evoked memories of her senior year winter formal and prom. She shook her head as she remembered how handsy both boys had been on the dance floor. She should've known better than to trust Olive to pick a decent date for her.

Flannel button-downs in every possible color hung on the steel rod attached to brackets on each opposing wall. Levi's, her favorite jeans, filled a wooden cubicle tucked into one of the closet's corners.

She grabbed her broken-in pair of Ariats, shoved them on her feet, then threaded her arms through her jacket. Their neighbor to the west, called to the state capital, was boarding his horse at the Sinclair Veterinary Clinic.

Many Texans were being called to Austin to work for the state's governor. The nation's situation was precarious. Texans had it easy compared to citizens residing in other states. Her state seemed to be the only one fighting against the president's martial law decree.

The horse needed exercise every day. A simple ride through the pasture in the cool night air might clear her jumbled mind. It would at least get her out of the suffocating house and out into the open. Enclosed spaces never concerned her before her abduction, but they bothered her now.

Laurel would appreciate the help with the horse. Although Bryan pitched in with the farm chores, she noticed he and Olive did more goofing off and flirting than work most of the time.

Olive acted different around Bryan. Sure, she still talked with no filter whatsoever and they bickered all the time. Yet, their arguments weren't really arguments. It looked more like some sort of cave man mating ritual. And Bryan still held flighty Olive's attention. She never stayed with the same guy for long.

A smile slid over her face. Olive was a notorious flirt and had more boyfriends in high school than she could keep track of. Her sister changed boyfriends more often than she changed clothes. The thought drew a dry laugh from her lips as she closed her bedroom door and walked down the stairs.

She skirted around the foyer's corner, through the kitchen, and slipped out the back door. Thankfully, no one was in the kitchen to ask questions. She just wanted to go for a ride without everyone freaking out. She couldn't step a toe out the door without at least one of her sisters or AJ knowing about it. They were being overprotective, and she understood why. It didn't make it any less annoying though.

The sorrel mare, used for herding cattle, trotted restlessly around the corral. Willow hooked a booted foot onto the lower wooden rail of the corral's fencing and swung herself over. The horse stopped to watch her, ears pricked in curiosity.

"Hello, Belle," she said, turning toward the horse with an outstretched hand.

The sorrel trotted over and stuck her velvety nose into her palm.

"Sorry, I don't have a treat for you. If you're good, I'll get you one when we're finished with our ride."

Grabbing the horse's halter, she led her out of the corral and into the barn. She took her well-worn saddle and blanket from its stand and hefted it onto Belle's back. The horse's ears flicked back, then pricked forward again.

"Good girl," she murmured encouragingly.

She cinched the saddle, slipped on the bridle, buckled it, then led Belle out of the barn. The full moon glowed brightly against the inky sky and millions of stars twinkled.

Riding at night had its risks, but right now, she craved a

distraction. She pulled a thick, cream-colored beanie from her jacket pocket and tugged it down over her head.

The horse stomped its front hoof into the dirt, chuffing out a breath. Excitement filled her as she swung herself into the saddle. Eager to feel the cool night air blow through her hair, she galloped out of the yard into the open prairie.

AJ LEANED against the couch and ran both hands through his hair.

"Stupid," he muttered. "Too fast, dumbass."

His ears perked, and he looked to the living room's entryway at the sound of heavy boots clomping against tile. Bryan sauntered into the room, his face set in a wide grin.

"So it's finally happened," he quipped. "You've realized you're a dumbass."

AJ scowled. "You've got Vulcan hearing, you know that?"

Bryan plopped down beside him. "What's got your tits in a twist?"

"Feck off," he snapped.

Bryan studied him a moment. "Seriously, what's up?"

Genuine concern radiated from his friend, and he appreciated it. But he wasn't sure he could talk about Willow and the knotty, messy ball of feelings residing in his chest. He hadn't sorted through it yet.

He huffed out a sharp breath. "It's complicated."

"All relationships are," Bryan said sagely.

"How the hell would you know?" he scoffed.

Bryan raised an eyebrow. "Oh, I know."

"I moved too fast with Willow," he blurted. "And"—he paused, rubbing the back of his neck—"I'm probably not the best guy for her anyway."

Bryan frowned. "What makes you say that?"

Quinn's face rushed into his mind faster than a running back racing toward the end zone. His feelings of unworthiness came from his relationship with her. No one knew what happened between them, not even Lacy. His sister was usually privy to his private life, mostly because she couldn't keep her nose out of his business. A point came where he gave up trying to keep anything a secret from her, the nosy beast.

However, the situation with Quinn had been different. All anyone knew, including his sister, was his girlfriend died a tragic death. But he knew the truth. And the truth had gnawed an ugly hole into his soul over the years. Maybe . . . maybe it was time to let go. He trusted Bryan and considered the man a brother after what they'd been through in Mexico City.

He shifted, uncomfortable with the idea of actually talking about Quinn. But what did he have to lose? Not a damn thing.

"Do you remember Quinn Eisley?" he asked, hating the slight tremor in his voice.

Bryan pursed his lips. "From high school?"

He cleared his throat. "Yeah."

"Kinda," he said without conviction. "She wasn't—" Bryan's voice faltered as understanding lit his face.

"She wasn't there long," he confirmed. "She died."

Bryan nodded. "I remember now. But the details of how she died are a little fuzzy."

"Her family moved to Shidler when we were Sophomores," he began. "Her stepdad worked for Chevron Oil."

"Okay," Bryan said, drawing out the word.

"She was so shy. It was painful to watch her trying to talk to someone. She didn't make many friends. I was one of the few she had. When we started dating, I spent time at her house. Her mom was nice enough. Her stepdad, though . . ."

He paused, gathering his thoughts. Quinn's stepdad was a real piece of work. Her real father had died a couple of years prior. She'd never told him how he'd passed. It was almost like she was afraid to talk about it.

"Her stepdad didn't like me," he admitted.

Bryan snorted. "I can't imagine why."

He rammed his fist into Bryan's shoulder.

"Ow," Bryan said, massaging his abused arm. "You just proved my point, shit ass."

"Hey, I was nice back then," he insisted, then sobered. "There was a reason he didn't like me."

"Why did he want to beat the shit out of you?" Bryan asked, crossing a leg over his knee.

"I started noticing bruises on Quinn. No one noticed them at school because they were strategically placed where her clothing would cover them."

Bryan shook his head. "Aw, shit."

"Things escalated with her stepdad. He forced her to break up with me. It was almost like he was jealous. We still saw each other at school, but I could tell something else was going on. She never did come right out and say it, but that bastard was abusing her."

Bryan leaned forward, letting his hands fall between his legs. "Go on," he urged.

"This went on for a couple of months. Then . . . I got a text from Quinn. I was at Jace's and left my phone on the charger in his room. By the time I read it, I knew it was too late to try and stop her. I jumped in my truck and went to her house, hoping I was wrong. But the state coroner's vehicle was parked in the driveway when I got there."

It crushed him when he realized she'd gone through with it. All the guilt and anger and brokenness from that day came flooding back. Sometimes, when he closed his eyes, he could still see the red and blue whirring lights of the state and county police vehicles.

"Was the text a suicide note?" Bryan guessed.

"Yeah," he responded hoarsely.

He'd never forget the short text that simply said, *I love you and I wanted you to know this isn't your fault. Don't try to stop me, AJ. I can't live like this anymore. I'm so grateful I met you. Q.*

Bryan held up a finger. "Wait, I remember this story now. Didn't the papers say her *stepdad* killed her?"

He lowered his head into his chest. "Yes, and that no-good son-of-a-bitch is in prison where he belongs."

Bryan's eyes widened. "You withheld evidence. Why?"

He shot to his feet, unable to sit still any longer. He paced to the fireplace, bracing his hands against it.

He'd watched as the Osage County sheriff walked Quinn's stepdad out of the house in handcuffs. It only took him seconds to realize her father was being charged with Quinn's death. The anger he felt toward her father still festered inside him, and he remembered the instant he decided to keep Quinn's suicide text to himself.

He waited for the guilt associated with the memories to surface. It didn't.

"He was raping her, Bryan," he shouted. "Every chance he got. He deserved to go to prison for life."

"They could've given him a death sentence. Would you have been okay with that?" Bryan asked, voice low and even.

He spun around and stared at his friend, anger smoldering in the pit of his stomach. "Yes, I would've."

Bryan shook his head, looking even more befuddled. "I still don't get why you think you're not good enough for Willow. Although, your track record with women makes more sense now," he admitted with a wry grin.

"I wasn't there for her. I should've stopped her. Stopped him. And then there's the whole letting-an-innocent-man-go-to-prison thing," he said, using air quotes around the word innocent.

Bryan tapped his fingers together. "It was her choice," he reasoned. "You're not at fault for that. As for the stepdad, I don't really blame you for what you did, and I don't think Willow would either."

"I'm not so sure about that."

Tears burned the back of his eyes, and he sniffed. He hadn't talked about this with anyone, and pain still pricked his heart. The grief for Quinn still lingered, but to his surprise, it had lessened.

However, if he wanted a relationship with Willow, he'd have to tell her about Quinn, and that wasn't something he was ready to do.

13

After a short fifteen-minute ride, Lacy and Jace made it to the Lighthouse Inn. Excitement squeezed Lacy's heart. Her knee bounced up and down at the idea of a job, a shower, and most importantly, food. She looked out the passenger window at three duplex cottages and one triplex cottage. They lined an exquisitely inlaid lane of dark red, burnt orange, and black brick.

Brown paint peeled off the cottages' sides. The wooden balusters holding up the small A-frame roofs buckled and splintered under the weight. It looked as if the tiniest breeze would knock them down like a house of cards. She instantly fell in love with the charming place despite its disrepair.

They drove toward a two-story house at the end of the lane. A short, stocky man in brown trousers and a brown-and-black-checked, flannel button-down sat in a white wicker rocker. One of his suspender straps holding up his pants fell down a bony shoulder as he whittled on a piece of wood.

The man's head snapped up as they approached. A frown carved grooves around his already wrinkled mouth.

Jace turned and gave her a smile that didn't reach his eyes. "You ready?"

"He doesn't look very happy," she commented dryly, trying to relieve some of the tension.

"He's probably wary of strangers. Desperate people will do anything for food." He grabbed her hand and gave it a reassuring squeeze. "Come on. Let's go."

She slid out the driver's side after him, nervousness replacing her excitement. If this man didn't hire them, they'd have no choice but to go to Tulare.

"Hi," Jace greeted the old man with an outstretched hand.

The man studied Jace's hand as if he was afraid it would turn into a snake and bite him.

Jace cleared his throat and dropped his hand. "Um, your brother—"

The old man's eyes flared, panic replacing his wariness. "What about my brother? Is he okay? What's happened?"

"Nothing," Jace reassured. "He sent us here."

The old man's shoulders sagged, dislodging the other suspender from his shoulder.

The man's silence gave Jace the opportunity to continue. "He thought you might need a couple of workers to help with the place."

The old man crossed his arms over his chest. "Where'd you meet my brother?" he asked, suspicion biting into his tone.

"Farmer's market in Carmel," she interjected, trying to sound friendly. "He gave us a jar of his honey."

The old man harumphed. "Old geezer shouldn't be working so hard. But he won't listen to me. He cares more about those blasted bee hives than his own kids." His shrewd eyes turned to Jace. "Got any carpentry experience? This place has gone to the dogs. I took a fall off a ladder a few years back, and the wife won't let me up on one now. Can't find anyone worth a pinch of salt willing to work. Everybody's looking for a handout."

"I've done some roofing, some dry wall and painting. I can repair fence too," Jace said, giving her a wink.

She stifled a laugh, remembering how much he hated

repairing fence. It seemed like a lifetime ago when he'd galloped onto the Monroe farm asking her for asylum. She'd given him such a hard time at first, but he never gave up on her, not once.

The old man eyed them both, measuring them up. She hated being assessed by a man who knew nothing about them or what they'd been through. They needed food and shelter. She needed some stability after her ordeal in Mexico City. Would the man hire them or send them on down the road? Acid built in her stomach. She placed a hand on her abdomen as a wave of nausea crashed over her.

The man finally held out his hand to Jace. "I'm Wyatt. Sorry for being rude, it's just that you can't be too careful nowadays. I can't tell you how many homeless people, desperate for anything, the wife and I have had to fight off."

She flinched. They were in the same predicament.

"We're not looking for a handout," she ground out defensively. "We'll work for food, room, and board." And a place to call home, she added silently.

Wyatt scratched the top of his head. "All right. I'll give you all a trial run. The wife would scold me if I didn't give you a chance, and I'd like to stay on the right side of my wife. That woman is the sweetest thing God ever made until she gets mad. Whoo-wee, she can scald the hide off a cat with her tongue."

Jace's lips twitched, and Lacy let out a soft chuckle.

She smiled at Wyatt. "She sounds great."

"Come on." Wyatt said, waving them forward.

Bone weary, they followed him to the front of the property to a two-story structure located beside the triplex. Wyatt punched in a code that unlocked the front door.

"My wife inherited this place. It's been in her family for generations. I can't tell you how many tourists have come through here. It's been hard on her to see it so run down."

They stepped in to a cozy downstairs space which served as a check-in and breakfast area. The stale scent of coffee and waffles wafted in the air, mixing with the dust motes. Wyatt walked through the lobby to a set of stairs at the back.

"Careful," Jace murmured, pointing to a crack in one of the wooden steps.

"The upstairs flat is the only place with a kitchen," Wyatt explained as they climbed. "Thought I'd set you up here. The cottages beside this building need the most work. You can spruce this place up too if you want."

The stairs groaned in protest with every step they took. A shiver ran down her spine. She couldn't help it. The sound reminded her of the doors that ominously creaked open in horror movies. Her overactive imagination wondered if the place was haunted.

The man's face, weathered from the wind and sun, marked him as a man who'd seen at least seven decades. Despite this, his hair was still mousy brown, and his whiskey-colored eyes stubbornly held on to the brightness of youth.

They followed Wyatt upstairs into an open floor plan that reminded her of a flat she'd seen once on a television show. The space was small, but the roof's skylights and the wide windows along the back end gave it an open, airy feeling.

The dingy walls needed a fresh coat of paint, and the small bar separating the kitchenette from the living area needed resurfacing.

"Think you can handle repairs like this?" Wyatt asked bluntly, waving a hand at the bar.

Jace shoved his hands into his front pockets and rocked back on the heels of his boots. "Yeah, I think so. If you have the supplies, we'll get it done."

Jace glanced at her for confirmation. She grinned and nodded, feeling like she could do anything as long as they were together.

"Well, I'll let you settle in. Come on up to the main house around six and the wife will have some stew made," Wyatt invited.

"Thanks," they said in unison.

Wyatt turned to leave, but Jace stopped him with a question that made her heart leap into her throat.

"Would you marry us?" Jace asked. "Your brother mentioned you used to do weddings here."

Surprise flickered across Wyatt's face. "Sure. Janice and I haven't had the pleasure of a wedding in years. What did you have in mind?"

Jace slid to her and wrapped a warm hand around hers. "Do you know anything about handfasting?"

Wyatt scratched the whiskers on his chin. "As a matter of fact, I do. Is that what you're wanting?"

"What do you think?" he asked her with an excited grin.

His buoyant mood was contagious, and she grinned back. "I'd love that."

"Tomorrow morning, then?" Wyatt asked, looking from Jace to her.

Jace leaned his head down and whispered, "Tomorrow?"

A delicious shiver danced down her neck in response to his warm breath against her ear. She didn't know how he made that one word sound so sensual. Her body tingled as she eagerly nodded her head.

"Tomorrow," Jace agreed, leaning forward to shake Wyatt's hand.

Wyatt walked to the stairs, then swiveled back toward them. "Feel free to explore the grounds. The view from the cliff is spectacular."

When the downstairs door slammed shut, Jace took her hand and led her to the wide-open window at the back of the flat. They watched Wyatt limp down the lane toward his own home.

"Do you want to start cleaning up here or go exploring?" he asked as he wrapped his arms around her waist, tucking her into his side.

She looked out the window. The day was still young, and she didn't want to spend it cooped up indoors. Work could wait until they'd eaten something more substantial than apples and honey.

"Let's go see the cliff," she decided.

They walked to the sheer cliff that dropped into the Pacific, each in speculative, yet comfortable, silence.

"Why do you want us to be handfast?" she finally asked. "Is it extra binding? Are you afraid I'll run away?" she teased.

Laughter rumbled up his chest. He smiled down at her, eyes twinkling.

"Will you run?" he challenged.

They stopped at the cliff's edge, and he beckoned her into his arms. She went without hesitation, wrapping her arms around his waist.

"Never again," she declared with feeling.

The day was mild, but by the sea, a cooler wind drove around them, bringing with it the strong scent of salt and fish.

"Glad to hear it." He rested his chin on top of her head and sighed. "My mom mentioned handfasting to me once. Her grandmother was handfast. I just thought maybe it would honor them if we were married in that way."

She raised her head and locked her eyes on his. "I think that's beautiful."

They spent the afternoon by the cliff, talking about their vows and the future. He still wanted her to talk to her parents, and she was slowly warming to the idea. Guilt accosted her heart when she pictured her wedding day. Her mom wouldn't be there to help her dress or do her hair and makeup. Her dad wouldn't walk her down the aisle. Her brother, AJ, wouldn't get to stand as best man for Jace. However, she wouldn't let the melancholy circling around her settle.

They watched the sun burn into the ocean, then walked back to the Inn much the same way as they'd left. She couldn't believe only a few hours remained until her wedding day.

THE SMALL OUTDOOR area the Gates used for weddings had been spruced up earlier that morning. Lacy's heart pinched as she looked over the empty space where rows of white benches would've been placed for family and friends. They were missing the happiest day of her life.

Determined not to let sadness ruin her big day, she drew in a deep breath. Her bare feet sunk into a deep green carpet of cool grass as she walked down the aisle toward Jace. Her breath caught in her throat as her eyes latched onto his. There had to be a word somewhere in the universe that was stronger than the word *love*. The English language didn't do what radiated from his eyes justice.

Mrs. Gate had strewn a variety of flower petals in shades of pink, red, yellow, and white all the way down to the white lattice arch where he waited. She couldn't imagine a life without him now. He was a part of her.

The morning sun warmed her bare shoulders as she glided to the end of the aisle. She turned to face the man who'd fought his way into her heart, the man who'd become as important to her as the air she breathed.

A soft breeze blew, catching the white wrap-around skirt she'd found in the house they'd occupied on Coranado Beach. She'd paired it with a simple sleeveless white top with black buttons down the front.

Jace smiled at her, his eyes tender and full of wonder. She smiled back, trying to swallow the huge lump in her throat. The gods had truly blessed her.

He wore a pair of well-washed, button-down Levi's and a solid black T-shirt. He still looked like a GQ model in the under-stated, simple outfit. The T-shirt stretched across his broad shoulders and the sleeves strained against the corded muscles in his arms. His face was clean-shaven, and he'd gotten a haircut from Mrs. Gate. Much to her chagrin, he'd cut off his shoulder-length hair, but she had to admit, the new, messy, bed-head style was super sexy.

"You ready?" he whispered.

She nodded, heart thundering, not trusting herself to speak without bursting into tears.

He grasped her right hand with his and Wyatt wrapped a three-strand braided cord firmly around their wrists. She loved the idea of incorporating the handfasting ceremony and Mr. Wynn knew the old tradition well, having performed many weddings on the Lighthouse property.

The gold strand caught her eye as it glistened in the sunlight, contrasting with the purple and pink in the braid.

"The gold strand," Wyatt explained, "represents unity, strength, and prosperity. May you always be unified, prosper in all your endeavors, and find strength in one another. Purple represents healing, health, and power. May you have a lifetime of good health and find the power within yourselves to live for each other. The light pink cord represents love, honor, truth, and happiness. I can see the love between you. Love is a powerful thing. May you be blessed with a lifetime of love and happiness."

Her toes curled into the pillow-soft grass as Jace continued to stare at her, his gaze heating with every passing second.

She raised her eyes briefly to the arch above their heads. It provided some shade due to the beautiful deep-purple clematis vine weaved into the lattice holes. Sunlight dappled through it, and she breathed in the sweet, warm fragrance of the vine. Her imagination couldn't have dreamed up a better place to marry the man who held her heart.

"The binding of hands represents the eternal bonds that hold you together," Wyatt said in a rich, confident voice. "This cord is a reminder of the bond you form today as you exchange your sacred vows."

Jace gently squeezed her right hand bound to his as Wyatt knotted the cord.

"I love you," he rasped and the emotion infused into the words settled over her.

Tears sprang into her eyes and her lips trembled. "I love you," she breathed out.

"As this knot is tied, so are your lives bound. All your love and dreams for one another are woven into this cord. May this binding serve as a firm foundation. May it provide strength in times of struggle and a constant source of light in difficult times."

Wyatt cleared his throat. "Now, in the sacred circle you've created, you may exchange your vows and rings if you have them."

Jace had asked for the amethyst ring he'd given her at Christmas right before the ceremony. He wanted to place it officially on her finger. Her ring finger felt naked without it, but she hadn't complained.

He fished it out of his front pocket with his free hand, eyes boring fiercely into hers. The lump in her throat grew, and she wondered how she'd manage to say her vows with it lodged firmly against her vocal cords.

"Lacy," he began, "I've thought a lot about what I'd say to you when this day finally came but . . ." He blew out a breath and smiled. "You're so damn beautiful, all the words I wanted to say have vanished. That's what you do to me every single time I look at you. I love you. You're the most courageous, strong-willed woman I've ever met, and I stand in awe of you. I adore you. I swear to you I'll spend the rest of my life trying to keep up with you."

She couldn't help the tears tracking down her cheeks. Her heart felt like it would explode. The words he said and the words that escaped him sank deep into her bones and settled there, strengthening her.

"We belong together. You and I are written in the stars," he continued, "and if there's such a thing as many lifetimes, I *know* we'll spend every single one of them loving each other. Through sickness and health, through good times and bad, I vow to be your friend, your lover, your rock. Always. From this breath until my last breath, I'm yours."

He slipped the cool, white gold band on her ring finger.

"With this ring, I thee wed," he said, grinning now. "I take you, Lacy Monroe as my wife, my friend, my lover, and my strength."

Wyatt's smile stretched wide across his tanned weathered face, then nodded encouragingly at her.

Jace dragged his thumb along her cheek, wiping away tears, and she let out a shuddering breath.

"Jace." Her voice wobbled and her throat convulsed as she swallowed hard. "I don't think I can express in words how much I love you. I love you more than all the stars in the night sky. I never believed in fate or destiny, until you. You're the one. You've always been the one. I was made to love you. It scares me sometimes how much I want you, how much I need you. When we're apart—"

Tears burned hot behind her eyes and her vocal cords froze as a tsunami wave of emotion rolled over her. Memories of her time in Mexico City were still fresh in her mind. She'd been ripped away from him by her uncle. It had been the worst time in her life.

She cleared her throat and continued. "It feels like half of me is missing. You're my better half, my reason, my strength. Through the beautiful times, through times of heartache, I vow to be your better half, your reason, your strength. Always. From this breath until my last breath, I'm yours."

She echoed his last line. It was perfect. It was theirs alone. His eyes shone as she brought their bound hands to her lips and kissed his knuckles.

"I don't have a ring for you. Yet." She drew in a deep breath. "I take you Jace Cooper as my husband, my lover, my protector. My everything."

Without waiting for Wyatt's declaration, "You may kiss the bride," Jace wrapped his free arm around her waist, drew her close, and lowered his lips onto hers. His lips were soft and sweet, the kiss, slow and alluring. His hand moved up her back and fisted into her hair, flowing freely down her back. She let out a soft, breathy noise as he deepened the kiss.

Wyatt cleared his throat and Jace lifted his head, breaking the kiss, having momentarily forgotten where they were.

"By the power vested in me by the State of California, I now pronounce you husband and wife," Wyatt concluded, chuckling softly.

His rotund, jolly faced wife waddled over and stood beside her husband, offering congratulations.

"I made a cake for this evening's meal," the woman announced proudly.

They offered their thanks to the couple with promises to be at supper promptly at six, then turned toward their flat.

Jace took her hands and laced his fingers through hers. "What do you want to do now, Mrs. Cooper?" he asked, grinning widely.

She grinned back, untangling her hand from his. She walked backward a few steps. "Catch me and find out."

With that, she took off into a sprint toward the cliff where she'd laid a blanket and a small picnic basket filled with fruit and sandwiches, courtesy of Mrs. Gate. Heavy footfall sounded behind her. She laughed, knowing she couldn't outrun him. Halfway to the edge, he caught her and swung her into his arms. Right where she wanted to be.

14

AJ and Bryan stood in companionable silence along the bank of a large pond on the Sinclair property. Cottonwood trees surrounded the water, their leafless, clapper claw branches hovered over the stillness, waiting to snatch anything that sprung from the water's dark depths.

Dark grey clouds hung low in the early morning sky, obscuring the anemic sun. A stiff breeze blew under AJ's thin T-shirt. Goose bumps rose over both arms and legs. He surveyed the little red-and-white bobber rising and falling with the harsh waves and sighed. He should reel it in and check the wriggling silver minnow he'd speared with a rusty hook. He jiggled the rod, then reeled it forward a few inches.

"You're too impatient," Bryan observed dryly.

"We're not going to catch anything," he griped, yanking the bobber forward again. "It's too damn windy."

"Maybe," Bryan replied.

He eyed his friend thoughtfully. He appreciated Bryan's help with Scott even though their investigation stalled like a bad engine. Scott was being careful. Either that, or he really didn't have anything to do with Willow's abduction, and the only thing he was guilty of was being a narcissistic asshole.

"Thanks for helping with Scott," he said. "What do you think about all this? Am I crazy for thinking he was involved in Willow's kidnapping?"

"Crazy? Definitely," Bryan said, smirking. "But the guy is sus. You're not wrong about that."

"I'd understand if you needed to leave," he said, watching Bryan's reaction closely. "I didn't even ask what you planned on doing now that we're free of my uncle."

"I've got nothing better to do at the moment," Bryan said, tugging on his line.

He gave Bryan a sidelong glance. "You don't want to go home? Your parents are still in Shidler, aren't they?"

Bryan's brows dipped. "Yeah, they're still there. And no. I don't want to go home."

He scratched his head. "Why not?"

He'd give anything to get back to Tulare where his parents waited, worrying a path in the living room's carpet, no doubt. He couldn't blame Lacy for not going home right away, but he should've gone back to explain everything that happened.

A dark shadow of doubt hovered around his thoughts as they shifted to Willow. She'd done nothing to encourage him to stay, and he was getting nowhere with his investigation. The push and pull dynamic of their relationship was confusing. Neither of them knew what to do with the feelings between them. Maybe it was time to move on. He needed to consider it at least.

"They don't want me to come back," Bryan said acerbically, interrupting his thoughts.

AJ reeled in his line, inspected the minnow, now dead, then cast it back out.

"Why wouldn't they want you to come home? Surely your mom—"

Bryan cut him off. "No. She doesn't. My mom and dad didn't agree with my decision to join the military when I graduated high school. Dad wanted me to stick around, but there was nothing for me in Shidler. What was I supposed to do? Become a welder? Not that there's anything wrong with being a welder. But I wanted to learn to fly. And I did," he finished, pride leaking into his tone.

AJ clapped him on the back. "I'm sure as hell glad you did. We would've been toast in Mexico City trying to escape in a car. Even that Corvette wouldn't have outrun Nieto's men."

Bryan gave a short laugh. "True. But I loved that car. Maybe I'll get me one," he mused.

"So, the senator paid you a lot of money to fly him around?" he asked, curiously.

"Yeah. For that and being his mole," Bryan answered, yanking his pole backward.

Bryan furiously cranked the reel. Water swirled as a large fish fought the forward motion on the line's end. The end of his pole bent toward the water.

He reeled in his own line, tossed his pole to the side, then ran down to the edge of the bank.

"Stop playin' around in the mud and grab him," Bryan ordered, cranking on the reel with all his might.

His boots sloshed in murky mud and water along the edge. "That's what I'm trying to do, you dumbass buffoon."

His boot slipped in the mud, and he teetered on one foot, arms splayed out for balance. Grunting, he righted himself, then reached into the water. He grabbed Bryan's line, and heaved a huge, largemouth bass onto the bank. He whistled. It was the biggest one he'd ever seen.

"Damn," he said, whistling. "That's got to be at least twenty-eight inches."

Bryan wiped sweat dripping from his brow with the back of his hand. "For sure. It's got to weigh at least thirteen pounds."

"You gonna keep him?" he asked, watching the large fish flop along the bank.

Bryan reached down and picked up the fish by its mouth. He looked him over, eyes squinted in thought.

"Nah," he finally decided. "He's too old. Probably tough as nails."

He removed the hook, careful not to rip the fish's mouth, and tossed him back.

Bryan reached into the minnow bucket and retrieved the last tiny bait fish. They'd caught precious few earlier that morning, but the day had been long, and he was glad to see the last one go.

"What did you do with all the money the senator paid you?" he asked, picking up on their conversation.

"It's in an account overseas," Bryan replied vaguely.

The tips of his mouth curved down. "How are you going to get it? There's no open bank anymore that I know of, not even in California. Almost everything's bartered or exchanged. Some still have physical, paper money they use, but it's mostly worthless."

"I'll charter a plane or find one to fly to the Cayman Islands," Bryan explained.

"Ah," he said in understanding. "You gonna live there?"

The hum and occasional pop of a four-wheeler engine carried on the wind. He glanced over his shoulder. Olive raced through the brown, dead grass, hair flying like a banner behind her. She looked like a goddess riding a chariot into battle.

He gave Bryan a shit-eating grin, punching him in the shoulder. "Here comes trouble."

Bryan stumbled sideways. "Knock it off, you stupid arse."

"Just thought you might wanna know your girlfriend's here," he taunted.

Bryan gave him a sidelong glance as he reeled in his line. "Shut it, dumbass."

Olive pulled up beside them and cut the engine. "What's kickin', little chicken?" she greeted with a grin aimed toward Bryan.

"You're so bizzare," Bryan said, rolling his eyes. "We're done here. Just used the last minnow."

"No luck?" she surmised, blowing off his disparaging remark.

"Bryan caught a nice sized largemouth bass," he informed her. "Tossed him back, though."

Olive's gaze connected with his, and the grin slipped from her face.

He grew uncomfortable under her silent stare. "What?" he demanded.

"You hurt my sister's feelings," she chastised.

He stooped over and picked up his rod to hide his surprise. "How?"

"You basically denied anything was going on between you two, which I know is a lie." She finished in an accusing tone.

He thought about the kiss they'd shared last night, and it was like a lightning strike to his heart. "We worked it out," he murmured, averting his eyes from her stern expression.

Olive let out an unladylike snort. "Oh really?"

He could still feel the soft warmth of her body against his, smell her light honeyed scent, and taste her full supple lips. The way her eyes connected with the deepest part of his soul almost undid him.

A sharp jab in his shoulder woke him from his thoughts. He turned to glare at Bryan.

Bryan raised a brow. "Your eyes glazed over like you were possessed by an alien or some shit. Where'd you go just now?"

"Nowhere," he retorted sharply.

Olive stared him down, impatience radiating from every pore. "Well?" she demanded.

He raised his free hand. "What?"

He'd missed everything she'd said daydreaming about Willow.

"Have you seen Willow this morning?" she practically shouted.

Panic seized his heart. "No. What's going on?"

The doubts about their relationship ghosted away on the wind when he thought of Willow in danger. If anything happened to her, he didn't know what he'd do. He dimly realized he was in deep shit when it came to her. Like a tractor beam, she drew him into her orbit. There was nothing he could do about it. All his thinking about leaving was meaningless.

"I really thought she'd be with you," Olive muttered, dragging her fingers through her tangled hair. "The horse we're boarding is missing. Laurel thinks Willow took her out last night and didn't come back."

"And you're just now looking for her?" he asked incredulously. "How could you just now notice your sister is missing?"

He wanted to strangle the girl as real fear dragged its bony claws down his back. What if Scott had gotten to her? What if she'd been thrown from the horse and was lying hurt somewhere?

"Do you realize Scott could have her?" he seethed, chest pumping up and down.

"I had no idea she'd even left the house, and Laurel thought she heard her come in last night," Olive defended, her tone weak.

"Calm down," Bryan said, hands pumping the air like a brake pedal.

He speared Olive with a scathing look. "Where have you looked so far?"

He secured his pole with a bungee cord onto the four-wheeler he'd ridden to the pond, then hopped onto the vehicle.

"The northern section along the highway. Laurel's searching behind the house. There's a creek Willow likes to visit down there," she said in a breathless voice.

Bryan walked over and placed a reassuring hand on Olive's shoulder. "We'll find her."

Olive's brown eyes tightened with worry and her lower lip trembled. "The last time we couldn't find her . . ." she choked out, not able to finish.

Bryan jumped onto his four-wheeler. "Come on, I'll help you look."

"I'll head out behind the pond," he said, pushing the button to start the engine.

It roared to life. Bryan and Olive started their four wheelers, then they all rode off in separate directions to look for Willow. Worry bit into him like a snake. He could feel its poison surging through his veins, burning them to ash. Where could she be?

His eyes swept over the open prairie. Bryan hadn't watched Scott's house last night. They both went to bed after their talk, agreeing that one night off of surveillance wouldn't hurt. What if Scott knew they'd been watching him and took the first opportunity he had to snatch her? He couldn't lose her like he'd lost Quinn. He wouldn't.

Wave after wave of helplessness assaulted him as he continued to search with no luck. He came to a fence line where the Sinclair property ended. He looked up and down the line, wondering which way to go next. He turned south. He'd follow the fence, then cut up through the creek back to the house.

Where the hell was Willow?

15

Willow watched the colors of early dawn stretch along the horizon. Dark clouds muted the otherwise brilliant orange and pink hues that streaked across the sky. She shivered. Mother nature decided to add a chilly wind as if the gloominess wasn't quite enough to express her thoughts on the already depressing morning. Her whole body quaked, trying to generate enough heat to keep warm.

She shifted her back against the craggy boulder, searching for a more comfortable position. The jagged rock cut into her spine and shoulder blades no matter which way she turned. She wrapped her hand around her right thigh and gently repositioned her lower leg. Her ankle swelled, tightening the skin around it.

"I can get through this," she muttered. "Someone will find me sooner or later."

She hoped it would be sooner. Otherwise, she'd have to think about moving. Somehow. She couldn't walk without help, but she could probably crawl.

She lifted her hand and felt blood still seeping from the gash along her hairline. It ran in rivulets down the side of her face half the night. Her hands were stained a dull, dirty red from applying pressure to the gaping cut. Her head throbbed in merciless tandem, the pain so intense she wished she had a machete. She'd lob it off right there.

She thought about the night before, wondering if she could've prevented her accident. In the waning twilight, coyotes began to howl and hunt for their dinner. She remembered turning the restless mare toward home, galloping along the creek's tree line.

The air was cool and soft against her cheeks as the mare's hooves pounded against the dirt. The tang of sweet grass, dried with the previous summer's hot temperatures, soothed her troubled mind.

Then a coyote raced out of the trees in front of her, barreling down on a frightened rabbit. The skittish mare reared onto its hind legs, releasing a shrill whinny. She clung to the saddle as the horse bolted into the trees, bucking like a prized bronco. Losing her grip, she tumbled out of the saddle and hit her head on the rock where she now rested.

The culprit of her predicament meandered through the trees near her, stopping every so often to lower her head, using large, yellow teeth to pull dead prairie grass from the ground. It would've been better for her if the damned horse had run home. At least then someone might've come looking for her.

"Go home!" she shouted, waving her hands at the careless horse. "Shoo!"

She still couldn't believe no one noticed she was missing yet.

Not even AJ. The thought caused her heart to sink. Had she driven him away?

She still couldn't erase the memory of his kiss. Every time she thought about it, her stomach tightened, and her lips tingled as if they too remembered his soft, inviting lips.

Alone in the darkness she could admit it to herself. She wanted him. The man was Mercury-level hot. She'd heard Olive talk about her sex life enough to light her imagination on fire. Again, she thought about the kiss they'd shared. What would it feel like to have his calloused, yet gentle, hands travel down the curves of her body?

She sucked in a sharp breath as a warm wave of desire crashed over her. Yeah, she wanted him more than anything. But, as he succinctly pointed out, she had trauma issues.

He said it didn't matter. But how could it not?

The night spent propped against the boulder had been miserable. Not to mention scary. She sat and listened to coyotes call to one another. Their howls echoed and bounced through the trees. It sounded as if they surrounded her. They were more scared of her than she was of them. She'd chanted that mantra to herself throughout the long night.

"What do you think, girl?" she'd asked the mare. "You think those coyotes will come and eat me like Little Red Riding Hood's grandma?"

The sudden sound of her scratchy, water-deprived voice startled her. It sounded unnatural, out of place with the nighttime's natural symphony, so she didn't speak again. It didn't matter. The horse ignored her anyway.

The shadowed eeriness of the trees, the darkness, and the howls caused an endless amount of goosebumps to erupt all over her body. The cold seeped into her bones, and the wind carried the scent of rain.

She'd slept in fitful spurts. Every time she closed her eyes, she dreamt of Scott. They'd be eating at the same restaurant in Laredo where she'd been kidnapped. However, the dream took an unexpected turn. Instead of two Mexicans waiting for her behind the restaurant, it was Scott. He'd shoved her into the black SUV.

The owl hooting in a tree nearby, every twig that snapped under a nighttime creature's paw caused her heart to jump into her throat. Would Scott find her here and kidnap her? What if he'd somehow found out she was missing?

The mare jerked her head up, ears pricked forward at the sound of a four-wheeler.

"Finally," she muttered.

Dread spread down her spine. What if it was Scott? She held her breath and listened intently until the quad's engine stopped at last.

"Willow!"

AJ's voice echoed through the trees. Her breath released in a relieved whoosh. Her heart went into overdrive at the sound of his voice, trying to pound its way out of her rib cage.

"Over here!" she shouted. "I'm over here!"

"Willow?"

His voice caused tears to spring into her eyes. She sniffed and swallowed the lump in her throat.

"Yeah! I'm through the trees," she responded, her voice raw and scratchy.

Branches snapped underfoot as he ran. He broke through the last of the brush. When his eyes landed on her, he sprinted to her, knees buckling as he landed by her side.

"Thank God," he breathed. "Where are you hurt?"

Without waiting for her answer, gentle hands began inspecting the gash on her forehead.

"Ow." She jerked, slapping his hand away on instinct.

He lowered his hand, and she saw uncertainty in his eyes. He shifted and dropped into a sitting position beside her.

Dammit, Willow, she thought. *He's just trying to help you.*

She mentally berated herself for reacting that way. If she continued to respond to him this way, she'd end up driving him away for sure.

"What the hell happened?" he asked, softly.

"The horse threw me. I haven't been thrown from a horse since I was a kid," she complained, embarrassment flooding her system. "My brain is trying to pound its way out of my skull."

"I can see that," he said evenly. "Where else are you hurt?"

"I think my ankle is broken," she muttered.

He studied her with solemn eyes. "I'm going to carry you to the four-wheeler. Okay?"

"Okay," she agreed, stretching out the word.

He rose to his knees, placing both hands on his thighs.

She hesitated, then without overthinking it, blurted, "I know I keep pushing you away. I don't mean to. I feel like I've kind of made a mess of things."

His eyes widened at the admission.

"I know you're scared of hurting me, but I didn't mind you touching my forehead. It just . . . hurts," she finished lamely.

He cupped her cheek. "You're right. But you're not the only one trying to figure stuff out. There's something I haven't told you. About me."

"What about you?" she asked, thinking there wasn't anything he could say about himself that would dissuade her heart from falling for him.

He pushed up and rose to his feet. "Another time," he deflected. "Right now, let's get you to your sister so she can patch you up."

He scooped her up like a lost puppy. She muffled a whimper as her ankle dangled in the air.

He winced. "Sorry, darlin'. I know it hurts."

"It's okay," she said, trying to breathe through the pain.

With gentle care, he deposited her onto the four-wheeler's seat. He swung his leg over and settled in behind her. The heat from his chest soaked into her back and his scent, warm and musky, enveloped her like an invisible cocoon. He leaned over her shoulder and pushed the start button. His body pressed into her as he leaned forward, grasping the handlebars. They lurched forward, racing over the rough terrain.

She wanted to snuggle against him, to lean her head back on his chest. Every muscle in her body ached from the toss off the horse's back, and she struggled to keep herself upright. His chest rose then fell with a sigh as he took one hand off the handle bar, wrapped it around her waist, and scooted her flush with his chest.

"Better?" he whispered in her ear as the wind rushed around them in a tunnel.

She nodded and leaned her head back. How had he known?

AJ pulled the ATV directly in front of the small clinic's door. She didn't think he'd set foot in the place since Laurel removed the bullet from his chest.

Laurel rushed out, the bell clanging wildly as the door flung open. Her older sister assessed the situation, eyes roving over her with an expertness that few ever achieved.

"What the hell?" Laurel admonished in her mother-knows-best voice. "How could you be so careless? How badly are you hurt?"

"I'm okay," she tried to assure her.

Laurel's eyes narrowed and speared her with a look that sliced straight through her. "I'll be the judge of that." Laurel turned to AJ. "Carry her inside."

It was a command not a request, and Willow's lips turned up in a half-smile. "My sister's kind of bossy."

His brow quirked up. "Ya think?"

She winced as AJ picked her up off the seat. "Sorry about that," he apologized.

Blood seeped into her mouth as she bit into her lip to keep from crying as he maneuvered her through the doorway. He sat her on the sterile, stainless-steel table with a gentleness that juxtaposed the toughness he projected. Her heart thudded against her rib cage when he crouched before her. Black hair fell against his forehead in a way that made her want to run her fingers through it.

His eyes lifted to hers. "Which ankle?"

"The right one," she answered, hardly able to breathe let alone speak.

The right ankle had swollen and filled the entire space around it. Getting the boot off was going to suck. He removed the left one, then picked up the right. His fingers moved, delicately pushing against the outer leather shell from the toes to the swollen area.

He grasped the heel with the other hand. "This is gonna hurt," he warned.

Laurel came out of the back room, pushing a stainless-steel cart with an array of supplies needed to close the gash on her forehead. She spotted a staple gun and shuddered. Those things were brutal.

"Don't jerk it off," Laurel warned. "We can cut it off if necessary."

"No," she objected, "Dad gave me these boots."

"Yeah, when you were in the eighth grade," Laurel shot back.

"But, I love these boots," she whined.

Laurel rolled her eyes at her little sister. "Those boots are old. No big loss."

"Maybe not to you," she muttered sullenly.

"What the hell were you thinking?" Laurel rebuked again. "You didn't tell anyone you'd left, much less where you were going. Do you know what you put us through? It was like you'd vanished all over again."

She lowered her eyes. The distress that'd driven her from the farm seemed minute now. Her actions had been dangerous, especially if AJ was right about Scott. What would he have done if he'd found her?

"I'm sorry," she said sincerely. "It won't happen again."

Her sister grunted. "See that it doesn't."

AJ gently tugged on the boot. It didn't budge. He rose to his feet and turned to Laurel.

"I think you'll need to cut it. I don't want to pull too hard," he said.

"No, Laurel," Willow said, scooting back on the table. "Please."

Laurel gave her a sympathetic look. "There's no way around it, honey. I'm sorry."

Laurel retrieved trauma sheers from the cart, bent down, and sliced through the leather. The boot fell to the floor with a soft thud.

"Dammit, Laurel," she grumbled.

Ignoring her, Laurel peeled off the sock, her expert fingers feeling around on the ankle.

"I don't think it's broken," Laurel observed. "But we'll X-ray it to be sure. Lie back so I can get a better look at your head."

Silent tears seeped from her closed eyelids as Laurel washed the gash out with saline solution. It trickled down her skull, soaking her hair with salt water, dirt, and blood. Laurel sponged Betadine inside and around the wound to disinfect it.

"I'm going to try to glue this. It's going to sting," Laurel warned, dabbing away excess disinfectant. "If it doesn't work, I'll have to staple it."

Laurel finished gluing and bandaging her head, then wheeled the table to the X-ray machine.

"Don't move," Laurel said, placing a lead apron over her chest.

Thankfully, the X-ray showed her ankle wasn't broken. Her sister grabbed some Coban wrap from the cart, and wound the long, brown elastic material around it in a compression wrap.

"Don't put any weight on your ankle until the swelling decreases," Laurel instructed, as she handed her a pair of crutches.

"Where'd you get these?" she asked curiously.

Laurel rolled her eyes. "Don't you remember when Olive got chased by that bull? She fell trying to run away from it and twisted her knee."

She shook her head. "Nope. I don't remember that."

"Well, you were probably too young to remember," Laurel conceded.

Laurel turned, plucked an Ibuprofen bottle from the cart, and shook out two pills. "Take these and let me know if it doesn't help and I'll get you something stronger."

"Thanks," she murmured, accepting the medicine.

Laurel turned to AJ. "Take her into the house and get her some ice for her ankle and a glass of water."

"Thanks, Laurie," she said, lowering her head. "I'm sorry I worried you."

Laurel's eyes sheened over with tears. "You're welcome. Now go lay down. Make sure you elevate that ankle."

She nodded, and hobbled out of the clinic, the crutches making soft thumping noises as she went. AJ followed close behind, steadying her a couple of times on the uneven walkway between the clinic and back door. When they reached the living room he helped her settle onto the couch.

He fluffed two throw pillows then placed them under her calf. Tears leaked from the corner of her eyes as he left to get her a glass of water. She blamed them on the pain but knew her tears stemmed more from emotions and being overly tired than her broken body.

She wiped them away, took a steadying breath and when he'd returned with the water, she had her emotions under control. She accepted the water with a subdued "thank you," and downed the pills.

"Rest," he said, brushing hair from her forehead with a gentle hand.

Her eyelids drooped on the command. "Okay," she mumbled, already half-asleep.

* * *

LATER THAT EVENING, Willow hopped on one foot out of the bathroom, steam billowing out behind her. She had thoroughly enjoyed the much needed bath. She'd actually found leaves and little sticks in her hair as she washed it. How embarrassing.

AJ leaned against the opposite wall, waiting for her.

"Are you ready to play whatever game Olive has planned?" he asked with a raised brow.

She grimaced. "No. But let's go anyway."

Olive gathered everyone in the living room, declaring they were duty bound to entertain her injured baby sister. She suspected Olive wanted an excuse to drink more than anything else. Under Laurel's watchful eye, Olive rarely got to break out their parent's cache of liquor.

She reached for the crutches she'd left outside the doorway.

"I'll carry you," he said, pushing off the wall.

She dipped her head. "You don't have to do that."

He chuckled. "I know I don't have to. I want to."

Before she could protest, he swept her up into his arms and carried her down the stairs into the living room. Talk about sweeping a girl off her feet! She wanted to fan her heated cheeks, but her hands were wrapped around his neck, so she buried her face in his chest instead.

Olive and Bryan sat on the floor around the well-used Chippendale coffee table. AJ placed her on the couch, then sat beside her. A reluctant Laurel stoked the crackling fire, blazing on the grate.

A full bottle of Crown and five shot glasses sat on top of the coffee table's cherrywood surface.

"Laurel, come on," Olive cajoled in a playful whine.

Laurel pushed a rocking chair from its spot near the fire to the table and sat with a loud, resigned sigh. "Okay, Olive. What's the game?"

Olive rubbed her hands together with an evil grin. "The game is Truth, Dare, or Drink. The rules are simple. You choose one of the three, but you can't choose Drink more than three times in a row. If you refuse, you lose."

"Who starts?" Bryan asked.

Olive produced a single die. "We roll for it. Highest number goes first."

She didn't want to play but knew it would be useless to argue when Olive got an idea in her head. Legally, she wasn't old enough to drink, but didn't think that excuse would work. She couldn't walk much less perform a Dare which left Truth, and she had a sneaking suspicion Olive wanted to bombard her with Truth questions about AJ.

Bryan won, rolling a six, and immediately challenged Olive. "Truth, Dare, or Drink?" he asked, eyes sparking with mischief.

Olive tapped her index finger against her lips in feigned thought. "Hmm. I guess I'll go with Dare."

Bryan grinned like a fiend. "I was hoping you'd say that. I dare you to smell my feet."

Olive scrunched her nose and punched his shoulder. "Ugh. Why? Why do you have to be so weird?"

Bryan turned toward Olive and removed his boots. He raised a foot, waggling his toes, clad in a dingy white tube sock.

"Come on. Just a sniff," he said, thoroughly enjoying the moment.

AJ huffed a laugh under his breath and leaned against her shoulder. "I know for a fact he hasn't taken a shower in at least two days."

Olive heard him and gave Bryan a horrified look. "You can't be serious."

"Oh, I'm serious," he pronounced with his brow cocked.

Olive deliberated a moment. "Fine," she said with a fiendish grin that promised retribution.

Bryan lifted his foot higher toward her nose. Olive grabbed his ankle and gave him an audacious look. Taking a deep, fortifying breath, her sister leaned her nose toward Bryan's wiggling toes, took a delicate sniff—and gagged.

"Oh my God," she gasped. "Your feet smell like cheese soaked in vinegar!"

Bryan beamed, taking the comment as a compliment. "Thanks. I put a lot of work into the smell, getting just the right cheese-to-vinegar ratio."

"Idiot," Olive snarked, shoving the offending foot away.

"Hey," he said in a playful voice. "No need for violence. Geez."

Olive rubbed her nose with the heel of her hand. "I'm next."

Anticipation mixed with dread zipped from the top of Willow's head down to her toes. She might get lucky. Olive could pick Bryan and pay him back for making her smell his feet. Which was genius.

"Okay," Olive began, looking around the circle. "I choose Willow."

She groaned. "No, pick someone else. Don't you want to pay Bryan back?"

"Way to throw me under the bus, Will," Bryan muttered.

"Willow, Truth, Dare, or Drink?" Olive challenged.

She slumped against the couch's cushioned back, thinking through her options. If she chose Truth, her sister would go for the jugular. But drinking? That wasn't the best idea either.

Throwing her hands up in surrender, she answered, "Truth."

Olive's eyes gleamed in the room's low light. "So, Willow, inquiring minds want to know. On a scale of one to ten, how hot do you think AJ is? And this is a two-part question, so buckle up, buttercup. Second, who's the better kisser, Scott or AJ?"

Her face flamed as AJ turned to stare at her with a mixture of amusement and curiosity. She balled her hands into fists. If she lied, Olive would know and make the situation worse by opening her big, fat mouth.

Staring at a picture on the wall of wild roses, blooming in riotous colors of red and orange, she braced herself. This was going to be painful.

Her heartbeat kicked up. "On a scale of one to ten, I think every female would agree AJ's a dime."

Olive wasn't fooled. "But the question wasn't what the female population thinks. What do you think?"

Her eyes narrowed on her sister. "I would have to agree."

"Hmm. So a ten? That's your answer?" Olive pushed with a wicked grin.

Anger began to simmer in her gut. "Yes," she bit out.

"And the next question? Remember, it's two-part," Olive reminded her. "Who kisses better, Will? AJ or Scott?"

"AJ," she whispered.

Olive cupped her ear. "What was that?"

She glanced at AJ who was still staring at her and cleared her throat. "AJ kisses better."

Olive clapped her hands in gleeful abandon. "My wittle sister's in wuv."

"Shut up, Liv," Willow warned, eyes narrowed.

AJ leaned into her. "Want to get out of here?" he asked quietly.

She nodded. "Definitely."

He picked her up, cradling her body against his chest, and headed for the hall.

"Hey, where are you going?" Bryan called after them.

"Somewhere quiet," AJ replied in a short, clipped voice.

"Ooo," Olive hooted. "We know what that means."

Bryan laughed and nudged her leg with his stockinged foot. "We could go somewhere quiet."

Olive slapped it away with an, "Eww."

She tuned out the lively mayhem from the living room as he walked across the foyer to the stairs. Leaning her head against his chest, she heard the rapid beat of his heart and smiled. At least one good thing had come from her being injured. She could get used to his arms around her. It scared her, yet she wanted to take the leap and fall for him.

16

The sun warmed Lacy's cheeks as she stepped out of the middle cabin of the triplex. She swiped the sweat beading on her forehead with the back of her hand. She'd cleaned the cabin top to bottom and needed a break before starting on the next one.

She'd never seen so many mice droppings in her life. Not even her grandma's old farmhouse had an infestation this bad. The little brown pellets were everywhere—in the kitchen cabinets, on the beds, and, the most bizarre place she found them, the bathtub.

The mice dropping's pungent, musky odor stuck in her nose like a sand burr. The house smelled clean now, like bleach mostly, because she'd used an entire bottle disinfecting the kitchen, bathroom, floors, and baseboards. Yet that distinct odor stubbornly remained in her nose-memory. Bleh. She sucked in fresh air through her nose, hoping it would quell the queasiness in her stomach.

A sudden shiver bolted down her spine, pricking the hairs on the back of her neck. She stepped off the porch, raised a hand to shield her eyes from the bright sunlight, and looked around. She had the uneasy feeling someone watched her.

Weird. Nothing seemed amiss so she shrugged off the apprehension clinging to her shoulders with a shudder.

A ladder, propped against the side of the cabin to her left, stretched to the roof's peak. She looked up. Jace stood on the top rung, replacing a rotted fascia board. His T-shirt was tucked into the back of his jeans, which hung low on his hips. His flexing biceps glistened with sweat as he hammered a nail in the new board.

The man was sinfully hot, and he was all hers. The urge to drag him off the ladder and back upstairs to their bed overwhelmed her but she took a deep breath and banked the fire his half-naked body stirred within her for this evening.

"Hey," she called up.

He looked down and grinned. "Hey, beautiful."

She scoffed at the comment. Her hair hung in a lopsided messy bun atop her head, and she wore a tie-dye T-shirt with the sleeves cut out. It looked like a dress on her, so she'd tied the excess material into a knot at her waist. Mr. Gate let them rummage through clothing left by customers over the years to work in, so they didn't ruin the precious few they had.

The small apple orchard on Mr. and Mrs. Gate's property already had new green leaves sprouting due to February's unseasonably warm weather. A walk among the heavenly fragrance of the budding apple blossoms was tempting.

"I was thinking about exploring the apple orchard. I seriously need a break from all the mice poop. Wanna come?"

He grabbed the nail he held in his mouth and pounded it into the board. "Sure. I'll finish this and meet you there."

"Okay," she agreed, and headed in the direction of the orchard.

Shock.
Confusion.
Pain.

FRAGMENTED THOUGHTS CHASED one another through Lacy's mind like a monkey chasing a weasel. Her brain latched onto that cliché, and she wanted to laugh. How absurd. Why would a monkey chase a weasel?

She tried to concentrate but couldn't hold onto any one thought for more than a second or two. Freeze-framed images flashed through her mind and then disappeared.

The sweet fragrance of an apple orchard in early spring.

Pain ricocheting from the back of her head.

Garbled words caught in a vortex sifted to her. Phrases floated around like tiny, annoying gnats. Impossible to swat away. Impossible to grasp.

It sounded as though her ears were flooded with fluid. Either that, or she was underwater, drowning. A spike of panic barreled up her middle. Was she dying?

A familiar voice, harsh and demanding, yelled, "Dammit, Lacy. Wake up!"

She knew that voice. Inwardly, she commanded her eyelids to open. They fluttered, feeling as if sand bags weighed them down. She whimpered and tried again.

A large, warm hand cupped her cheek. "Come on, that's it."

Jace's voice softened, and she responded to his encouragement. One eyelid cracked open. Then the other. His blurry face came into view. She blinked and her vision cleared.

The mattress dipped as he sat beside her. Water, wrung from a washcloth, splashed back into a basin that sat on the small nightstand by the bed. With tender care, he laid the cool cloth on her forehead.

She tried to speak but couldn't get her frozen vocal cords to obey. Her eyes darted to the nightstand where a glass of water sat. Jace followed her gaze. He picked up the cup and wrapped a hand around her head.

Sharp pain stole her breath as he eased her head up to drink from the glass.

"I'm sorry," he murmured softly.

She took a small sip, then pushed the glass from her lips. "What happened?"

Her voice cracked and came out in nothing more than a harsh whisper.

"I'm not sure," he hedged, eyes tight with concern. "I was hoping you'd remember."

The light illuminating the darkened room hurt her eyes. She closed them and tried to remember. The last thing that came to mind was walking through the apple orchard.

"I was walking through the trees," she whispered, remembering again the orchard's fragrance.

Even in early March, the trees showed the promising signs of spring. Millions of buds formed on the trees' naked branches. A few pink blossoms had even burst open, their sweet, floral scent infusing the air. The dry ground crunched softly beneath her feet as she walked among the rows.

He brushed strands of hair from her face. "I know. I was coming to meet you. Do you remember anything else?"

"Not much," she admitted, frustrated she couldn't recall those memories.

They were shadows at the edge of her mind, unformed apparitions only seen in one's peripheral vision. There, but not quite there.

"How do you feel?" he asked.

"I'm fine," she assured him, although she wasn't sure that was entirely true.

He rose, and she tracked his movements through the room with tired, pain-filled eyes. He readied for bed, removing the white, cotton T-shirt, which revealed the hard, defined lines of his stomach. No matter how many times she saw his body, it still affected her the same way. Fireflies took flight inside her. The lightning they carried set her blood on fire. Injured or not, she still craved him.

Sitting on his side of the bed, he tugged off his boots. They plunked to the floor one at a time. He unbuttoned his thread-bare Levis and dumped them on the floor.

She laid back the covers, and he climbed in beside her. When he reached for her, she willingly slid into the warmth and safety of his arms. His calloused hand reached under her T-shirt and rested just below her belly button. His touch stole her breath. She arched into his touch.

"Don't get too excited," he said with a low chuckle. "You're hurt."

She let out an exaggerated sigh. "Only married a week and a half, and you've lost that lovin' feeling."

His breath came hot against her ear as he responded, "Nice try. Now close your eyes and get some rest. I'll wake you in an hour or two in case you have a concussion."

She didn't tell him they were already shut, didn't even mumble a reply as sleep overtook her.

LACY WAS BACK at her grandmother's farmhouse, the place where she'd been sexually assaulted by Jace's brother, Zach. Her heart thumped wildly against her rib cage as she hid behind the old leather couch. A hurricane of adrenaline and the fight-flight-or-freeze instinct raged inside her. She tried to move, but fear held her hostage.

The scene switched to the apple orchard. The sun-warmed wind blew softly against her cheeks. A stick snapped behind her and she turned around with a smile, expecting Jace to be there, but the path behind her was empty.

She couldn't shake the sense of someone's leering eyes watching her. She suppressed a shudder and kept walking.

Warning bells pealed inside her. Someone was following her. She adjusted her course back toward the clearing.

As she veered left, a man came into view. He was small, lean, and walked with a feminine style many women never achieved. He strolled toward her with a mysterious smile on his face. The man's mustache curled up on the sides and his dark hair was oiled and parted down the middle. The image he cast made her think of the old western movies she used to watch with her grandpa.

"Who are you?" she asked warily.

He stopped and cocked his head to the side. "A friend of your father's. And Jace's."

Realization struck her as his softly spoken words sank in. Dammit. Her father—no uncle, she stubbornly corrected herself —hadn't listened to her warning. Thomas Monroe had sent Widdowson after her.

Fury swept over her. "Widow."

The name ripped from her lips with disdain.

His smile widened as he gave her an elaborate bow. "Of course."

"What do you want?" she asked, nails digging into the palm of her hands.

He took a step forward. "You. And Jace," he added as an afterthought. "Your father needs you home. Your mother, you see, she's—"

"I don't give a shit about what he needs or what she needs!" she shouted. "And that is not my home."

Widdowson took another step toward her, and she took a step back. Her eyes swept over him in quick assessment. She could probably outrun him. In a split second, she turned and ran. The little man was faster than she'd anticipated, gaining ground quickly. Her pulse spiked. She pushed herself to run faster.

But it wasn't enough. Pain ruptured up the back of her neck, and she crashed to the ground. Skin peeled back as her cheek skidded across dirt, sticks, and last season's dead leaves. He'd struck her from behind.

A scream tore from her throat. She bolted up, fully awake.

Jace sat up, disoriented. "What? What's the matter?"

His strong arms wrapped around her shaking form, and cradled her against his chest.

He smoothed hair from her face. "It was just a nightmare," he murmured.

"No," she sniffed. "It wasn't. I know what happened."

The muscles in his arms flexed. "In the orchard?"

She nodded.

"Who was it?"

Her eyes darted up to his. "Widow."

17

Fear's iron hand gripped Lacy by the throat and squeezed. Squeezed until the air she breathed became nothing but a trickle. In and out, she fought for every breath that wheezed through her lungs.

Widow was here.

Her eyes locked onto Jace's and the panic, the terror she felt, shone through his eyes as if they'd stepped onto a landmine together.

Jace had been an intimate part of her life for months. They'd been to hell and back, and in that time, she'd never seen him visibly shaken. Until now.

"We have to go," he said, pulling away from her. "Now."

He threw back the covers and sprang out of bed, collecting his strewn clothing from the floor. He shrugged into his T-shirt, pulled on his jeans, then sat on the bed to tug on his boots.

She watched him in shocked silence, unable to move. Where would they go?

"Lacy, get dressed," he commanded.

His harsh tone filtered through the thick haze of dread that descended upon her as if she wore a reaper's cloak. She scooted to the bed's edge, but when she stood the world tilted and spun like an old-fashioned wooden top. Her body pitched forward despite her efforts to stand straight without wobbling.

Jace caught her before she face-planted onto the floor.

"You have a concussion," he said, helping her sit back on the bed. "I'll help you dress."

"Do we have to go now?" she asked as she lifted a hand to her aching forehead. "Widow knows we're here. If he was going to do something, don't you think he would've done it by now?"

His eyes darkened. "Widow is unpredictable, so there's no way of knowing. What did he say to you? Do you remember?"

She lowered her head into her hands. "My uncle sent him. He said, 'Your father wants you home.'"

He stopped in his tracks. "If he wanted to take you back, he could've easily done it. Why did he leave you?"

Good question, she mused, lifting her eyes to his. "Is he toying with us? Do you think he's still around?"

"Yeah, I do," he confirmed as he swiveled around on his boot heels.

He gathered her jeans and shoes scattered on the floor, then bent before her. The light from the bedside lamp shone on his dark walnut hair. She ran a hand through it as he threaded her jeans over her feet and up her legs. He glanced up at her, and those eyes that never ceased to arrest her softened.

"Lay down and lift your butt," he said with an amused smile.

She rolled her eyes and lowered herself, careful not to go too fast. Her head pounded in protest at the movement. He dragged her jeans over her hips, briefly running a warm calloused hand over her lower abdomen. Her breath caught, but all he did was zip and button her jeans.

"We have to go," he reminded her, lowering his body over hers. "But you know, the way you're so easily aroused by my touch is a real turn-on."

He nuzzled her neck as his hands grasped hers and gently lifted them above her head.

"You're teasing me," she said on a gasp as he nipped her lower lip. "Not fair."

"Yeah, I am," he admitted as he slowly slid his way down her body.

"Jerk." She tried and failed to sound sincere.

He chuckled softly as he slid her worn pair of Converse onto her feet.

"Do we need to take anything?" he asked.

"Our bags are packed and in the closet," she told him.

He quirked a brow.

"Never hurts to be prepared," she said with a slight smile.

He retrieved them, slung both over one shoulder, then went to the bed where she waited. "Ready?" he asked, offering her a hand up.

She grasped his hand in hers. "Not really. Where will we go?"

He tugged her to her feet. "We'll head southeast."

Her narrowed eyes shot to his. "To Tulare?"

He tugged her forward and they were off, hurrying through the cottage, turning off the lights as they went. Jace stopped at the counter and scratched out a quick note to the Gates who'd been so kind to them.

A sudden thought froze her to the spot. "Widow won't hurt Mr. and Mrs. Gate will he?"

A frown settled on his face and deepened the lines between his eyes. "I hope not. That's one of the reasons we need to leave. So they'll be safe."

They closed the cottage door, and a feeling of remorse over-took her. She liked it here, better than anywhere else she'd been in her limited trips over the years. As they descended the steps, she placed a hand on his arm to steady herself.

"Can we come back?" she asked as tears burned the back of her throat.

"We'll see," he hedged. "If it's at all possible, I'd like to come back too."

Her torn heart was soothed by his words. "Thank you."

He tossed their bags into the truck bed, opened the passenger door and helped her up.

They drove toward the rising sun. She rolled down her window, closed her eyes, and let the cool breeze blow against her face.

Had Widow seen them leave? A shudder raced up her spine. The thought of that man stalking them, watching their every move, unnerved her. Had he seen Jace dress her, or the kisses they'd shared?

They were headed to Tulare, toward her parents, who owed her one hell of an explanation. They hadn't told her she'd been adopted, hadn't shared the fact that Senator Thomas Monroe was her real father. Why? She dreaded the confrontation but knew Jace was right. She wouldn't rest until she had answers.

18

AJ laughed softly as he watched Willow struggle to stay awake. He'd swept her into his arms and carried her up the stairs to her bedroom. Refusing to watch her struggle with the crutches was the excuse he used, but he'd loved every minute her warm body snuggled against his chest.

He'd given her privacy and turned his back as she changed into an oversized T-shirt and boxers. When she finished, she limped over on bare feet and placed her small hand in his. He helped her into bed and then propped himself up on the headboard beside her.

"You didn't have to answer Olive," he said, breaking the silence.

The silence wasn't uncomfortable, but he wanted to learn more about her. It still unnerved him when he thought about commitment. He'd need to tell her about Quinn.

Her pillow rustled as she slid down and snuggled beneath the covers. The pink comforter, stuffed with downy feathers, was silky soft and warm beneath his calloused hands. Its warmth helped stave off the room's chilly air.

She gave him a sidelong glance. "I know."

Her cheeks bloomed red as he slid down the headboard and

scooted closer to her. He turned his body toward her and brushed a strand of hair from her face.

"Well thank you for the compliment," he said softly.

Her lips tipped in a small smile. "You're surprisingly humble."

"What do you mean?"

"What I mean," she began slowly, "is that you're nice to look at and I think you know it."

"Ah," he said, comprehending what she didn't say. "So, Scott thinks he's God's gift to women, huh?"

"I'm not comparing you to Scott," she said with a frown.

He arched a brow. "Aren't you, though?"

"How many relationships have you had?" she challenged, changing the subject.

"Relationships?" he hedged, squirming a little.

He could answer the question with relative ease. But would it be a lie by omission? The idea didn't set well with him, yet he didn't want to answer with brutal honesty either. He'd only been in one relationship, but his *relations* with women were vast. Something he'd become increasingly ashamed of the more he got to know Willow.

Her lips twitched. "Yes. Relationships. It's not a hard question."

It was.

"Technically?" he hedged in a teasing tone.

"Oh my God, just answer the question, AJ," she burst out on a laugh. "I'm not going to judge you."

He rose on an elbow, propped his head on his hand, and looked down at her. "No judgments, huh?"

"None whatsoever," she assured, placing a soft hand on top of his.

He sighed. "I've only been in one relationship and it . . ."

Quinn's face materialized before him as it always did when he thought of her. His heart pinched at the painful reminder.

Her face softened as she studied his face. "It didn't end well?"

"No," he said, voice cracking.

He cleared his throat, and she squeezed his hand in reassurance.

"After that I didn't have *relationships,* I had—"

A wide grin spread across her face, and it threw him off center. It wasn't the reaction he expected.

"You were a one-and-done kinda guy?" she asked, eyes glinting with mischief.

"Not really," he grumbled in denial. "I just wasn't looking to get serious with anyone."

She nodded, a contemplative look crossing her face.

"Does that bother you?" he asked quietly.

She shrugged. "No. I was thinking about Olive. You are alike in a lot of ways."

He snorted. "How so?"

"She got burned in a relationship," she explained, locking her gaze on his. "Now, she dates someone a time or two, then cuts them loose. I think she's scared to try again."

His eyebrows rose in surprise.

A short rap came from the door, cutting their conversation short. Bryan stepped into the room.

"What?" AJ snapped as the leash on his temper broke free at the intrusion.

Bryan frowned. "Laurel wants to talk."

And that tanked his mood altogether.

"About Nieto?" he guessed, unable to keep the bite from his tone.

Bryan shrugged his shoulders. "Don't shoot the messenger."

He cursed under his breath and stood with a glance at Willow, wishing they could continue their conversation. He raked a hand through his hair. Laurel wanted to discuss Nieto. Again. She'd battered him over the last few weeks with questions, ultimatums, threats, and it had intensified within the last couple of days. Anything she thought would get him to change his mind about helping her.

"I'll be back," he told Willow. "I want to finish our talk."

"Okay," she agreed, snuggling down into the covers.

He smiled at her, glad she had time to relax, then turned and walked out with Bryan in tow.

They trudged down the stairs to the living room. Olive had switched from the floor to the couch. She sprawled out, arms hanging akimbo and jaw slightly slackened. She hiccupped and giggled as her eyes lit on Bryan. Bryan rolled his eyes but sat down beside her.

AJ took a seat on the floor and leaned back against the couch.

"We're going after Nieto," Laurel stated in a determined, no-nonsense voice.

"No," AJ said flatly. "We're not. Why are we still talking about this? It's crazy to think you could even get close enough to Nieto to kill him. You can't. And offering yourself up as one of his girls—"

To his surprise, she agreed. "Bryan's going to get some of his military friends to help."

AJ groaned and glanced up at Bryan. "Tell me you didn't."

Bryan sighed, a resigned look on his face. "They were going to do this with or without our help."

"It's suicide," AJ half-shouted.

"I'll leave in the morning," Bryan said, ignoring AJ's protests. "Senator Monroe stationed two friends of mine in Austin. I'll be back within the day."

"After you get these buddies of yours, then what?" AJ queried, frustration bubbling over.

"Then," Laurel interjected, "we'll come up with a plan."

"It better not involve Willow," AJ warned.

The slow thump, thump, thump of Willow's crutches echoed across the room as she entered.

"I'm going," Willow announced. "I want to help. This is my fight more than anyone else's."

AJ's gaze locked with hers. "Don't do this," he pleaded.

Anger simmered in her eyes. "How many girls has he hurt?

How many more will continue to be taken and sold at his hands? I can't in good conscience stand by and do nothing. And I can fight my own battles, AJ. It's not your decision. You don't have to go."

His heart sank. "Like hell I don't. If you go, I go."

"Oi! All for one and one for all!" Olive said in a jovial British accent.

"Sober up," Laurel snapped.

"I'm oh-kay," Olive said with another hiccup. "No worries."

The ding-dong of the doorbell rang and everyone froze. The sun had set hours ago, and time stretched the night toward the midnight mark. The fire in the grate popped and sizzled. A sense of unease filled the space between everyone in the room. Still, no one moved to answer.

The bell rang again, then the harsh *bang, bang, bang* of a fist on wood shook the solid door on its hinges. Laurel stood, ran nervous hands down her jeans, and walked to the door. AJ rose, tiptoed to Willow, and helped her sit in the rocker.

He couldn't imagine who would be on the other side of the door. His eyes darted around the room, searching for something, anything to defend them. He zeroed in on the poker by the fireplace. He quickly snatched it from its stand.

As soon as the door cracked open, the person on the other side gave it a shove so hard it caused Laurel to lose her balance. She stumbled backward but regained her balance before toppling to the floor.

"What do you want?" Laurel asked the person hidden behind the wall separating the living area and foyer.

Scott barreled into the room, eyes glazed and wild as they landed on Willow. A slow smile crept across his face as he sauntered over to her. AJ stepped deftly in front of the rocker, blocking her from Scott's view.

"Get out of my way," Scott seethed, pointing his finger in AJ's face. "You've been nothing but trouble since the moment you got here."

Willow's hand gently but firmly pushed AJ far enough to the side so she could see Scott's face. His feet, however, remained rooted in front of her.

"What do you want, Scott? We broke up, remember?"

She fired her questions at him in a calm, even manner.

Scott extended a hand toward her. "Come for a drive with me. We can work this out."

AJ knocked it aside. "She's not going anywhere with you."

"I can speak for myself," Willow said, reminding him of her earlier statement.

He knew she could fight for herself well enough, but an overwhelming desire to protect her rose in a powerful wave. She could berate him later. Now, all he wanted to do was get rid of the vermin standing in front of him.

"There's nothing to work out. It's over."

Willow's frosty tone sent a shiver down his back. The look on Scott's face turned desperate.

"Please," Scott begged. "I just want to talk."

Willow placed a hand on his shoulder. "AJ?"

"Yeah?" he asked, eyes never leaving Scott.

"Will you please show Scott the door?"

He smirked. "Sure darlin'."

AJ grabbed Scott's forearm and jerked him forward.

Scott wrenched out of his grasp. "Alright," he hissed, then turned to Willow. "This isn't over."

AJ opened the door. "Yeah, it is." He shoved Scott over the threshold, slamming it with a satisfying bang.

"What the hell?" Laurel's voice shook with anger.

Bryan rose and stood by AJ. "Should we follow him?"

"Yeah," AJ responded, tone flat. "I have a feeling we'll finally find out what's going on."

19

Downtown Cotulla at night was darker than a black hole. Not one street lamp battled against the night. AJ felt the light's absence as if it morphed into a living, breathing entity. He sensed it skulking in the blinding blackness, stalking them like a panther.

He couldn't shake the disturbing images as he and Bryan drove down the main drag. The inky beast swallowed the truck's headlights, rendering them ineffectual. Unease skittered down his back. Even the cheerless quarter moon was suppressed by this murky darkness.

At the Main Street's north end, light leaked from a storefront window onto the paved sidewalk. A beacon, announcing someone was brave enough to venture out into the black shadows.

Bryan's head bobbed toward the light. "Think that's where he went?"

They'd followed the dust trail Scott's little hot rod left behind to the edge of town where the gravel road ended. Then Scott disappeared, nothing more than a menacing shadow melting into the night. This left them no choice but to drive up and down each street.

"It's our best shot," AJ replied with a shrug.

Bryan made a sharp left turn, then a right down the alley behind the lit building. He killed the headlights and cut the engine. Debilitating darkness engulfed the building still several yards away.

AJ searched under the truck's bench seat for a flashlight. Not finding one, he popped open the glove box and felt around until he found a small imitation Mag Light. He punched the crusty black button. Its bulb produced a beam of dim yellow light that sputtered anytime he moved it. Better than nothing.

The combination of nerves and the sour odor of takeout food permeating the truck caused the acid in his stomach to churn. The truck, stolen from an old woman when they'd rescued Lacy and Willow from Nieto's clutches weeks earlier, still smelled of stale French fry grease.

"What's the plan?" Bryan asked.

Good question. He'd never felt so inadequate. What the hell did they think they were doing skulking around in the dark like Batman and Robin? He didn't suffer from superhero syndrome. No delusions of grandeur filled his mind. A realist by nature, he knew the odds of their success in this endeavor were slim to none. They'd walk away from this giant fiasc-a-pade with nothing.

He blew out a breath through pursed lips, ridding himself of the negative thoughts. Failure wasn't an option. He needed to know what Scott was doing.

"I'll go check it out," AJ volunteered, clicking the flashlight's button on and off.

He hated to wait. For anything. The thought of sitting as a lookout made the skin on his legs itch as if an army of ants marched in happy abandon up and down his pant legs. He'd waited out in the desert in Mexico City, lying in the hot, gritty sand, waiting for Nieto to make a move, and got a scorpion sting for his trouble.

Bryan nodded. "If you're not back in ten, I'll come check things out."

He leaped out of the truck and skirted down the alley as fast as the flashlight's stingy light would allow. The perfume of rotting food added to his queasiness, so he breathed through his mouth to stay the convulsive urge to throw up. He tripped over a plastic pop bottle, bumped his hip into the sharp edge of a garbage bin, and made an orange tom cat jump five feet in the air with his back arched. The cat walked away hissing in displeasure.

He spotted a fire escape on the side of the targeted building. He grabbed the lower rung and pulled. It came down with a loud screech, causing his heart to beat in a wild rhythm against his rib cage.

Way to go. He had all the stealth of a gaggle of children playing in a school yard.

He pressed against the side of the building and waited a few seconds in case the noise brought someone out to investigate.

When no one materialized, he grabbed a rung and started climbing. His chest protested the strain against the still healing bullet wound. It served as a grim reminder that if they did go back to Mexico City, they'd likely all be killed. It was stupid to think otherwise, but he'd been decidedly outvoted.

At the top stood a door leading into the upper level of the structure. He jiggled the door's rusty knob, but it wouldn't budge. Dammit. Why hadn't he ever learned to pick a lock?

His gaze shot up, searching for another way inside. He swept the flashlight's beam slowly across the structure's upper level to the right of the small fire escape.

Not finding an opening, he cursed under his breath. How the hell was he going to get inside?

Sweeping the light across the building's other side, the beam landed on a window midway down the brick wall. A narrow crumbling ledge circled the building. Could he scale the ledge to the window? It was a stupid idea. But if Scott was inside, he might be able to get some answers.

Taking a large, steadying breath, he tested the ledge, gingerly placing some weight on it with his boot. A few pebbles broke loose and fell to the ground. Shit. If he died tonight, he was going to be pissed. His finger tips strained to hold onto the grooves between the bricks. His ears rang as adrenaline swam through his veins.

"Don't look down," he muttered under his breath. "Don't do it."

He looked down.

His heart stuttered and his stomach dropped like he was riding a roller coaster. A large garbage bin full of boxes and bagged trash loomed underneath. The drop wouldn't kill him, but it would hurt like hell. He let out the breath he was holding and decided it was worth the risk to try.

Getting a firm hold between the bricks, he took a cautious step onto the meager ledge. It didn't give way. He didn't plummet to his death. That was a good thing. He rolled his shoulders, trying to ease the tension tying his muscles into knots.

After a few seconds, he forced himself to scoot toward the window, hugging the building's side like a leech on skin. His cheek scraped the rough brick as he inched sideways. Sweat beaded on his forehead and the ringing in his ears transformed into a roar.

Finally, he stopped underneath the window, gathering enough courage to pry a hand from his death-grip on the brick wall. He sucked in oxygen, reached up and dug his fingers under the windowsill. The muscles in his arms flexed with the strain to lift the wooden frame while trying to keep his precious balance. It screeched as he shoved it open.

Relief flooded him as he gripped the splintery wooden sill and hauled himself inside. He tumbled onto the dusty wooden floor.

Strained voices carried from the lower level. Someone was here, but was it Scott?

Light shone from a wide, wooden staircase. He inched toward it, stopping just short of placing a foot on the first step. The old wood looked as if it'd creak and pop under the slightest pressure.

An angry man's voice filtered up the staircase. "The package must be returned, and you have failed to retrieve it. Do you understand the consequences if our client doesn't get what he's asked for?"

No one answered.

"Why haven't you delivered?" the harsh voice demanded with impatience.

The response confirmed his suspicion.

"I—I'm sorry, father," a whiny voice stuttered.

His heart lurched into a gallop as he recognized Scott's voice.

He leaned forward, straining to hear everything.

"There's two guys getting in the way," Scott continued. "It's too difficult. I can't get her alone. She's always with someone."

"Getting in the way," the man mused in a mocking voice. "Do you realize things will escalate from difficult to impossible if we don't make good on our promise?"

The loud crack of an open hand against skin made AJ flinch.

His heart raced as the puzzle pieces fell into place. Scott worked for his father. The *she* they were talking about was Willow. It had to be. And Scott's father was involved in trafficking girls.

"If you don't retrieve that girl within the next seventy-two hours we're screwed," Scott's father continued. "We're supposed to deliver her to Laredo. The man himself will be there. We *cannot* fail."

"Yes, Father," Scott replied, tone meek and submissive.

"Take Diego," Scott's father commanded. "And Scott, do whatever it takes to get her back. We stand to lose a lot more than money if you don't."

He knew it. They wanted Willow.

He hastily backed toward the exit.

As his heel lowered, the floor's wooden plank popped under his weight. The sound reverberated through the building like a gunshot. His pulse skyrocketed.

"Someone's upstairs," Scott's father boomed. "Go! Check it out."

He didn't stick around to hear anything else and bolted. Never mind being stealthy. He unlocked the door, wrenched it open, and flung himself down the fire escape. The slick bottom of his boots slipped on a rung, and he tumbled down the last few feet. Fire lit his ribs and chest like a bonfire as his feet jolted on the pavement. He couldn't get a full breath into his lungs, but he pressed on, running through the dark alley.

The truck's engine roared to life and Bryan moved forward to meet him.

He jumped in and before he'd even shut the door, shouted, "Go! Hurry!"

The truck lurched forward, the passenger door slamming shut with the sudden movement.

"What the hell happened?" Bryan asked as they raced down the alley.

The tires skidded on loose pebbles as Bryan turned the corner.

"Holy shit," AJ said through short gulping breaths, clutching his chest.

He leaned back and tried to slow his breathing.

"Holy shit!"

"What?" Bryan demanded.

"I'm pretty sure," he wheezed, "Scott is the one who had Willow kidnapped. His father is in on it too."

Bryan cursed.

"That's not all," he rasped out, still trying to gain control of his breathing. "Scott's been trying to kidnap her again. His father talked about a man wanting the girl back. Willow has to be the girl he's referring to. And the man he talked about? I think it's Nieto."

"That changes the game," Bryan muttered.

"Sure as shit does," he agreed. "And I think I know where Nieto is going to be in the next seventy-two hours."

"Where?" Bryan demanded.

"Laredo."

"Laurel will want to move on this information," Bryan said. "Which might interfere with going to Austin for help."

"We need to find out where in Laredo that meeting will be. Got any ideas?" AJ asked, tossing the dead flashlight into the floor board.

"Not yet," Bryan said. "We really need help. I'm not a war strategist. I was just a soldier, following orders."

"Well, we've gotta think of something. Nothing's gonna stop Laurel."

Bryan grunted his agreement.

They had to come up with a plan to get Nieto without getting everyone killed or captured. Nieto wanted Willow back. How could he persuade Willow to stay out of the fight?

20

Lacy nestled against Jace's side, eyes closed, praying for the three-hour drive from The Lighthouse Inn to Tulare to last longer. A lifetime would suit her fine.

The sun peeked over the horizon, kissing her cheeks with heat magnified by the truck's windows. Jace moved one hand off the wheel to rest on her thigh. Her heart warmed at his reassuring touch.

The noise of the tires grating against asphalt along with the sun's rays created a soothing effect which should've allowed her to sleep. But she couldn't silence her thoughts. They kept circling around faster and faster. *Why didn't they tell me I was adopted?*

Jace tried to reason with her. He thought she should give her parents a chance to explain their justification for not telling her. Her heart wouldn't listen, though. She couldn't forgive them, she just wasn't ready yet.

Forgiveness was always in the best interest of the forgiver, not the person to whom you were bestowing the forgiveness. She knew that, and the logical part of her brain also knew Emmett and Lila Monroe didn't tell her about her adoption because they were trying to protect her.

Good friggin' call.

That much she could admit. The cunning Thomas Monroe left her at the mercy of a human trafficker, for God's sake. What kind of father would allow their daughter to be sold as a sex slave? The fact he did told her a lot about his character and what lengths he was willing to go to get what he wanted. She couldn't imagine what it would've been like to grow up with Thomas Monroe as a father.

Which led to another thought. What kind of mother would give away her child? The short time she'd spent with Thomas Monroe's wife, Geneviève, from San Antonio where they'd kidnapped her, to the Monroe Farm, was not enough time to form an opinion. Most of that time she'd spent ignoring the woman. She had a hunch there was more to the story she didn't know.

Did she want to know?

Jace gave her thigh a short squeeze. "Breathe, baby."

She sucked in a long breath through her nose, counted to five, then slowly released it. Repeating the process a couple more times slowed her heart rate from a wild gallop to a more normal cadence.

"You okay?" he asked quietly.

"No . . . yeah." A short sardonic laugh escaped her lips. "Hell, I don't know."

She leaned her head back against the truck's bench seat and closed her eyes. The sun's rays danced beneath her eyelids as if faeries frolicked in gleeful abandonment upon them.

"You'll get there," he said. "I have faith in you."

Her eyes popped open, and she snorted. "Your faith may be misplaced because I have serious doubts."

"About?" he prompted.

"I seriously doubt my parents," she began, using air quotes around the word *parents*, "will say anything to change my mind. They should've told me, despite the fact they were trying to protect me. Look how well that turned out."

He gave her a sidelong glance. "True. Forgiving them will have to be your choice."

"I know that," she shot back, irritated he'd voiced her earlier thoughts. "To forgive, or not to forgive? That is the question."

"Smartass," he quipped, trying to lighten her mood.

Looking over her shoulder she asked, "Have you seen anyone following us?"

"No, but we need to assume Widow knows where we're going. He probably took an alternate route."

"Do you think Widow knows where my parents live?" she asked, disbelief lacing her tone.

Jace kept his eyes on the road, but his brows tipped down. "He knew where *we* were. The man is ruthless. We can't underestimate him. Or your uncle. We have to assume they know everything."

"We can't stay with my parents, can we?" she guessed.

"No. It's too dangerous."

"What are we going to do? Keep running?"

"For now. After we check on AJ and tell your parents what's going on, we'll stop in Perry to see Edwards and Cat and the rest of our friends."

"Won't we put them in danger?"

"Oklahoma is the last place Widow would expect us to go. But we won't stay long. I just want to check in with Edwards, make sure he's okay."

"Okay," she agreed, but knew it would be hard for her to leave Cat again.

She'd never been close to Hailey or Ethan in high school, and she'd never met Gracie or Matty before their appearance at the farm. But they had become her friends even though Hailey tested her patience at first. The girl eventually accepted the fact the world she once knew was gone. The thought of seeing all of them again lifted her spirits.

Then she thought of Travis. He'd disappeared from the farm

with her horse, Acer, and never returned. Without a doubt, she knew Travis had the skills to take care of himself. It just sucked he left without saying goodbye. Given their history, she expected more from him.

"What happened to Travis?" she asked softly. "I know you told me he left with Acer. What you didn't tell me was why."

Jace let out a heavy sigh. "I was angry, frustrated with the whole situation. I was trying to give your uncle the slip so I could find you."

She appreciated him not calling Thomas Monroe her father. She set her eyes on his profile, listening intently.

"I took it out on him," he admitted. A little well-placed shame crossed his face. "I baited him into an argument. Not my finest moment. I—"

She laid her head against his shoulder when he hesitated. "I'm not going to be mad. I just want to know why he didn't stick around to make sure I was okay."

"Do you know why your relationship with him didn't work out?" he asked, surprising her with what sounded like a change of subject.

"Do you?" she countered, seriously doubting he knew the reason.

He raked a hand through his hair and said with a sigh, "Yeah."

She groaned. "Please don't tell me AJ had anything to do with it."

"No, it wasn't AJ. Or me for that matter," he added.

"Why?" she prompted.

When he hesitated too long with an answer, she nudged his leg with hers.

"His father didn't approve of your relationship," he said.

The low timbre of his voice, soft yet firm, reminded her of the way he spoke to his horse when it was skittish or spooked.

She leaned back to look at him. His face was inscrutable. She didn't understand. Travis's parents had always been nice to her and her family. They'd been good neighbors.

"I don't get it," she said. "Travis's parents were always nice to me."

"I doubt they had a problem with you being his friend," Jace paused, rubbing the back of his neck, "they just didn't want you to be anything more."

She shook her head. "Why?"

He glanced at her, then leaned down and pressed a kiss to her forehead. "You're not native."

Her eyebrows rose. "I'm not what?"

"Your skin isn't brown enough," he said bluntly. "And honestly? I'm glad. If you hadn't broken up with him—"

"I would've found my way to you, Jace," she said, cutting him off. "I knew Travis wasn't the one. We were better friends than anything else."

After they'd started dating, she'd noticed a change in Travis. He stood her up more times than not, but he always came back with a believable excuse. That wasn't why she broke up with him though. On an instinctual level, she knew he wasn't her forever.

"I think Travis would disagree," he countered.

"I still don't understand what this has to do with Travis leaving," she muttered.

"We were fighting over you when your brother showed up, and he sort of piled on. I don't blame Travis for leaving."

"Okay," she said simply, deciding to drop the subject. It was a moot point anyway. Travis had to find his own way.

"Okay?" he parroted.

She shrugged. "Yeah."

The conversation had taken her mind off the impending confrontation with her parents and the fact they were being chased across the country by a madman. A madman that her biological father had sicced on them.

She could feel the rage boiling inside her over the fact Thomas Monroe hadn't heeded her warning. Why couldn't he leave her alone? She'd threatened to kill him if he came after her or one of her friends. As much as she despised the man, she didn't actually want to kill him or anyone else. He knew it and had called her on it.

Widow was stalking them, toying with them. Would he be waiting in Tulare?

21

There was nothing to do but think during the long drive, and Lacy's thoughts ran the gamut. Childhood memories, both good and bad, flooded her in a torrential downpour. Every conjured memory contained her parents loving her, guiding her, disciplining her. They taught her how to love and how to forgive. Those memories chipped away her resolve to stay angry at them.

The directions AJ left in the glovebox to her parent's new home eventually led them to a winding gravel drive on the outskirts of Tulare.

Jace stopped, jumped out, and opened a swinging, black iron gate.

He climbed back into the driver's seat, slammed the door, and turned to her. "You ready for this?"

She shrugged, leaning her head back against the bench seat. "Not really. But let's go anyway."

He turned, cupped her cheeks in his hands and said, "You got this."

She nodded. He leaned his forehead against hers, then turned and placed the truck in gear.

They pulled through the gate and followed the drive up a small hill. It ended in front of a sprawling, grey brick house. A dark-stained balcony overlooking a greening pasture jutted out the east side.

Early morning sun shone on Emmett Monroe's salt-and-pepper hair as he sat on the deck in a white wicker chair, sipping from a large coffee mug. He watched them pull to a stop and cut the engine. He stood, gave them a short wave, then disappeared inside.

She turned to Jace. "I wonder if he recognized you."

Jace unbuckled his belt. "AJ would've told them I'm with you," he reasoned.

She reached down to unbuckle her seat belt. It stuck. She tried again with more pressure, but the button felt welded to the buckle.

Sweat pricked her scalp. The need to escape pressed all the air from her lungs. She felt like a fly caught in a spider's sticky web. She wasn't ready for this. Not yet. Loving childhood memories didn't erase the hurt they'd caused with their deception.

Panic poured over her like hot tar and singed her nerves as her fingers fumbled, trying again to release the belt. It didn't budge. She jerked on the strap, then let out a sharp yelp as it snapped back and struck her across the face.

Before she melted down completely, Jace reached around, released the belt from the buckle, and let it slip harmlessly between them.

Instead of leaning back, he pressed forward, brushing soft lips against hers, once, twice, until her body relaxed into his.

"I love you," he murmured in a gravelly voice that sent a burst of heat to her center.

She wrapped her arms around his neck, pulling him closer. "Love you."

His eyes darkened and he kissed her again. She surrendered to it as his fingers sank into her hair. A small whimper escaped her when he lifted his head too soon. He glanced back at the porch, a slow smile sliding across his face. He turned back to her.

"We have company," he murmured, motioning behind him with a nod.

She craned her neck around him to see her mother and father standing on the porch. Her father crossed his arms against his chest, eyes narrowed.

The absence of his body's warmth against hers as he leaned back into the driver's seat left her feeling bereft, alone, like a dark wind suddenly swept across her soul.

He gave her a wink and said, "We better go."

She crossed her arms against her chest. "I'm not ready."

He framed her face between his hands, brushing his thumb across her temple. "Come on. It won't be that bad. We'll tell them we're married first."

"That's a hell of an icebreaker," she muttered, opening the door, and climbing down from the truck.

Jace jumped down, rounded the hood, and shut her door. He placed a hand against the small of her back as they approached her parents.

Her mother greeted them with a soft smile. Her father, however, looked like a volcano about to erupt. A disapproving scowl formed hard lines around her father's eyes and mouth. Her mother patted his shoulder, and their eyes locked. Something passed between them. Her father's shoulders relaxed, and he let out a loud sigh.

Her mom walked down the steps and gathered her into a warm embrace.

Tears clogged her throat. "It's good to see you, Mom," she choked out.

Her mom stroked the length of her hair. "Aw, baby. I'm glad you're here. We've been so worried. We've missed you."

Over her mother's shoulder, she watched Jace walk up the steps and stretch out his hand to her father. Emmett stared at him too long to be polite and for a moment she thought he'd refuse to shake Jace's hand. But, her father reluctantly gave in.

"How you been doin' Jace?" her father asked dryly, pumping Jace's arm up and down.

"Fine, sir," Jace replied. "You have a nice place here."

Emmett dropped Jace's hand, staring at AJ's truck. "Where's my son?"

Shock spilled over her.

AJ wasn't here?

She disentangled herself from her mother's arms and went to stand beside Jace. Her father stepped forward and caught her in a crushing bear hug before she could ask about her brother.

"Hi, Daddy," she rasped out, struggling to breathe.

He released her, stepped back, and looked her over from head to toe. "You okay?"

His concern touched her but also reminded her of the hard conversation ahead about her adoption.

"Yeah. I'm okay," she answered. "AJ isn't here?"

"He went to get you," her father replied, frowning.

Her parents knew nothing about what'd happened to her since they'd parted ways last summer. The courage she'd mustered wilted a little at the thought of telling them about Mexico City and Thomas Monroe's involvement.

"He did, but—"

She trailed off, unable to continue. This wasn't the way she wanted to start their talk.

Her mother's face filled with panic. "Is he okay? Is he—"

"He's fine," Jace interjected. "It's a long story."

Her mother's relief was palpable as she walked up the steps and opened the front door. "Let's have some coffee on the deck. We can talk there."

They walked through the spacious living room and stopped for coffee in the kitchen. Her mother motioned to coffee mugs hanging on one of those contraptions that looked like a wooden tree.

"Help yourself," her mother said with a pleased expression, glancing between the two of them.

It was hard to wrap her mind around the fact her mother knew about Jace's interest in her. Her mother had stepped in and told Jace to wait until she was older to ask her out. By the look her mother gave them now, it seemed she was delighted with the match.

Jace plucked off two mugs from the tree, both a pleasant blue with a white-and-red stripe rimming the top. He filled their mugs, pouring a generous amount of cream into hers.

They stepped out the French doors. Bright sunshine spilled onto the deck, a beautiful waterfall of yellow and gold. The air hinted of sweet grass and manure. Four white, wicker chairs with bright red cushions sat around a round glass table. A matching settee was pushed against the deck's side railing.

Emmett and Lila carried their mugs of steaming coffee to the settee and sat down. Her father placed a hand on her mother's knee. He watched her and Jace with sharp eyes as they scooted two chairs from the table to sit across from them.

Jace sat and placed his mug onto the deck's floor. Lacy did the same. Uncomfortable silence stretched between the two couples. It scraped like sandpaper across her skin. She rubbed sweaty hands on her jeans, heart jumping like a grasshopper across hot cement.

Her dad continued to scrutinize Jace, but her mother smiled with warmth at them both.

A strangled cough escaped her father as his eyes landed on the amethyst ring on her finger.

Jace chuckled softly.

Heat burned up her neck and she nudged his shoulder with hers. "Stop," she whispered.

"What's going on between you two?" her father demanded.

"We have some news," Jace began.

"He's too old for you, Lacy," her father interrupted, then turned to Jace. "You're too old for her."

"Emmett," Lila chided. "He isn't too old."

"He's AJ's age," Emmett blustered.

Lacy leaned into Jace for support. "It's too late, Dad. We're married."

Emmett sprang up. "The hell you are!"

Lila grabbed his hand and tugged. "Emmett."

Her father slumped back into the settee, shaking his head.

"Congratulations," her mother offered sincerely.

Emmett's head whipped to Lila. "Why don't you act surprised?"

"Because I pay attention," she snapped. "This boy has been in love with our daughter for years. The fact he waited until she graduated high school before asking her out says a lot about his character."

Emmett harumphed.

"Oh, Em. He's a good boy from a good family. You know that," Lila said in a softer tone.

Emmett turned from his wife to stare at Jace. "You better treat her right. If I hear you've raised a hand against her—"

"Emmett," her mother interrupted disapprovingly.

Emmett glanced at Lila. "No, dammit. Let me finish." He turned back to Jace. "If I hear you've so much as raised your voice at my little girl, you'll regret it."

"Daddy!" Lacy exclaimed, mortified.

"I give you my word," Jace said somberly. "I love her."

Emmett's shoulders finally relaxed, and a corner of his mouth raised into a half-smile. "Well, I guess she could've done worse."

LACY'S PARENTS looked as if they'd been obliterated. Tears streamed down her mother's cheeks. The muscle in her father's jaw ticked, his expression hard and unyielding.

She hated hurting them with the truth. But they deserved to know all that had happened to her leading up to their arrival in

Tulare. Mexico City had been difficult for her to relive. She rushed through the story, leaving out some details that were more sensitive. There was no need to tell them how Nieto tried to seduce her, or the way he'd touched her.

She told them about the farm, her new friends, and how the Military Police made their lives miserable, trying to starve them into submission. Zach's assault on her, she omitted. It felt unnecessary to reopen that particular wound and the knowledge would only hurt them. And Jace. He didn't need to dwell on Zach or the fact he'd killed him. It was over, in the past, and it needed to stay there. Buried for good.

"But AJ's okay?" her mother asked again, leaning into her father.

Emmett wrapped an arm around his wife, scooting her closer. She nestled her head against his broad chest.

"He was recovering when I left," Lacy answered, unable to keep the ring of uncertainty from her tone.

AJ should be home by now. What could've kept him away?

"Bryan went to get him. I'm sure they'll turn up," Jace assured her parents.

She took a deep breath and dove into the subject she wanted to avoid. "There's something else I found out I think you should know."

A mixture of curiosity and concern crossed her parents' faces. Her mother gave her an encouraging nod to continue.

"One of the things I did to escape Uncle Tommy, I'm not proud of," she admitted, and told them how she and Bryan had kidnapped Geneviève.

A deep V formed between her mother's brows. "How did that help you with Thomas?"

"Geneviève is his only weakness," she explained.

Her father snorted, shifting on the settee.

She glanced at her father. "He'd do anything for her, and I knew that."

"How?" her mother asked in confusion. "You don't know your aunt and uncle that well."

"After he stopped Jace and I at the Mexico border, I had a pretty good idea. I smarted off to him about her and he lost his mind over it."

"He hit Lacy," Jace added in a harsh tone.

She inclined her head toward Jace and whispered, "They didn't need to know that."

Emmett looked like a rocket on a launch pad. Anger poured off of him in waves. Her mother laid a comforting hand on his shoulder.

"I'm fine," she said. "But when I exchanged Geneviève for our freedom, he told me something."

Lila locked eyes with Emmett. He leaned over and kissed her forehead, murmuring something Lacy didn't catch.

"Am I adopted?" she asked. "Is Uncle Tommy my real dad?"

The Band-Aid she'd applied to her broken heart ripped off with the question. Their expression, a mixture of fear and regret, was answer enough.

"How could you not tell me?" she demanded, hurt bleeding into her tone.

"We were trying to protect you," her mother said quietly. "Geneviève isn't a stable woman. And Thomas—"

Her mother's voice trailed off. There was nothing they could say that would make the situation better. She'd guessed as much about Geneviève. The woman seemed fragile, both in a physical and mental sense.

"We're sorry," her father said, eyes begging her for forgiveness.

"It's okay, Dad. I—"

A loud boom shook the deck. Emmett and Jace sprang up at the same time and rushed to the rail. Lacy and her mother followed.

A surge of hot air forced them all backward as bits of metal and glass blasted the side of the house. Jace hovered over her, protecting her from the spray of glass and metal raining down on them.

Fear slithered up her spine causing her to shiver. "Widow," she whispered.

Widow had blown up AJ's truck.

22

Night's darkest hour reluctantly released its hold when Willow opened her eyes. Dawn's light filtered through her closed gingham curtains, washing her room in an array of monochrome greys. AJ, who'd crept into her bed late last night, stirred and scooted closer to her. Because he usually ended up in bed with her most nights anyway, they'd given up on the pretense of sleeping in separate beds.

Before she could move, AJ slid a hand under the covers, still warm from deep sleep, and placed it on her leg. Her eyes connected with his, and he gave a slight shake of his head. A warning.

Then she heard it. Outside her window the air was eerily silent, as if nature still hadn't awoken from its nighttime slumber. The trellis her father had built for her mother's climbing blood-red roses knocked against the side of the house in a rhythmic *tap, tap*. When the harsh Texas wind blew with unforgiving force across the prairie, the trellis would bang in an irregular tempo.

This sounded different.

Someone was attempting to climb the trellis to her window.

AJ's lips brushed her ear. "Go get Bryan," he whispered.

She swallowed hard, nodded, and slipped out of bed. The

wooden floor, cold and uninviting under her bare feet, creaked as she tiptoed to the door. The door's brass knob turned with ease. She opened it and slid through the crack.

She limped as fast as she could to the room Bryan occupied. It was vacant, so she checked Olive's room, but found no sleeping figure under the rumpled covers.

Where the hell were they?

She hobbled down the stairs to the living room and found Bryan and Olive sleeping on the couch. Bryan's slack arm was flung around Olive's waist.

Biting her lip against the pain in her ankle, she rushed to the couch and shook Bryan's shoulder. "Wake up," she whispered.

He didn't move, didn't even crack open an eyelid.

"Hey," she said, shaking harder. "Wake up."

He grunted, shifted closer to Olive, and started snoring.

Frustrated, she leaned down into his ear. "Wake up!" she whispered in a harsh, demanding voice.

He flung an arm out, which she dodged by ducking her head. "Go away, Ma. I don't have school today," he mumbled, voice slurred with sleep.

Despite the circumstances, she laughed softly. "I'm not your mother. Get up. AJ needs you."

When he didn't respond, she placed both hands against his back and shoved him into Olive.

This maneuver woke Olive who succinctly pushed Bryan off the couch. He tumbled to the floor at Willow's feet, letting out a loud, "Umph."

"There you are," she said dryly. "Get up."

"Why?" Bryan grumbled.

He looked around owlishly, rubbing his eyes with the back of his hands.

"Because someone is trying to break into the house. AJ sent me to get you," she informed him, a sense of urgency thrumming inside her.

That grabbed his attention. "Where's AJ?"

"My room. They're climbing the trellis."

He exchanged a look with Olive, rose to his feet and took off toward the stairs.

Olive scrubbed a hand down her face and swung her feet to the floor. "Better stay down here, Will."

Willow turned her back on her sister and started for the stairs.

A loud bang, followed by a crash of shattering glass, met her as she bounded into her room. AJ and Scott had fallen into her vanity, breaking the mirror. Makeup and other beauty products from the drawer littered the carpet.

As AJ glanced her way, Scott aimed a punch straight into AJ's jaw. He cursed, shoving Scott face first into the floor, pinning him in place.

"Grab something so I can tie his hands," AJ said, blood dripping from his nose.

She cast a glance around the room. "Like what?" she asked, flustered.

On the other side of the room, Bryan cornered Diego.

"I don't know," AJ grunted as Scott elbowed him in the ribs. "A shirt?"

Olive ran into the room, carrying a length of rope and a pistol. "Thought you might need these," she said, handing them over to Bryan.

AJ dragged Scott off the floor and shoved him against the wall. He grabbed Scott's arms and wrenched them behind his back.

Scott struggled against AJ's iron grip. "You sorry sonofabitch," he hissed. "You have no idea who you're messing with. My father—"

AJ scoffed and rammed his head against the wall. Bryan tackled Diego to the ground.

Willow stood and watched the scene play out like a movie reel. She hated violence. Yet it surrounded her on all sides. It was as if she couldn't escape its nightmarish hold on her life. Memories from Mexico City surged forward, leaving her momentarily paralyzed.

She remembered her ears ringing from her head hitting the hotel's glass table where Nieto had taken her and Lacy. She could still smell John's rancid breath on her neck right before he bit her. She bent over, bracing her hands on her knees, trying to breathe.

Bryan tied Diego's hands behind his back, led him to her bed, and forced him into a sitting position. Diego spat in Bryan's face.

The loud crack of Bryan's hand across Diego's face jolted her out of the horrifying memories.

AJ watched her closely and when their eyes met said in a soft voice, "It's okay, Willow."

She nodded, opened her closet, and grabbed the first flannel button-down hanging on the crossbar. She held the sleeves and wound the shirt up like she did with a kitchen towel when she wanted to smack one of her sisters.

"That's not going to work," Olive told her, then ran out the door.

Her sister returned with a zip tie, handed it to AJ to secure Scott's wrists.

"Hey," Scott grunted. "That's too tight, you motherfu—"

"Watch your mouth," AJ interrupted, "before I break your jaw."

AJ manhandled Scott to the bed, dumping him beside his friend.

Olive went and stood by Bryan, then folded her arms across her chest and asked Scott, "What's going on?"

Willow watched her ex as he tried to formulate an answer. AJ stepped back and took her hand, weaving their fingers together.

Scott's eyes narrowed on the action. "I just wanted a chance to talk to Willow without *him* in my way," he said, bobbing his head toward AJ.

"Bullshit," Olive shot back. "Why'd you bring Diego with you? You don't need him to talk to my sister."

"I think it's time you told Willow the truth," AJ challenged Scott.

Confused, she turned to stare at AJ. What did he know that she didn't?

"There's nothing to tell," Scott answered sullenly.

Bryan pulled the pistol out of his back waistband and aimed it at Scott.

"What are you gonna do? Blow my brains out?" Scott yelled.

Willow cocked her head as acid burned a hole in her stomach. "What did you do, Scott?"

Scott's face turned into an ugly mask of fury and desperation. "Fine. You want the truth? Well, here it is."

Willow stumbled back a step at the blast of hate he directed at her. AJ wrapped a protective arm around her waist and pulled her close to his side.

He leaned over and murmured, "I got you."

Scott snorted. "I never wanted to ask you out. Diego saw you first at our graduation and thought my father's client would like you."

"Shut up," Diego hissed.

But Scott continued as if he hadn't heard his friend's warning. "Like I'd ever date you," he scoffed. "Please. You look like a homeless person."

Willow dipped her head, embarrassed. It was true. She didn't pay much attention to fashion, choosing comfort over style.

"That's enough," AJ warned before Scott could continue berating her. "Get to the point."

Scott smirked. "Diego took a picture of you at graduation. My father showed it to his client, and his client thought you'd be good for business."

Dread filled the pit of her stomach. "What client?"

Her ears roared and black spots dotted her vision. Had Scott sold her? To Nieto?

"It was my father's idea for me to date you. I followed you for days, learning your routine." Scott rolled his eyes. "Some routine. All you did was paint and help your dad around here. Dumb luck on my part you finally went to the gas station. It was a perfect chance to run into you. So I took it."

Her head spun. Why had she gone to the gas station that day? She couldn't even remember.

"What client?" she repeated through clenched teeth.

Scott let out a deprecating laugh. "Oh, I think you know."

"I want to hear you say it," she bit out.

"Why?"

She stepped out of AJ's embrace toward Scott. "Because I want you to own up to what you did."

Scott studied her as if trying to calculate what she'd do if he told her. She folded her arms across her chest to hide her hands balled into fists.

"You should thank me for going out with you. I elevated your social status," he bragged, expression turning haughty.

She leaned down in his face. "Who was it Scott?"

"Nieto," he answered, staring at her with cold, flat eyes.

She stepped back, holding in the rage. At that moment she couldn't figure out who she was the most furious with, Scott or herself. How could she have been so blind?

"So why keep up the facade?" she asked, a sudden thought occurring to her. "Why have you been so desperate to talk to me? Get me out of the house?"

Diego laughed. "You stupid bitch."

AJ's simmering eyes locked on Diego. "Don't call her that."

"Nieto paid a lot of money for you," Diego continued as if AJ hadn't spoken. "You think you could just walk away? Escape? No. He wants you back."

Willow felt the blood drain from her face. She stumbled back into AJ, her world going dark.

23

Gritty, black smoke plumed into the sky, saturating the air around Lacy, Jace, and her parents with the pungent stench of burning oil. The force of the blast blew the truck doors off the cab. Shattered glass covered the ground and glistened like ice in the sunlight.

Lacy covered her mouth with a shaky hand as she stepped onto the front porch. She stared at the wreckage, unable to move. Her pulse skittered.

Widow was here.

This was his calling card, his way of toying with them again. She was catching on to the diabolical man's method of operation, which was instilling fear into his victims before he finally pounced.

Jace walked out and stood beside her, slipping an arm around her waist. The precious articles of clothing they'd scavenged and the brightly colored cord from their marriage ceremony were gone. There was nothing left but the blackened, hulled-out cab and the truck bed bent in a twisted, inverted V shape.

Shit. AJ was gonna be pissed about the truck. What were they going to do now? How would they get back to Texas? A kaleidoscope of fragmented thoughts raced through her mind.

She burrowed her face into Jace's side, breathing in his familiar scent, willing her mind to calm.

Jace tightened his grip around her waist. He leaned down and placed a kiss on the top of her head.

"It's okay," he murmured. "We're okay."

"Who the hell would do this?" her father demanded as he burst out the front door. "We should search the area."

Jace shook his head. "You won't find him."

Emmett turned on his boot heel back toward the porch where Jace stood. "You know who did this?"

Jace scrubbed a hand over his face. "Yeah. Thomas sent a guy named Widdowson after Lacy."

Emmett's jaw hardened. "To kill her?"

"I don't think so, Dad," she responded quickly. "Widow had plenty of opportunities to kill me, but he hasn't."

"Why do this? If Thomas wants you back, why didn't he come himself?"

Good question. All this was a show of power. Dominance.

"I think he's proving a point. I threatened him, and he obviously didn't like it."

"You threatened him? How?" her father asked, using the authoritative voice that always made her limbs quake.

Heat flushed her face. She shouldn't feel shame or guilt over what she'd done to her uncle. He deserved it.

Yet, she did.

Kidnapping her aunt to use as leverage was dishonorable. It hit below the belt, and she knew it. She'd sunk to his level to free herself and her friends. And then threatened to kill him if he came looking for her.

She bent her head, studying the puke stain on her shoe and said quietly, "I told him I'd kill him if he came after me."

After a long moment her dad said, "That's my girl."

She raised her eyes, surprised at his reaction. He walked up the steps and pulled her into a hug. She leaned into his strong chest, and he patted the top of her head like he used to do when she was little.

Relief washed over her, relaxing the tightened muscles in her neck. She breathed in his scent, pine with a hint of leather, and peace filled her heart.

"I love you, Daddy," she whispered softly.

His arms tightened around her, and he sniffed. "Me too, doll. And I'm sorry for what you went through. I never should've left you there or trusted my brother to do the right thing by you."

She lifted her head and offered him a small smile. "It's okay. I found Jace and he's worth everything."

Her dad rested his chin on the top of her head. "Honey, judging by the look in that boy's eyes, he would've followed you here."

"I'd follow her anywhere," Jace agreed solemnly.

She stepped out of her dad's embrace. "We need to go. You're in danger as long as we're here. Widow won't stop."

"Where will you go?" her mother asked, concern tightening the crow's feet around her eyes.

She gave her mother's tightly clasped hands a gentle squeeze and then turned to look at Jace. Their eyes locked, a silent agreement passing between them.

"We have to make a stop in Oklahoma," Jace answered.

"But we'll go to Texas," she added. "We'll find AJ."

Emmett walked down the steps. "Give me an hour to replace the truck."

"Hurry, Dad," she urged.

Sticking around another hour was risky. She didn't know what Widow had planned for them next, but they needed to go. Fear pricked her scalp as if a million tiny needles were being gouged into her skin. Every minute they stayed pushed them closer to Widow's end game, and she knew he'd kill whoever got between him and her.

"MY GOD, it's good to see you," Cat gushed as she held Lacy in a tight embrace outside Edward's two-story farmhouse. "Come in and I'll get you something to eat."

Cat's strong arms felt solid, comforting, like an island Lacy could take refuge in. She held onto the familiarity she'd missed a moment longer, lying her head on the older woman's shoulder. Cat clucked her tongue and stroked a soft hand down her cheek.

"I really missed you, Cat," she said, swallowing around the lump in her throat.

"*Liebes,*" Cat murmured, using her native German tongue. "I missed you too."

She released the older woman and stepped back. A wide smile bloomed across her face as she took in her countenance. She looked genuinely happy. Cat's chestnut hair, streaked with silver, fell against her shoulders in soft waves. It gave the older woman a younger air and softened her face.

"You look great," she commented with a knowing look. "Living at Edwards' place seems to suit you."

"It does," Cat agreed, giving her a wide smile.

Jace pocketed the fob to the new slate-grey Chevy Silverado and followed them inside.

AJ would be pleased with his new ride. It had all the bells and whistles he could play with. Her father had bartered a year's worth of milk for it to the man who owned one of the Chevy dealerships in Tulare. The man's daughter was pregnant. Milk was hard to come by and no one had the means to buy a vehicle anymore.

As they walked into the kitchen, Cat turned and placed both hands on Jace's cheeks.

"You've done a good job taking care of our girl," Cat said in a soft voice. "Thank you."

Cat released Jace and turned to Edwards. "Look what the Cat dragged in," she said, sarcastically.

Edwards sat at the kitchen table, cleaning what looked like a carburetor to her amateur eyes. His bushy silver brows lifted in surprise. He set his tools down and wiped his hands on a greasy shop towel.

"Well, would ya look at that!" he exclaimed.

"Hey, Edwards," Jace greeted in a tired voice.

"Good to see ya," the older man said with a grin.

Jace dropped into the chair beside Edwards. "What're you doing?"

"Cleaning this damn carburetor."

Jace drove the twenty-one-hour drive straight through, only stopping when he needed fuel. Her father had filled two fifty-five-gallon drums with gasoline and showed Jace how to siphon the gas from the drum to the truck's fuel tank. Emmett had parted with a few gold coins for the gasoline.

She planned to drive the remaining distance to Cotulla after their short visit with their Oklahoma family.

Cat placed her hands on her hips. "It looks like you both could use a good meal."

"Jace needs a nap," Lacy commented dryly after watching Jace yawn five times in a row.

"You know where the bed is," Edwards said, motioning to the door off the kitchen.

Jace waved him off. "Nah, I can sleep in the truck."

Lacy tuned out the men at the table and their conversation about cars and their damn parts. She walked to Cat who busied herself at the stove, heating a cast-iron skillet.

The older woman's face fell as she turned to Lacy. "You're not staying?"

She smiled sadly. "We can't."

As Cat prepared a quick meal of scrambled eggs and biscuits, Lacy told Cat about being held hostage in Mexico City, the miraculous rescue her brother and Bryan pulled off, and the devastating news about Thomas Monroe being her biological father.

"My brother and Bryan found us at a party Nieto was throwing. AJ ended up being shot by Raul."

Cat shoved a pan of biscuits in the oven and slammed the door. She swung around, hands on her hips. Her brows turned down in an angry V.

"I can't believe I helped that arsehole escape," Cat muttered.

"It's not your fault. AJ shot him. I have no idea if he lived or not," she said quietly. "That's one reason we need to leave. AJ was supposed to go back home to California, and he didn't."

Cat wiped the flour from her hands on the bottom of her apron. "Can you get the honey down for me?"

She turned a slow circle. "Where is it?"

"In that middle cabinet," Cat said, waving a hand in the general direction.

"Anyway, by the time we got to Bryan's helicopter, Nieto's men had caught up with us. They shot a hole in the gas tank, and we ended up making an emergency landing in the middle of nowhere. We had to hike our way out with AJ shot. A girl I met in Nieto's underground cell, Willow, escaped with us. She took us to a ranch her family owns in Cotulla. I hope AJ and Bryan are still there and not in trouble somewhere," she finished, exhaling loudly.

She handed Cat the honey, then went to the sink to wash her hands of the sticky residue left on the jar.

"For the love of tits and trucks," Cat exclaimed, shaking her head. "What a clusterfuck."

"And now," she concluded, "my uncle-slash-father sent that maniac Widow after me."

Cat's grey eyes darkened in anger. "Why?"

The why of it placed a heavy mantle of guilt on her shoulders. She'd treated her aunt, who was also her biological mother, abominably when she'd kidnapped her and used her against her uncle. Widow tried to tell her about her mother's mental condition, but she refused to listen. That didn't make her less culpable though. She knew. Deep down she knew Geneviève needed to unburden herself by telling her side of the whole adoption story. She didn't want to tell Cat about any of it, so she lied.

"I don't know," she muttered, hating the bitter taste of deception on her tongue.

"Have you considered staying? There's strength in numbers," Cat suggested.

She heaved a sigh. "And put everyone in danger? No."

"Then what?" Cat asked in exasperation. "You run circles around the country until he eventually catches you?"

The scenario seemed ridiculous, but Cat did have a point.

The smell of baking biscuits made her mouth water. She was hungry and tired, both physically and mentally.

"I need to see my brother before I can think of anything else. I need to know he's okay," she said, avoiding Cat's question.

Guilt slammed into her over leaving her brother. What if he'd developed complications? The thought sucked the oxygen from her lungs.

"You can't run forever," Cat said in her pragmatic way.

As if she needed to be reminded.

Cat pulled the pan with piping hot biscuits from the oven and served them with scrambled eggs. She placed a fresh dollop of butter in the center of the table along with the honey.

She placed a stack of blue and white Corel plates at the end of the table for Cat. She picked one up, placed a biscuit and some eggs onto the plate, and handed it to Jace.

"Thanks, darlin'," he said, then glanced at Cat. "Where'd you get the butter?"

"Ethan and Hailey are in charge of milking the cow and churning the butter," Edwards answered as Cat handed him a steaming plate of food.

Matty barreled through the door, Castiel quick on his heels. "I smell biscuits!" he shouted.

Cat held out a hand to the dog and gave a sharp command in German. Lacy recognized the word "stop." Castiel dug his claws into the worn wooden floor, flopping his butt down in obedience.

Matty skidded to a stop. "Lacy, you're back!" he exclaimed.

Cat turned in time to see Matty reaching for a biscuit. She slapped his hand away.

"Go wash up," Cat instructed the boy with a smile.

Matty lifted his dirt-stained face to Cat's, returning her smile. "Yes, ma'am."

"Wash your face, too," Cat hollered as Matty raced off to the bathroom."

"'Kay," Matty threw over his shoulder.

Castiel turned his bear-like face toward Lacy. Without warning, he lunged straight into her lap. His giant tongue licked her cheek, her ear, her nose, but when he moved to her mouth, she turned her head away.

"Yuck. Enough," she told the dog, laughing. "I missed you too."

She patted his head, gave him a gentle nudge, and he bounded to the ground. He placed his head on her knee, his deep brown eyes begging her to pet him.

Matty returned, plopped down at the large wooden table with a plate, and dug into the meal as if it were his last. His ruddy cheeks glowed with health. He'd improved by leaps and bounds since she'd last seen him. He'd almost died last fall due to pneumonia complications. If she and Travis hadn't broken into Shidler's pharmacy, he would've died.

"Hey, Matty," she greeted with a chuckle as he wolfed down a huge forkful of eggs.

He took a huge bite from his biscuit and asked, "Where y'all been?"

"All over," she evaded, not wanting to burden the boy with details.

"Are ya stayin'? Edwards and Ethan rounded up a few stray horses. I'm in charge of the horse barn," he declared, eyes gleaming brightly.

"We can't stay. But I'll come and look at your horses before we leave," she told him.

The boy nodded, continuing to shovel food into his mouth.

Gracie glided into the room cradling her newborn baby close to her chest. Her eyes widened as she took in the company at the table.

"Hey, guys," she greeted as she sat down, voice soft and even.

The baby gurgled, waiving a plump fist in the air.

Gracie had been held in one of the government's work camps. Dylan, the traitorous bastard who'd lived at the farm with them, had made a deal with her uncle to rescue her.

She was glad Gracie had been rescued but hated Dylan. He'd helped Widow torture Jace. She never should've given him a second chance when he'd betrayed the group at the farm. He did it all to rescue Gracie. She understood that. It just didn't absolve him for the methods he'd used. Ends didn't always justify the means.

Jace gave the girl an encouraging smile as he reached over to grasp the baby's waving hand.

"Hi, Gracie," he said. "How's the little one?"

Gracie gazed down at the little bundle in her arms, face glowing. "Josie is happy and healthy. She almost sleeps through the night now."

Cat rose from the table and gathered Josie in her arms. "Get something to eat," she urged the young mother.

She looked around the table and smiled even though her heart ached. Jace caught her eye and grinned. He loved being back among their friends as much as she did.

"Where's Hailey and Ethan?" Jace asked.

"On a supply run," Edwards answered.

"Hailey's expecting now," Cat added.

Tears gathered in her eyes, happy for Hailey. "She's probably over the moon."

Cat chuckled. "Yes, she's giddy as a goose but a little scared after watching Gracie give birth."

Gracie smiled. "It's so worth it though."

She looked at Gracie thoughtfully. "Have you heard from Dylan?"

Gracie stiffened. "No."

Dylan was probably still working for her uncle. She let the subject drop but wondered what the girl's hardened expression meant.

Matty pushed his plate aside and turned to her. "You ready to look at those horses?"

"Sure," she agreed, rising from the table, then turned to Jace. "Wanna come?"

"Nah," he said, waving her off, "I'll stay and catch up with Edwards."

As Matty led the way to the barn with Castiel trotting by his side, she couldn't help wondering about her own horse. She missed their rides, the powerful way his hooves flew underneath her when she gave him free rein. Someday she'd have a horse again.

She shoved thoughts of the future aside and focused on the present. As much as she wanted to stay, they couldn't linger here. Her brother took precedence above everything else. Worry and the foreboding feeling something wasn't right with AJ pestered her until it was all she could think about.

Cat walked into the barn a few minutes later, her casual gait unhurried, but something in the older woman's eyes told her she had something pressing on her mind. Cat leaned against a stall, willing to wait and watch.

Lacy gave an older sorrel mare an affectionate rub between the eyes.

"You're doing a great job with the horses, Matt," she praised. "Edwards should be proud of you. Is he teaching you a lot?"

From the corner of her eye, she saw Cat smile softly. The woman she'd grown to love and think of as a second mother seemed genuinely happy. The knowledge caused her heart to settle and some of the worry she had for her friends disappeared. They were making a life for themselves here, not merely existing like they did at the farm.

"Yup," Matty responded, "he's teaching me how to shoe them. Did you know he has his own forge?"

The excitement in the boy's voice was only eclipsed by the shine in his sweet, brown eyes.

Her eyes widened. "No, I didn't. So you can make your own horseshoes?"

His head bobbed up and down.

Before the boy could launch into an explanation of the inner workings of the forge, she reached out and wrapped him in a hug.

"I'll see you later," she told him. "I've got to go now, okay?"

He stepped out of her embrace with ruddy cheeks. "Will you come back?"

She ruffled the top of Matty's head. "I don't know, kiddo. I hope so."

She pivoted around to Cat with a raised brow. Cat motioned for her to follow, and they stepped out of the barn into the bright sunshine. Jace stood by the truck talking with Edwards. As if he could sense her eyes on him, his head turned in her direction. He gave her a smile that accentuated the dimple in his cheek. She sucked in a breath at that heart-stopping smile. Warmth filled her center.

Cat cleared her throat. "You two certainly haven't lost any chemistry."

The dry comment cleared some of the hazy desire flooding her system. Not all of it, though. She let out a sigh and turned her attention back to her friend.

"What's up," she asked, stuffing her hands into the back pockets of her jeans.

Cat's shrewd eyes narrowed. "How are you feeling?"

The question took her aback and her brows dipped in confusion.

"Fine. Why do you ask?"

"You seem . . . different. There's something . . ." Cat muttered.

"I mean, I have been battling some nausea," she admitted, "but that's because—"

She didn't want to get into a whole conversation about how she'd gotten a concussion. Without thought, she reached up and rubbed the sore knot still evident on her head. Widow had clocked her good.

Why was Cat so interested in how she'd been feeling? Then realization struck.

Cat's keen eyes sharpened like a blade. "I think—"

She held out a hand, eyes narrowed on the older woman. "Don't say it."

She knew the look in Cat's eyes and didn't want to hear her say, "You're pregnant."

24

Thomas Monroe sat on the back porch steps of his childhood home, eyes bleary and unfocused. He'd sent his assistant, William, to check on the men at the camp in the pasture. He couldn't stand the boy's presence one minute longer. He'd never been a man prone to violence. The right words, used with timely precision, were a much more effective way to get his point across. William, however, was testing that theory. The boy hovered.

Tires crunched on the gravel drive, but the noise barely registered. Nothing mattered now. Not his quest to take over the country and set it back to its former glory, and certainly not finding Lacy. He no longer had the will to soldier on. In the back of his mind, he knew he needed to pick himself up and continue his mission, but right now, he wanted to wallow.

A car door slammed shut. Widdowson sauntered up and stood in front of him.

"Why did you call me back?" Widow asked, clearly annoyed.

Monroe had a few cell phones that still worked. Contraband, stolen from the president. The president hadn't shut down all cell towers, recognizing the need to communicate with the National Guard and other key players in his effort to reset the economy. Monroe had given one to Widow to keep track of the man's progress.

He narrowed his eyes. "Do I need a reason?"

"I was almost ready to snatch your niece," Widow rebuffed.

"You were taking too long," he snapped.

Widow smirked. "My methods take time. I don't simply grab and go. If you wanted that, you should've sent one of your militia men."

The man was unhinged.

"It doesn't matter now," he muttered. "Nothing matters."

Widow's shrewd eyes studied him. "What happened? Where's Geneviève?"

He closed his eyes, trying to shut out the pain of reality. "Inside."

Understanding and a hint of true sympathy filtered through Widow's tone as he said, "I'm sorry."

He took a deep breath and opened his eyes. "I need you for something else now."

"What about your niece?" Widow asked.

"Never mind her," he said dismissively, batting a hand through the air. "We'll deal with her later. I have a meeting with Nieto."

Widow perked up. "Where?"

"Laredo."

"What do you need me for?" Widow asked, once again the picture of sheer boredom.

Raking a hand through his hair, he said, "Right now, I need you to take care of Gen. I can't go back in there."

Admitting weakness, any weakness, to Widow wasn't something he relished. But it wasn't like the diabolical man could use Gen, his only true weakness, against him anymore. Like his own daughter had done.

She was gone. She'd found his razor, slit her wrists, following the raised scars from her previous attempt like a roadmap.

He had to come to terms with it, pick himself up, and go on.

The war with the president wouldn't wait for him to grieve. He'd grieve when he was dead.

Some called his resistance a dereliction, a rebellion. It wasn't. He was launching the biggest revolution since the Revolutionary War. He was an apostate, not an anarchist. He still believed in democracy as the best way to govern the United States.

Widow moved past him and walked inside. His fingers fumbled inside his shirt pocket for the pack of cigarettes. He pulled the last one from the pack, crumpling the paper and cellophane into a tight ball.

He stood, tossed the ball aside, then reached for the lighter in his pants pocket. He flicked the lighter and lit the tip.

Widow walked back out and said, "I'll go get some men to help."

He nodded, fighting the tears clogging his throat.

"Where do you want her?" Widow asked, his voice flat and devoid of emotion.

He wondered if the man felt anything at all. Widow was a cut-and-dried, straight-from-the-book psychopath.

"There," he said, pointing to his mother's garden.

Gen would be close to him there. He needed her near. She was his whole universe.

"Fine. And after that?" Widow questioned.

"We go to Laredo."

25

AJ caught Willow before her limp body hit the floor.

"Willow!" Olive gasped, pitching forward, arms outstretched toward her sister.

"I've got her," he assured, infusing a calmness into his tone he didn't feel.

She couldn't weigh more than a hundred pounds soaking wet. He scooped her up, cradling her in his arms. He stared down at her, his chest tightening. She was so pale. Her porcelain skin looked almost translucent in the lamplight. Long, dark lashes rested in half-moons across her cheeks. They stood in stark contrast to her ashen face.

Her body needed more time to heal from the trauma of being Nieto's prisoner for four months. She'd gained several pounds since their return but needed to gain more. The visible bruises continued to fade, turning a greenish yellow. He wondered about the mental bruises he couldn't see.

"You got this?" he asked Bryan brusquely.

"Yeah, I got this," Bryan confirmed, giving Diego a menacing look.

Turning, he left and walked the short distance to his bedroom. He couldn't share the same space with Scott right now or he'd kill him. And digging a hole deep enough to hide the body would be an inconvenience at the moment. Not that the bastard didn't deserve it. Shit. It took all his self-control not to turn around and beat him bloody.

He stepped into his bedroom, and kicked the door closed with his boot so hard it rattled the hinges.

"Get your shit together," he muttered to himself, walking to the bed.

Willow's eyelids fluttered open as he laid her down. Her eyes widened as she glanced around the room and color quickly returned to her cheeks. She lifted her gaze to his and he watched in rapt fascination as she bit her lower lip. He swore it was the sexiest thing he'd ever seen. He shouldn't be thinking of kissing her right now, but damn him straight to hell, he couldn't think of anything else.

He turned away from her and the plump lip she held hostage between her teeth and tried like hell to get his raging hormones under control. Schooling his features, he pivoted back around.

"I fainted," she said with a sheepish grin.

"Yeah, you did. Scared the life out of me. You dropped so fast I barely caught you before you hit the floor. You do that a lot? Or was that just for me?" he teased, returning her charming grin. "You don't have to fake passing out to get my arms around you, darlin'."

He hoped his lighthearted teasing masked the growing desire pumping through his veins at an alarming rate. He should be ashamed.

Her cheeks turned crimson as he sat beside her. The mattress dipped, rolling her body until her hip rested against his. An electric current buzzed between them like he'd stuck his finger into an electrical socket.

"I don't pass out a lot," she grumbled, propping up on one elbow. "And I didn't do it for you. I'm embarrassed, and I hate the fact Scott saw me. As if he needed another reason to think I'm weak."

The anger he'd thrown on the backburner flared to life. He hoped Bryan was rag-dolling Scott's ass. His heart pinched at the thought of Willow feeling weak. She was far from it. It took endurance and a strong mind to withstand the hell, the sexual abuse she'd been through in Mexico City.

"You're not weak, Willow," he said, infusing reassurance into each word. "You're brave and strong, and after everything you've been through, you're still so damn sweet it makes my heart ache."

She shook her head in denial. "I think you're mistaking sweet for stupidity. Or naiveté. How could I not see what a horrible person he is? Beneath his fake, shiny veneer, he's nothing but a black hole that almost sucked the life out of me."

She lowered her eyes, fidgeting with the faded blue comforter's hem. He caught the shadow of shame creep over her before she shuttered her expression, and his heart cracked.

He placed his hand on her hip and squeezed gently. "You're not stupid. He knew how to play you and used your inexperience against you."

"So, not stupid," she said uncertainly, lifting her doubt-filled gaze to his. "Just naïve."

"That's nothing to feel ashamed of," he said with conviction.

"It's nothing to be proud of either," she retorted sourly.

He nudged her over, then laid beside her, stretching both arms above his head. The pull on his ribs sent the now familiar twinge of pain up his chest.

The black T-shirt he wore rode up, revealing part of his washboard stomach. He lowered hooded eyes and watched Willow.

Damn, she was the whole package. The girl-next-door sweetness just added to her allure. What he couldn't stand to see was the doubt and self-loathing in her eyes. He knew it stemmed not only from Scott but also her time spent in captivity.

God, that term sounded awful. She'd been treated like a caged animal. Nieto and the man who bought her tried to strip her of her humanity. They took away her basic rights and treated her like an animal to be used at their whim.

Scott started all of this. If anyone deserved to be punished, it was him. His anger threatened to boil over as he recalled Scott's critical description of her. Who the hell cared how she dressed? She could wear a gunny sack and she'd still be gorgeous.

He wouldn't care. From her captivating eyes and soft blond curls down to the subtle curves of her body, she was stunning.

Her gaze traveled from his bare stomach up to his face, cheeks burning. A war waged in her eyes as she studied him. He stayed silent, wondering what she was thinking.

"AJ," she said quietly.

"Yeah?" he responded in a low, gravelly voice.

"I don't know what to do with you, or how to do *this*," she said, motioning between them with her hand.

His brows furrowed. "What do you mean?"

She sighed and tore her gaze from his. "Despite everything I've been through, I'm not *experienced*. The only experience I've had with sex was"—she cleared her throat—"well, you know what it was."

A bright sheen covered her eyes as she trailed off.

"I know. But sex isn't all there is to a relationship," he said in quiet reassurance.

She blew out a frustrated breath. "How would I know? Scott's the only guy who bothered to ask me out. And he's right. I do look like a homeless person most of the time."

A spike of anger arrowed straight through his heart at the hurt in her voice. He could beat Scott bloody and not feel an ounce of remorse. Damn him for making her feel like she was anything less than perfect.

He stifled his anger at Scott and focused on Willow. What was she trying to say?

"He's a moron," AJ said dryly. "I wouldn't give a squirt of piss for his opinion."

Her lips tipped into a wan smile. "He is, but—"

He turned to face her. "There's no 'but' to it. Tell me what you meant when you said you don't know what to do with me."

A sudden thought caused his heart to plummet. Had she changed her mind about him? He still needed to talk to her about Quinn. Maybe she could tell he was hiding something from her.

Her shoulders slumped in resignation. "I don't know how to act with you."

Curiosity replaced some of his fear. "How to act? What exactly do you want, Willow?"

Their gazes collided. "I want you. I want to—"

Her rushed words stopped and the tormented look on her face shredded him. He reached out and tucked a wayward strand of hair behind her ear.

"What do you want to do? Just tell me," he encouraged, tone gentle.

She flopped onto her back and stared at the ceiling. "I want to touch you, kiss you. Do all the things a normal girl would do without horrible memories ruining it."

The longing in her voice almost broke him. Sadness and a sense of loss settled on his shoulders in a raw and almost violent wave. So much had been stolen from her. He knew pursuing a relationship with her would take work. He wasn't lazy and was willing to put in the time and effort. She was worth it.

Tears ran down the side of her face, pooling in her ear. He reached over and gently wiped them away with his thumb. Slowly, he rose and leaned over her. She turned her head from his probing gaze, but he grasped her chin and turned her head back.

"You can touch me whenever you feel like it," he said with a seductive smile. "We can go slow. Those awful memories will fade. We'll replace them. I want you to be able to trust me, trust I'll never hurt you. It'll take time. We'll find our way. I promise. And"—he waggled his eyebrows— "we can practice. A lot."

A slow smile bloomed across her face, lighting her eyes. "Practice, huh?"

"Hell, yeah," he said with enthusiasm, giving her a wink.

"I do trust you," she said, lowering her eyes.

He swallowed hard. "There's something we need to talk about."

"Okay," she said, looking up at him with uncertainty. "About what?"

God, he hated the doubt spreading across her face. He wished there was another way, but he had to talk to her about Quinn. Their relationship couldn't begin with anything less than complete honesty.

He took a deep breath and dove in. "Me. There's things you should—"

He was cut short when Laurel burst into the room. Her hair, a disheveled mess, matched the sour expression on her face.

"What the hell is going on around here?" she fumed.

Willow flinched at Laurel's rough tone. She started to sit up, but he slid his hand from her hip to her shoulder and gently held her in place.

"Willow and I are talking," he said evenly.

"Ugh," Laurel slapped her hand against her forehead. "I can see that. Why are Scott and Diego tied up in Willow's room?"

Willow sat up, leaning against the headboard. "Laurel is feral until she's had coffee."

He coughed, trying to cover his laughter. "Yeah, I can see that."

"What. Is. Going. On?" she asked, enunciating each word.

"Scott and Diego broke into Willow's room through the window. Both guys climbed the trellis," he said, tone clipped with a hint of annoyance bleeding through.

"Why?" Laurel asked, taken aback. "I know he acted rude last night when he barged in, but I never thought of him as a real threat."

The tension radiating from Willow was palpable as she stared at her sister, long and hard. Her body vibrated, shaking against him like an unbalanced tire on the freeway. He brought his hand to the nape of her neck, gently massaging her tense muscles in a soothing, rhythmic motion. She leaned into his touch.

"Is anyone going to answer me?" Laurel erupted.

"He sold me to Nieto, Laurel," Willow seethed. "He's not the person you thought he was."

"His father's in on it too," he added. "Apparently Nieto wants his investment back and Scott and Diego were supposed to deliver Willow to Scott's father. They're meeting Nieto in Laredo."

Laurel stood in the doorway like a wax statue in one of those tourist attraction museums. He knew the woman had preferred Scott as a favorable match for Willow. She'd made a snap judgment of AJ from the beginning, and it wasn't a favorable one. It must've been a shock to realize she'd been so utterly wrong about both men.

Laurel's gaze snapped to his and in a low, deadly voice, said, "I'm going to kill him."

He leaned over and kissed Willow's forehead. "Stay here and rest. I'll be right back." He rose and strode out the door with Laurel.

AJ WINCED as Bryan rammed his large fist into Scott's mangled face. Blood splattered from Scott's nose onto Bryan's forearm. Bryan ignored his bloody, swollen knuckles and continued pounding Scott's face.

He knew Bryan would beat both men until one of them talked. He wondered if Bryan learned the art of interrogation from the military, or if it was just an inherent caveman instinct.

Willow's comforter was peppered with a fine mist of blood spatter. The fan blew the scent of salt, rust, and sweat around the room, filling the small space with a pungent sickening smell.

"Tell us where the meeting is!" Bryan shouted, spittle flying onto Scott's crushed cheek.

Bryan had already worked over Diego. The guy leaned sideways. His bruised and battered face rested against the headboard. Blood pooled onto the comforter from his broken nose.

"He can't tell you what he doesn't know," Diego slurred.

Diego's left eye had swollen shut. He struggled to keep the right one focused on Bryan. Bryan swiveled from Scott to Diego.

"But you *do* know," Bryan accused. "Tell us what you know, and I'll stop pounding your faces into ground meat."

Diego's head drooped. "If I tell you, I'm dead."

"Not if we kill Nieto," he interjected. "Tell us where the meeting is."

Diego let out a strangled laugh. "And if I don't?"

"Then I guess you're dead either way," he shrugged indifferently.

"If he tells you, will you let us go?" Scott choked out.

Laurel, still in the silent, deadly mode in which she left his room, walked over, lifted Scott's head, and spat in his face. "You deserve to die for what you did to my sister."

He was beginning to worry about Laurel. She hadn't said a word about the information Willow divulged about Scott. Usually, she blustered around, shouting at everyone they better get on board with her plans to kill the man who'd hurt her sister. Now, she silently seethed, which scared him.

"I'm sorry," Scott sniveled. "It wasn't my fault. When my father gives an order, it's obeyed. No matter what. I had no choice."

"Had no choice?" Laurel's lip curled in a sneer. "There's always a choice. This *is* your fault!"

Laurel cocked back her arm, ready to punch his face, but Olive caught it before she could strike.

"Let Bryan and AJ handle this," Olive warned.

Laurel shook her head, body shaking, arm straining against Olive's hold.

"I know you, Laurie, and this isn't you," Olive insisted. "Don't stoop to his level."

Laurel took a deep breath and said, "You're wrong. This *is* me. This is who I've had to become. There's no other way to get justice."

But Laurel's shoulders slumped in defeat as she lowered her arm.

Bryan bent down and withdrew a black tactical knife from his boot. "If one of you doesn't tell us where the damn meeting is, I'll peel your fingernails off. Then I'll cut off your fingers, one knuckle at a time."

Scott bent over and wretched on the floor. Unable to restore his balance, he toppled forward, landing in the brown, chunky sickness. Bryan bent over, grabbed Scott under his arms, and heaved him back on the bed.

He grimaced. Sickness matted Scott's hair and stuck to the side of his left cheek.

"Better start talking," Bryan warned.

"Who will you start with?" he asked Bryan. "Scott?"

Scott whimpered. "Please, no. Please, no," he begged.

"Yeah," Bryan agreed. "Scott's a good place to start."

Bryan lifted the pistol from his waistband and handed it to Laurel. "Can you watch Diego?"

Laurel took the gun and checked the safety. "Of course."

AJ hauled Scott to his feet. "Let's go."

"Where are you taking me?" Scott screeched, eyes wild. "Diego, please! Please!"

He shoved Scott through the doorway. "He can't help you now. Unless he tells us where the meeting is."

Scott screamed at Diego all the way down the stairs. When they entered the kitchen, tears streaked down the man's broken face and snot ran from his nose in a steady, gelatinous stream. AJ pulled out a kitchen chair and forced Scott to sit. He remained behind the chair, and wondered if Bryan would really peel off the guy's fingernails.

Bryan pulled a chair close to Scott and sat. He leaned over and cut the zip tie from Scott's hands with his knife.

Bryan grabbed Scott's right hand and slammed it onto the kitchen table. Scott struggled against Bryan's hold, trying to rise from the chair but AJ shoved him back into the seat.

"Stop struggling," he demanded.

"I'm curious," Bryan drawled conversationally. "Are you right- or left-handed?"

"R-rright," Scott stuttered, snot falling out of his nose like a waterfall.

"Perfect," Bryan said, eyes cold and flat.

He'd spent a lot of time with Bryan and knew the man's character. But if he hadn't, he just might've been scared shitless right now.

The putrid scent of vomit and sweat wafted off of Scott like they were heat waves rolling off of asphalt in triple-digit heat. He turned his head, breathing through his mouth. God, the man smelled as if death took a dump on him and steamrolled right over him.

Bryan picked up the knife he'd laid on the table and checked the blade's sharpness with his thumb.

"You're gonna have to hold still," Bryan instructed Scott, "or this is gonna hurt a hell of a lot more."

Scott's eyes widened and he bolted upright. AJ shoved him back into the seat again. He reached around and wrenched Scott's free hand behind his back and held firm. The angle would pop Scott's shoulder out of place if he struggled.

"Please. Please. I'd tell you if I knew," Scott blubbered. "Please don't do this!"

Bryan slid the knife's tip under Scott's right index finger. Scott screamed in earnest, his face contorted in pain as Bryan slid the knife all the way under the bed of the nail. Blood stained the blade as it ran down the side and dribbled onto the tabletop.

Olive burst into the room, chest heaving. "Stop! Diego told us where the meeting is."

AJ watched Olive sprint into the kitchen, and skid to a stop. The slick, tiled floor caused the soles of her worn boots to lose their grip, and she slammed into the side of the refrigerator with a muted thud. Her chest rose up and down in rapid succession as she tried to catch her breath.

"Where will they be?" he asked, shifting his stance behind Scott's chair.

Eyes bright with fervor, Olive quickly assessed the room. When her eyes lasered in on Bryan and the knife he held inside Scott's fingernail, her mouth opened and closed like a fish out of water.

"Where's the meeting, Olive?" he repeated with barely restrained impatience.

He rolled his stiff shoulders, trying to loosen the knots that had formed along his neck.

Bryan's hand stilled as he glanced over at Olive, but he held the knife steady under Scott's nail. Scott's head fell to his chest, his breaths short and labored. Bryan's open palm cracked against Scott's cheek.

"Wake up," he commanded in a booming voice when Scott's eyelids slid shut.

"Damn, Bry," Olive managed, shaking her head in disbelief.

Bryan shrugged off the comment. "Someone's gotta do the dirty work."

Scott roused and glared at Bryan. "When my father finds out what you've done, you're a dead man."

"Ooo," Bryan mocked. "I'm shaking in my boots."

"Bloody hell," AJ muttered under his breath.

Recovering somewhat, Olive placed a hand on Bryan's shoulder and gave him a pointed look. "You can stop being Mr. Double-oh-seven now."

Bryan rolled his eyes as he removed the blade. "Fine."

Bryan wiped off the bloody blade on the hem of his jeans, then placed it on the table. Olive grabbed a chair, scooted it beside Bryan, and sat beside him. He turned to look at her and his expression softened.

"You okay?" Olive asked, taking Bryan's large hand in her smaller one.

"Yeah," Bryan responded gruffly. "I'm good."

AJ let go of Scott's hand, more relieved than he'd like to admit. Despite his reputation for getting into fights and starting bar brawls, he hated violence. And as much as he wanted Scott to pay for selling Willow to Nieto, seeing the man tortured made him physically ill.

He'd never seen Bryan in full military mode before. The guy was hair-raising scary. Bryan might've told Olive he was okay, but the tightness around his friend's eyes and the crease between his brows told a different story.

Scott held his hand to his chest, sobbing loudly. Blood from his finger soaked the front of his light-blue, designer polo shirt.

"My dad is gonna kill all of you for this," Scott fumed.

Olive's lip curled into a snarl as she turned and stared at Scott. "Shut up. No one wants to hear your whiny-ass voice anymore."

Bryan folded his arms across his chest, a ghost of a smile playing around his lips.

"The meeting is tomorrow at St. Peter the Apostle Church," Olive continued. "Diego didn't know what time, though," Olive informed them over Scott's continued proclamations of impending doom and death.

"What are we going to do with him?" he asked motioning to Scott. "And Diego. We can't just let them go. They'll run right to Scott's dad. And we can't take them with us."

"My dad—" Scott started.

"Yeah, yeah. Your dad's gonna murder us, blah, blah, blah," Bryan mocked. "Give it a rest. You're not going anywhere."

Olive snapped her fingers. "I know what we can do. We can lock them in the old storm cellar behind the barn."

"Can you lock it from the outside?" Bryan asked.

"I think so," Olive mused. "I'll ask Laurel. If not, we can find a way."

Bryan stared at Olive's back as she left the kitchen.

He cocked his head. "Man, you've got it bad."

Bryan ran a hand through his hair, a crooked smile on his face. "Maybe."

"She's got a mouth on her. Sure you can handle that?"

"I don't know," Bryan admitted. "But I sure as hell want to find out."

WILLOW LIFTED her head from AJ's pillow. Her eyelids fluttered as she fought the grogginess weighing her down. She reached a hand out, felt the cold bed sheets beside her, and knew AJ hadn't returned yet. Thin curtains hung against an inky window pane. Night had fallen.

A loud shout outside the door jerked her into full consciousness. What the hell was going on?

"Move!" she heard AJ yell.

Someone shouted an obscenity in response. Diego maybe?

She propped up on her elbow, preparing to get up when a

body crashed through the door. Diego fell inside with a loud thump.

She gave him a hard, calculated look as she rose from the bed. Fury engulfed her. She hated him and every other person who'd been involved in her kidnapping.

Hate fueled her anger and before she even made the conscious decision to do it, she stomped on his face. The cartilage in his nose crunched under her heel. Blood poured from his nose, giving her a wicked sense of satisfaction.

She glanced up. AJ stood in the doorway with a grin plastered to his perfect, symmetrical face.

"Getting out all your aggression?" he asked dryly.

She snorted. "Hardly. I wish I had boots on."

"A baby could stomp harder than you," Diego sneered.

She kicked him in the stomach, then leaned over him and said in a low voice, "You're a dead man."

"I think you stomped on his face pretty good." AJ pointed down at Diego with an impish grin. "I think you broke his nose."

Diego's dark brown eyes turned black as his upturned gaze locked on her. "There's nowhere you can hide that Nieto can't find you."

The statement hit her chest like a landmine blast. Was it true? If they didn't succeed in killing Nieto, would she have to run for the rest of her life?

"Shut your mouth," AJ growled. "Or I'll be more than happy to shut it for you. Get up."

AJ yanked on Diego's arm. Diego struggled against the force, cursing loudly in Spanish, but he was no match for AJ's strength. AJ hauled Diego to his feet and started down the hall. Diego stumbled, not fully gaining his balance. AJ stopped, steadied the man, and then continued.

She followed at a snail's pace, smiling wistfully at AJ's backside as he disappeared down the stairs. Next time he insisted on carrying her, she wouldn't object.

When she reached the kitchen, it was empty. The kitchen

table's surface was stained with blood. What the hell? Cold air whistled through the back door, chilling her bare feet.

A debate warred within her. Should she try to follow? They'd all left through the back door, not even bothering to shut it. Her numb toes reminded her she wore no shoes. However, curiosity won out and she hobbled out the back door.

Standing on the back porch step, she surveyed the yard. Darkness swallowed the barn. She couldn't see anything standing here. No light shone through the clinic's windows. It was as though everyone had disappeared into thin air.

The night's stillness unnerved her. No critters rustled in the nearby woods. Even the nocturnal barn owls, usually out hunting the grounds for mice, rabbits, or whatever they could find, were absent.

Her eyes swept over the pasture and locked onto a flashlight bobbing in the distance. It flicked back and forth, scouring the ground for obstacles. The group came into view, Laurel leading the way.

"You're awake," Olive said, trudging up the steps. "You missed all the excitement."

"What happened?" she asked.

"Scott and Diego are locked in the storm cellar," Olive answered.

Anxiety punched her in the chest, and she swayed forward.

What if they escaped?

She acted like Scott's presence didn't affect her, but it did. Deep down, it terrified her to think what would've happened if AJ hadn't been in her room when Scott and Diego climbed in through her window.

AJ stepped in front of her, placing his hands on her waist to steady her. "Hey, you okay?"

She nodded, running a shaky hand through her hair. The elastic band had slipped from her hair during her nap. Now it flowed down her back in a riotous display of wavy blond curls.

"They can't get out," AJ assured her. "It's locked from the outside."

She took a deep breath. "Okay."

AJ cupped her cheeks, and his eyes bore into hers. "I won't leave your side. You're safe with me."

Warmth flowed into her bloodstream, eliminating the night's chill. She wanted to kiss him for saying that. Forgetting the audience standing at the bottom of the porch steps, she tentatively leaned forward and brushed her lips against his. His eyes went wide. He moved a hand to the nape of her neck and returned the kiss.

Laurel cleared her throat. "It's freezing out here and you're blocking the door."

AJ lifted his head, breaking contact. Immediately, she felt the loss of his warm, soft lips against hers. Wanting him was unexpected. She never thought she'd be able to feel this way after four months of sexual abuse. But by some miracle, she did.

AJ wrapped his arm around her waist. "Let's go inside."

The group followed. The welcoming scent of fresh coffee filled the kitchen. Olive spoke to Bryan in low tones while Laurel prepared steaming mugs for everyone.

"We need to leave in the morning. You don't have time to go to Austin now," Olive said.

Bryan nodded his agreement as he sat down at the table. He patted his knee, his eyes trained on Olive. Olive smirked but sat on his lap.

She cocked a brow at her sister. "Interesting."

"Zip it," Olive muttered.

Smiling softly, she returned her attention to AJ who'd placed a hand in hers, threading their fingers together. Her stomach fluttered like butterflies in a meadow, flitting from flower to flower. The new sensation enveloped her. It was a feeling she could get addicted to, but she needed to take things at a slower pace. The past four months had left its mark on her, no matter how badly she wished it otherwise.

Besides, he'd said they needed to talk. The way he said it made her uneasy. There was something in his past he kept well hidden. What could it be? There wasn't anything the man could do or say at this point to sway her heart from falling for him. Even if it meant falling off a cliff.

She glanced up and swore his cat-green eyes glowed. "You said we needed to talk."

"I did," he returned with a bemused smile.

"I don't want to go back to my room," she said, shuddering.

The broken furniture and glass scattered all over her carpet was a sobering reminder she'd almost been kidnapped again. The blood spatter everywhere, and the puke smell turned her stomach. Her room would need to be sanitized by the CDC before she'd step foot in it again.

"You can stay in mine," AJ offered, squeezing her hand.

"Thanks," she said on a relieved sigh.

"And don't worry," he added with a smile, "I'll be the perfect gentleman."

She cocked a brow. "The *perfect* gentleman?"

Her boldness in the way she teased him surprised her. She'd never acted this way, never knew she had it in herself to flirt. The thought pleased her.

His smile widened. "Of course. However, *you* can ravage me anytime you want."

Heat bloomed across her face. Biting her lower lip, she tried to formulate a come-back, but his intense stare distracted her.

He leaned down and whispered in her ear, "But you'll have to stop biting your lower lip. It makes me want to kiss you."

A knock on the back door silenced the group. On instinct, she shifted closer to AJ, molding herself to his side.

Laurel took a deep breath, wiped her hands on a kitchen towel, and went to the door.

What if it was Scott's father? What would they do?

"Did anyone think to hide Scott's truck?" she asked AJ in a low voice.

He nodded. "Bryan drove it down into the woods."

Relief swept through her. "Good."

Laurel opened the door.

Her brows rose in disbelief. "Lacy?"

AJ moved forward, dragging her with him. He dropped her hand and engulfed his sister in a tight hug. Jace stood close behind her.

"Thank God you're okay," Lacy said against her brother's shoulder. "Mom and Dad are worried sick."

AJ leaned back. "You've seen them?"

"Yes," she said with a small smile.

AJ released her, a frown creasing his brow. "Lacy, Bryan told me everything. How're you doing?"

She didn't know what AJ meant, but it sounded serious. Stepping up boldly, she took his hand in hers. Lacy eyed the action, looking at her, curiosity in her bright green eyes.

Jace stepped in the door and closed it behind him. "We have a problem."

AJ's head whipped his direction. "With what?"

"Widow is after Lacy," Jace informed AJ.

Bryan cursed. "What the hell for?"

"Wait. What?" AJ said raising a hand in the air. "The insane psycho freak who tortured you?"

"Yeah. Monroe wants her to visit Geneviève," Jace said, raking a hand through his messy hair. "He blew up your truck, AJ."

How in the world had their situation gotten worse? She went and gave Lacy a hug.

"We'll figure this out," she promised.

Lacy returned Willow's hug, noting the restored strength in the girl's arms. It felt as if she'd known her a lifetime. After everything they'd been through, the bond they shared was stronger than any other relationship in her life, save Jace.

"I've missed you," she told Willow sincerely.

The scent of coffee and cinnamon saturated the kitchen area, causing her mouth to water. It reminded her of Christmas morning, waking to cinnamon rolls and coffee with so much cream the liquid turned into a light shade of brown sugar.

Willow drew back, eyes glistening with tears. "Me too."

They sniffed in unison, laughed, and hugged again. She'd been close to a few girls in school, her childhood chums she rode bikes with all over Kaw City, swam at the beach, and spent hours in the woods climbing trees. Yet none of those relationships were as strong as the connection she had with Willow. Their bond had been forged in fire.

Jace stepped around the girls. AJ stuck his hand out and they grasped arms at the elbows, their free arms wrapping around each other. Lacy smiled over Willow's shoulder, watching them.

They'd greeted each other that way since they were boys chasing grasshoppers.

Lacy released Willow with a wide, knowing smile. "What have you been up to?"

Willow's eyes darted to AJ. "Um . . ."

"Aww, come on," she teased, giving her a knowing look. "You can tell me."

AJ sidled up beside Willow and weaved his fingers through hers. "You've been here two seconds, Lace. Mind your own."

His hard tone didn't match the grin on his face nor the spark in his eyes. It drew her up short. AJ was notorious for playing the field. He never settled on one woman, stringing at least two along at a time.

Her senses sharpened as her gaze flicked between the two of them. This seemed different. The sweet blush on Willow's face told her the girl had already fallen for her brother. The way her brother possessively claimed Willow's hand and how his adoring gaze lingered on the girl spoke volumes. He'd fallen too.

She smirked at her brother. "That's okay. I can already tell what's been going on."

"No, you can't," her brother scoffed.

Willow shifted from one foot to the other. "Are you okay with . . ." She trailed off, a lost look crossing her features.

"I—"

"We don't need her permission," AJ stated, cutting her off.

Letting out a huff, she tried again. "What I was going to say—"

"She's important to me, AJ," Willow retorted. "I want her blessing."

"He could've asked me what I thought about the two of you getting involved with each other," Laurel interjected with an icy tone as she poured Bryan another cup of coffee.

"Because we don't need anyone's permission," AJ blustered.

Her eyes darted from person to person as the conversation passed around the room like a ping pong ball.

"She has a point," Olive said sagely, leaning against the granite bar that separated the kitchen from the dining area.

Bryan snickered, lowering himself onto a bar stool. "We didn't ask Laurel either."

Olive's gaze snapped to his. "Because there's nothing going on."

Bryan gave her an arch look. "Really?"

"I think it's GREAT!" she shouted over everyone.

AJ snapped his mouth shut on a retort as the room fell silent. All eyes turned her direction.

"Well, God damn," she muttered. "It's like a three-ringed circus in here."

AJ rolled his eyes. "Jace, control your woman, would ya?"

Jace walked over and stood behind her, wrapping his arms around her waist. She leaned against his chest, soaking up his warmth.

He leaned down, resting his chin on her shoulder. She sighed, contentment spreading through her like warm whiskey.

Turning his head, he whispered in her ear, "*Can* I control you, Lacy?"

His teasing words didn't match the low and sensual undertone of his voice. The control he insinuated had nothing to do with AJ's smart remark. Her body tingled with anticipation in response.

"No," she denied weakly.

He laughed softly. "Deny, deny, deny."

"Hey, break it up," AJ said in a playful voice. "That's my sister."

"We have something to tell you all," Jace returned evenly as he grasped her left hand and held it out.

The light from the overhead ceiling fan caught the diamonds around the large princess cut amethyst. It was a beautiful ring Jace had made for her before they'd even got together. It fit her perfectly.

AJ's eyes narrowed on the ring, then turned and raised an accusing brow at Jace. "What did you do?"

Jace's chest rumbled with laughter against her back. "We tied the knot. Literally."

"I have no idea what that means," AJ grumbled, shaking his head.

"We got married, dumbass," Jace supplied.

"What the hell?" AJ snapped, his face a mixture of disbelief and concern. "Why?"

Jace's arms tightened reflexively around her as if he thought AJ would drag her away from him.

"You knew my intentions," Jace reminded him. "Back at the farm we talked about it."

AJ threw up his hands and blustered, "The hell we did. You finally fessed up about loving her. You didn't say anything about marrying her the first chance you got."

Jace stiffened at his friend's accusing tone. "Where did you think this was going?"

AJ sighed and muttered, "Shit." He turned his probing gaze on her. "Didn't you want to wait until we could all be there?"

She shrugged. "We had an opportunity, so we took it."

"How'd Dad take it?" AJ asked, looking directly at Jace. "You did tell Mom and Dad, right?"

"We did," she affirmed.

Pain swift as an arrow shot through her chest. She didn't see how she could ever get used to the idea she was adopted. And the fact that her parents hadn't told her still stung no matter how logical their argument had been.

A war raged inside her, tugging her one way then another. One side of her argued vehemently that her parents should've told her about the adoption. The other side simply asked, what would the knowledge ultimately have changed in her life?

"Congratulations, man," Bryan interjected, slapping Jace's back. He turned to her with a wide smile and added, "I'm happy for you both."

"I'm so happy for you, Lacy," Willow beamed.

Laurel rapped a wooden spoon against the kitchen table, and all eyes turned her direction. She didn't know Laurel well. The only interaction she'd had with the woman was when she removed the bullet from AJ's chest. The woman saved her brother, and she was grateful. But she couldn't help thinking Laurel had a rough edge to her and a personality that demanded control.

Laurel stood at the head of the table like a captain at the helm of a ship. Her sloe eyes swept around the room, making eye contact with everyone.

"We need to nail down a plan." Laurel's commanding voice filled every space of the room.

"How?" Olive huffed, drawing out a chair at the table and flopping down. "We don't have enough information to 'nail down a plan,'" she mocked, using air quotes.

Bryan, seated at the bar drinking his third cup of coffee, said, "She's right."

Laurel shot him a warning look. "You can stop agreeing with everything my sister says."

"He never agrees with me," Olive said, indignantly.

"Yes, I do," Bryan disagreed with a sarcastic grin.

Once everyone was seated, Laurel plowed forward. "We know where Nieto will be, but not when, so we'll need to watch the church until he shows. We should leave in the morning. Early."

Jace held up a hand, and his head cocked to the side in the familiar way she loved when he was trying to figure out something.

"Hold on a sec. What the hell is going on?"

"Well, for starters, Willow's boyfriend, Scott, sold her to Nieto," AJ said, anger simmering in his tone.

She sucked in a sharp breath. Willow's gut instinct was correct. They'd talked about her boyfriend during their time confined in the hotel where Nieto often held his girls. Willow had been suspicious of her boyfriend but had no evidence to back up how she felt.

She caught Willow's gaze and gave her a confirming nod. "You were right," she murmured.

"Let's get back on point," Laurel said, reining back in everyone's attention.

She filled them in on how Nieto wanted Willow back, and their plans to kill him.

"Let me get this straight," Jace started, kneading his temples. "Scott is Willow's boyfriend, and he tried to kidnap her. You have him and Diego locked in your storm cellar. Who the hell is Diego?"

"Scott isn't Willow's boyfriend anymore," AJ corrected.

Olive smirked. "Yeah, that's the takeaway."

Willow narrowed her eyes, shooting daggers at her sister. "Shut up, Liv," she said through clenched teeth.

Bryan turned to Jace. "As far as we know, Diego is the liaison between Scott's father and Nieto. The two have been doing the dirty work for the big dogs."

"How are you going to kill Nieto?" Jace asked, puzzled. "He'll be heavily guarded, right? You'd need someone willing and able to take that shot, and you've done no recon."

Going after Nieto was risky. She understood why Laurel and the others felt like they had to do it. Even she felt like killing him if she dwelled on what he'd done to her. It just didn't make sense to take the risk. What would it ultimately accomplish? Killing Nieto wouldn't change the past and it sure as hell wouldn't wipe the slate clean.

It was a stupid idea. Someone was bound to get injured or killed. A strong sense of foreboding settled on her shoulders. She leaned against Jace, needing to touch him, draw from his strength. He placed his arm around the back of her chair. His warm hand rested on her shoulder, and his fingers played with the ends of her hair.

"This is a crappy idea," she said, forcing herself to speak in a low, even tone. "You're going in half-cocked with no plan, and you have absolutely *no* idea how dangerous this man is. You'd need a solid plan with a team who knew what they were doing to take him out. Someone's going to get hurt or killed if you go after him this way."

The room erupted in voices competing with one another to be heard. Leaning back in her chair, she let the cacophony swirl around her. The majority wouldn't change their minds. She knew it before she spoke, but she had to try.

In the middle of the chaos, she turned to Jace. "I don't want to do this."

He let his hand slip from her shoulder and sighed. "I know."

She took a moment to study her husband. His face was an inscrutable mask, but underneath she could sense his agitation.

"You're not going to walk away from this are you?"

He squeezed his eyes shut, opened them, and gave her a pleading look. "I can't. Bryan and your brother risked everything to save you. How can I not help them do the same for Willow? And you, for that matter. Nieto might come for you next."

"I just have a bad feeling about this, Jace."

He leaned over and rested his forehead against hers in solidarity. "We'll be okay."

She puffed out a breath through pursed lips. "Yeah, we will."

The discussion continued. Plans were sketched out, thrown out, and drawn up again. Somewhere along the way, she laid her head down on the table. The last thing they'd settled on before sleep claimed her was they were leaving at dawn.

28

AJ frowned as he watched Willow hobble woodenly from the kitchen. His gaze skirted around the room. Laurel and Olive went their separate ways after their team meeting, as Laurel put it, to prepare for the Laredo mission.

His sister's sleeping form snagged his attention. Her head was nestled between her arms just like she'd slept as a kid, and his heart softened. She was safe. And he was so damn grateful for it.

Jace and Bryan stood with him, discussing weapons. Tuning them out, he glanced back at Willow.

"Let's get everything together," Jace suggested. "We can see what we're working with."

"Good idea," Bryan agreed. "Meet y'all back here in ten?"

"Sounds good," Jace said, nudging AJ.

"What?" he snapped.

With a raised eyebrow, Jace asked, "You listening?"

"Gather your gear. You know, guns, clips, ammo, that sort of stuff," Bryan added, his voice tinged with mockery.

Willow had made painfully slow progress. He couldn't let her hobble all the way up the stairs to her bedroom.

"Sure, sure," he said, waving a dismissive hand. "I gotta take care of something first."

"We don't have time for you to 'take care of something,'" Bryan taunted.

He gave him a droll look. "Not that, dumbass. I'm gonna help Willow back upstairs."

"She needs to stay here," Jace said, face grave. "She's injured and a liability. It's stupid to bring the one thing Nieto wants. If this blows sideways, he'll take her."

"I know. But leaving her here by herself with those two idiots in the storm cellar? That's not an option."

"So stay with her," Jace suggested.

"She won't agree to that," he said, shaking his head.

But God, he wished she would. He'd ignore the burning obligation to go and stay with her, even though he knew the group needed his help. He'd do anything to keep her safe.

"Why not?" Jace asked.

Bryan scowled. "Because the Sinclair women are stubborn, mule-headed, sometimes violent—"

Someone cleared their throat, and Bryan stumbled to a stop as a chilling wind swept inside.

All three men turned toward the back door. Olive slammed it shut with a loud crash that rattled the kitchen windowpanes.

Her brows turned down into an angry V and her foot tapped in a staccato rhythm on the ceramic tiled floor. "I dare you to finish that sentence."

Bryan stood in slack-jawed speechlessness, staring at Olive.

He laughed and jabbed him in the ribs. "Go on. Finish."

Jace leaned into Bryan's space and added, "She does look a little violent. I think she wants to stab you."

Olive huffed and marched through the room. Bryan started after her.

"Sucks to be you," he said on a laugh.

"Not helpful," Bryan shot back over his shoulder.

"Get your gear," Jace hollered at Bryan's retreating back.

Bryan turned and flipped them the bird as he followed Olive into the living room.

"I'll be right back," AJ told Jace.

He headed to Willow who'd stopped at the bottom of the staircase. Her wild blonde hair fell below slumped shoulders. Her whole demeanor screamed defeat. Shit, he hated that.

"Need some help?" he asked softly, coming up behind her.

Sighing heavily, she nodded. "If I could just lean—"

He wrapped his arms underneath her legs and waist, then lifted her into his arms. She let out a surprised squeak. Totally adorable. The soft feel of her body against his chest quickened his breath. Carrying her wasn't necessary. He could've helped her walk on her own. But she was as addictive to him as aged whiskey, and he wasn't going to pass up an opportunity to have her in his arms.

"My room?" he asked as he topped the stairs.

"Yeah."

Her one-word answer sounded soft and breathy. His eyes locked on hers. One corner of his mouth tipped up, and he winked. Her lips parted in surprise, heat rushing to her cheeks.

He walked through his open door to the small bed. The lumpy mattress creaked in protest as he laid her down. He turned and shut the door with a soft click.

She looked up at him, eyes filled with expectation. "Can we talk now?"

His heartrate spiked. He hadn't forgotten they needed to talk. He'd hoped she wouldn't remember . . . which was just a dick move. And a cowardly one. The thought strengthened his resolve to tell her everything about Quinn. He wasn't a coward and wouldn't start being one now.

Quinn. The name tumbled around his brain like a kid kicking a tin can along a sidewalk. Telling the truth had its risks. A host of questions and fears joined the noise. What if she rejected him after he'd told her everything? Just thinking about losing her caused a pain in his soul so deep he knew it'd haunt him for the rest of his life.

Willow scooted over and patted the space beside her. "Will you sit with me?"

He shook off the fears threatening to get the better of him, and said, "Sure."

He sat and swung his long legs onto the mattress. The bed, so narrow their sides touched, protested with creaks and groans as he adjusted himself into a comfortable position.

She gave him an uncertain look. "Do you want to talk more about what happened to me in Mexico City?"

"No," he answered quickly to put her at ease. "Unless you need to talk about it?"

She took a deep breath and then blew it out through her nose. "I've told you everything that matters. The rest . . . the rest is dark and messy."

Wrapping an arm around her waist, he drew her closer. "I'm here for the dark and messy. I promise you I can handle it. You're not alone."

He watched as his words sank in. She finally lifted her eyes to his. Those mesmerizing eyes that captivated him from the beginning. He could get lost in them, happily drown in them. She was his siren, his addiction.

"What are we to each other, AJ?" she asked, quietly.

Man up, he chided himself, refusing to let fear take root in his heart. She wanted a label, needed one, and he understood why. It represented a measure of security, finality, and after everything she'd been through, it wasn't too much for her to ask of him.

He leaned over and with a feather-light touch brushed his lips against hers.

"Willow," he breathed. "I want you. Never for one second doubt it. But I need to be completely honest with you before we label what's going on between us."

He sat back, lifting his eyes to the ceiling. This was hard no matter how you sliced it.

She placed a soft, petite hand on his thigh. "Tell me what you think I need to know. I'll listen."

He dragged in a deep breath. "I told you I didn't do relationships, remember?"

"I remember," she said, holding his gaze.

The blackness at the window had softened to a dull grey. Night sounds began to die as nocturnal animals scurried home to sleep away the day. He'd need to hurry his story. They were leaving at dawn, and he seriously doubted Laurel would put her plans on hold so he could finish telling Willow about the worst mistake of his life.

"I had a girlfriend once. I was a freshman in high school when Quinn moved to town. Dark haired, petite, awkward as hell," he said, huffing a laugh. "I felt sorry for her because no one seemed to notice she existed at school."

"You do have a type," she muttered.

He tightened his arm around her waist. "The best type."

"So sappy," she said as she leaned her head on his shoulder. "Go on."

He told her everything about his relationship with Quinn, how far he'd fallen for the dark-haired girl, and how her stepfather abused her. Then stuttered to a stop when he came to the text message Quinn left him.

She lifted her head and studied him with sorrow-filled eyes. "What happened to her, AJ?"

A lump formed in his throat, and he swallowed hard. Hot tears burned the back of his eyelids, but he didn't let one escape. The part of him that condemned himself cruelly lectured he had no right to tears, because it was his fault she was dead.

She'd texted him. It didn't matter she'd absolved him of guilt by telling him not to stop her. It was a cry for help. He believed that with his whole heart because he just couldn't accept she'd been so willing to die. He'd failed to show her the light at the end of her dark tunnel.

He cleared his throat and steadied his voice.

"I was at Jace's on a Saturday afternoon. He wanted to work on the tree fort we'd built. A storm had blown off part of the roof. My phone died, so I left it on a charger in Jace's room. When I got back . . ."

The message she'd left took shape in his mind.

I love you and I wanted you to know this isn't your fault. Don't try to stop me, AJ. I can't live like this anymore. I'm so grateful I met you. &

Willow placed a soft hand against his cheek and turned his head to her. It lifted the temporary fog from his thoughts.

Her eyes tightened. "What happened when you got back?"

A rough noise escaped his throat. He closed his eyes, fighting the emotional tide beating against his mental levee. Constructed over the years, layer by layer, it hid him from the worst of the hurt. But in the process it hardened everything inside him. It only started to crumble when he met Willow.

She turned her body toward him. Placing her hand on his shoulders, she swung her leg over, straddling him. Shock whipped through him, which turned to hunger in a heartbeat as she settled herself down on his thighs.

Resting her forehead on his, she whispered, "I'm so sorry this is causing you pain."

He nodded, unable to speak over the lump in his throat.

"Take your time," she said. "Or don't tell me. I don't need to know this, AJ."

"You do," he said, voice hoarse. "It might . . . it might change your mind about me."

She sat back, face somber. "I promise you it won't. But I'll listen."

Taking a deep breath, he gathered himself enough to continue.

"When I took my phone off the charger, I noticed a message

from Quinn. It said . . ." He squeezed his eyelids shut and forced out the truth. "She was going to take her own life."

She inhaled sharply.

"I tried to reach her in time, but when I got to her house, the sheriff and state police were already there."

"I don't know what to say," she murmured, lying her head on his shoulder.

"The thing is, Quinn didn't leave a note for her mom. And the way she died, well, it looked suspicious."

She raised up. "How? Was it not ruled a suicide?"

His eyes darted to the ceiling again, wishing God would grant him absolution. But the universe wasn't that kind. He'd always bear this burden to some degree.

He huffed. "Turns out her mother knew the stepdad was abusing her, so they all concluded he killed her. He got life in prison without parole."

He watched her trace the dots together and knew the moment she figured it out.

"Oh," she said, nodding slowly. "You didn't come forward and show the police the suicide text."

"No, I didn't."

She placed her hands against his cheeks, forcing him to look at her. "And you thought if I knew, I'd what? Judge you? Think you were a horrible person? Tell you to take a hike?"

"Essentially," he admitted, unable to mask the shame.

"Dumbass," she said, her lips tipping in a small smile.

"But," he sputtered.

"AJ," she began with a sigh. "Was it unethical to withhold evidence? Yeah, it was. Did you do the right thing by Quinn? I think you did. Who knows what that man would've done if allowed to go free. He's paying for what he did to his stepdaughter. It might not be ethically correct, but it is morally correct."

He stared at her in stunned silence. Her words blasted through the wall around his heart, and he felt it disintegrate.

Love for her swelled, filling his chest until he thought it might burst. A lightning bolt of understanding hit him. It wasn't just the tug, the attraction between them. He was in love with Willow.

Mine, his heart whispered as he took in every detail, every curve and plane of her face. But was she ready to hear it?

29

"Hey, asshole," Bryan's loud baritone voice filtered in through the closed door. "Get down here and help."

Willow laughed at AJ's scowl but crawled off his lap so he could get up. He snagged her by the waist and pulled her back.

"Where are you going? I like you right here," he told her with a teasing smirk.

His eyes darkened as his gaze traveled over her face. Her breath caught as he reached up and tucked a disobedient curl behind her ear. She felt her heart stumble over the tender gesture and before she could check herself or talk herself out of it, she leaned down and pressed her lips to his.

A tremor ran through his body. His response brought her satisfaction and, surprisingly, made her feel empowered. It thrilled her to know she could draw that kind of response from him. A part of her still couldn't believe he wanted her. With his looks, his choice of women was limitless, yet he seemed to want *her*.

She drew back as he threaded his fingers through her wavy hair. She closed her eyes as the heat of desire ignited her senses. Every nerve ending was sensitive to his touch.

On a soft growl, he leaned in. "Willow?"

"Yeah?" she managed, licking her lips.

His lips hovered close, his breath mingling with hers. They were addictive, and his taste was a drug she couldn't refuse.

"I'm going to kiss you," he breathed right before his lips claimed hers.

Footsteps tromped up the stairs. He let out a long-suffering groan and raised his head.

"Dammit," he muttered. "I need more time with you."

"Me too," she agreed as she slid off his lap onto the bed.

He braced his hands on his knees and rose. The longing lingering in his eyes as he looked down on her mirrored her own feelings.

Bryan pounded on the door. "Open up!"

"Go away," he groused.

"Come on, man. Don't make me come in there," Bryan warned.

"Fine," AJ ground out between his teeth.

He leaned down and smoothed the same stubborn curl out of her face.

"We have a job to do," she reminded him, rising from the bed.

He let out an exaggerated sigh. "I know."

She opened her closet, retrieved a black zip-up hoodie, and a pair of black Puma running shoes.

"Get your shit together. Let's go," Bryan shouted, giving the door one last beat that caused the hinges to rattle.

AJ cursed loudly. "Hold on, you friggin' douche canoe."

She slipped into her shoes, opened the door, and slid past Bryan. The pain in her ankle had settled into a dull throb. Halfway down the stairs, Bryan and AJ caught up to her.

"Ankle better?" AJ asked, slowing his pace to hers.

She nodded, trying to assuage the concerned look in his eyes.

"Go on," she insisted, giving him a playful shove forward. "I can get to the kitchen without you carrying me. I'm not helpless, you know."

Bryan grabbed the front of AJ's T-shirt on his way by, nearly causing him to lose his balance.

"You heard the lady. Come on," Bryan urged. "Kissy-kissy time is over."

AJ shoved Bryan down a step. "Let go of my shirt you idiot or we'll both fall."

Bryan released the material with a snort and continued his downward trot. "Maybe you'd fall. I have impeccable balance," he threw over his shoulder.

AJ turned back to her. "You sure you can make it?"

"Yes," she insisted. "You can't carry me everywhere."

He stopped on the step below her, so they were eye level. "Is that a challenge?"

Fire raced inside her at his intense stare. He was the arsonist, she was the blaze. He could raze her to ashes, destroy her in more ways than one, and she'd hand him the match to do it.

"No," she managed, pushing him aside.

He said nothing as he offered his arm to her. His idea of a compromise, no doubt, so she took it. When they reached the bottom, she delicately removed her arm.

"Thank you," she said, avoiding his gaze.

He dipped his head. "You're welcome."

She stared at his backside as he walked into the kitchen. Did the man have a flaw at all? It seemed unfair the universe paired them together. To her, they were a lopsided match.

Her brow furrowed as Scott's words rushed back. *Like I'd ever date you. Please. You look like a homeless person.*

Her hand lifted to her ponytail hanging slightly askew from her nap, and her eyes drifted down to the pair of Adidas track pants she'd had since her freshman year of high school. Paint spatter in various shades dotted the black material.

And then it happened.

The black swirling vortex of ugly pain and anger breached

the dam she'd constructed during her captivity, bit by painstaking bit. Everything that happened to her had been shoved behind the dam. Every single abhorrent touch, every word used to hurt her, she'd crammed behind that wall.

Haggard breaths sent shards of pain through her chest. Thoughts churned and spun out. Why had she been targeted? Why? She wanted to scream, to rage at the sky, at God, at Scott. Her skin burned, felt too tight, as if she didn't belong inside her body anymore.

Without thinking, she moved to the downstairs bathroom off the kitchen. Standing in front of the sink, she stared into the mirror at a total stranger. She didn't recognize the bright eyes staring back at her. She turned on the cold water, splashing it onto her heated cheeks. Muffled voices from the kitchen filtered through the door, but she didn't bother trying to discern them.

Opening the cabinet drawer under the sink, she rummaged around for a brush. She swore there'd been one in there just last week. A small pair of pointy black scissors caught her attention. She picked them up, put her thumb and index finger through the small holes, and squeezed. Chop, chop, chop. What the hell were these for anyway?

She studied the scissors, noting the tip's sharpness by pricking her thumb. They were small but would do some serious damage if wielded correctly. Would they cut through Scott's hair? With all the gel crap he plastered on every morning, it was doubtful. The thought of chopping his stupid hairdo sent a jolt of tingling satisfaction right down her spine.

Stepping out of the bathroom, scissors in hand, she moved through the living room to the bowl of keys by the front door. She rummaged through them until she found the set of spare padlock keys, then slipped out of the house without being spotted by anyone. One of the keys would surely unlock the door to the storm cellar where Scott and Diego were being held.

They were still tied up, right? She'd sneak in and chop off Scott's hair, which was directly linked to his overinflated ego. If she caused him pain, hers would lessen. It made perfect sense. Maybe she'd jab one of his eyes out too. Maybe.

"I've been thinking about the layout of the church," AJ began addressing the group sitting around the table. "I think we should assume the library will be closed, so we won't be able to access any kind of blue prints."

Bryan, Jace, Olive, Laurel, and Lacy sat at the table in various stages of thought. Bryan gulped down his coffee, sucking in air through his teeth.

He rolled his eyes at his friend's method of drinking coffee. Weird.

"Why do you think that?" Laurel asked.

"Because Texas is barely functioning as a state. They won't waste resources on keeping a library open, or any city offices that could help with municipal records," Lacy muttered.

He didn't know what the hell was wrong with his sister. She'd been in a sour mood since she woke up from her nap at the table.

"What's your problem?" he asked, staring down his sister with his all too familiar big-brother glare.

Lacy lifted her shoulder in a careless shrug but didn't comment.

"We need a working knowledge of the building before Nieto gets there," Bryan stated.

Olive leaned her chair back on two legs. "We could ask for a tour."

Bryan snapped his fingers. "That might work."

"Olive, put your seat down," Laurel chided.

Olive let out an exaggerated huff, but her chair came back down on all fours with a loud bang.

AJ swiveled around in his seat, looking out the kitchen entry way for Willow. Where the devil had she gone? He thought he'd heard her in the bathroom a few moments ago.

He scooted his chair back and rose.

"Where are you going?" Bryan asked. "We still need to—"

"Y'all keep talking. I'll be right back. I'm just going to check on Willow."

"She's in the bathroom," Olive said, motioning to the far wall adjoining the kitchen and bathroom.

"Not anymore," he said, walking out.

He checked the bathroom just in case. The door stood open, and light from the bar across the mirror shone against water droplets on the counter. He jogged out and took the stairs two at a time back to his bedroom. No dice. He checked every room upstairs, then went back down and inspected the downstairs rooms.

He strode back into the kitchen. "She's gone."

Laurel glanced at him. "What do you mean she's gone? She can't be. I gave her strict orders to rest."

He rolled his eyes. As if Willow would give two shits about her sister's orders. She had a stubborn streak that ran as big and wide as his sister's. It just took a more subtle form. Willow's introverted nature masked it well. But it was there.

"Well, she is," he insisted, making his way out the back door.

"Dammit. Where'd she run off to now?" Olive muttered, following close on his heels.

"I have an idea," he said, not slowing his pace.

They jogged past the barn, rounded the far corner, and skidded to a stop. The cellar doors were thrown open. A pitiful wail echoed up the chamber as they drew closer.

"Why was I targeted?" Willow demanded, tone harsh.

It didn't sound like her at all. He paused at the stairs and looked back at Olive. Her face drained of color at the sound of Willow's voice.

They moved down the stairs on quiet feet. What had happened between the time they'd spent in his room until now?

He stopped as a soft, *snip, snip, snip* sound grabbed his attention. Olive bumped into his back. He turned and placed his index finger to his lips.

There it was again. The snipping sound scissors made when cutting paper, or . . . He took the last few steps quickly.

"Please, don't," Scott pleaded.

He stopped a few feet from the bottom. Olive shoved her way around him and skidded to an abrupt halt.

"Aww, for fuck's sake, Will," Olive said with an exasperation he shared.

He stood and stared, his brain offering no words as he took in the scene. Scott and Diego were tied to two steel folding chairs. Willow walked a circle around Scott, chopping off his hair down to the scalp. He didn't know whether to laugh or be deeply disturbed. Scott looked like he'd caught the mange from a pack of wild dogs.

Willow barely acknowledged her sister's words. She glanced up, then kept hacking away at Scott's blond locks.

When he noticed the blood on Diego's legs and the deep gash in his cheek, he stepped into Willow's space. Drawing up behind her, he put his arms around her waist and gently tugged her back.

"Let me go, AJ," she growled.

She jabbed an elbow into his ribs. Lightning hot pain streaked across his vision, and he sucked in a sharp breath. She twisted and squirmed, but he held on, tightening his grip.

"I mean it!" she shrieked. "Let go of me!"

"Not until you tell me what's going on," he responded in a reasonable tone.

Olive took tentative steps toward her sister. "Let me have the scissors, Will."

Willow's head jerked to Olive. "No. Not until they tell me why. Why did they have to choose me?"

Diego's head lifted and he glared at her with hate, causing his dark brown eyes to blacken.

"*Puta.* We chose you because you fit the profile. Boss wanted a blondie with a tight bod."

Olive turned and landed a right hook to the side of Diego's cheek hard enough to split the skin.

Diego laughed low in his throat. "You think I care what you do to me? Even if we escape, we're dead without *you*," he finished, staring at Willow.

Trying to block everything out except Willow, he grasped her chin and drew her eyes back to him.

"Whatcha doin', sweetheart?" he asked in a soft, even tone. "Talk to me."

His voice contradicted how he felt. Inside, he was a mess. Why would she do this? Had she become completely unhinged? How had he missed it?

Willow narrowed her eyes at him. "I'm not crazy. I just . . . I need answers."

He sighed. "I don't think you'll ever have an answer that justifies what you've gone through. What else is bothering you? What triggered all this?"

Her eyes darted to the sod floor, packed down so tightly it shone against the lights along the wall. Blond hair carpeted the space around Scott's chair.

"You never did answer my question, you know," she said quietly.

His brain buzzed, trying to ferret out what question she'd asked him in the last twenty-four hours. He came up blank. They'd talked about Quinn, but he'd answered all her questions. What had he failed to answer?

He gave his head a slight shake. "What question?"

Scott rocked back and forth in his chair, wailing loudly.

"Knock it off," Diego commanded.

"That bitch cut my hair," he bawled.

"Yeah, well, she stabbed me a couple of times and you don't hear me howling like a scalded cat."

"Let's go back in the house," he suggested.

Olive reached out and took the scissors from her sister. Willow slumped against him and sighed in total resignation.

"Come on," he urged, taking a step forward.

As they moved up the stairs and out of the storm cellar, he mulled over what question she'd asked him. He couldn't think of one thing. When they reached the back porch steps, he stopped and let Olive retreat into the house. He sat on the bottom step and patted the space beside him.

"Sit down and let's talk."

Willow crossed her arms. "I don't want to. Don't you have to get back in there? We're about to leave."

The sun peeked over the horizon causing the landscape to glow with golden hues. A south wind rustled the trees in the distance. The days were slowly warming, the temperatures climbing out of winter's freezer.

"I want to settle this first," he said, patting the space beside him again. "Don't be stubborn. You remind me of my sister."

The last comment drew a smile from her, at least.

"Oh, you like that idea?" he asked with an arched brow, deciding to roll with it.

Her smile grew as she sat down. "Yeah, I do. Your sister is—"

"Cranky," he interjected.

She laughed outright at that. "She's wonderfully outspoken and bold and brave."

"And you're not?" he asked.

"No. I'm not," she stated flatly.

"I think you're selling yourself short."

She swiveled around to face him. "I'm not. AJ, we're just . . ."

He watched the struggle on her face as she fought to continue. His heart plummeted at the tone in her voice, but he remained silent, letting her talk.

"We're different. I don't know how to explain it." She fumbled with her ponytail, trying to straighten it. "We're a lopsided match."

Whoa. That was the last thing he expected her to say. What the hell would make her think that?

His brows furrowed. "What do you mean?"

She tightened her ponytail with frustrated force and dropped her hands into her lap.

"I'm . . . I—" She stuttered to a stop.

"What question did I not answer, Willow?" he asked with a patience he didn't know he possessed.

Picking at a sliver of wood on the steps, she answered, head bowed, "What are we to each other?"

He sat in silence beside her. Now he remembered the question, but he thought he gave her an answer. As he turned over everything she said, it dawned on him. Scott and his big, fat mouth. That stupid asshole's words must've impacted her more than he realized. Her actions in the storm cellar made a little more sense now.

He picked up her hands and intertwined their fingers together. She didn't resist, but her eyes held questions.

He held up their hands. "See our fingers laced together?"

She nodded.

"Our souls are laced together the same way. You want to know what we are to each other? You're mine, Willow, and I'm yours. This," he emphasized, pointing between them, "is forever."

"But I'm not beautiful like Lacy or pretty like my sisters. I don't get it," she finished, tears tracking down her cheeks.

Frustration built inside him. How the hell could she not see how gorgeous she was?

"Willow, take me at my word. You are the most beautiful woman I've ever met."

She snorted. "Like hell."

"Why would I lie?" he asked, cocking a brow at her. "I've met plenty of women to compare you to and trust me when I say you're beautiful. Inside and out."

"I think maybe your brain was deprived of oxygen when you were shot," she responded sarcastically.

"Dammit, Willow," he exploded, heat racing to the tips of his ears. "Listen to me very carefully."

"Why?" she asked, turning her head away from him.

"Look at me," he demanded, waiting until her gaze locked with his. "I am in love with you."

He enunciated each word, trying to drive his point home.

"What?" she asked faintly, eyes growing wide.

He forged on. "There is no one else. There will be no one else. You're it. You're the one. You're *my* person. And I want to be yours."

30

Tears pricked Lacy's eyes. Never in a million years did she think she'd ever hear her brother confess his love to any woman. There'd only been one girlfriend in AJ's life, and she'd died tragically at the hand of her stepfather. After Quinn . . . well there was no *after*.

AJ buried his feelings deeper than Mariana's Trench, careful not to show too much emotion. He kept his head bowed at Quinn's funeral, left a single daisy on her casket at the graveside because they were her favorite, then never spoke of her again. Everyone thought he'd recovered from the tragedy quickly. Even their parents quit watching for signs of depression in him after a few months.

She knew better. Her brother's uncharacteristic silence about Quinn after her death spoke volumes. Over the years she tried to get him to open up, but he always found a way to evade or deflect the conversation. Added to that, her brother turned into the quintessential playboy, playing the field like a professional hockey player.

So, the words she overheard him speak to Willow was a balm to a long forgotten ache in her soul. When it sounded like he'd finished talking, she zipped up her dark grey hoodie and opened the back door. As she trotted down the steps, she gave her brother a jaunty smile and a thumbs up.

AJ scowled back at her. "Were you listening to us talk?"

She stopped in her tracks. Holding onto the stair's wooden railing, she turned back to face the couple.

"Maybe," she shrugged, feigning indifference.

A smile played around her lips.

"You've got no shame," he muttered, giving her one of his get-lost looks.

She stuck her tongue out at him which drew a giggle from Willow. She bounded off the last step, flipped her hair over her shoulder, and took a step in the direction of the corral.

"Where are you going?" her brother asked. "We're about to leave."

"None of your business," she said over her shoulder, jutting out her chin.

"Well, don't go far," he advised.

"Can you just leave me alone for one second?" she exploded. "Quit telling me what to do. I just need—"

She stopped and placed a hand on her heated cheeks. Air. She needed air. It's what drove her outside. The cool breeze whipped her hair back into her face, but she didn't care. She closed her eyes a moment and breathed in the crisp morning. The fragrance of dew on freshly cut grass, warming in the rising sun filled her lungs.

"Fine," AJ said, raising his hands in surrender. "Do what you want."

AJ and Willow rose from the steps and walked back into the kitchen, leaving her alone. She needed to think, to process what they were about to do. She shook her head, unable to dispel her ruminations. They were all insane if they thought they'd catch Nieto with his pants down around his ankles.

The pitiful collection of guns and ammo everyone had gathered sat in the middle of the kitchen table which consisted of two shotguns, one AR-15 rifle, a 40 Smith and Wesson, and a

Glock 17. Five guns. And an assortment of stored ammunition garnered from the Sinclair's gun safe.

It wouldn't be enough fire power to take down Nieto and his men who carried automatic weapons. He'd have a lot of men in his security detail. How the hell were they supposed to get past them? It would make all their plans moot if they couldn't accomplish that one gargantuan task.

In essence, they were screwed.

The thought of killing anyone drove bile up her throat. She'd been nauseated ever since they'd left California. She blamed it on stress. On finding out she was adopted. On being hunted by Widow. Now, she blamed it on anger.

It couldn't possibly be what Cat suggested, although her ability to sense when a woman was pregnant was usually spot on. She squashed the inner voice chirping away that she and Jace hadn't exactly been careful to prevent a pregnancy. Raking a hand through her tangled hair, she wondered why in the world they hadn't been more careful.

She knew what pregnancy felt like, having experienced it before. She placed a hand over her flat abdomen. Could she be? Her monthly flux had never been normal, so it was hard to determine if she was late.

It wasn't that she didn't want a baby with Jace someday, she just didn't think they were ready. Their present situation seemed to punctuate her point. What would Jace think if she told him she might be pregnant? His overprotective nature would go into overdrive, she was certain of that. Which meant he'd make her stay at the Sinclair Ranch while the others went to Laredo.

Dammit. Although she didn't want to do this, didn't want to be a part of any more killing, she wouldn't let Jace go without her. She also understood the danger Willow was in and would continue to be in if Nieto wasn't stopped. But killing left a stain on the soul no matter how justifiable.

A horse trotted restlessly inside the corral. The wooden poles were worn smooth with age. She ran a hand along the silky wood and stepped up on the lowest pole.

She missed her horse, Acer, and hoped Travis fed him apples every once in a while. Life only a year ago had been different, almost decadent in comparison to her life now. Jace had told her more than once this wasn't the life he'd envisioned for them. Would they run from Widow for the rest of their lives?

She huffed. The solution to that problem? Simple. Go back to the farm. But the thought of giving in to Thomas Monroe set her teeth on edge.

Jace sidled up beside her, leaned over the top pole, and let his arms dangle over the rail.

"Thinking hard?" he asked in a teasing tone.

She sighed, turning to face him. "I don't want to go to Laredo."

"I know," he acknowledged.

"We don't have enough fire power."

"I know."

The back door slammed. She glanced over her shoulder. The group began loading the trucks, shuffling outside with the measly supply of ammo and guns. Olive's strident voice carried the short distance to them, insisting Bryan drive the Sinclair truck.

"You can't drive that old stolen hunk of junk," Olive stated firmly. "Our truck is newer."

"I kinda like that old truck," Bryan retorted.

"You can't be serious!" Olive shouted.

It still bugged her they'd stolen that truck from the old woman after their helicopter crashed in the middle of nowhere. They'd just escaped from Mexico City where Nieto had held her and Willow hostage. Bryan had maneuvered the shot-up chopper over the border before it crashed.

They'd been on foot after that with Bryan carrying a barely conscious AJ on his back. They'd been desperate. And desperation often caused people to make hard choices. Choices they wouldn't consider under normal circumstances. Like stealing a car. Or going after a madman with no chance of surviving.

She tuned out their conversation and gave Jace her full attention. "We have our own problems. What about Widow?"

"There's nothing we can do about Widow until he makes another move," he said practically.

She jumped to the ground, restless and annoyed. "This is a bad idea. They have no idea what they're walking into. We're not trained for this, for God's sake."

His face turned somber. "You can always stay here, Lace."

She whirled around. "You would separate us? After *everything* we've been through?"

He stepped off the corral pole and turned to face her. Red tinged his high cheekbones, and his cobalt eyes darkened to midnight blue.

"Do you have any idea how much your brother and Bryan risked to save you?" he asked in a deceptively even tone.

"That's not the point," she argued.

"It's exactly the point!" he shouted, the reins on his control slipping. He ran a hand through his hair. "Lacy, you are my life, and I owe them mine for saving you. This is a debt I need to honor. I can't walk away from this. I won't."

Hopeless frustration ran through her veins like poison. There was no changing his mind. She could risk telling him she might be pregnant but dismissed the idea. She wouldn't burden his mind with it. It would serve only to distract him.

"You'd seriously leave me behind with Widow somewhere out there?" she challenged. "He won't stop hunting me. You know he won't."

"We'll deal with that after this," he said evenly.

"We don't have enough information, Jace," she said harshly, refusing to give up. "Who is Nieto meeting anyway? Nieto's security will be tight. It won't be easy to get around them or take them out."

"Scott and Diego didn't know who would be at the meeting," he admitted. "But we've been through things just as tough."

"Because we had no choice!" she shouted. "I didn't ask to be kidnapped, but I did what I had to do to survive and escape. No choice there. We have a choice here. We're the ones instigating this fight—that we have little chance of winning, by the way. How am I the only one that sees that?"

Out of breath, she dragged in oxygen, one lungful after another.

He rubbed the back of his neck. "I don't think the others see it like that. To them, they have no choice but to go after the man responsible for trafficking Willow. They're after justice. They want Nieto to pay for what he's done."

She threw her arms out wide. "Fine," she bit out. "I give up."

His eyes softened. "Is this our first official fight as a married couple?"

One corner of her lip twitched, but she refused to give him the satisfaction of a smile.

"You two finished fighting yet?" AJ hollered from the gravel drive beside his new truck.

"Shut up, AJ," she lobbed back, crossing her arms.

Jace stepped into her space, leaned in, and whispered, "You owe me."

"Owe you what?" she grumbled, still feeling querulous.

"Make-up sex, of course," he said, giving her a wicked grin.

"Oh my God," she muttered, cheeks heating as she walked away from him toward AJ's truck.

His laughter at her back caused her strides to lengthen. What a frustrating man! How she could love him to distraction and want to punch him in the nose at the same time was a pure mystery to her. His provocative words sent an electric current straight through her. If she turned around, she'd jump into his arms, wrap her legs around his waist, and kiss him, no matter who was watching.

She opened the truck cab's passenger door and hurled herself onto the bench seat. She'd go on this reckless mission, but she'd go under fierce protest.

AJ poked his head inside. "Get in the front."

"Why?"

"Because I want to sit in the back with Willow."

She rolled her eyes but crawled over the console.

"Watch your feet," AJ complained. "I don't want your footprints all over my new truck."

"Bite me," she muttered, plopping herself down with a huff.

"Up yours," AJ retorted with a good-natured grin.

Jace jumped in the driver's seat while AJ and Willow slid into the back seat.

Jace's gaze was grim as he said, "I'm sorry, Lace."

Her heart softened a fraction. This crazy, insane situation wasn't his fault, and it was unfair of her to blame him.

"I know," she murmured.

The white Sinclair truck in front of them inched forward. The diesel engine blew black smoke out of the tail pipes into their windshield momentarily blinding them.

A fitting, albeit ironic metaphor. They were walking into a dangerous situation completely blind.

31

Willow took a deep breath, blew it out through pursed lips, her heart tapping an erratic dance. Seeing Nieto again, the man who'd caused her so much pain, sent her spiraling like a whirlpool in the ocean.

Then there was AJ. She sat in the truck's back seat tucked into AJ's side with his arm wrapped securely around her. His warmth seeped into her. Soap and a fragrant woodsy scent unique to AJ enveloped her. The combination was heady. She found herself wanting to run her fingers through his midnight hair and nuzzle his neck, but staring straight ahead was all she could manage.

Anxiety chewed through her nerves causing heat to prick the back of her neck. Why was she so nervous? Oh yeah. Because AJ told her he loved her, and she had no idea how to respond. She did warn him she was inexperienced when it came to relationships.

"How come you don't want to drive your new truck, AJ?" Lacy taunted with a smirk.

"Turn around," AJ ordered, narrowing his eyes at his sister.

Willow tuned in to their conversation. Lacy ignored her brother, and turned to grin mischievously at her.

"Watch this one, Willow," Lacy cautioned in a playful tone. "He's super bossy. Remember what I told you?"

Her lips turned down at the painful reminder of Mexico City. The only good thing to come of it was her bond with Lacy. And AJ, she admitted. Then she remembered something Lacy had said and burst into laughter.

His brows rose. "That good, huh? You gonna let me in on the joke?"

She crossed her arms, trying to look serious. "She said you'd steamroll right over me."

"What the hell is that supposed to mean?" he asked, glaring at his sister.

Lacy tilted her head. "What do you think, Mr. My Way or the Highway?"

"Please turn around," AJ pleaded. "I don't think Jace would appreciate it very much if I throttled you."

Lacy let out a gusty huff but turned around, affording them a modicum of privacy. Jace chuckled and placed a hand on her knee.

"Why didn't you want to drive?" Willow asked, deftly changing the subject. "This truck is awesome."

The black leather beneath her fingertips felt supple and silky to the touch. The new-car smell permeated the cab, and she sniffed in appreciation.

"I'll have plenty of time to drive," he commented. "Besides, I wanted us to have a chance to talk."

Unease slithered up her spine. What else could he possibly want to talk about? She usually avoided confrontation like a rabbit evading a hungry hawk.

Scott and Diego, and what she'd done to them, was a closed subject. She didn't want to think about *why* she'd gone into a Harley Quinn revenge spiral. She wouldn't speak of it again. It was done. She couldn't change it, so what was the point of discussing it?

The satisfaction of cutting Scott's hair dwindled swiftly, and shame stepped in to take its place. When all her rage leaked out, she realized her actions had nothing to do with justice and everything to do with getting even.

"About what?" she asked stiffly. "We already talked."

"Well," he hedged, drawing out the word. "We never finished our conversation about us."

She could feign ignorance, but she knew what he meant. Still, she didn't make it easy and turned her head toward the window. A soft, resigned sigh escaped her. Avoiding the subject was cowardly but feeling helpless because she didn't know how to express her feelings was worse.

Texas prairie flew by in a dull, brown blur. It would take about an hour to reach Laredo. He grasped her chin and gently turned her head back to him while she contemplated the likelihood of quashing this conversation.

Squeezing her eyes shut for a moment, she summoned her composure. Lines puckered his forehead in genuine concern. What was he thinking? Was he worried she'd go off the deep end again and somehow jeopardize the mission? If he knew how screwed up she really was, he might lose interest in her.

"Come on," he implored. "Talk to me."

"Do we have to do this now? Shouldn't we be concentrating on what's ahead?" she asked, desperately trying to deflect.

Although, thinking about what awaited them in Laredo caused panic to rise to the surface. She'd put confronting Nieto in a locked box inside her head and stubbornly refused to think about it. She knew it was there, though. Its dark oily presence seeped out like a blinding fog, roiling around the darkest depths of her consciousness.

As if he could read her thoughts, he said, "If we talk about what's ahead, it'll make your anxiety worse. Tell me what you're thinking. About us."

"You—you," she stammered, frustrated at him and herself.

Why couldn't she be normal? A typical eighteen-year-old girl would snuggle next to him or hold his hand or kiss him. The last thought brought a flush to her cheeks.

"Breathe, darlin'," he reminded her gently.

Desperate to say something, she blurted the first thing on her mind.

"Look at me, AJ," she hissed, trying to contain her emotions. "I don't give a shit about how I dress, my hair's a mess most of the time. Not to mention, I'm shy. I don't know how to do relationships. I'm just not girlfriend material."

Tears stung her eyes. She sniffed and furiously swiped at one that had the audacity to escape.

"Do you think so little of me?" he asked softly.

She shook her head. "I just don't know how you're so sure of your feelings for me. We haven't known each other very long—"

He interrupted her by closing the small space between them and crushing his lips against hers. She gasped, her heart taking off like a rocket. The kiss erupted like an instant inferno, burning her from the inside out. The instant his tongue touched hers, she melted into his embrace and lost herself.

Sensing her surrender, a low rumble of approval vibrated through his chest. His hands threaded into her hair, tilting her head for better access. Heat built within her core, and she met his kiss with the same intensity. She could barely contain the flame of desire he'd ignited inside her.

He finally lifted his head and drew in a ragged breath. His eyes, darkened with desire, bore into hers.

"Do you understand now?"

She swallowed hard, heat engulfing her cheeks. "That was intense. Have you—have you been holding back?"

"Yeah, I have," he said, evenly. "Did I scare you?"

"No," she admitted. "I liked it."

"I'll remember that," he promised. "We'll learn the whole relationship thing together, go at a pace you're comfortable with. I can be patient."

A snort from the front interrupted him, and he slapped the back of Lacy's seat.

"Just sayin'," Lacy mumbled, flipping her braids over her shoulder.

Because she was tired of talking about the subject, she nodded her agreement. Hashing out the same problem over and over hadn't done her any good. He took her nod at face value, dropping the subject.

She leaned her head against his shoulder, willing her mind and body to relax.

"My mom and dad," he began without preamble, "knew each other in high school, but never dated. My dad told me once, the first moment he saw her, he knew she was the one. It scared him. So, of course he avoided her."

"Didn't they grow up together?" she asked, wondering why he felt the need to tell her about his parents.

"Nah. Mom's dad moved to Shidler when she was a sophomore in high school. He worked in the oil field, and they moved around a lot. Her mother took off on them when she was twelve, leaving her dad to raise her."

"That's sad," she said softly. "I can't imagine growing up without my mom. I miss her."

"Yeah," he agreed, eyes glazing over for a moment. "Anyway, her dad promised they'd stay in Shidler until she graduated. So she tried out for basketball, cheerleading, and wrote for the school paper. She made friends and was soon one of the most popular girls in school."

"Must be nice," she mumbled. "My sisters were like that."

"My dad played football and had a small circle of friends. He dated off and on, nothing too serious. Until he saw her. My mom didn't date until her senior year, then she started dating one of the guys from the football team. Still, he didn't approach her until their graduation."

"Why?"

"I don't know. He never explained that part. But when he

finally got the nerve to talk to her, she said, 'Well, it's about time. What took you so long?'"

"She knew?"

"Yup. She'd felt the pull, that connection between them every time they crossed paths, but she said if he didn't have the balls to approach her, he wasn't worth her time."

"Harsh," she commented without rancor. "Why are you telling me this?"

He gave her a lopsided grin. "To this day it's hard to be around them sometimes. They still love each other after all these years, and they're not afraid to show it."

"Ugh," Lacy muttered without turning around. "He speaks the truth. I remember one time—"

He knocked his fist against the back of her seat again.

"This isn't your conversation," he said through gritted teeth.

Willow laughed and without realizing it, wrapped both arms around his waist.

"My point is this," he continued, giving one last glare at the back of Lacy's head. "I know you're the one. Just like my dad knew. I couldn't walk away from you if I tried. I never thought I'd find the kind of love my parents share. Until you."

"What about Quinn?" The question slipped out before she could censor herself.

Her breath caught. She closed her eyes as embarrassment crashed into her. *Why?* she mentally berated herself. Why couldn't she keep her mouth shut? She withdrew her hands and slapped them into her face. He'd bared his soul, given his heart to her. And that was her response?

He tugged on her wrist, trying to dislodge the hand cemented to her cheek. "What about Quinn?"

She peeked through her fingers and saw his lips quirk into a smile. He seemed amused at her self-induced discomfort. Which irritated her into finishing what she started.

"Did you feel that way about her?"

He leaned into her space. "Look at me so I can answer you."

Slowly she lowered her hands. "You don't have to. I don't know why I even asked about her."

He took a deep breath. "I don't mind."

"You sure?" she asked even though he sounded sincere.

"Quinn was in my life for a season, and I'll never regret the time I spent with her. I did love her."

The girl was dead so why did a sharp stab of jealousy slice through her at his admission?

"But she is my past. You are my present and my future. So, to answer your question. No. I didn't feel this way about her."

He picked up her hand and placed it over his thundering heart.

"We are inevitable, Willow."

Something inside her began to transform. Feelings of resentment over what happened to her began to sway. If she hadn't gone through hell, she never would've met AJ. Hell was just the price she had to pay for the love he offered. And she was beginning to think it was worth it.

32

AJ noticed the change in Willow by the way her expression softened, and her eyes widened. Finally. Relief coursed through him as the constant tension in his shoulders lifted. She understood he meant what he said. He loved her.

And he knew she loved him too. He didn't need those three words from her at the moment. She wasn't ready to give them, still grappling with trust issues and insecurity. It would take time to sort out, and he looked forward to spending every moment with her. If it took a lifetime, he'd give her forever.

She leaned her head on his shoulder. Her whole body relaxed into his, melting into him like warm chocolate. He rested his chin on her head. The scent of her apple shampoo wafted from her hair, filling his senses. He swallowed a groan. God, he loved her smell. He stretched his legs out in front of him, soaking up the moment, willing it to last.

All too soon they'd be in Laredo, thrust into a situation with which he didn't agree. They were poking a bear with a mighty short stick. Worry stabbed a sharp, pointy fingernail into his almost healed bullet wound and twisted. He reached up and rubbed the heel of his hand against the injury. The odds of someone getting shot, or worse killed, was too high and he didn't want to speculate on those numbers.

Their "team meetings" as Laurel called them, had accomplished little. No one wanted to admit it, but they were winging it. Having no idea what lie ahead of them made planning pointless. Everything hinged on the information they gathered once they arrived.

He must've nodded off. When he opened his eyes, they'd parked along the road across from St. Peter the Apostle Church in Laredo. The meeting site. The church stood tall and proud against an otherwise dismal neighborhood. The wide, red brick steps leading to the entrance sat in stark relief against the white brick of the church. An old, abandoned building with boarded up windows across the street to the right lent to the impoverished atmosphere.

The street was deserted, devoid of motorist and pedestrian alike. Their trucks, parked along the curb, stood out like a sore thumb. They couldn't stay parked here indefinitely. They'd need to find a more inconspicuous spot.

Willow cast solemn eyes up at him, and his heart stumbled.

He gave her a sleepy smile, stretched his legs, and said, "Hey, beautiful."

Her eyes lit with pleasure and her cheeks flushed. "Hey."

"Sorry I fell asleep," he apologized. "Turns out, I'm pretty boring company, huh?"

"I wasn't bored," she said, shyly, casting her eyes away from his.

He studied her face. She acted embarrassed. Curiosity burned inside him. What thoughts were running through her pretty head?

"Why weren't you bored, Willow?" he asked in a low, gravelly voice.

She met his gaze, eyes sparking with amusement.

"I like watching you sleep," she said with a shy smile.

He wanted to pull her onto his lap, but now wasn't the time.

Keeping her safe was the only thing he could think of and the only thing that mattered to him. This was sure to blow sideways. He couldn't think of a scenario in which it didn't. If it was his last act on earth, he'd keep her out of Nieto's clutches.

Dipping his head, he buried his face against her neck and breathed in deeply, comforting himself with her unique, citrusy scent.

Bryan sidled up to the driver's side and rapped two knuckles on the window.

Jace rolled it down. "What's the plan?"

Lacy crossed her arms, frowned, and studied the church across the street. "We don't *have* a plan," she mumbled.

Jace reached across the back of the seat, giving her shoulder a comforting squeeze.

AJ could feel the agitation radiating off his sister. It took on a life of its own as if her tension had turned the stifling air into a poltergeist.

"I'm going to go read the bulletin board. See if there's anything going on today," Bryan answered, giving Lacy a questioning glance. "Wanna come check it out with me, Lace?"

The outdoor bulletin board planted at the base of the wide, rounded stairs would have the church's weekly schedule posted along with various events happening around the neighborhood.

Lacy heaved an exaggerated breath and reached for the door handle. "Sure. Why not?"

Her gloomy tone concerned him. It could infect the group. They couldn't start with a defeated attitude.

Giving her something to do might release some of her pent-up anxiety. Maybe it would be enough to expel her infectious pessimism. Bryan had gotten to know her over the past few months. Enough to realize she needed a distraction. He'd have to thank Bryan later.

"Careful," Jace cautioned as she stepped down.

Worry leaked from Jace's tone. He could relate, not wanting to let Willow out of his sight. All his overprotectiveness seemed to transfer from his sister onto Willow. He'd need to work on turning down the volume on that particular emotion, knowing it came across as overbearing and controlling. Navigating his relationship with Willow was challenging enough without adding in *Operation Annihilating Nieto*.

Lacy shot Jace a reproachful look. "It's across the street. You will be able to see me the whole time."

Unaffected by her sarcastic tone, Jace lifted a shoulder and said in a reasonable tone, "Still. Be alert. Anything could happen."

Bryan walked over to Lacy. "Ready?"

She nodded. They walked to the curb. Bryan looked both ways for cars, then stepped into the deserted street. A gust of wind blew bits of paper and a plastic grocery bag along the curb. An aluminum can skipped across the pavement with a *tink, tink, tink* as it traveled at the wind's command.

Bryan grabbed her hand and pulled her forward. As they jogged across, she pulled her hand away from his and punched him playfully in the arm.

"There's a pair I never thought I'd see team up," he commented, leaning forward to watch his sister. "She hated him in high school, said he was a conceited prick."

Jace turned to look at AJ. "I owe him big time. He really came through when you guys helped her escape."

"And when they kidnapped Aunt Geneviève," he added with an eye roll. "Those two are dangerous together unsupervised."

Jace chuckled. "No shit."

Bryan and Lacy studied the board then turned and walked back to the curb. Lacy nodded at something Bryan said as they crossed the vacant street.

Lacy opened the door and jumped inside. "Well, there's a Saturday night mass tonight at six. If their meeting is held then, we could follow the crowd inside without drawing attention."

The way in might be easy, but getting out would be a different story. They had to assume Nieto would post guards around the building. Unless they could use the church goers as a shield, which was out of the question, they'd be fish in a barrel trying to escape. The guards would pick them off as soon as they stepped out the door.

"We need an exit strategy. Someone will need to mark potential exits around the building," AJ added. "When we get inside, we'll have to figure out how to find the meeting place. This will be un-orchestrated and sloppy."

Jace nodded. "When Nieto gets here, we'll need to assess how many men he has with him and how to eliminate as many as possible without calling the cavalry down on our heads."

He rubbed his forehead with the heel of his hand, trying to relieve some of the tension building into a massive headache. This had too many variables that could go wrong, too many scenarios in which Willow or Lacy could be taken again.

Olive joined Bryan at the window. "What's the tea, Skippy McGee?"

Bryan snorted. "You're so bizarre."

Olive gave him a saccharine smile, folded her hands under her chin, and touted, "Sticks and stones."

Bryan's lips twitched, but he didn't comment further.

"There's a mass tonight at six," Lacy reported.

Olive pursed her lips. "They could be using mass as a cover for their meeting. Let me go get Laurel."

Before anyone could respond, she turned and walked to the Sinclair truck and poked her head inside the passenger door window.

"Great," AJ said with fake enthusiasm. "Get the drill sergeant."

Willow poked him in the side with her index finger, a look of mock horror on her face. "Don't call my sister names."

He laughed without repentance. "The shoe damn well fits her."

"Shh, here they come," Lacy said, glancing back at them.

He shook his head, not caring if Laurel heard him. The

woman rubbed him the wrong way. Laurel treated Willow like a child, refusing to listen to her little sister's opinion on targeting Nieto. If she had, they might not be sitting here, contemplating the best way to die. A *TikTok* video flashed through his mind along with the stupid tune, ". . . *dumb ways to die*." Attempting to kill a high-profile drug and trafficking lord definitely qualified.

Olive returned with Laurel in tow, speaking to her sister using her hands to emphasize her point. He couldn't hear the conversation, but Jace could.

"What the hell are they talking about?" he asked.

"Clothes," Jace replied in confusion.

"Olive wants to go shopping for mass," Willow guessed. "She's a certified shopaholic."

Willow's eyes drifted to the track pants she wore and frowned. He could tell Scott's hateful words about her clothing still bothered her.

He leaned down and whispered, "You're the most beautiful woman in the room no matter what you wear."

"Yeah," Willow scoffed. "I'm sure the Archbishop would think my paint-splattered track pants the height of fashion."

He chuckled but let the subject drop, knowing he could only push so far.

Olive returned to the window with Laurel. "Okay, if we're going to mass—"

"We don't know if the meeting will take place during mass or not," Lacy interrupted, determined to be the devil's advocate by arguing about everything.

"But we should be prepared if it does," Olive retorted. "So, we need clothes. We can't go to church looking like hobos. We need to blend."

"She has a point," Bryan agreed.

"Whah-pah!" AJ burst, cracking an imaginary whip in the air with his hand.

Jace chuckled. Bryan would agree with anything Olive said.

Bryan craned his neck around Jace's head and glared at him. "Seriously?"

He opened his mouth to reply, but his sister cut him off.

"Who's going to watch the church while we shop?" Lacy countered. "They could slip in while we're gone, and then this whole trip would be pointless."

"That's what I said," Laurel added, folding her arms against her chest.

Bryan's brows scrunched together in thought. "I'll stay back and watch."

Lacy shook her head. "What if you need help? You won't be able to contact us while we're gone."

Most of the time, he considered cell phones to be a pain in the ass. Once his mother had bought him the damn thing when he turned twelve, she expected an immediate response to texts and phone calls. Now, he'd give almost anything for one. Powering down cell phone towers and the internet was the first thing the government did after the economy crashed. Which was just another way to control the population.

"How long is this going to take?" Bryan asked, glancing at Olive. "Never mind. Dumb question. Y'all will need to hurry."

"I'll stay back with Bryan," Laurel said with finality. "AJ and Jace, if you could find a sporting goods or hardware store, we could get some more ammunition."

"You won't be able to buy guns, but a knife or two wouldn't hurt," Lacy mused, tapping her index finger against her lip.

"I hate to be a wet blanket," AJ started, "but how are we going to get all this stuff? By stealing it?"

"I brought money," Olive announced, bouncing on the balls of her feet. "Mom and Dad left us well prepared. So let's go."

"It's important you hurry," Laurel cautioned Olive. "This isn't for pleasure. One store. Get in and out. You know my size."

Olive snapped her fingers and turned to Bryan. "I'll need your size."

Bryan rattled off his sizes, emphasizing the length of his pants.

He grinned, remembering Mexico City where they'd stolen two suits from a vacation home. They had to dress to the nines to get in to Nieto's trafficking party to rescue the girls. The pants had been too short for both of them, and Bryan's dress shirt had ruffles.

"Yeah, make sure Bryan's shirt has ruffles on it. Oh, and pastel pink or purple really brings out the muddy brown in his eyes," he goaded with a smirk.

Bryan's eyes narrowed at him through the window. "Dude. That was a low blow."

"Just keeping it real, brother," he said, smiling wide.

Olive opened the back passenger door and slid in beside Willow, then slammed the door so hard he swore his teeth rattled.

She leaned over her sister, waggling her eyebrows. "Cozy, huh?"

He rolled his eyes. The girl was unhinged.

Willow's eyes shot daggers at her sister. "Can you just . . . tone it down a little? This isn't a game, Liv. What we're doing here is serious."

Olive shrugged. "Everything's a game."

Olive's flippant attitude bugged him. Did she have a death wish? She'd be a liability to the group if she didn't take what they were about to do seriously.

Jace looked at the back row through the rear-view mirror. "Where am I going?"

"Jump back on I-35 north. An outlet mall is just a few minutes up the road. You can drop us off at the Calvin Klein store," Olive answered.

"She shops a lot," Willow explained when Jace's brows rose to his hairline.

"What can I say?" Olive said, defensiveness creeping into her tone. "All girls love to shop."

"Not all girls," Willow and Lacy said in unison.

Lacy turned and gave Willow a fist bump.

Olive huffed and crossed her arms. "Fun suckers."

"I just think this is a waste of time," Lacy shot back. "Who gives a flying fu—"

"Okay," he interrupted before his sister could finish, "everyone take a breath."

"You take a breath," Lacy sniped.

"Look," Jace interjected, infusing patience into his voice. "Nieto knows what you, Willow, AJ, and Bryan look like. The more we blend with the crowd, the better off we'll be. If you stick out for any reason, he'll spot you, then our cover's blown."

"Fine," Lacy huffed. "But we seriously need to hurry."

They pulled into the outlet strip into a parking spot near Olive's requested store. It took them roughly three minutes to get to the mall. Good. The quicker the better.

"There's an Academy Sports on up I-35," Olive told Jace.

"Splitting up is a bad idea," Jace muttered.

"It's the fastest way to get this done," he replied, grasping the door handle.

Jace's brows turned down, etching a deep V between his eyes. Lacy leaned over, placed a hand around his neck, and drew him into a kiss a brother shouldn't *ever* have to see.

"Come on," he griped. "I'll have to pour bleach in my eyes if you guys don't knock it off."

He opened the passenger door, hopped out, and opened Lacy's door. Lacy broke away from Jace and gave him a reassuring smile.

"We'll be quick," Lacy promised.

Jace gave her another quick kiss. "We'll be right back. Stay with the girls and don't separate for any reason."

"God, you guys are worse than Mom and Dad," he groaned.

Lacy laughed at her brother's discomfort. "Move, dumbass, so I can get out."

He stepped back and swept his arm out wide and bowed. "There you go, princess."

Lacy glared at him as she jumped out. Olive handed Jace some money, then took off toward the store. Willow and Lacy followed a few steps behind.

He hopped into the passenger seat, and Jace pulled out of the lot. It took longer than three minutes to find the sporting goods store. He bounced his knee up and down. This was a mistake. They shouldn't have split up.

"Come on," Jace muttered, swinging his door open. "Let's get this done."

They hurried to the back of the store where the ammo was located. Jace went to the counter and rattled off what they needed to the wide-eyed, young clerk. The poor guy looked like he'd just started working and knew nothing about guns or ammunition.

As the clerk searched through boxes, he walked down the aisle that contained knives, sharpeners, machetes, pepper spray, basically anything needed for self-defense. He stopped and studied a Smith and Wesson fixed blade knife, wondering if Willow knew how to use one.

Would it be more dangerous to give Willow a weapon she didn't know how to use? However, leaving her defenseless didn't feel right, so he picked up two, one for Willow and one for Lacy, and joined Jace at the counter.

The clerk handed over the boxes of bullets. "You guys going hunting?"

He gave the nosy clerk a sharp look. "Guess you could say that. Nice day for it."

They made their purchases and left the store. Jace sped back to the mall, pushing the gas pedal to the floor.

Urgency thrummed through him. Blood raced through his veins with every harsh heartbeat. He could hear it roaring in his ears. The feeling that something had gone horribly wrong nagged at him. The tires grinding against the asphalt shredded his last nerve.

Jace pulled into the lot and turned toward the Calvin Klein store. Willow and Olive rushed out before the truck rolled to a stop, bags slung over their arms. They flung the passenger door open, threw their bags into the floorboard, and jumped inside.

Jace's hands white-knuckled the steering wheel and he let out a low growl. "Where's Lacy?"

Tears formed in Willow's eyes. "We don't know."

33

L acy picked a dark-green, chiffon dress from the rack, held it against her body, and looked down. The high-neck bodice clasped around the throat, showcasing the popular cold shoulder sleeves. The high-low front hem fell right above her knees, leaving the back to fall mid-calf which gave the dress a fun flair.

She loved it. The price tag hanging from the inside label almost changed her mind. However, the Sinclair's were paying. She shrugged, slung it over her forearm, looking around the store for Willow and Olive.

Not seeing them, she let out a low groan. Olive tried on at least three outfits already. What else did she find? They were two racks over a few minutes ago. Deciding to check the dressing room located along the far wall, she took a step forward.

A cold hand clamped down on her shoulder from behind.

Her heart seized as she stumbled to a stop. She tried to take a breath, but it died in her throat.

"We meet again," crooned a smooth voice.

The bitter taste of fear coated the back of her mouth. She tried to swallow, but her throat constricted. Air wheezed painfully in and out of her lungs. Time slowed and she heard every gasping breath in her ears.

"Widow," she managed, voice barely audible.

She forced in a deep breath and let it out in slow puffs through pursed lips.

"Very good," he said, his cloying tone mocking her.

She tried to shrug off his hand and turn around, but the man took a step closer. His fingers dug between her collarbone and shoulder joint, bruising the skin. She caught a whiff of the faint, yet distinct, smell of lavender pomade mixed with stale cologne.

Bending, she reached for the knife always strapped to the lower part of her right leg. It wasn't there. Dammit. She'd lost it when Widow blew AJ's truck to pieces.

He yanked her back to a standing position, his grip tightening on her shoulder. She jerked to the left, trying to dislodge his hand.

He leaned in, placing his lips against her ear and tsked. "No, no. You're going to be a good girl and come quietly."

He pulled a gun from the inside pocket of his tan trench coat and jammed the slim barrel to her lower back. Her knees wobbled. She needed to keep a cool head. She could get through this.

Just count. Breathe.

"What do you want, Widow?" she asked, trying to sound more confident than she felt.

He pushed her forward. "You're asking the wrong question."

His hand slid from her shoulder to her forearm as he sidled up beside her. She winced as his long fingernails dug into the tender underside of her arm.

He dragged her as she stumbled one step behind him. She tried to keep up with his brisk pace, weaving their way through the racks of clothing to the store's front door. A rack's arm scraped her side and shuddered from the impact.

She let out a muffled, "Umph."

He stopped abruptly when they reached the door.

. . .

"Put the dress down," he demanded.

Her sweaty hands clung to the fabric like a lifeline. The alarm would go off if she stepped outside with the dress which might give her a chance to run. He reached around and tried to rip it from her grasp.

An older saleswoman looked up from the cash register behind the sales desk. She walked around the counter and strode forward, her black pumps clacking against the shiny tile floor. Her brown hair was coiffed into a French twist, and her pink lips turned down as her eyes flicked from Widow to her.

"Is there a problem, ma'am?" the woman inquired.

She opened her mouth to answer but Widow cut in, "Of course not. My wife and I were just leaving."

The woman arched a penciled-in brow at Widow. "Excuse me, but I wasn't speaking to you."

Her cultured voice dripped with disdain. She looked condescendingly at Widow as if he was a piece of gum she'd like to scrape off her shoe.

Widow stiffened at the woman's tone and straightened his shoulders. She felt his barely concealed anger at being challenged as he shifted to the side, poking the hidden gun's barrel into her ribcage with extra force.

"I—I'm fine," she stuttered, not meeting the woman's gaze.

Widow let go of her arm long enough to tug on the dress. With a great deal of reluctance, she let it go. He graciously handed the garment back to the woman, then secured her arm in his grasp once more.

"My wife has expensive taste," he said in a degrading tone.

The saleswoman turned a sympathetic gaze to her. "Are you sure you're all right?"

The lady probably assumed she was in an abusive relationship. Widow dug the gun deeper into her side. A warning. She held in the gasp that wanted to escape and gave the woman the best smile she could manage.

"I'm fine," she said, quietly, again looking away to avoid the woman's probing gaze.

The woman looked uncertainly between them, and opened her mouth to say something else, but Widow turned her toward the exit.

"Let's go, dear," Widow said, opening the door.

She had no choice but to follow. They stepped out into the cool morning air. A light breeze blew white cirrus clouds along the horizon. A murder of crows landed in the parking lot, their caws echoing on the wind. They began pecking at the ground, searching for food.

"How are you even here?" she asked as she searched the lot for anyone who could help.

AJ and Jace hadn't made it back yet. The few cars parked in the lot were empty. Widow steered her with an iron grip toward her uncle's black Cadillac.

"Your father has a meeting with an acquaintance of yours," he answered, tone clipped.

"My *uncle* is meeting with Nieto? Why?" She stressed the word uncle, unable to let his snide comment slide. "And how did you know I was here?"

Thomas Monroe would never be her father. He just happened to be her sperm donor.

"You and your friends parked in front of the church. You didn't even try to hide," he sneered in disgust. "Your father sent me to scout the church before the meeting. I saw you and couldn't pass up the opportunity fate sent my way."

Widow had stumbled onto her location by accident. The thought soured her stomach. He slipped the gun back into his inner coat pocket, opened the passenger door, and shoved her inside. Her butt hit the seat so hard her breath whooshed from her lungs.

"Buckle up," he said, tone sharp. "If you try to run, I'll shoot you."

She rubbed her throbbing forearm where he'd manhandled her. There'd probably be a bruised imprint of his fingers there if she looked.

"Where are you taking me?" she asked, trying to stall as she pulled the seatbelt over her shoulder.

If she could hold him up long enough, maybe her brother and Jace would show. A long shot and wishful thinking on her part, but she had to try.

He laughed. The unhinged sound caused the hair to stand up along the back of her neck.

"I'm debating that very question. I'm fascinated by you, and I'd like to see if I could break you."

The statement sunk into her skin like toxic water. She fascinated him. How?

He took a step back and started to slam the door.

"Wait," she said, holding her hand against the black door panel. "How do I fascinate you?"

He stopped. Good. She needed to stall, keep him talking somehow, but his intense scrutiny sent tiny ant-like sensations running up and down her arms and legs. Maybe she shouldn't have asked the question. It was as if a blinding spotlight had been pointed straight at her. What if he decided to torture her like he had Jace?

Her heart raced, but she held still and counted the birds in the lot. Thirteen. Thirteen crows.

"You don't seem like the kind of person to break easily. You're frighteningly self-aware for a girl your age. I'm just wondering how long it would take before you shattered and what the key to that would be. I'm afraid after observing you these past weeks, the answer is too easy."

She stared at him in horror. He wanted to torture her just to see how long it would take to break her? Acid burned the back of her throat. It *was* too easy.

Her key was Jace.

She'd do anything, even give up her life to keep him safe. Out of Widow's clutches. Jace had suffered enough when Widow used the waterboarding technique to torture him. She'd arrived at the Monroe farm soon after with Geneviève and rescued him.

"Yes, too easy. So, I'll take you to your father," he murmured, stroking his thin mustache. "He called me off your trail, you know," he added as an afterthought.

Wait. What? Her temper flared.

"Then what the hell are you doing?" she shouted. "Let me go!"

Her fingers slipped down to the belt buckle. If she timed it right, she might be able to release the belt and jump out as he was driving. It would hurt like hell but shooting her would become more difficult.

"Don't you want to know why he called me off?" Widow asked, a sinister glint lighting up his otherwise dull brown eyes.

She feigned indifference. "Not really."

Widow slammed the door, rounded the hood, and slipped inside. She scanned the lot. Her brother and Jace still hadn't shown up.

What was taking them so long?

Starting the ignition, he put the car in drive and pulled out of the lot. He gave her a sidelong glance, a smile playing around his lips.

She'd amused him. The thought fueled the fury racing through her veins. He wanted a reaction from her. In some ways, Widow reminded her of Nieto. Were all sadistic bastards narcissists?

"Hmm," he murmured. "To tell or not to tell."

He tapped his finger on the steering wheel. She counted the annoying *tap, tap, tap*, as he pulled onto the I-35 ramp.

"You seem nervous," she observed, nodding toward his hand on the wheel. "Are you afraid of my uncle?"

She asked the question wondering if it would trigger some sort of reaction from him.

He rolled his eyes and sniffed. "No."

He said no, but his body stiffened at the question.

"If he told you to stop hunting me, aren't you afraid he'll be angry when you show up with me?"

Pushing him was risky. He could just pick up the gun he'd placed in his lap and shoot her. Something told her he wouldn't though. He was playing an angle of his own. Whether it be simple curiosity, or some sort of grudge against her uncle, she didn't know.

His lips turned down in annoyance. He didn't answer her question. Interesting.

Widow sped along the interstate, oblivious of the speed limit. The likelihood of being stopped by a police officer was nil. Texas still functioned as a state, but every city- or state-run department had been scaled down to conserve resources.

The Cadillac zipped onto an off-ramp, and Widow turned the car toward the giant Holiday Inn sign. It towered over the cluster of other smaller chain hotels.

He parked, cut the engine, and stepped out. She'd missed her opportunity to run, but he'd driven too fast to think about jumping. Opening her car door, he pointed the gun at her chest, not bothering to hide it.

"Out," Widow ordered.

She unbuckled the safety belt and got out. Trepidation hovered over her, its ghost-like fingers swirling in and out of her head. She was terrified of her uncle. What would he do with her?

They walked under an awning to a set of stairs leading to the hotel's upper level. Widow stopped at room 213 and inserted a key card into the door's metal reader. The green light flashed. He opened the door and shoved her inside.

A cloud of smoke rushed toward the open door. The air, thick with the pungent smell of cigarettes and stale coffee, threatened to suffocate her. Through the haze, she saw her uncle at a small work desk against the wall to her right. A cigarette dangled from his hand. Dark bags circled the man's eyes. He looked haggard, as if he'd aged twenty years in the few weeks since she'd last seen him.

Thomas looked at Widow, then his tired eyes shifted to her. He stiffened and anger flashed across his face.

"What the hell is she doing here?" he bellowed.

He stood, the sudden movement knocking over the wooden chair with a mustard yellow cushion.

"I thought—" Widow started.

"You thought," Thomas sneered. "That was your first mistake. I don't pay you to think. I pay you to follow orders. I ordered you to scout the church and instead you come back with . . . *her*."

"I did scout the church," Widow returned, easily. "And found her and her friends parked on the street by the church."

Her uncle didn't interrupt, so Widow continued.

"We should probably find out what they're up to," he reasoned, "although I think it's fairly obvious."

Thomas narrowed his eyes at her. "Why are you in Laredo?"

She mashed her lips together and crossed her arms over her chest.

"He can make you talk," her uncle threatened, pointing to Widow.

She rolled her eyes and opened her mouth to speak but an open hand cracked against the side of her face. Stars exploded in the back of her eyes. She stumbled. Reaching out a hand, she caught herself against the wall.

"Do not disrespect me by rolling your eyes at me. I won't tolerate it," her uncle spat.

Her cheek stung as if a thousand pins had been stuck into the side of her face. Anxiety clawed her chest, causing spasms of pain to ripple through it. Her uncle would turn her over to Widow without batting an eye.

Thomas stood before her, ramrod straight. He looked every

bit the tyrant she knew him to be. The expectant look on his face irked her.

"Well?" he demanded, "Why are you here?"

She stiffened as he leaned into her space. His sour breath, a medley of coffee, cigarettes, and garlic, assaulted her nose.

"I was going to tell you," she gritted out between clenched teeth, "but didn't get a chance to because I got the bejesus slapped out of me."

Thomas's eyes darkened and his nostrils flared. "Watch yourself. I don't like your smart mouth."

She swallowed her retort and summoned all the inner peace that remained inside her.

She took a deep, calming breath. "When I was rescued from Nieto, we also rescued a girl named Willow. He'd done horrible things to her, and her sisters want Nieto to pay for his crimes. That's why we're here."

He took a few steps back. His brows turned down as he digested the information. He raised an index finger to his pursed lips.

"Fools," he muttered in disgust. "All your friends will be killed."

She canted her head to the side. "Maybe. But it's worth a try, don't you think?"

Widow strode over, hands clasped in front of him. "What to do with you now?" he mused.

Thomas huffed. "I don't need her anymore."

His answer drew her up short. Curiosity stirred inside her. He'd changed his mind? After all the trouble he'd gone through to get her back? It didn't make sense.

"Why?" she asked, unable to stop herself.

Her uncle closed his eyes, and his shoulders bowed forward. When he opened them, a bright sheen covered his brown irises.

"My wife is dead," he said, devoid of all emotion.

34

L acy's mind whirred like a computer processor, trying to download a file too large for its capacity. Geneviève was dead?

"H—, how?" she stuttered.

As angry as she was with her birth parents, she hadn't wished them harm. Not really. She had threatened to kill Thomas Monroe if he came after her and if push came to shove, she'd probably do it if it meant protecting those she loved. But she'd hate it.

Her heart thumped painfully against her rib cage. She'd never have the chance to give Geneviève her forgiveness for giving her up. Her birth mother died thinking she hated her. Now, she'd never get to know Geneviève. If that was something she decided she wanted.

"What does it matter to you?" her uncle asked, the tang of bitterness so palpable, she could almost taste it on her tongue.

She reached out and placed a hand on her uncle's forearm. "Please, just tell me."

Her uncle let out an exhausted sigh. He turned away from her, walked over and righted the chair he'd been sitting in, and lowered himself onto the mustard cushion. His elbows thumped onto the table, and he lowered his head into his hands.

She walked over and sat in the matching chair on the opposite side. Images of her aunt the last time she'd seen her flashed through her mind. Then she remembered something. She'd wondered about it at the time but didn't want to ask the woman anything about the thick, angry scars running from her wrist halfway to her elbow. Now that she'd thought it through, it seemed fairly obvious what those scars represented.

Widow walked to the small, mustard-colored sofa, picked up the remote and turned on the television. Its low hum broke the silence stifling her lungs. The outdated room looked like it had been plucked out of a 1960's *Ladies Home Journal*.

After several minutes, she thought he wasn't going to answer. Her mind leapt from one possibility to another. Had Geneviève been sick? Was she in an accident? Then, it circled back to the most obvious answer. Suicide. The thought burdened her like an anchor chained to her soul. Was it her fault because she'd rejected her? Suddenly, she didn't want to know the answer.

On top of everything else, this might be the straw that broke her. She let out a self-deprecating huff at the thought. Widow wouldn't have to torture her for her to break. She was already broken.

Widow glanced up from the sitcom on the television. "Just tell the girl."

Monroe gave Widow a disgruntled glare, then turned his penetrating gaze on her. He ran a hand through his thinning, greasy hair. It looked as if he hadn't showered in days. Not that it would help the smell. The hotel room reeked of cigarette smoke. It sunk into the thick wine-colored drapes covering the window, giving them a dingy look. Lack of natural light and the smoky haze gave the room a depressing, animal cave vibe.

Monroe squeezed his eyelids shut. "She took her own life."

She strained to hear the barely audible words. When they registered, her heart sank.

"The same way she tried before?" she asked carefully.

"How did you know about that?" he asked, eyes sharpening.

"How could she miss it?" Widow answered for her.

"How?" her uncle demanded. "Did Gen tell you?"

Widow snorted, but directed his attention back to his show before Monroe could berate him. Laughter from the sitcom echoed through the room.

"No," she answered. "She didn't, but I . . . I saw the scars on her wrists."

She lowered her eyes to the small table. The uneven Formica surface made to look like real wood had warped. Rings stained the top along with blackened scorch marks from unattended cigarettes. Evidence left by many customers who'd come and gone over the years.

Monroe sighed heavily. Something akin to pity filled her heart for the man. It surprised her. Geneviève was his whole world. Now he had nothing.

"I left her alone," Monroe admitted. "For just a few minutes. I didn't think she'd—"

His Adam's apple bobbed up and down as he stammered to a stop.

She didn't need to know the details, so she nodded and looked away again. It was painful to watch him. Agony rippled off of him in waves.

"It's all your fault," Monroe seethed.

She stilled. He blamed her. Of course he did. He couldn't possibly be at fault for anything. Anger rose swiftly at the accusation. How dare he blame her? Barbed allegations of her own burned on the tip of her tongue. She choked them down and clasped her hands together under the table to stop them from shaking.

Widow rose from the couch and strolled over. "You know," he began casually, "Nieto might find her valuable. She was involved in his son's shooting, after all."

Monroe's gaze snapped in Widow's direction. Widow had piqued his interest.

"We could take her with us to the meeting. Use her as leverage," Widow suggested.

Cold dread filled the pit of her stomach at the thought of being under Nieto's control again. The man wouldn't be as tolerant of her as he'd been before. She wouldn't have another opportunity to stab him. He'd make sure of it.

Flashbacks of her time in captivity rained down on her. The dank underground cell with its rusty sink and horrid hole used as a toilet flashed through her mind and threatened to settle there. The smell. She'd never forget the putrid, sour odor that sunk into her clothes, hair, and skin like cheap perfume.

Monroe tapped an index finger on the table in swift succession, his eyes focused on the far wall in front of him. He was mulling over the idea of using her as leverage against Nieto. An exchange. Military support for her life. Panic squeezed its tight fist around her mind like a vise, causing her head to thump and her ears to ring. She couldn't survive being Nieto's prisoner. Not again.

She needed to think. If they took her to the meeting, the others would see her. Her thoughts flitted to Jace, then to AJ and Bryan. They'd be in a position to rescue her. Their own plan to kill Nieto might be compromised with her in the way. But they'd put her first. The tension between her eyes began to ease. They wouldn't allow her to leave the meeting with Nieto.

Monroe's darkened eyes landed on her. He seemed conflicted as if an angel and a devil were on each shoulder debating the issue of turning her over to Nieto.

Why was this such a hard decision for him to make? He didn't care about her as a daughter or a niece. He'd proven that already. But what argument did the angel on his shoulder have?

She tried to swallow against the dryness in her mouth. "Geneviève wouldn't approve."

The room's stillness seemed to amplify her quiet statement. Both Monroe and Widow stared at her.

Widow's eyebrows rose to his hairline.

Monroe frowned, his salt and pepper mustache dipping down below his jawline. "Don't you dare speak her name," he spat.

"We need this ace up our sleeve," Widow persisted, sensing he might be losing the argument. "We don't have anything else. You already turned over all the gold we had."

Monroe whipped his head to Widow at the slight censure. Monroe had made a mistake paying Nieto before he'd gotten an ironclad agreement from him. What did he expect? The man was a drug runner and sex trafficker, for God's sake.

Widow's statement seemed to turn the tide against her. She watched her uncle's eyes harden with resolve.

"Fine," Monroe muttered. "We'll take her along. But I don't want to use her if we don't have to."

Surprise scuttled through her. He said he wouldn't use her unless it was necessary. Which it would be. Nieto was a lot of things—cruel, shrewd—but he wasn't a fool. If Nieto wanted her back, he'd use the opportunity to his advantage.

It would take all her wits to come out on the other side of this unscathed. She took a moment to send a silent plea for help to whatever god was listening. She'd take all the help she could get.

She shifted in her seat. "Why are you doing this?"

The need to understand the man drove her to ask the question. What was more important than his own daughter?

Monroe scrubbed a hand across his face. "Did you encounter a checkpoint when you drove into Laredo?"

"No," she said, drawing out the word. "Why do you ask?"

"I did that," he stated, pride causing his shoulders to straighten. "Do you think you could've driven into New York like that? Or any other city in this country?"

Her tired brain couldn't make the connection. What did checkpoints have to do with why he thought garnering an army from Nieto was more important than his own niece? Or daughter. She shook her head. Whatever. She was so confused.

Monroe stared at her as if waiting for a light to appear above her head. She wasn't a cartoon character, and a damn light bulb wasn't going to illuminate above her head.

She raised a hand in the air, brows lifted. "So?"

"Dear God," Monroe muttered. "How can you be so obtuse?"

Her head jerked back at the insult as if he'd physically slapped her. "Obtuse?"

The word came out on a screech as incredulity rose within her. He had the audacity to call her stupid.

"Yes, God dammit, obtuse," he thundered. "If the president is allowed to sweep across the country unchallenged, the rights you're accustomed to will disappear. This nation will cease to be a democracy."

She took a deep breath and absorbed the information. "You're an anarchist," she concluded.

Monroe slammed a hand down on the table's uneven surface. "No! What I'm trying to start is not a rebellion. It's a revolution against despotism. It's a complete rejection of their form of government. It's our constitutional right to throw off any form of government that would impede our rights to freedom."

Widow turned and stretched his legs across the sofa. His eyes landed on hers. Did his face have any other expression besides that stupid, annoying smirk?

"Call it apostasy if you have to put a name on it," Widow threw in, laying his head back against the sofa's arm.

"No one asked you," Monroe growled, and turned back to her. "Are we done?"

For some reason, his question smarted. She couldn't understand why, nor did she have the mental ability to analyze it.

"I just want to understand," she said, carefully masking the hurt from her face and tone.

She wouldn't give him the satisfaction of knowing he had that kind of power over her.

"Understand what?"

His irritation ground her gears. "Why my life means nothing to you!" she shouted.

His expression smoothed out. "The needs of the many outweigh those of the one."

She didn't think her heart could break any more than it already had. From being assaulted by Jace's brother, Zach, to being kidnapped and threatened by Nieto, her heart was pretty much decimated.

She was wrong.

Monroe's words rang in her ears like a death knell. It was the nail cinching the coffin closed.

Her life meant nothing to him. Her life was forfeit.

35

***

AJ thought if it was physically possible, Jace would've blown apart all over the truck's interior.

"What the hell do you mean, *you don't know?*" Jace exploded.

He rubbed the back of his neck as he studied Willow, who flinched at the man's explosive comment. This was bad. Worse than bad. Cataclysmic. Who would've snatched his sister? She wouldn't have left the store on her own.

Willow bit her inside cheek. "I'm sorry," she said, quietly.

"It's not your fault," he responded immediately.

"Willow and I stepped into the dressing room. We were only gone a minute, I swear," Olive said, eyes round, pupils blown wide.

Jace let out a low growl. "You were supposed to stay together."

"Look," he broke in, "Casting blame won't get my sister back."

Jace nodded tersely, lips pressed into a grim line.

"Did you ask the sales person if they saw anything?" he asked, hoping someone could give them a clue.

Willow dragged a hand through her ponytail. "Yeah, we did.

The lady said she left with some man. The man said Lacy was his wife."

Jace cursed and hit the steering wheel with the palm of his hand.

"What did the man look like? Did she say?" he questioned, trying to steady his breathing.

Details mattered. The more they knew, the closer they'd be to finding Lacy.

Willow gave him an odd look. "She said the man was short and slender, well dressed, and had a mustache. She also said his black hair looked like an oil slick."

"I believe she used the word 'dandy' to describe him," Olive said with repulsion.

The description weeded out his uncle. He wasn't short or slender. The man was an inch or two over six feet, and well-built for a man in his late fifties. The description didn't fit Nieto either.

Jace cursed. "It's Widow. He's been tracking us all over the country. She was worried about it, and I didn't listen."

He remembered Jace mentioning it when they arrived at the Sinclair Ranch but hadn't given it another thought. He should've paid more attention to his sister's problem. What could he have done differently though?

He slumped against the seat's backrest and cursed.

"If he harms one hair on her head, I . . ." Jace ran a shaky hand through his hair, not finishing his thought.

"I know," he commiserated. His uncle was a certified prick, always had been according to his dad. "Why can't he leave well enough alone?" he muttered under his breath.

"So, where does that leave us?" Olive asked.

Jace threw the truck in gear and pealed out of the lot. "Sitting here won't do us any good. We need to get back to Bryan and Laurel."

He closed his eyes, trying to concentrate through his rising panic. Why would his uncle's demented errand boy be in Laredo? The timing was too convenient.

The key in a game of chess was to think like your adversary, stay two moves ahead, and try to outmatch them. Thomas Monroe was a man who didn't like to lose, and Lacy had bested him when she kidnapped his wife. Obviously, the man hadn't let that go, so this had to be his counter move.

Then something occurred to him. Could his uncle be meeting with Nieto? Was that why he and his lackey were here?

He voiced his thoughts to Jace. "Hey, you don't think Monroe's here in Laredo do you?"

"I was just asking myself the same question," Jace said as he pulled up to the church.

Olive jumped out of the back seat the moment Jace placed it in park and ran to the other truck. Willow shifted beside him, her distress evident by the creases cutting lines across her forehead.

He rubbed a soothing hand down her arm. "It's okay. It's not your fault."

Willow twisted her hands in her lap. "I just . . . If anything happens to her . . ."

She let the sentence hang, wrapping her arms around her middle. He wanted to reassure her, tell her nothing bad would happen to his sister. But this game was dangerous and there was no guarantee any of them would come out on the other side unscathed. In fact, if they calculated the odds . . .

He let the thought go. Nothing good would come of focusing on their dismal odds.

Jace rolled down the window as Bryan, Laurel, and Olive approached the truck. They couldn't loiter outside the church. It looked too suspect. But where could they go?

Bryan's concerned gaze focused on Jace as he asked, "Are you sure it's Widow?"

Olive must've given Bryan and Laurel a report on what happened.

Jace nodded. "The description the sales lady gave was spot on. It makes sense. He's been tracking us. He found Lacy taking a walk and knocked her out, then blew up AJ's truck. That was in California."

"He catch up to you in Oklahoma?" he asked, absorbing the new information.

It rattled him to think Widow had been that close to his sister before this. Close enough to abduct her. But why didn't he?

"No, but we didn't stay long enough. He must've tracked us here," Jace said.

"Why didn't he just take her in California?" he asked, putting a voice to the disturbing thought.

Jace let out a heavy breath. "I don't know. He could've. It was a close call. Too close."

He scratched his head. "He's playing with you. Like a damn cat with a mouse."

"That's the only explanation we could come up with. Blowing up your truck was ballsy of him," Jace responded thoughtfully.

Trying to come up with a reasonable explanation was a waste of time. Who knew the inner workings of a mad man's mind? AJ certainly didn't.

His attention returned to the three outside the window. They needed to move locations before someone noticed them.

He waved a hand to the back seat where he and Willow sat, then at the empty front seat. "Hey, can y'all get in? We don't want to attract attention."

Laurel walked around the hood and got into the front passenger seat. He scooted closer to Willow to make room for Olive and Bryan. He patted his knee.

"Sit on my lap," he suggested.

A blush crept up Willow's neck to her cheeks, but she scooted over and sat between his legs. His arms wrapped around her middle. He slid her back against him, trying to stretch out his cramped legs. It was a tight fit, but he wasn't complaining.

She laid her head back against his chest. The urge to bury his nose in her hair almost got the better of him.

Bryan and Olive slid into the back seat. Olive slammed the door.

"Damn," he couldn't help commenting. "What did that door ever do to you? It's like you're trying to kill it."

Laurel craned her neck around to look at Olive. "See? You do slam doors too hard. It makes the people around you cringe."

Olive shrugged off the criticism. "Are we going to look for Lacy or what?" she asked as her knee bounced up and down.

The girl had to have some sort of attention deficit hyperactivity disorder. It was like she couldn't sit still to save her life. He hoped it wouldn't be a liability. They'd be waiting a while.

"No," Jace answered quietly. "Our best bet is to wait and see if she shows up here. If she doesn't, then we'll backtrack."

"If we wait too long, we'll lose any chance of getting her back quickly," Laurel pointed out in her no-nonsense way.

"It's already gone," he muttered. "The border's right here. A few hours at this point won't make much difference."

"It makes sense that Monroe's here to meet with Nieto. She'll show," Bryan said with a confidence he envied.

"I'm counting on it," Jace muttered.

Silence rained down on the group as they watched the church. A northern wind blew trash along the side of the street. Winter held onto the area by a single claw, batting at spring's attempts to warm the landscape with wintry storm clouds.

AJ's eyelids slid shut, enjoying Willow's relaxed body against his. Her breathing evened out and he knew she'd slipped into sleep.

"I'm hungry," Olive announced suddenly, causing Willow to jerk awake.

Damn, the girl was a menace.

Bryan turned and smiled at her. "You read my mind, baby."

"Don't call me baby," Olive groused, but a smile played around her lips.

Laurel let out a long-suffering sigh. "Can't you wait?"

"No," Olive said firmly. "Plus I have to pee."

"I'm not leaving," Jace said. "So if you guys want to go grab something, I'll stay."

Olive turned a pleading look at her older sister. "Please, Laurel. This is so boring. I'm going stir crazy."

He could agree with the crazy part. Between the three sisters, Olive was the attention seeker. He wondered if it was a middle child thing. Laurel took charge and Willow allowed herself to become background noise, a fly on the wall. He was the oldest, so he understood Laurel's desire for control.

Laurel, Olive, and Bryan decided to go on a food run and bathroom break. The group had voted on burgers, so they wouldn't be gone too long. Most of the City of Laredo's fast-food restaurants were open for business. He'd noticed an Arby's and McDonalds were open during their drive down the interstate. His stomach rumbled in anticipation. It'd been a while since the group had their last meal.

Willow roused herself from her sleepy state and tried to slide over to the empty space beside him. His arms tightened around her waist.

"Nuh-uh," he objected. "Please stay."

Willow turned to look at him. "Aren't you cramped?"

He leaned forward and brushed his lips against hers. "Nope," he whispered against her mouth.

Jace cleared his throat. "Um, if you two lovebirds are finished—"

AJ snorted. "Look who's talking. You and my sister are the worst."

Jace pointed toward the church. "No, dumbass. Look who just showed. That's him, right? It has to be him."

Nieto strolled down the sidewalk like a royal. Two guards flanked his six. He paused at the bottom of the steps, turned, and spoke to the men, then walked up to the door. The men followed but didn't go inside. They stationed themselves by the door, crossing their beefy arms against their broad chests.

"Mass isn't for another couple of hours," he said as he craned his neck around Willow for a better view.

"I can't believe he only brought two guards. Think there are more around back?" Jace asked.

"Probably. What should we do? Move the truck?" he asked.

Jace started the truck and crept down the block, made a U turn, and parked along the opposite curb. The view wasn't as good, but they were out of the guard's line of sight.

The Sinclair truck rumbled down the street, made a U turn and parked behind them.

The burgers arrived, but he had no appetite now. His stomach soured at what they faced. Bryan was good at recon. He could check the back of the church without being detected. Then they could make plans from there.

As soon as Willow saw Nieto, her lungs seized. She fought to drag in a tight gasping breath. What had Lacy said about breathing and counting? She couldn't remember, but tried again, taking a deep breath through her nose, then letting it out slowly through pursed lips.

AJ rubbed her back in slow circles up and down her spine. He knew.

He leaned into her and whispered, "It's going to be okay. Breathe."

She nodded and took another deep breath, all the while berating herself for being so weak. She needed to conquer the fear coursing through her veins. It clouded her clarity.

"Only a fool would walk into something like this unafraid," AJ said, voice low so only she could hear.

The comment bolstered her courage and soothed her ragged nerves. She turned her head to look at him. His brows lowered into a deep-set V. His concern caused tears to form and burn the back of her eyelids. She leaned into him, burying her head in his neck. The low vibration that rumbled from his chest warmed the deepest part of her.

She loved this man. Was it too soon to feel this way? Her

parents would say yes but she knew her own heart. So why couldn't she tell him? She hadn't responded to AJ when he'd declared his love for her. She was a coward. Always scared of something.

The back passenger door swung open before she could act on the impulse to tell him. Olive hopped inside, followed by Bryan who set two paper bags full of burgers onto his lap. The aroma of onions and grilled meat wafted from the bag, along with the tangy scent of mustard and ketchup. It smelled divine.

Laurel swung herself into the front seat, lowering a plastic bag to the floor board. "Any changes?" she asked Jace.

Bryan opened a bag and handed each of them a burger loaded with cheese, onions, lettuce, tomatoes, and pickles. The other brown bag held crispy, golden fries.

"Thanks, my man," AJ said, releasing his hold on her.

Jace unwrapped his burger before answering Laurel. "Yeah. Nieto's inside the church."

"We saw the men standing in front," Laurel said, not surprised by the news. "They come with him?"

"Yeah," AJ answered. "We need to check the back of the church to see if there are more of them, but we were waiting for you guys to get back."

Laurel nodded and passed out water bottles from the plastic bag. The group's discussion became background noise. Laurel droned on with a pep talk, trying to bolster everyone's courage. She munched on a fry and concentrated on blocking out her sister's grating voice.

Soon after the burgers and fries disappeared, Bryan left to scout the church's perimeter. He returned soon after with a dismal report. Two men guarded the back entrance and two had disappeared inside. With the two men stationed in front that equaled six men total. Six trained men experienced in killing against three guys and three women, all untrained with the exception of Bryan.

Time slowed. Each second passed in time with her heart

beat. *Thump, thump*. One second. *Thump, thump*. Two seconds. *Thump, thump*. Three seconds. Her hyper-focused nerves frayed in the truck cab's silence. She bounced her knee in an attempt to decrease the anxiety zinging up and down her spine.

Finally, cars began parking in the lot across from the church. People filtered in the front doors for the evening mass.

"Let's go change," Olive suggested, picking up the garment bags that laid flat on the floor board.

Olive gave the guys jeans and button-down shirts, then grabbed the remaining clothes and opened the door.

"Come on," she motioned to Willow and Laurel. "Let's go change in our truck."

They walked in strained silence. No one spoke as they changed into dress clothes. She'd picked a pair of black, dressy jeans and a sleek, blue-grey top that hung off one shoulder. The store happened to have a pair of black knee-high boots with heels short enough not to trip her up. They were kick-ass.

Conservative Laurel chose a grey pencil skirt with a matching jacket. Olive's choice was a bit bolder. She chose a black flirty one-piece pant suit that fit her personality to a T.

Olive insisted on brushing out Willow's tangled hair and twisted it into a messy bun. A stab of envy assaulted Willow as she looked at both of her sister's brunette hair lying in perfect waves against their shoulders.

The guys had finished changing when they returned.

AJ handed her a sheathed knife with two nylon leg straps attached. "Buckle this on your right leg, within easy reach."

"On the outside of my jeans? Won't people notice?" she asked, taking the knife out to test its sharpness.

"You're going to need to be able to access it easily. This is the best way. I doubt anyone will notice if you strap it on the inside of your calf. It should blend in with your black jeans."

His eyes raked over her, and her breath hitched at his intense stare.

"Stellar choice, by the way."

"Thanks," she mumbled, not knowing how to accept the compliment.

She'd never gotten many, so it seemed foreign to her ears. He meant what he said though. It was obvious by the raw hunger in his eyes.

Bryan gave the Glock 17 with a holster and loaded clip to Laurel. "Strap this to your hip. Make sure your jacket covers it up."

The loaded 40 Smith and Wesson went to Jace. He tucked it into his back waistband under his shirt.

"Jace, you walk in with Laurel and Willow," Bryan continued.

"Wait," AJ interrupted. "I don't think Willow should go inside. Nieto knows her face. He doesn't know Jace, Olive, or Laurel. Send Olive inside instead."

AJ handed Olive the knife he'd gotten for his sister. "Strap this on."

Olive scrunched her nose. "This is totally going to throw off my outfit," she complained.

Ignoring her, Bryan continued, "Since we can't go in with rifles and shotguns slung over our shoulders, we'll find another way inside."

"Where?" Laurel asked.

Bryan rubbed the back of his neck. "The church has a basement. I saw an open window on the far side while I was scouting. It will be a tight fit, but I think we can make it. Don't fire your weapon unless absolutely necessary," he cautioned. "Jace and I are the only ones with silencers. Let one of us fire on Nieto. The shot will be muted, and we don't want the church goers to panic."

"How are we going to get Lacy?" Willow asked, anxiety building as she heard Bryan's plan.

"I don't know yet," Bryan admitted. "You three going into the church are going to have to find a way downstairs to the basement. That's where they'll probably meet. We'll find you and go from there. Be prepared for anything."

The group dispersed. Olive, Jace, and Laurel walked up the church steps and disappeared inside.

AJ jumped into the driver's seat and turned over the engine. "We need to move closer to that open window."

Bryan opened the passenger door and jumped down. "I'll move the other truck."

AJ nodded and pulled out onto the street. He passed the church, made a right turn and parked around the block. Bryan followed, then ran back to AJ's truck.

Bryan opened the passenger door. "Ready?" he asked as he grabbed the AR rifle from behind the back passenger seat.

Bryan loaded the clip and slung it over his shoulder. He slid one of her family's shotguns out next and handed a box of shells to AJ.

"How the hell am I supposed to carry these?" AJ asked, staring at the back of Bryan's head.

Bryan turned around and handed him a fanny pack that looked like it had time traveled straight from the '80's.

AJ groaned. "Is this all you have?"

"Suck it up, buttercup," Bryan said with a smirk.

"Fine," he muttered, strapping on the blue, tie-dye pack with a neon green zipper.

He unzipped the pack, dumped in the shells, then tossed the box into the truck's bed.

Bryan turned to close the door, but she placed a hand on his arm, stopping him.

"I can take the other shotgun," she announced with confidence.

Bryan trained a skeptical eye on her. "You sure?"

She huffed. "I'm a native Texan who grew up on a ranch. What do you think?"

Bryan lifted a brow at her sarcasm. "Okay, okay, no need to get snarky." He turned to AJ. "Do all Texans have an over-inflated ego?"

To lift the tense mood, AJ bantered back. "Oh yeah. They

can't help it though. They all believe their own BS about everything being bigger in Texas."

A stormy look crossed her face. What the hell were they doing? Insulting the whole state of Texas?

She crossed her arms. "What the hell?"

Bryan and AJ grinned at each other, then Bryan said, "Well, it's not your fault you aren't an Oklahoman. You know why they say Oklahoma's so windy, don't you?"

She gave Bryan an arch look. "I have no idea."

"It's because Kansas blows and Texas sucks," he replied with a tongue-in-cheek grin.

AJ and Bryan fist bumped each other.

Surprised laughter burst from her chest, dispelling some of the tension at the base of her neck.

Bryan handed her the last shotgun with a box of shells and a small, black backpack.

"Hey," AJ whined, "Why didn't you give me the backpack?"

"Because," Bryan said with a mocking grin, "the fanny pack makes you look so pretty."

Bryan batted his eyelashes at AJ who promptly lifted his middle finger in the air.

Impatience built inside her. She shifted her feet as they continued to throw insults at each other.

"Can we go?" she finally asked, unable to take the suspense any longer.

They turned in unison to stare at her. Bryan's lips stretched into a wide smile.

"Sure, sure," Bryan said breezily.

AJ stepped over and gave her shoulders a squeeze. "It'll be okay." His voice turned serious. "Stay with me. Don't leave my side, okay?"

She nodded and they started down the sidewalk toward the back of the church.

37

The strong odor of paint fumes leaked out of the open basement window. AJ squatted down and peered inside. Wet paint covered the walls of the empty room in a nondescript beige.

He looked up at Bryan and grimaced. "The walls are wet with paint."

"That explains the open window," Bryan said.

"You think the painters will be back?" he asked as a shiver rolled down his back.

His sister said when you felt a shiver along your back someone was walking over your grave. The thought squeezed his already tight chest. Was it an omen? He couldn't go into this situation thinking he was going to die.

"Hey, you okay?" Bryan asked, nudging his shoulder.

The question stated with genuine concern knocked him out of his funk. Bryan didn't normally ask questions like that, much less express concern.

"Aren't you worried the painters will come back?" he couldn't help asking. "If they catch us, this whole thing will be blown."

Bryan shrugged as if it were a non-issue. "I'll go in first. You can hand me the weapons."

He took the AR rifle from Bryan. It clanked against his shotgun as he slung it over his shoulder.

Bryan bent down on his knees and lifted the window up to its full height. He slipped his legs in first, then shimmied his upper body through the window. The window's lower sash, a thin strip of aluminum, scraped Bryan's torso as he wiggled his large frame through the small space.

He heard Bryan's boots hit the tile floor and the man's, "Umph," as the rest of him tumbled to the ground.

Kneeling at the window, he stuck his head inside. "Make it?" he whispered with a grin.

Beige paint streaked up the back of Bryan's new jeans and his salmon-colored button-down, which was an improvement to the shirt's horrid color. Paint matted clumps of his hair together.

Bryan stood below the window. "Hand down the weapons."

"You have a stripe down your back like Pepé Le Pew," he couldn't help but snark as he lowered the AR rifle through the window.

Bryan cocked a brow and sniffed both arm pits. "Smell like him too," he smarted off.

"We know that," he shot back as he swung the shotgun off his shoulder and lowered it down.

Willow handed him the last weapon.

As he lowered it into Bryan's hands, Willow bent down and whispered, "Get up."

He rose to his feet and looked around. One of Nieto's men walked their way.

Willow shoved him against the wall in front of the window, rose on the tips of her toes, and crashed her lips into his.

Although he knew what she was doing, it didn't stop the powerful shot of lust that barreled through him like an Indie 500 race car. He managed to crack open an eyelid and caught the guard snickering in his peripheral vision.

Willow's hands fisted the front of his shirt as she continued to assault his senses. He kept an eye on the guard watching them until the stout man holstered the pistol he'd drawn and finally turned and walked back around the corner.

He leaned back, breaking the kiss, his breath ragged. "Good distraction."

Her face flushed. "Anytime," she said, boldly.

"Hey, if you two are finished, let's go," Bryan hissed from below.

He leveled her a serious look. "You ready for this?"

Her face sobered, and she nodded once. Despite the nod, he could see her confidence slipping.

He helped Willow through. Her tiny body had no problem maneuvering into the room below. After she'd cleared the space and stepped back, he lowered himself inside. His shirt rode up to his chest as he forced himself through the tiny window. The metal sill scraped his bare back, and he felt the sticky, cold paint on the wall as he slid down.

Bryan cracked open the door and scanned the narrow hallway outside. "Looks clear. I'll go find what room Nieto's in. Be right back."

Bryan slipped from the room, softly closing the door behind him.

The gravity of their situation hit him like a freight train. He shifted his weight from one foot to the other. He hated to wait. He'd rather be in on the action. His mom often accused him of having FOMO, fear of missing out. The acronym didn't fit this time because he'd rather miss out on this whole situation.

The thought triggered another of his mom and dad sitting on the deck of their new home. He wondered what they were doing right now and what they would think of their plans to take out Nieto. He gave himself a mental shake, shutting down those thoughts.

After too much time passed, he huffed out a breath and walked to the door. Turning the knob slowly, he started to crack it open when Bryan pushed his way through. His body knocked against the wall with a dull thud.

"What the hell?" Bryan hissed.

"I was coming to see where you were. You were gone too long," he answered, straightening himself to his full height.

Bryan shook his head. "Dumbass," he muttered.

"Asshole," he bit back.

"What did you find?" Willow asked quietly.

Bryan turned to her as if he'd forgotten her existence. "If you turn right down the hall, there's double doors to the left. I think that's where Nieto is. I heard men inside talking in Spanish. As of right now, there are no guards outside the door. I think they're inside with Nieto. If you turn right and walk to the end of the hallway, there's stairs on the right that lead up to another hallway that separates the bathrooms and classrooms from the sanctuary. Jace, Olive, and Laurel should find us without a problem."

"So now what?" he asked, impatience pricking his scalp.

"We need to wait for Jace and the girls. Jace and I will go in first. If there's only two guards inside, we can neutralize them, then deal with Nieto," Bryan responded, pacing to the window.

"What do you mean 'neutralize'?" Willow asked with a frown.

"We should keep our loss of life to a minimum if we can," Bryan said, rubbing his palms against his temples. "These paint fumes are brutal."

"Should I go upstairs to the bathroom and wait for my sisters?" Willow asked. "I could show them the way down."

"No," AJ responded sharply. "You're staying with me."

She rounded on him. "I'm not helpless, you know. I can shoot a gun as good as y'all can."

He wanted to grin at her declaration but thought it unwise. Bryan, however, had no qualms grinning and spouting the first thing that came to mind.

"Should we call you Annie Oakley?" Bryan teased.

Willow's chin raised a fraction. "I might not be able to out-shoot you, *Bryan*," she said, drawing out his name, "but I bet I can do better than Jace and AJ."

Bryan's grin stretched wider. "Oh-ho! A challenge. I love it."

Bryan's body went rigid as his eyes darted from Willow to the door.

"What is it?" he asked.

Bryan put a finger to his lips, and whispered, "Someone's coming. I really, really want to come back to this conversation when we're on the other side of this."

AJ strode to Willow and stood in front of her. "Stay behind me," he instructed, muscles coiled like a spring ready to snap.

Tremors shook her body as she pressed close to his back.

She took a step back as he slung the shotgun off his shoulder and pointed it at the door. Bryan did the same. Tension hung thick in the air as they waited.

And waited.

38

Two sentinels stood, one on each side of the church's back door, holding AR rifles across their chests. A totally normal thing to see, Lacy thought with so much sarcasm it begged to be said aloud. Even if this was Texas, no one expected to see hit men with rifles drawn in the open, and at a church no less.

Thomas Monroe led their group of three toward the back door where the men with the rifles stood guard. Widow took up the spot at the end which left her sandwiched between two psychos with nowhere to run.

Monroe said something to the guards. She didn't catch his words because he'd leaned in with his voice tuned low. The guards nodded, and moved aside so they could enter.

When they'd driven past the church's front door a few moments ago, she noted the trucks were missing. Had they hidden them somewhere? Her heart plummeted to her toes.

Or had they left?

In her soul, she knew Jace wouldn't leave her. Neither would AJ or Bryan for that matter. But where were they? Uneasiness shivered up and down her spine as crafty as a slithering snake. It sunk its fangs into her neck with wicked glee. She stretched her shoulders, trying to dispel the feeling. She needed to lay eyes on Jace and her friends again to verify they were safe.

They walked through the door into a narrow hallway. The faint odor of paint fumes lingered in the air.

Monroe stopped at a set of double doors. Head held high, he opened them and strode through like the damn King of England. It amazed her how often he overthought his importance.

Widow nudged her in the back, urging her forward. Her feet suddenly felt rooted to the spot. She licked her lips. Her mouth felt like she'd been chewing cotton. Was Nieto beyond those doors? Her stomach churned with a witch's brew of acid and bile. Beads of sweat broke out along her hairline.

Widow grabbed her arm in the exact spot he'd used earlier to manhandle her out of the clothing store, leaving it bruised and sore. She suppressed a wince. He shook her hard and shoved her through the doors.

"Go," Widow demanded, clearly irritated he had to put out the effort to make her move.

Her eyes darted around the room until they connected with a pair of bright, brown eyes filled with unholy delight.

Nieto sat at the end of a long conference table. His feet rested, crossed at the ankles, on the table's modern black top. His posture remained relaxed with his arms in his lap. His lips quirked upward as he dropped his feet to the floor with a muted thud.

Rising, he held out a hand in a welcoming gesture. "Come, come," he said.

His silky-smooth voice slithered along her skin. Her whole body revolted at the oily evil sound.

"Move," Widow ordered in a voice that promised retribution if she didn't.

Still, it was hard to take the first step toward the table where Nieto waited. He was a spider, waiting patiently for his prey to come close enough to ensnare. She forced her feet forward.

At the same time, Widow shoved her, causing her to trip over her feet. Stumbling, she caught herself on a chair that sat opposite Nieto.

Nieto continued to watch her, his smile inching wider with every passing second.

Monroe took a seat to Nieto's right at the modern-style table. The shiny black top sat on three triangle shaped legs spaced evenly across the bottom. The white leather high-back chairs looked too futuristic and seemed out of place in the centuries-old church. Widow ushered her toward the seat next to her uncle and slid into the chair on her other side.

She grimaced. Sandwiched in again. Tamping down the overwhelming desire to squirm in her seat like a toddler was almost impossible. She shifted, uncomfortable under Nieto's regard and Widow's hostile presence to her left. Her foot twitched involuntarily, banging her knee on the underside of the table. She swallowed a curse, rubbing her smarting knee.

"I have to say," Nieto began in his thick Spanish accent, waving a hand her direction, "this is a surprise."

"I'm here to talk to you about our deal. Not *her*," Monroe said, his nose wrinkling as he reduced her to nothing but a pronoun.

He couldn't say her name, couldn't acknowledge her as a niece or daughter. How pathetic.

Nieto's features hardened. "Our deal was void the moment my son was shot."

A muscle in Monroe's jaw ticked. A myriad of emotions crossed the man's face, but frustration and anger seemed to take front and center. Monroe was usually the one dictating deals, the one in control. His loss of dominance knocked him sideways.

"I'm sorry about your son," Monroe began in a placating tone, "but can't we—"

The double doors crashed open, each swinging toward the wall, hitting the two guards stationed there. The guards stumbled back, but regained their balance, reacting quickly. They drew their weapons, but they were too slow.

As soon as she saw Jace and Bryan barrel through the door, she threw herself on the floor, her knees cracking on the vinyl tiles. She covered her head with her arms against the muted *pop, pop* of firing weapons.

Lifting her head a fraction, she peeked between the table's triangular legs. Bryan shot the guard on the right in both knee caps and in the right shoulder. Jace contended with the one on the left. The guard lunged for Jace's weapon. Jace fired twice in quick succession, hitting the man in the right and left shoulder.

The guard's weapons clattered to the floor as they fell, screaming in pain. Blood spattered the light wood of the double doors. Bryan slid their guns across the floor with his foot. They skimmed across the tiles and out the wide-open doorway. He raised the butt of his gun, and rammed it down on one guard's head, then the other. The force of the blows knocked them out.

Her heart pounded in her ears. Everything sounded like it was being filtered through a wind tunnel. She needed to get to Jace, get behind their line of fire, their protection.

The gunfire ceased. Angry shouts became a cacophony of background noise in her roaring ears.

She crawled forward, but a hand clamped down on her ankle like a steel shackle. She tried to grab hold of the table leg in front of her. Her fingers slipped on the sleek surface unable to get a handhold around the slick base.

Her nails scraped the floor, cracking open as Widow dragged her backward. She kicked out with her free foot, nicking Widow's chin. In a surprising show of strength, he jerked her back until her body lay sprawled underneath his legs.

"JACE!"

She screamed his name so loud it felt like her vocal cords tore. Widow grabbed the back of her shirt and yanked her up, banging her head against the bottom of the table. Pain exploded in a shower of white light behind her eyelids. Nausea hit her with the instant urge to throw up.

Nieto shouted something in Spanish. As Widow dragged her to a standing position, she saw the gun in Nieto's hand.

It was pointed at Jace.

Her ankles felt like Jello, and she wobbled to the side. Her hand instinctively reached out for something solid to catch her but found nothing but air. Widow's hold on her shirt kept her from falling on her face.

"No!" she screamed. "No, no, no!"

Then Olive strode into the room flanked by AJ and Laurel, her shotgun pointed at Nieto. Laurel drew her pistol from its holder and trained it on the man as well.

"Drop the gun," Olive demanded, tone low and angry. "Now!"

"No," Nieto responded with a smirk.

She watched in fascinated horror as Olive racked the shotgun and raised it eye level.

"Olive, no!" Laurel shouted.

But it was too late.

Olive pulled the trigger with zero hesitation.

The blast hurt her ears. She covered them with her hands and screamed.

Nieto stumbled backward, dropping his pistol as the scatter-shot penetrated his chest. Blood bloomed across his white suit jacket. His hand instinctively moved to cover the wound. His lips moved without sound. A gurgle surged from his chest and blood trickled out of his mouth as his body buckled.

Her eyes darted from Nieto to Olive who'd crumpled onto the hard, unforgiving floor.

What the hell happened?

Her brain raced. There had been two gunshots.

Bryan let out a strangled, guttural cry as he rushed to Olive, now motionless on the cold, hard floor. "God, no," he said, dropping to his knees beside her.

She watched, horrified, as Bryan drew Olive into his arms. He rocked back and forth, hugging her body to him.

Laurel knelt beside him, stroking Olive's hair, weeping silently.

Olive was dead.

The bullet pierced her chest, blasting through her heart.

Monroe stood and whispered something to Widow. Widow shoved her directly in front of him with Monroe tucked in behind him.

They were using her as a human shield to escape.

She jerked her arm, kicked backward, and connected with one of Widow's shins. He let out a curse but didn't let go. She rammed an elbow into his gut.

"God dammit," Widow yelled, shoving her forward.

Widow took another step. They were inching toward the door.

Jace stood motionless, staring at Olive's dead body. Willow clung to AJ's arm, shoulders shaking with the sobs.

"Jace!" she screamed again.

He jerked his head to her, and his eyes widened. He raised the pistol into firing position.

"Let her go, Widow," he ordered in a low voice full of determination.

Widow cackled. "Or what? You going to try to shoot me with your girlfriend standing in front of me? I don't think so."

"That's my *wife*, you sadistic bastard. Let her go."

"Wife, girlfriend. What's the difference?" Widow tossed back as if a gun pointed at his head was as natural as the sun rising in the east.

"We'll let you leave peacefully," Jace bargained. "Those gunshots were probably heard upstairs. Nieto's men are coming, and I want to be gone when they get here."

She jerked and twisted, thrashing against Widow. "Just shoot him!" she growled.

"'Just shoot him,'" Widow mocked in a high-pitched voice. "Please. He won't shoot."

As the last word left Widow's mouth, his grip loosened.

The silencer on Jace's pistol muffled the deafening report as it fired. Widow fell backward into Monroe.

The bullet hit its mark. Gruesome blood and brains sprayed down on her and Monroe, but she didn't notice. She was free.

She bolted forward and hurled herself into Jace's arms. The pistol clattered to the floor as he dropped it to catch her. Tears streamed down her face as she latched onto him, wrapping her legs around his waist. Her arms encircled his neck. She buried her face there and breathed in his familiar, comforting scent.

"Take me home, Jace," she sobbed. "I want to go home."

His gentle hand rubbed up and down her back. "I'll take you anywhere," he promised.

He heaved a deep sigh as his arms tightened around her. As his heart slowed to its normal beat, so did hers. Her eyes felt puffy, her throat dry and scratchy, but she was safe in his arms.

Then she remembered her uncle. Damn him for doing this to her. Again.

She turned her head to face Monroe. "Go," she said, voice gravelly and raw. "I *never* want to see you again. Do you hear me?"

He gave a curt nod, opened his mouth to speak, then snapped it shut. He turned without a word to the door and strode out.

39

The room's silence pressed down like heavy weights on AJ's chest. His breaths rasped out fast and harsh. His ears were numb from the gunfire. All he could hear was the internal thumping of his heart as it pumped adrenaline through his system, and each breath as it left his jittery body.

His eyes tracked around the room, his brain desperate to make sense of what just happened.

Thump, thump. Whoosh. Blood pooled on the floor. Olive's blood. Nieto's blood.

Thump, thump. Whoosh. Bryan held Olive's limp body crushed against his chest. Blood stained his cheekbone and smeared his forehead.

Thump, thump. Whoosh. Warmth soaked into the back of his shirt. Willow's tears from her face pressed to his back, hiding from the grisly scene.

Thump, thump. Whoosh.

Thump, thump. Whoosh.

No one moved. Time froze, encasing everyone in ice. Laurel's hand, tangled in Olive's long brunette hair, stilled like an arm on a marble statue.

Olive's death was a blur. Everything had happened in lightning succession. Could they've done something different? He hadn't been outside with the others when she'd made the rash decision to rush in and kill Nieto. God, he wished he could rewind time, go back and do things differently. His heart felt like it'd been pummeled by a heavyweight competing for the championship.

He blinked once. Twice.

Time hadn't stopped.

The haze of shock receded, and his surroundings came into focus. Muted noises from above began to filter into his ears, into his conscious thought.

They needed to go.

The guards stationed outside banged on the back door, shouting in furious Spanish. One of them would run to the church's front entrance to get inside.

They had minutes to get the hell out of there. If that.

How much time had passed since Olive and Nieto shot each other?

Shouts and screams from the churchgoers upstairs filtered down as they stampeded out of the church. Hopefully, the crowd would slow Nieto's men from rushing down the stairs.

With cell phone towers out of commission and no land lines available, the only way to contact whatever police force Laredo still had would need to be done in person. That would buy them some time. But not much.

"We've got to get out of here. *Now*," AJ stressed.

His voice cracked like a whip against the silence's resistance as if breaking the sound barrier. Silent tears rolled down Bryan's stubbled cheeks as he raised his head.

Bryan turned his head and wiped his nose on his sleeve. "Okay. Yeah."

As if Laurel's world suddenly came back online, she wiped her cheeks with the back of her hands, and rose to her feet. Her shoulders slumped forward as she turned her stricken face to Bryan.

"Can you carry her?" Laurel asked, voice scratchy and hoarse.

He jogged to the open doors to check the hallway. "It's clear out here, but I hear footsteps on the stairs. Come on, guys. Let's go."

"I got her," Bryan mumbled, voice breaking on the last word.

Jace gently shoved Lacy forward. "We gotta go," he urged.

Bryan lifted Olive into his arms, cradling her against his chest. Her head lolled back. A sob escaped him as he adjusted it to lay on his shoulder.

"I got you, baby," Bryan whispered.

Someone had closed her eyes. Blood soaked into Bryan's shirt, dripping down his arm into the blood puddled on the floor.

He hated to think about it, but where were they going to put her once they escaped the church? It seemed crass to just lay her in the truck bed.

As if reading his mind, Bryan said as the group moved on swift feet out the door, "I'll ride in the truck bed with her."

Laurel nodded her thanks, then her face crumpled as a violent sob shook her body.

"Hurry," he pressed. "Someone's coming down the stairs!"

They raced down the hallway to the back exit. Bryan trailed the group with Olive, jogging a few feet behind them.

It only took seconds to reach the exit, but it felt like an eternity. Their movements lagged like a film out of sync with the sound.

At the door, he held up a hand, pressing his ear against the grey metal door. He didn't hear a thing.

"How are we gonna get out of here?" Jace asked, at a loss. "We've got to assume at least one of those guards is alerting the others which leaves one out there," he whispered. "They wouldn't leave this door unguarded."

The somber group looked shell-shocked. Willow and Laurel leaned against each other, sniffling. Lacy held onto Jace as if her life depended on it. None of them had the mental capacity to make a single decision. They'd left all their weapons back in the room, which proved none of them were thinking with a clear head. He'd need a gun to get them out of the church.

He cleared his throat. "I'll run back and get Jace's gun, then go out first."

He raced down the hallway, back to the bloody crime scene they'd left behind, and quickly located the gun with the silencer. It lay on the floor where Jace dropped it to catch his sister. He bent down and retrieved it. Checking the chamber, he racked it and stuffed it into his back waistband.

A shiver shot up his spine. Someone was checking the rooms, one by one. Cautiously, he peered out the door and looked both ways. The coast was clear, but whoever was down here was in the next room.

He sprinted back and worked his way through the group to the door without a word. Pushing all self-doubt aside, he mentally fortified himself for the battle ahead. The odds of them getting past the remaining guard outside were against them.

Willow reached for him and pulled his arm against her chest as he passed. Her breaths shallow and fast.

"Willow," he said, gentling his voice. "I'll be okay. This is a piece of cake. A walk in the park," he lied.

She shook her head with vehemence and tightened her hold on him. He leaned down, pressed a chaste kiss to her forehead, and gave her what he hoped was a confident smile. It felt foreign on his face, as if it didn't belong there.

"For God's sake, Will, stop it," Laurel reprimanded in a harsh whisper.

He glared at the eldest sister. "She doesn't need that right now. Leave her alone. Better yet, just stop talking."

Laurel's head jerked back as if he'd physically struck her. He thought for a moment she'd retaliate, but she just closed her mouth with a frown.

He ran a hand down Willow's jawline, his thumb caressing her cheek. "I'll be all right," he repeated. "Let me go."

She nodded, releasing her grip on his arm. "Be careful," she whispered, eyes glistening with tears.

"Be right back," he told her.

The door handle felt cold against his palm as he turned it. He pushed it open, not giving himself a chance to hesitate.

The guard outside had an assault rifle trained on him the second he stepped out into the sunlight.

He raised his hands and took a step back just as the door clicked shut.

"Whoa," he breathed under his breath in disbelief.

His eyes widened in horror as he took in the jagged scar running from the burly guard's hairline down to his left eyebrow. It gave the man a menacing air. Panic rose inside him like a monstrous spectrum, scraping its long, ugly claws up his back. What was his play here?

"Who are you?" the man demanded in a heavy Spanish accent. "Let me in the door."

The guard's voice sounded like he'd had a gravel and glass sandwich for lunch and washed it down with a mug full of sand.

His heart pounded like a runaway freight train as he took a step forward, trying to push his way past the man. He didn't have to pretend to panic.

He held his arm up like a shield and shouted, "Get the hell out of my way! I need to get out of here!"

He could brawl with the best of them. He wasn't linebacker strong, wide-built with bulky muscles like Bryan, but he could scrape his way to a win almost every time. But those were bar fights with drunken idiots. Fighting this guard who looked like he'd trained in mixed martial arts? The hulking man would wipe the State of Texas with his ass, then hand it to him. But he had to try something.

The guard's nostrils flared. "Take another step and I'll shoot."

He froze when the man's stance shifted into full firing mode. His eyes darted around frenetically, searching for an alternate escape route. He didn't feel like getting shot again.

"Look, I'm just trying to get out of here," he explained as he tried to calm his harsh breathing. "We heard gunfire upstairs, and I couldn't get out the front door, so—"

The man sighed, muttered something in Spanish, and took a side-step to the left. "*Salir.* Go," he commanded, motioning with the rifle for him to pass.

He walked past the guard, careful not to look him directly in the eye. Then, the guard turned his back on him, drew his weapon, and aimed it at the door. Holy shit. The man was going to fire at the lock. He couldn't let him get inside where his friends waited.

He drew the gun from his waistband. Without giving himself a fraction of a second to think, he aimed and pulled the trigger three times.

One shot struck the man's shoulder, causing him to lose his grip on the rifle. It clattered to the ground. The next shot grazed the man's hip, ripping a scream from his throat. The last one hit the guard square in the back, and he finally dropped to his knees like a lumbering giant.

He ran forward, raised the butt of his gun, and brought it down hard on the guard's head. The man fell forward, unconscious.

He knocked on the door. "It's clear! Let's go!"

The group charged out, racing down the alley for the trucks they'd parked down the street. He chanced a look over his shoulder. No one followed. The relief he felt almost buckled his knees.

Bryan lagged a few feet behind the group with Olive. His face, set in lines of determination, was red and the muscles in his neck bulged under the strain. His heart broke for his friend, for the man who'd become like a brother to him. He couldn't imagine losing Willow.

Thoughts bombarded him as his mind tried to make sense of Olive's death. Olive had become something special to Bryan during the long weeks spent at the Sinclair Ranch. They'd done chores together, drank, bickered, and played together. A bond had formed. For the first time in Bryan's life, he'd let someone in. And that was a hell of a big deal because the man was a steel trap when it came to his feelings, his past.

They turned and sprinted down another alley. He looked at the street looming ahead of them. The alleyways had partially hidden them from anyone bothering to pay attention to a group running fast and furious down an alley with a dead body.

Finally, the trucks came into view. He pushed himself harder. His heart hammered double-time at the exertion.

Reaching his truck, he wrenched the door open and threw himself into the driver's seat. He pushed the start button, and the engine roared to life.

In the rearview mirror, he saw Laurel hopping into the driver's seat of the Sinclair truck. Willow rounded their hood, avoiding the truck bed where Bryan and Jace were loading Olive, and got into the front passenger seat. His heart sank a little, but he understood her need to be with her sister.

When Jace finished helping Bryan, he and Lacy sprinted to the truck, opened the back door, and slid inside.

"Everyone ready?" he asked, eyeing them through the mirror.

Lacy looked wrecked. He'd almost forgotten her kidnapping ordeal. Jace pulled her close and she laid her head against his shoulder.

"How're you holding up, girl?" he asked softly.

He pulled out and drove at a normal speed down the street, not wanting to attract attention. When the interstate turn-off came into view, his chest expanded. They were practically home free.

When they turned onto the Interstate 35 on ramp, he took his eyes off the road long enough to look at his sister through the mirror again. She gazed back at him with a sad smile.

"I'll get there," she said quietly in answer to his question.

Her eyes, normally a pretty, forest green, were dull and had dark purple circles underneath them. The weight of the world lingered in her gaze. His heavy heart sank even deeper. He hated to see his sister hurting.

Her bastard father had walked away from her without saying a word. What a coward. His uncle had made no effort to try and make things right, smooth things over with his biological daughter. He didn't know why he expected things to be different. Maybe because his uncle had always seemed so sophisticated and put-together. Leaving a mess behind seemed beneath him somehow.

"Geneviève is dead."

Lacy had spoken so quietly, he almost missed it.

Questions bombarded his brain, but the look on Lacy's face had him biting his tongue.

"I'm so sorry," was all he allowed himself to say.

He'd talk to her later, after the dust settled.

She nodded at him, then closed her eyes.

40

By the time the group arrived back at Sinclair Ranch, night had fallen. A moonless sky left the prairie pitch black. The absolute absence of light caused the little hairs on the back of AJ's neck to rise. It was unnerving, which added to the uneasiness already crawling over his skin. The darkness illuminated the stars twinkling in the vast, endless sky. Stars shined brighter in Texas, he noted absently.

AJ parked his truck behind Laurel's in front of the small veterinary clinic. He cut the engine and sat in the stillness. When Laurel and Willow exited their truck, he pulled the handle, pushed his door open, and jumped down.

He walked on leaden feet toward Bryan who knelt in the Sinclair's truck bed, staring down at Olive's body.

"I'll help you move her inside," he said, hoarsely.

The look on his friend's face tore his heart. Willow's soft sobs as she leaned into Laurel for support ripped it completely from his chest. He cleared his throat, trying to swallow around the huge lump lodged there.

The silence feasted on their somber mood as he and Bryan carefully moved her body from the truck into the clinic.

He tried to talk to Bryan, but his friend just shook his head and waved him off without saying a word. He'd never seen Bryan so devastated. And it worried him.

Afterward, he found Jace by his truck and helped him unload the weapons. Silence stretched between them. A heavy sigh escaped him as he laid the last of the ammo down onto the kitchen table. The bullets rattled in the box, triggering the sound of gunfire in his head. Two pops in quick succession had felled Olive and Nieto. Would the gruesome scene ever fade from his memory?

He felt the weight of Jace's stare as his friend asked, "You okay?"

Giving his friend a strained smile, he said, "Yeah. Just worried about Willow. And Bryan," he added.

"What about those guys in the storm cellar?" Jace asked.

He followed his friend out the back door and down the back porch steps into the yard.

"Honestly? I forgot all about them," he admitted, feeling no guilt at all.

They could rot down there for all he cared.

"We should let them go," Jace said, trepidation cracking his voice. "Wonder how that's gonna go. Should we take one of the guns down with us?"

"Nah," he said, shaking his head. "They won't give us any trouble."

He didn't think they would, anyway.

They walked around the barn, and he stumbled to a stop at what he saw. Jace drew up beside him, and they both stared, dumbfounded, at the open cellar doors.

Jace glanced his way, worry furrowing his brows. He shifted his feet on the dry prairie grass, using the toe of his boot to dig out a rock lodged in the dirt. They could stand there and contemplate their life choices by leaving Scott and Diego unguarded, or they could go down and try to ferret out what happened.

"Let's check it out," he decided.

Jace nodded, flicked on his flashlight, and led the way down the stairs. Silence hung thick along with the dust motes floating in the flashlight's yellow beam. The narrow strip of light swept the room as they descended the last step.

Jace rubbed a hand over his mouth. "Scott's father didn't show up at the meeting with Nieto. He must've decided looking for his son was more important."

"Good riddance," he muttered, staring at the empty chairs, then added with a twist of bitterness, "I don't think his motives were that altruistic. He didn't have Willow. That's why Scott's father ghosted Nieto."

"Should we be worried they'll come after Laurel and Willow after this?" Jace asked. "People like Scott and his dad are ruthless. They'll want payback."

They retreated up the steps where he slammed the door closed with a satisfying thwack.

"I don't know. Maybe." He rubbed the back of his neck. "If Scott's father is scared of Nieto, he probably took his son and Diego and ran."

The thought plagued him as they picked their way back to the house and continued throughout the night. He slept in fits and starts with Willow tucked into his side on the couch. She hadn't wanted to go to bed, so they ended up staying in the living room.

When she awoke screaming for Olive, he drew her closer and whispered reassuring words to her battered heart.

"It's okay, Willow," he said gently. "I got you."

She turned in his arms to face him. "Kiss me, AJ. Make me forget."

His heart skipped a beat. She didn't have to ask him twice. He lowered his head, his lips hovering over hers as he breathed in the air she exhaled.

"So damn sweet," he murmured, kissing her like she asked.

When she finally fell into a fitful sleep, his mind took over. He needed to talk to her about what he planned to do next. His hand gently stroked along her spine, up her neck and then down to the dip in her back.

His mother and father must be out of their minds with worry. Especially his mom. Returning to California had always been his end game. As much as he liked the Sinclair Ranch, it wasn't home.

His eyes drifted to her face. In sleep, the worry lines along her brow relaxed and the innocence of youth returned. A lock of blond curls fell against her brow. He brushed it back, careful not to wake her.

He wanted to take her with him. But how could he ask her to go and leave Laurel right after losing her sister? More importantly, how could he leave without her? The conundrum left him confused and irritable.

His eyes lifted to the ceiling. Whatever decision he made would suck.

He could go, check on his parents, then come back. Out of all the scenarios running through his head, that one seemed to be the most logical choice. Asking Willow to choose between Laurel and himself seemed cruel. He couldn't do it. He wouldn't. Letting out a long-suffering sigh, he stared into the grey darkness until sleep finally took him.

"ARE you sure you have to leave?" Willow asked Lacy with a sliver of hope set in her eyes.

Both girls stood on the back porch, watching the horse in the corral trot in restless circles. The sun, growing warmer each day, hung directly above their heads. A nice southern breeze blew her hair away from her sweaty neck. The tidy black dress shirt and pants Laurel insisted she wear today soaked up the sun's rays like a dry sponge.

She tried and failed to keep her eyes from straying to the fresh mound of dirt lying underneath the live oak tree in the backyard. Tears burned her eyelids. She did her best to brush them off, but they'd buried Olive only a few hours ago and the pain slicing through her heart hadn't abated. She wondered if it ever would.

Lacy leaned against the porch's wooden railing and sighed. "Yeah. I want to go home."

"Where's that?" she asked, refocusing her attention on her friend. "Oklahoma?"

Lacy snorted with derision. "No. I'll never live in Oklahoma again. Too many painful memories."

"Where then? California with your parents?"

Lacy winced at the word "parents," and she immediately chided herself for not being more sensitive.

"I'm sorry," she said sincerely. "You know . . . about everything that happened."

Lacy let out a self-deprecating laugh. "It's okay. I'm getting used to the idea of having an asshole for a bio dad."

Lacy's flippant words didn't fool her.

"I'm sorry about Geneviève too."

Lacy gave a little shrug. "I can't change Geneviève's decision. And I've decided it won't define the rest of my life. I get to choose who I'm going to be. Jace deserves better than a wife burdened with misplaced guilt and anger."

She marveled at her friend's wisdom. There was a nugget of truth in what she said for her as well.

Lacy continued, a true smile lighting her face. "And to answer your question, yes to California. But we're not staying with my parents. Jace and I want to go back to Pacific Grove. It's where we got married."

She nodded, letting a comfortable silence fall between them. When the group arrived from Laredo last night they'd been completely and irrevocably wrecked. A small part of her wanted to blame Laurel for Olive's death. If her older sister had only listened to her, Olive would still be alive, and Bryan wouldn't be shut in the barn, his heart broken into a million pieces.

It would be so easy to lose herself in feelings of resentment, easier to blame someone for the unbearable pain residing in her chest. But it wasn't fair. Olive agreed with Laurel's plan, and her sister had been reckless. Laurel wasn't completely at fault. They all were. And that's what she couldn't quite accept.

"What about you?" Lacy asked, eyes trained in the distance.

The question startled her. "What do you mean?"

Lacy looked down at her, surprise flickering across her face. "Oh, um, I just wondered what your plans were now."

Lacy let the last word fall. A contemplative look crossed her face, as if she still had more to say.

"To be honest, I hadn't really thought about it," she muttered.

The loss of Olive consumed her thoughts, leaving room for little else.

Had she assumed AJ would stay on the Sinclair Ranch with her? Yeah, she had. Stupid, really, considering they hadn't discussed it. In fact, AJ never spoke about plans after the mission at all. A niggling worry began in her mind. What if her assumption was wrong?

"My idiot brother," Lacy mumbled under her breath.

Her eyes snapped up. "Do you know something I don't?"

What would she do if AJ went back to California? Would he even ask her to go? Her thoughts turned to Laurel, and spiraled downward. Could she leave her sister alone on the ranch? A tug-of-war began inside her heart, loyalty to Laurel on one side and love for AJ on the other.

Lacy scrubbed her weary face with the palm of her hand. "He's going back to California."

The words settled in her chest like a lead ball. Blood rushed to her face as anger flashed through her. He should've told her. What was he going to do? Avoid her and sneak out in the dead of night like a coward? Why bother getting to know her at all?

Then panic replaced some of the anger. He didn't know she

loved him. She hadn't told him even though she'd had plenty of chances. What if . . .

She jumped when Lacy placed a warm hand on her shoulder. "Don't fly off the handle. I'm sure he's waiting for what he considers the right time. He probably didn't want to worry you with his plans because of . . . well, because of Olive."

An uncharacteristic *harumph* escaped her. "I can't believe he hasn't said anything."

Lacy's arms wrapped around her in a crushing hug. "I'm going to miss you, Willow."

She returned the embrace, a sad smile tugging at her lips. "Me too."

Lacy stepped back, swiping at a stray tear. "I'm gonna go find Jace. We need to hit the road."

"Be careful," she said, walking down the porch steps.

"Always," Lacy responded, disappearing inside the house.

The horse whinnied as she approached the corral. She stepped up on the lowest rail, resting her arms on the top, her heart a tangled mess. The horse trotted over and stuck a velvety nose in her face.

She gave the horse a wan smile, rubbing her between the eyes. "Yeah, yeah. I know you need exercise, but it will be a while before I take you out again."

The horse snorted as if she understood the meaning behind Willow's words, trotted off to the far side of the corral, and succinctly turned its back on her.

She needed time to gather her thoughts, search her heart for answers. What did she really want? The answer jumped out at her as soon as the question formed. AJ. She wanted AJ. But could she really leave Laurel all alone? The pain of Olive's death was too fresh, and she knew Laurel blamed herself. There was no easy answer. She jumped off the rail and headed toward the house, her heart still conflicted.

41

AJ walked up the back porch steps, deep in thought. Bryan had sequestered himself in the barn right after Olive's funeral, insisting he needed to finish her grave marker. AJ tried talking to Bryan about leaving, but he was silent on the subject. He didn't want to abandon his friend, yet he couldn't force Bryan to do anything he didn't want to do. There was no easy answer.

Willow stood alone on the deck staring at the live oak tree, her face a mask of pain. Even with her nose, red and puffy from crying, she was still the most beautiful woman he'd ever laid eyes on. He wished he could erase her anguish, or carry it for her somehow, but no one could escape grief when a loved one died.

Fighting the process only produced more suffering. He knew from personal experience. It took him years to accept Quinn's death. Even after he'd accepted the inevitability of it, he didn't deal well with the fallout.

He reached the top step and lingered there, wondering what to say. He needed to talk to her about his plans. The timing sucked, and he hated the position he was putting her in.

He leaned his long arms over the porch rail. Squinting against the sunlight, he trained his eyes on Willow's profile.

"Hey, beautiful."

She turned to face him, lightning flashing from her stormy blue-grey eyes. She was angry with him, and it was damn cute. His lips turned up into an amused smile, which only deepened her frown.

"Uh," he started, trying his dead level best to dampen his grin, "are you mad at me, Willow?"

She slammed a palm down on the wooden railing. "Why would I be mad at you, AJ? Hmm?"

"I . . . well." He stammered to a stop.

Why *would* she be mad at him? He searched his brain for some *faux paus* he'd committed but drew a blank.

"Um," he began again. "I don't know?"

The statement rolled off his tongue sounding more like a question. He shifted uncomfortably, having no idea how to handle this. He'd never had a woman angry with him before. Except his sister. And mother. Well, it wasn't often he had a woman mad at him.

She huffed, turning her gaze away from him. "When were you going to tell me you're leaving?" she asked in a deceptively quiet tone.

Ah, shit. He scrubbed a hand down his face. He knew he'd waited too long to tell her.

He sighed in resignation. "There just never seemed like a good time to bring up the subject."

"Well, hearing it from your sister hurt," she admitted.

"Dammit," he muttered under his breath. "I'm sorry."

He looked up at the wispy cirrus clouds skating across the light blue sky. Starlings flew in a murmuration, diving and swooping, creating figure eights in the bright sunlight.

"Are you really leaving?" Willow's voice trembled like she was afraid of the answer.

He rubbed the back of his neck, trying to catch her gaze, but she kept it locked on the live oak tree.

"When I left California to find my sister," he began, fumbling for a place to start, "I had no idea it would end like this. I had to go to Mexico City with Bryan to rescue her from a sex trafficker for God's sakes. I've been stung by a scorpion, shot in the chest."

He paused to take a breath and gather his thoughts. The beginning of his journey seemed the best place to start explaining why he had to go back to California.

Willow turned to face him. He locked his gaze with hers. Some of the storm clouds in her eyes cleared, but he could tell she was still troubled. And hurt.

"Go on," she urged.

"Then I met you," he said, voice thick with emotion, "and you turned my world on its face. The first time I saw you in that parking garage, it was like the wind had been knocked out of me and somehow I just knew. I knew you were the one."

He stepped into her space and placed a hand on her cheek. She leaned into his palm and closed her eyes.

"I love you, AJ," she whispered.

He froze. His breath lodged against the sudden lump in his throat. She'd finally admitted it. The words sucker-punched him in the chest in the best way. He grabbed the front of her black blouse, pulled her toward him, and wrapped his arms around her waist.

"Finally," he breathed.

He wanted to throw up his fist and shout *yes* to the heavens. The love, joy, the absolute relief he felt at hearing her say those three little words craved a release. He took a deep breath and tried to contain his feelings, but he couldn't hold back the mile-wide smile on his face.

She conceded a small smile of her own. "Have you been waiting for me to say it?"

He barked out a laugh. "Yes, and you took your damn sweet time about it too."

The smile dropped from her face. "But you're leaving."

He sighed. "I have to go check on my parents, Will. They'll be wondering about me. I'd ask you to come with me, but—"

She laid her head on his chest, the words seeming to mollify her somewhat.

"But what?" she prompted.

"I didn't want to place you in a position where you had to choose between me and your sister."

"Ask me," she demanded. "Give me the choice."

He leaned back, placed two fingers under her chin, and lifted her face to look at him. He searched her eyes for a moment.

"Will you come with me to California? We don't have as much land as you do here, but it's green with rolling hills. It's beautiful."

His voice held an excited, hopeful tone, but even though she'd wanted him to ask, he still saw the conflict warring inside her.

She stepped out of his embrace. "I need to talk to Laurel. I don't know—"

"It's okay," he said, taking hold of her hand and squeezing lightly. "I get it."

She gave him a grateful smile and started to reply when Bryan walked out of the barn with a wooden cross.

42

A J watched Bryan trudge to Olive's fresh grave as if he were walking toward his own death. His heart plummeted at the look of total devastation on Bryan's face. There wasn't a damn thing he could do to ease his friend's pain, and it left him feeling helpless.

Quinn's image was burned inside his eyelids. It was like when he looked directly at a lightbulb, then closed his eyes. An exact replica of that lightbulb would be etched on his eyelids every time. He knew what it was like to lose the girl you loved. Your heart never truly healed, it just learned to beat on.

Willow turned and ran into the house, returning with Laurel a few seconds later.

"What's he doing?" Laurel asked with a frown as she tracked Bryan's slow progress.

"He made a cross to mark Olive's grave," Willow answered softly.

They walked down the porch steps to the tree where Bryan hammered the cross into the ground. He trailed behind, letting the sisters have their space.

Laurel sucked in a sharp breath, her face red and blotchy from crying. "Thank you, Bryan," she whispered.

Bryan gave a curt nod and swung the mallet down on the wooden cross one last time. The dull thud echoed in the space between them as the vertical pole sunk into the soft earth. The finality of it hit him square in the chest as he watched Bryan.

The mallet fell from Bryan's hand. He dropped to his knees into the dark, upturned soil, his head bent low. Olive was gone.

They'd gone to Laredo to kill Nieto and by some miracle succeeded. But the cost was high. Too high. The universe always demanded balance. A life for a life. Now, silence reigned in Olive's absence, a painful reminder that beautiful brash soul no longer walked among them.

The group stood in silence, each with their own memories of Olive. He admired Bryan's simple cross made from the fallen branch of an oak tree he'd found by the creek. Bryan had stripped the bark and sanded it to silky perfection. Willow had given Bryan a wood burning kit and stain leftover from one of her art projects. Bryan burned Olive's name and her birth and death dates into the wood.

When the silence became more than he could bear, he leaned in and kissed Willow's brow, gave Bryan's shoulder a squeeze, and walked back to the house.

In the kitchen, he started a new pot of coffee, then sat at the kitchen table, head in his hands. Would Willow go with him to California? The thought evoked both excitement and fear.

Lacy and Jace opened the back door, walked in, and joined him at the table. He raised his head and set thoughts of Willow aside to concentrate on his little sister. A level of satisfaction and contentment surrounded her. Jace was good for her.

"We're leaving," Lacy said without preamble.

His face fell. He hoped they'd travel to California together.

"Now?" he asked with more irritation than he meant. "I thought we'd ride together."

Some of the spark in Lacy's eyes dimmed. "We're not going back to Mom and Dad's, AJ."

His eyes widened. "Why not?"

He couldn't imagine where else they'd go. Not to mention how hurt their parents would be if Lacy and Jace didn't return. He knew his sister still struggled with the idea of being adopted. It didn't matter to him who her parents were. She was his baby sister and always would be.

Jace placed his hand over Lacy's on the table in a show of solidarity. "We're going back to Pacific Grove. An elderly couple there owns an inn and offered us jobs."

"But Mom and Dad have plenty of work for—"

"I promised Lacy," Jace cut in firmly.

AJ heard the resolve in his best friend's voice. Jace would do anything for his sister, and he couldn't begrudge him for it. Although their mom and dad would be disappointed, maybe bringing Willow with him would assuage some of their distress. The thought lightened his heart.

"What truck are you taking if you're not riding with me?" he asked.

Self-reproach flashed across Lacy's face. "The white one we stole."

AJ narrowed his eyes. "Thought you wanted that returned to the old lady."

"Yeah, well, desperate times," Lacy snarked.

Jace chuckled and patted her hand. "If there were another option, we'd take it, but we really need to get out of here."

"I get it," he conceded.

And he really did. He couldn't leave Texas and the disturbing events they'd been through fast enough. He was ready to saddle a horse and play cowboy again, rounding up cattle and fixing fences for his dad. He was ready to breathe without so many burdens weighing down his chest.

The image of Willow riding her own horse beside him filled him with excitement. It felt right and his heart burgeoned with hope that she'd say yes and come with him.

"What about Bryan?" Lacy asked, bringing him back down to earth.

"I don't know," he said with a furrowed brow.

Jace rose from the table and held his hand out to him. He grasped it, and Jace pulled him up into their signature hug.

"Be careful," he said, trying to keep the sadness at bay. "And make sure my sister visits us often."

"Will do," Jace agreed.

Lacy walked over and gave him a hug. "Love you, AJ."

He leaned back, saw tears in his sister's eyes, and his heart squeezed. He never could stand to see her cry.

"Love you too, sis," he said, patting the top of her head affectionately.

She sniffed and stepped back. Jace wrapped an arm around her waist and tugged her to the door. He watched them walk out with the satisfaction of knowing his sister was in good hands. The best hands.

Bryan passed them on their way out. Lacy hugged him goodbye and Jace shook his hand. After their farewells, Bryan stepped over the threshold, stomped his feet to rid his shoes of any dirt or mud, and walked into the kitchen.

Bryan shuffled to the sink and turned on the water. He scrubbed his hands and face with dish soap, then dried them on one of Laurel's white kitchen towels.

He grimaced when Bryan pulled the white towel, now streaked with dirt, away from his face. Laurel would have Bryan's head on a pike for that.

Bryan poured himself a large mug of coffee. Leaning against the sink, his friend took a noisy gulp of the hot liquid, sucking in air through his teeth.

Weirdest thing he ever saw.

AJ could sense Bryan had something on his mind, so he contented himself by watching his friend repeat his strange coffee drinking habit.

After Bryan emptied half the mug, he wandered over to the table, pulled out a chair, and sat. He plunked the mug onto the table and let out a long sigh.

"I'm staying here," Bryan said in a quiet, steady voice.

"Why?" he asked, genuinely curious as to why he'd even want to stay.

Bryan ran a hand through his hair, dampened from splashing water on his face.

"Laurel can't run the ranch by herself. Ol—" Bryan stammered to a stop, swallowing hard. "Olive did all the work of a ranch hand. I'm going to stay and help."

He nodded, bringing his index finger to his pursed lips. "What about your plans to go get your money? Monroe paid you a lot to be his beck-and-call pilot."

"It will still be there when I'm ready," Bryan said in his no-nonsense way.

With Bryan staying at the ranch, he wondered if it would influence Willow's decision to go with him.

"Does Laurel know you're staying?" he asked, the idea Willow might actually go with him taking root.

"Yeah. We argued about it at first, but she came around, saw it made good sense," Bryan answered.

Willow popped her head around the corner of the kitchen doorway that led to the rest of the house.

"Can I talk to you for a sec?" she asked, eyes focused on AJ.

"Sure," he responded, scraping the legs across the tile floor as he pushed back his chair.

He joined her at the doorway where she took his hand and led him into the living area. She plopped down on the couch, pulling him down with her. He chuckled when he almost landed in her lap.

"What's up?" he asked, repositioning himself beside her.

"Well," she hedged, dipping her eyes to their joined hands.

She seemed nervous, shy even. He hadn't seen her this way since they first met. It piqued his curiosity.

He took his free hand and lifted her chin. "Well?"

"I talked to Laurel just now and she—"

Willow's eyes darted to the side as she stuttered to a stop.

Her cheeks flushed a pretty pink and her lips turned down at the ends, obviously struggling with her thoughts.

He laughed softly. "What's up with you? Why are you embarrassed?"

"Do you still want me to go with you?" she blurted.

"You know I do."

"Laurel doesn't want me to stay if my heart's somewhere else." She locked her stunning eyes with his. "And since I don't own my heart anymore . . ."

She drew out the last sentence, letting it hang, suspended between them.

"Who owns your heart, Willow?" he asked in a low, husky voice.

Leaning forward, she rested her forehead on his. "You do," she answered on a soft breath.

He inhaled her breath, her answer, letting it settle deep in his bones. The joy he felt in that exact moment was one he never wanted to forget, so he let her words brand him, sear into his brain.

He leaned in, brushing his lips softly over hers in a slow, sensual kiss. When he broke the kiss at last, they were both breathless.

"You've made me very happy," he breathed, kissing the nape of her neck.

"When are we leaving?" she asked, excitement edging her words.

"After," he mumbled, kissing his way up her neck to her jawline.

"After what?" she asked, voice barely above a whisper.

"This," he answered as he gracefully got to his feet.

He swept her into his arms and headed for the stairs. He wanted to show her just how happy she'd made him. He'd spend the rest of his life cherishing the gift of her heart. And that started right now.

43

The cliff overlooking the Pacific Ocean near the Lighthouse Inn was even more beautiful than Lacy remembered. She placed her bare toes just over the edge and curled them up tight. Spreading her arms like eagle's wings, she drew in a lungful of air, closed her eyes, and smiled. The scent of salt and seaweed was so strong she could almost taste it.

The mild wind blew her long raven-black hair from her shoulders. The sun warmed her cheeks. Her heart beat a normal cadence in her chest. This overwhelming feeling blooming inside her was what true peace and contentment felt like. She remembered this kind of happiness growing up and her physical body, as well as her mind, metaphorically sagged with relief. She could finally rest.

She felt Jace's presence before he spoke and knew what he was about to say. She dropped her arms to her sides.

"Are you trying to put me in an early grave?" he asked gruffly.

She craned her neck back to look at him and gave him a wide smile.

"Don't harsh my mellow," she quipped. "You know if you get right to the edge of this cliff, close your eyes, and spread your arms out like this," she said, demonstrating, "it feels like you're flying."

He laughed despite the concern on his face. "As long as you don't fly over the edge," he commented dryly.

It took Lacy and Jace over a week to cross the country from the Sinclair Ranch to Pacific Grove. They took as many back roads as possible while keeping in line with west bound Interstate 10.

Nighttime stars shone against the inky sky as they skirted below Phoenix to drop onto Interstate 8. She'd rolled the window down and let the cool desert air blow in her face, marveling at its dryness.

But this right here? Where the sky kissed the ocean and became one large, unending being? It was heaven.

He walked up behind her, wrapping his arms securely around her waist. He took a step back and spun her around in a 180-degree circle. She let out a shriek. Laughing, she turned and wrapped her arms around his neck.

"A little warning next time," she admonished, still laughing.

He nuzzled her neck, breathing in deeply. "I'd never let you fall."

"I know," she said, curling the ends of his hair at the nape of his neck around her finger.

He pulled her down to the ground with him, settling her on his lap. She leaned back against his chest.

They sat in the afternoon sunshine, talking in sporadic intervals, and loving every moment spent together. After some time had passed in companionable silence, Lacy knew it was time.

In a quiet voice, she spoke. "Jace?"

Leaned back on his elbows, eyes closed, soaking in the sun, he murmured, "Hmm?"

"I need to tell you something."

He leaned over and brushed a strand of hair from her eyes and waited for her to continue.

"I—I'm pregnant," she stammered.

She felt him stiffen beside her. His gaze lingered on her, and she wondered what he was thinking.

Then his handsome face burst into a huge smile. "Are you sure?"

"Yeah, pretty sure," she said on a half-laugh. "So you're not upset?"

He took her face between the palms of his hands. "Upset? No. I'm elated. Scared too. But damn proud you're carrying my child."

She scooted closer to him and leaned her head against his shoulder. "Thank God," she breathed.

"You're not upset are you? Or worried you might miscarry again?" he asked in an anxious tone. "You're going to have to eat better."

And here we go, she thought with an eye roll.

"No, I'm not upset. I'm leaving the past in the past."

When she'd first arrived at the Monroe farm, which seemed like eons ago, not mere months, she'd been assaulted by Jace's brother, Zach. Then she found out she was pregnant but miscarried a few weeks later.

She couldn't deny the whole ordeal left her scarred. However, after everything else that followed, she decided life was just too damn short to wallow in pain.

"And," she continued, "Cat said it was unlikely I'd miscarry again."

"Wait," he said, voice dropping an octave. "How long have you known about this?"

She winced. "Um, Cat pulled me aside before we left Oklahoma. You know she has a sixth sense about these things. She suspected I was pregnant."

His nostrils flared. "And you didn't tell me *why?*"

"I was working up the courage to tell you on the way to Texas. I swear I was. But when we got there, everything was just so screwed up. If you'd known I was pregnant, you wouldn't have let me help and that didn't feel right to me," she finished lamely.

"You put our child and yourself at risk. You were kidnapped for Christ's sake. What if you'd been drugged or beaten?" He shook his head. "It was reckless, Lacy."

His words lanced through her heart like a poison-tipped arrow. Tears welled in her eyes as regret washed over her.

She bowed her head. "I'm sorry. It was a mistake, I'll admit. But I wasn't drugged or beaten."

He huffed. "So, All's well that ends well?"

Her lips twitched. "Something like that."

He snorted. "What the hell am I gonna do with you?"

She placed both hands against his cheeks and whispered, "Love me."

He leaned forward, fastening his lips to hers. His hand cradled the back of her head and the other fell to her lower abdomen.

"Dammit," he breathed against her lips. "You make it hard to stay angry with you."

She leaned back, her eyes capturing his. "That's because we were made to love each other not fight. I love you, Jace."

He sighed. "Love you, too."

His hand remained on her abdomen, fingers spread, as if waiting to feel something.

"You know it's way too early to feel him kick or move around," she informed him.

He cocked his head, and she couldn't help remembering when he first showed up at the farm. He'd made the exact same head gesture. How things had changed since then. She shook off the memory with a smile.

"Him?" he asked curiously.

"Yeah, I think it's a boy," she replied.

A bright sheen appeared over his eyes. "Really?"

She nodded. "Mm-hmm."

"Have any names picked out yet?" He shifted his hand on her abdomen to the left with a look of wonder in his eyes.

"Actually," she said, carefully, "I think we should name him Jacob after your father."

She saw the moment her words hit home. He jumped up and turned his back to her, shoulders hunched forward.

Rising to her feet, she walked over and wrapped her arms around him from behind. He was still grieving the death of his parents. Sometimes it felt as if they'd lived a thousand lifetimes in the past year.

So many changes hit them in swift succession. Jace lost his parents, then killed his brother, Zach. He'd been blackmailed, pressed into the Texas militia, tortured, and beaten.

She'd been raped, gotten pregnant, miscarried. She'd been kidnapped by a sex-trafficker. All staggering, life-altering events they hadn't had a chance to fully process yet.

"Are you okay?" she asked quietly. "We don't have to name him after your father if it hurts you."

He turned and tipped her chin up. The reddened tip of his nose was the only indication he'd been crying.

"Are you kidding? I think the name is perfect," he responded, running his fingers lightly down her cheek.

A fountain of relief poured over her. "I was also thinking about naming him after my brother."

His eyes snapped to hers, catching on quickly.

"Adam Jacob?" he burst out incredulously. "No way. One AJ in the family is enough, don't you think?"

She laughed. "I'm kidding."

He grabbed her hand, laced his fingers with hers, and started walking back to the Inn.

"Seriously, though. Do you have another name in mind?" he asked.

"No, not really. You can come up with the middle name. As long as it's not weird or anything," she qualified.

He winked at her. "I'll do my best not to name him something weird like Nimrod or Gryphon."

She burst into a fit of giggles. "For the love of God, not Nimrod."

They continued to bounce strange names back and forth. The whole conversation struck her as surreal. For the first time in months, her life seemed semi-normal. She knew life with Jace would never be dull, and she found herself looking forward to their baby.

Whatever came next, she knew she wouldn't face it alone. Jace would be by her side, weathering life's storms and celebrating every single joyous moment in between.

A NOTE FROM THE AUTHOR

"I want you to be alive"

— LOGIC, FROM 1-800-273-8255

Suicide not only affects the victim but also has a devastating impact on those who are left behind to survive it. This is a subject that has deeply influenced my family. However, those are not my stories to tell. I will say if you know someone who needs help, please say something.

Your words and actions might save someone's life.

If you are in crisis, please reach out and tell someone or call 988 to be connected to a trained professional. Please, take a ";" (pause).

ACKNOWLEDGMENTS

I had no idea when I began writing Lacy and Jace's story in *Asylum* I'd end up with a trilogy! The journey has been educational. The road was paved with lots of tears of frustration, arguments with my best friend and editor, Judy Stohr, and to be honest, struggles of self-worth. At times, I thought I was a genius, but mostly I wondered who the heck would even read this? Judy has been there every step of the way, encouraging me to continue. I never could've accomplished writing the Asylum Trilogy without her unwavering support and advice.

I'd like to thank Bill and Lara Bernhardt. They've been with me throughout this entire journey. Their kindness and willingness to help aspiring authors is extraordinary. Their writer's retreats are phenomenal! They are the true GOAT.

And a big thanks to all the readers who invested their time in reading these books. I hope the story of Lacy and Jace, AJ and Willow, and the amazing supporting cast both entertained you and caused you to stop and think about the social issues plaguing our country today.

I'm a little sad to see my characters go. They've been a part of my life for many years now. I'll miss Lacy and her snarky attitude, Jace and his unwavering love for her. The best relationships you're ever going to find are in books and I find writing them to be cathartic. But, I know there are new characters full of love and adventures to write, and I am looking forward to new beginnings.

I'll see y'all on the other side!

ABOUT THE AUTHOR

Susy Smith is a celebrated dystopian storyteller, author, and curriculum specialist for the Kanza Tribe in Oklahoma. Armed with a deep understanding of language, the resilience of the human spirit, and a bachelor's degree in English, she weaves captivating, award-winning stories that leave readers wanting more.

Smith's literary journey commenced with *Asylum*, a gripping novel that clinched the 2020 WriterCon contest in the novel category. Her second installment in the series, *Ascendant*, won numerous awards in the sci-fi dystopian category, including first place in the fall 2023 Bookfest awards. She wraps up the series with her newest novel, *Allegiance*, which probes the intricacies of survival, the dark side of human nature, and ultimately what it means to be truly free.

In addition to her novels, Smith occasionally crafts poetry, adding a unique dimension to her diverse repertoire. Her authentic writing style echoes her experiences living in a small Oklahoma town with her husband and four grown children.

ALSO BY SUSY SMITH

Asylum

Ascendant